Society Dawning
A Sovereign Magi Society novel
Book 1

T.J. Vensarn

ISBN-10: 0692578706
ISBN-13: 978-0-692-57870-4

Cover design by TJ Vensarn.
Artwork by: Nadica Boshkovska
Check out author TJ Vensarn online at www.vensarn.com
Check out the artist's gallery online at
http://theswanmaiden.deviantart.com/gallery/

Acknowledgments

I would like to thank my wonderful wife for her support, suggestions, patience, and encouragement throughout the process of writing this book.

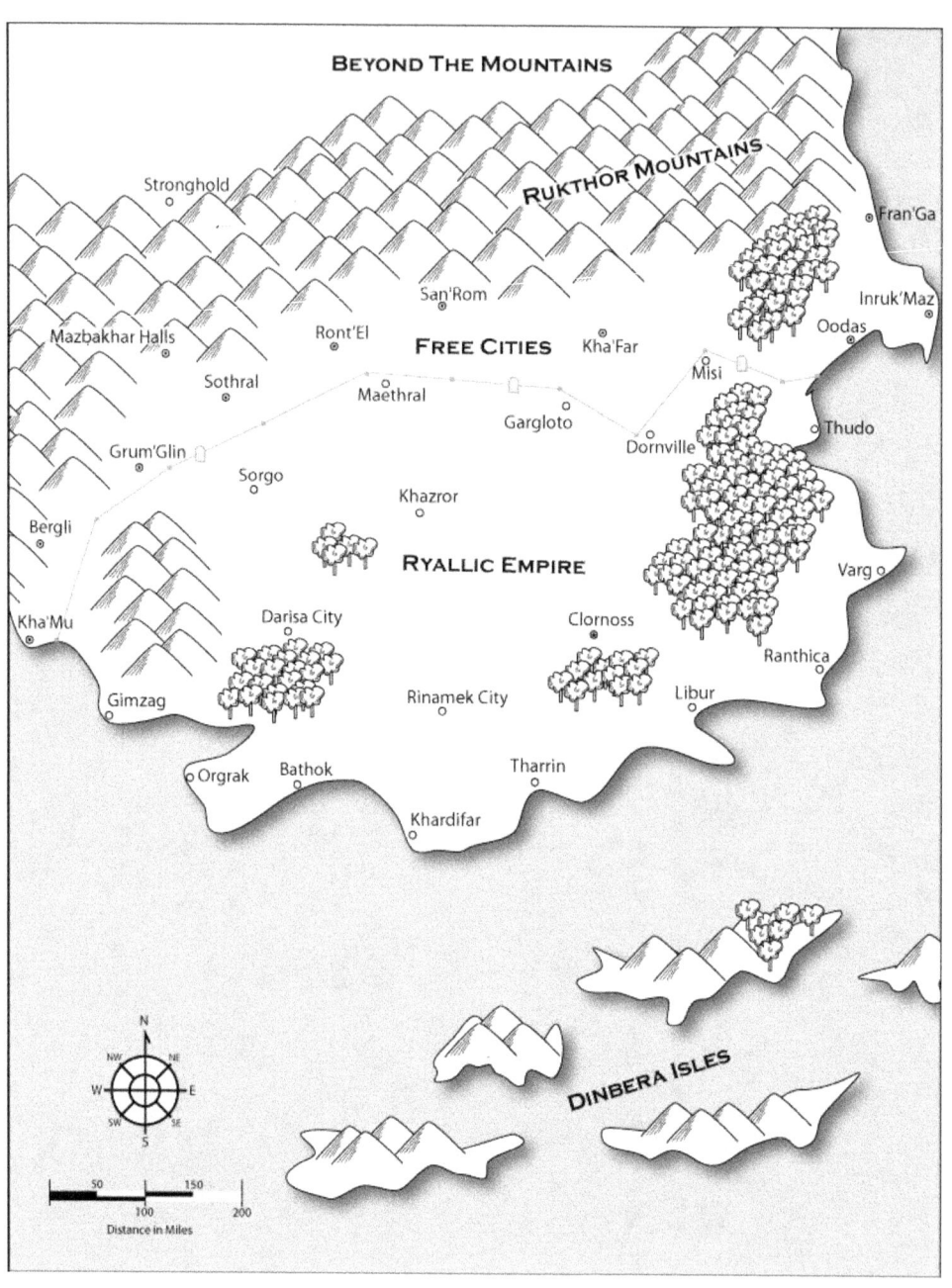

Chapter 1

Sarge

He had walked around the vast meadow of dead grass and searched for the headstone for several hours. Several dozen cattle mooed and eyed him suspiciously as he walked about. It wasn't a headstone in the traditional sense of the word, but that's what he called them for lack of a better word. Finally, he gave up and looked around for somewhere comfortable to sit and wait for darkness. Half a mile or so to the west was a farm house, so he headed that way.

He walked up to the barn, tossed his bag on a barrel, and dug out his recorder. It was a small woodwind musical instrument a little shorter than his forearm. He hopped up onto the barrel, leaned back against the barn, and started playing a happy melody.

Sarge was a middle-aged man, of average height. A lifetime of military service and battles had toned his muscles, and formed him into a man with an intimidating physique. His light blond hair stood out in contrast to his sun-darkened skin, and he kept it cut short whenever possible. Battle scars crisscrossed his arms and he had several small scars on his face as well. He wore an old tattered cloak with strange markings on the front edges. It was brown on the hood, shoulders, and top half and it was white on the bottom half.

After a while, a young woman came out of the farmhouse holding a dagger and walked towards him quickly. Two small girls followed her out the house and she turned and yelled at them to get back inside. Sarge groaned internally as the woman walked up. He really didn't have the patience to put up with people's nonsense. He just wanted to take care of business and be on his way. He had been tracking a necromancer and its undead spawn, the Awakened, for a couple of fortnights. He had finally caught up to them, and it was time to kill the necromancer and then find somewhere nice for an ale and a soft bed.

The woman stopped a few feet from him and held the dagger pointed at him. She demanded, "Who are you? Why are you sitting next to my barn?"

He ignored her and played his recorder. He wasn't sure how much she knew about what was going on in the region. If she already knew the horrible things that happened to her nearest neighbors, then she should have already fled.

The woman raised her voice, "Answer me, dammit! Did you bring the monsters that killed the Hyles family?"

He lowered the instrument and asked, "Why don't people ever flee when monsters are coming to eat them? Did you at least think about packing up and taking your family to safety?"

Without lowering the dagger she said, "We will defend our home! We're prepared to fight!"

"Well I suppose that settles it. But are you prepared to watch the Awakened kill your daughters? They're adorable little girls. They would have grown into lovely lasses. I suppose that is the way of the world sometimes. Now, if you'll excuse me, I was in the middle of a song." He put the recorder back to his lips and resumed his song.

By this point the woman was so angry that her cheeks were red. She had both fists on her hips and her chest was puffed out in indignation. "How dare you threaten my family? If you're here when my husband returns he'll send you straight to Khalius!" She turned and stormed back to the house.

Sarge had never been a very religious man. Sure, he said his devotions on the holy days and gave coins to the temples when he could. When he was being honest with himself he wasn't entirely sure that he believed in the whole 'Eternal Paradise' and 'Fiery Pits of Khalius' stories. He did choose to believe that overall he was a good person. If the teachings of the gods were real then he was confident that he would someday enjoy Eternal Paradise. The fiery pits of Khalius just weren't his style.

An hour later a horse and rider walked quickly up the dirt road to the farm. The woman came out of the house to meet her husband, with the two little girls right on her heels. She ran up to the man on horseback, talked to him, and pointed at Sarge. The man galloped his horse to the barn and jumped down to confront him. The man drew a short sword and said, "Hail stranger, you threatened my family? I oughta run you through!"

Sarge paused his happy song long enough to casually say, "Go away."

The farmer reached out with his free hand to grab Sarge by the wrist and pull him from the barrel. Sarge blocked the farmer's hand away, and jab punched him in the face very quickly, hard enough to cause the farmer to stagger backwards and drop his sword! The punch was quick enough that he only missed a single note in his song.

The man rubbed his nose, and saw that it was bleeding slightly. He picked up his sword and rushed forward. "Draw your weapon!"

Sarge stopped playing, "Listen Bub you've got six, maybe seven, hours of daylight. Then a whole bunch of Awakened are going to climb outta the ground over there. If you're still here you're all going to die, just like your neighbors down the way, and their neighbors beyond that."

The farmer seemed to lose some of his temper, "Was it you? Did you bring the monsters?"

Sarge's jaw dropped in disbelief, and he wiped his hand down his face in frustration. After a brief pause he answered, "Don't be an idiot! I'm hunting them! I've tracked this 'mancer for fortnights now. I'm not sure where they'll appear, and I won't have time to save your hides while I'm trying to kill the 'mancer. So pack up your pretty little wife and the kiddos, and get them somewhere safe for the night."

The farmer looked like he was going to say something else, and finally he turned around and walked over to his wife, and they walked into the house.

Several hours later the sun was just starting to vanish over the horizon. The farmer and his family hitched a wagon to the horse, packed some things into the wagon, and rode away. Sarge stuffed the recorder back into his bag, and stashed his pack behind a barrel for safekeeping while he took care of business. He wished he had a better idea where the headstone was, so he'd know where the hole would open up when the necromancer and his Awakened spawn returned to the world of the living.

He walked out into the field, watching for the tell-tale flash of purplish light. The minutes went by slowly as the shadows gradually grew longer and darkness set in. Then he saw it off to his right. He was a hundred yards too far west, unfortunately, so he completely lost the element of surprise. The moon was bright and some dim light still remained in the sunset, so he could see the Awakened as they climbed out of the hole and spread out in all directions. He wasn't sure which shadowy figure was the necromancer, but he knew it had to be one of them because the Awakened couldn't be very far from the necromancer that controlled them. He didn't know what the necromancers were looking for, but they were certainly searching for something. The number of attacks on farmers and ranchers had increased drastically over the past year, and after each killing the necromancers ransacked the homes in search of something.

3

The first Awakened that was coming at him was not even human; it was some sort of bear. Clearly it had been dead for some time, and most of its fur was no longer in place. The poor creature's eyes glowed red dimly, as did the eyes of all of the Awakened when the necromancers enchanted them. As soon as it saw him it started charging him, screaming a fierce, otherworldly, shrieking howl. He was walking straight towards the undead beast, carrying his long sword in one hand and a short sword in the other. Both swords had strange symbols carved in the blades, similar to the symbols sewn into the front edges of his cloak. He whispered something under his breath and the strange symbols started to dimly glow light blue.

The Awakened bear raced towards him, and as he quickly lunged right the bear lunged forward after him, trying to bite him in the side. Sarge drove his short sword deep into the side of the bear's face. Then, leaving the sword in the bear, Sarge redirected his motion. He jumped into the air, spun, twisted, and then landed on the beast's back. He thrust the long sword into the massive monster's chest, careful to slice between the ribs. The bear reared up and tried to throw him off!

"Where's your sarding heart?" Sarge shouted. He struggled to cling to the creature as he retracted, redirected, and then thrust the sword into the chest of the Awakened bear repeatedly, desperately trying to find the beast's heart. He heard the screeching howls of other Awakened getting closer and knew that he had to hurry or this was going to be a very bad night. He growled, "Aw, come on, damya!"

He leapt from the bear's back and rolled through the grass in a ball. The bear quickly pounced on him; its large maw slammed shut just inches from his face. Lying on his back, Sarge dodged from side to side, each time barely avoiding the Awakened's deadly teeth. The bear reared up and Sarge finally had the opening he needed. He shoved the long sword up under the ribcage into the bear's chest and towards its throat. This time the enchanted blade found the creature's heart and the Awakened bear fell lifelessly to the ground. Sarge managed to roll away quickly as he saw the bear falling.

He stood up and yanked his short sword from the bear's head just in time to spin and drive it directly into the heart of an Awakened human that was about to claw at him from behind.

Suddenly Sarge was a blur of motion. Years of practice, aided by his magical powers, turned his movements into a flurry of unimaginable speed. Several Awakened approached in a pack and he dispatched them all in quick succession. He thrust, ducked, spun and parried attacks in a series of fluid motions. For several seconds it was as if he was a beautiful dancer spinning and lunging this way and that, each motion ending with the hilt of his sword sticking from another undead's chest.

In seconds, six Awakened lay motionless at his feet. With the immediate threat gone, he looked to the bear that still had his long sword buried in its chest. He circled the bear quickly to see if there was an easy way at the sword, but there wasn't. He pushed the bear to try to roll it over. Glancing over his shoulder, he saw the necromancer approaching. Sarge shoved the bear corpse with all of his might, "Give me my sword, damya!" He shouted with a grunt, and finally he was able to roll the bear to the side enough that he could slide his sword out.

He looked up in time to see a purple ball of magical power streaking at his head! He raised the short sword quickly, and the magic orb hit the sword. Purple light danced around the sword and then seemed to dissipate into the glowing symbols on the blade. He turned to face the evil spell caster that he had been tracking for so long. He was wearing long black robes and his face was hidden within the cowl. Sarge imagined that the vile man was smirking at him, anxiously waiting the moment he could add Sarge to his growing platoon of Awakened.

The necromancer lifted his staff and pointed the end with a purple glow towards Sarge. A steady stream of purple magic raced towards him. He flipped his short sword to the left, and it landed point-down in the ground a few feet away. Then he started a quick vertical spin with his long sword, changing to a reverse grip on the sword as he did so. At the end of the spin he stepped back into a low fighting posture and started spinning his sword in front of him in the *Butterfly of Death*. Technically speaking, the motion actually looked more like a noble man's bow tie. No self-respecting warrior wanted to execute a sword movement called the *Bow Tie*, so instead it was a *butterfly*.

The rapid spinning pattern of the sword formed a blur of motion in front of him. It was almost mesmerizing, and even as he faced his deadly opponent he heard his instructor in his ear encouraging calm and smooth patterns.

The first purple orb smacked into his blade as the blade made its defensive pattern before him. The force of the magic orb changed the sword's balance briefly and altered his pattern slightly, but Sarge was ready for it and adjusted. One after another the orbs slammed into the protective butterfly of blurred-sword dancing in front of him, each time the orb spread

5

down the sword blade and dissipated into the symbols.

Several of the Awakened, which had originally scattered, were now headed towards him. If he didn't end this quickly he'd be trying to fight undead and the necromancer at the same time.

Slowing the *Butterfly of Death* slightly, he changed the flow of the dance. With another spin of the sword, Sarge directed the blade skillfully behind his back and passed it to his left hand as he spun to his right. A purple orb streaked past him, just barely missing his head as he moved out of the way. He continued his spinning motion and grabbed a dagger from his belt. A steady line of orbs zipped past as he spun, each one getting closer than the last. The spinning motion left him kneeling on the ground, several feet to the right of where he had been. He leaned forward and tossed his dagger through the air towards the necromancer. Without waiting to see if it hit, he leapt to the left and rolled across the ground smoothly. With a step and another quick leap, he landed with a roll close enough to his short sword to pluck it from the ground easily as he stood up from his roll.

He raised his swords defensively just in case his dagger had missed its mark, but the necromancer lay on the ground where he expected to see him. All of the Awakened fell to the ground at once. Without the terrible spell caster animating them, they returned to the lifeless corpses that they should be. Sarge walked over to the necromancer and kicked him in the head to make sure he was dead. He reached down and retrieved his dagger. Then he took a few moments to clean each of his blades on the dead spell caster's robes before putting them to rest in their scabbards.

With a closer look, he realized that this necromancer was a woman. This wasn't the first time that he had killed a necromancer who turned out to be a woman. He wondered if the other Magi had noticed an increase in how often the necromancers were female.

He had hoped that this necromancer would have something on her person hinting at what she was searching for, but this one was no more help than the last. Her pouch contained a good amount of coin, and that always helped. Unfortunately, there was nothing else on this one to help him.

The next morning Sarge left the farm and started his long walk to the nearest city, the Free City of Ront'El. As he walked he looked north and saw the Rukthor Mountains standing tall and imposing. They were so huge that they looked nearby, even though he would have to travel many miles to the north just to reach the foothills. The view was beautiful, and rarely a day went past where he didn't sit for at least a few moments to admire the beauty of the mountains. They stretched across the entire length of the known lands. The mountains held no known paths to whatever lay to the north of them, and Sarge had never met anyone who had ever traveled beyond them.

Looking to the south, he saw the massive wall far off in the distance. Even from this far away it was impressive. It extended from the sea in the west all the way to the sea in the east, separating the Free Cities from their much feared and hated neighbor to the south. The Ryallic Empire was a massive realm, encompassing all of the land south of the Free Cities. Sarge had met the soldiers of the Ryallic Empire on the field of battle long ago, and it was not an experience that he wanted to repeat. He pushed that dreadful memory from his mind and focused on his walk.

Many hours later, as the sun started to sink lower in the evening sky, he walked into the Free City of Ront'El. He hadn't spent much time in this city, so he didn't have any friends or contacts here and would need to find an inn. Luckily the necromancer fattened his coin purse considerably, so he could afford to splurge some. Within a few minutes of entering town he found the *Pouting Goblin Inn*. It was dark and smoky inside, but that didn't bother Sarge any.

There were several open tables so he picked one near the door and climbed up onto the stool. It was a tall table, with four tall stools placed around it. As he arranged his packs beneath the table a sexy voice said, "What'ya want, sugar?"

He looked up and was slightly disappointed. The serving wench had the seductive voice of a forest nymph, but the face of a mildly attractive goblin. He glanced down at her low-cut dress and nodded his final approval. The tall stool put his eyes at the perfect height to admire her ample bosom. He smiled and replied, "Well darling, what do you got for a mischievous old Magi who's been on the road for a long time?"

She smiled back at him and said, "You need a strong ale, and some of Vinni's famous elk stew."

"Not exactly what I had in mind, but it'll work." He winked at her as she hurried off.

A short time later she returned with a mug of ale and a large bowl of stew. He hoped that the stew tasted as good as it smelled. The serving wench set the food and drink before him and then said, "I'm done at eight bells, darling. Maybe I'll meet a mischievous old Magi who'll show me a good time after work?" She winked at him and walked off.

The stew tasted every bit as good as it smelled. Sarge quickly ate the delicious elk stew and was about to ask the serving wench for another bowl when he noticed a man across the room looking at him. He reached over and took a drink of the ale. He closed his eyes and enjoyed the burn. It wasn't the best ale, but it was much better than pond water. Sarge kept a wary eye on the man and enjoyed the first decent ale he'd had in far too long. Eventually, the man moved over and sat down at his table. Sarge drank his ale and pretended not to notice the man sitting at the table across from him.

The man asked, "You a Magi?"

Sarge straightened his cloak and looked at the man, "Let me guess, the Magi cloak gave me away?"

"I thought the Magi were all dead."

"It's a long story. Now go away, willya Bub? I'm trying to enjoy an intimate moment with my ale."

"Have you heard about the Awakened spawn pillaging again? Seems like it's getting more common."

"Don't know what's got them worked up again. I killed a 'mancer just to the east of here, so the dead should stay dead for a while. Now, I would like to relax and enjoy the spoils of victory."

The man looked relieved, and very impressed. "You killed a necromancer, all on your own? Impressive! What about the one near Grum'Glin?"

Sarge sat up straighter, and put the mug down on the table, "A necromancer was seen near Grum'Glin?"

The man nodded quickly, "A merchant came through the other day talking about it."

"Dammit!" Sarge swallowed the rest of his ale in several quick gulps.

Then he stood up and flipped a coin to the bar wench. With a frown he said, "The good time will have to wait, sweetheart." He made his way quickly to the door, and headed into town to find someone who sold horses. He had been looking forward to a hot bath and a warm bar wench. That would have to wait. Grum'Glin was far to the west, and it would take him a long time to get there. Now that he had a few coins he could buy a new horse, and that would speed up his journey a bit.

Chapter 2

Rissyl

It was a beautiful day in Sorgo. Located in the northwestern part of the Ryallic Empire, the winters in Sorgo were much colder than in the cities far to the south. It was the month of Early-Spring, so the frozen nights and cold days were finally starting to release their hold on the lands, and spring was beginning to take hold. The trees were getting their early season buds, and soon the flowers would bloom and the grass would turn lush and green. Off in the distance some storm clouds lingered, bringing the promise of rain and the threat of storms. For now the temperature was perfect, and it wasn't raining. Rissyl sat on the top of a stone wall, leaning against the outside of his family's home. A young man in his late teens, he was average height and slightly more than average girth. He liked to think of himself as strong or big-boned, but truth be told he was slightly squishy. He thought he was a decent looking guy, and he was proud of his strong jaw line that was a common trait of the men of his family. His curly light-brown hair was overdue for a cut, and the stiff spring breeze kept blowing it into his face.

Rissyl loved the view from up there. His family's home was on one of the highest hills in this section of the city, and he could see much of the city sprawling out before him. His house was in the northern section of the Garden District of Sorgo, and he felt that this was probably the best place in the world to grow up. It was referred to as the Garden District because of the many flower gardens in the streets and plazas in this part of the city. It was a place set aside for the Gentry. Those well-to-do folks who made up part of the upper class, and worked as merchants, artisans, bankers, lesser bureaucrats and that sort of thing.

Looking to the south he could see the Chancery, the city district where the chancellor's palace was located. The Chancery also had offices for the various bureaucrats who ran the city. While the lesser bureaucrats, magistrates like his father, were considered Gentry and lived in the Garden District. Aristocrats, the powerful folks who ran things, were the city ministers and they all had villas and manor houses outside of the city. He thought that it would be great to live like that someday, but he wasn't sure that he was interested in imperial politics, so he might have to settle for a nice house in the Garden District.

Not far to the west he could see the large wall that separated the Garden and Chancery Districts in the east from the rest of the city to the west. He could see the guards at the north gate keeping the district safe from ne'er-do-wells and vagabonds who might try to slip in and cause problems. He wasn't exactly sure what a ne'er-do-well or a vagabond was, but his parents complained about them often so clearly the guards should keep them out of his district if at all possible.

Then he noticed a group of children in a plaza a few blocks away. At first he thought they were playing, but then he started to realize they were pick-pockets. Judging by their mismatched and badly out of style clothing he assumed they were Denizens, the fancy term for commoners. He shook his head slowly and wondered why Denizen children would be in the Garden District. He wasn't sure how they could even get in without their parents.

His father often talked about Denizens using their children as pick-pockets, because people were less likely to be suspicious of children. Rissyl didn't understand how parents could do that to their own children since the punishment for pick-pocketing was typically ten years as a Dreg. Dregs were slaves, but no one was supposed to call them slaves. What kind of parent would risk their child spending ten years as a Dreg? If the rants of his father were any indication, those kinds of people were destined to be Dregs. Even after their term was over, most of them ended up breaking some law and ending up becoming a Dreg once again.

Sometimes he got frustrated that his parents both worked long hours, and sometimes it seemed like fortnights since the last time they have had any fun-time together. However, he knew that his parents would never expect him or his sister to turn to crime on the street. Even if they lived in the Commons District as Denizens, his parents would never do that. They would just work hard to be a good blacksmith, tanner, or something to make enough coin to put food on the table. He thought everyone should do that, instead of turning to crime and ending up a Dreg. He thought that it would be a rotten life to work dreadfully hard all day long and earn nothing for it. It would be awful to be someone's property. He couldn't even imagine what it would be like to live in the Dross. The Dross was located on the far west side of the Commons, and it was a walled and heavily guarded district where many of the Dregs lived. Some Dregs lived with a Lord, like his family's servants who lived at his home. Most Dregs lived in the Dross and worked each day on farms or building roads or something similar.

He shivered at these awful thoughts as he watched one of the children approach a man who was walking down the street. Rissyl couldn't see exactly what was happening because a tree was partially blocking his view, but he was fairly sure that one of the children just tried, or succeeded, to pick the man's pocket. Rissyl looked around for the sentinels. He expected them to come by at any moment to put an end to the children's crimes. He felt that no Gentry deserved to be robbed by Denizens, especially not in the middle of the Garden District. He couldn't believe the nerve of some of these filthy people.

He heard the voice of his best friend call his name from the other side of his yard. Rissyl shouted, "I'm back here, Urg!" A moment later, Burga stepped around the corner and into the rear yard. He was a skinny boy of average height, with short brownish blond hair and mischievous grey eyes. He was wearing a stylish blue tunic and a new pair of breeches.

"Hey Riz, you eat lunch yet?" Burga climbed up onto the stone wall as he talked. He sat on the wall with both feet hanging off the same side so he could look at Rissyl and see the scene below that was captivating Rissyl's attention.

"Nope. Check that out." He pointed towards the children down the street, "Denizen children I think, right here in The Gardens. Picking pockets or something?"

"Whoa! If the sentinels catch them, do you think they'll make them Dregs and sell them right there on the spot? Maybe we could buy one? I still have most of my Ryallic Victory Festival money." Burga flashed a huge grin at his friend.

Rissyl made a face as if he'd tasted something nasty, "I don't know Urg, and I don't think that's something to joke about. Technically, they are people still."

"Unless they become a Dreg, then we could buy them."

"You aren't old enough to own Dregs."

Burga ignored his point. They sat quietly watching for a long time. Finally Rissyl said, "Look at them, they're young aren't they? Do you think they're teens yet?"

Burga shrugged, "Don't know, I can't tell. Does it matter?"

Rissyl supposed that it probably didn't matter. He had heard his dad talk about kids as young as nine or ten years old becoming Dregs. Occasionally, Denizens started clamoring about laws that needed changed to protect

11

children from becoming Dregs at an early age, but they always seemed to quiet back down when it was suggested that the parents become Dregs instead of their children when the children break the laws.

"Speaking of Dregs, your new Dreg's got huge diddies!" Burga flashed him a huge grin.

Rissyl felt uncomfortable talking about one of his family's Dregs like that, especially where they might hear. "Yes, they are hard to miss."

Burga leaned over and said quietly, "So, did you sard her yet?"

"What?"

"You know, did you sleep with her yet?"

"By the gods, Urg! I know what it means! Do you kiss your mother with that mouth?"

He grinned and said, "Not until I've washed it out with soap."

Rissyl shook his head, "My father would knock my teeth out if he heard me swear like that."

Burga turned away and started looking towards the market. He smacked Rissyl in the chest. "Look there, sentinels!"

Rissyl looked where his friend was pointing, and sure enough there was a squad of sentinels. They were all on horseback. Each wore a shiny platemail chest piece with a mixture of chainmail and plates covering the rest of the body. The chain-plate mixture gave the sentinels a good amount of protection, while still providing much more ease of movement than full battle armor, or so Rissyl's father once explained. They wore an open-face helm and a tabard. One of them, the sentinel captain, wore a blue and black tabard with white and gold highlights. The other three wore a blue and black tabard. All four of the sentinels were riding in the general direction of the Denizen children.

Burga tugged his sleeve and said, "Come on, let's go watch!"

"We are not buying one!" Rissyl pulled his arm away and gave his friend a stern look.

"Fine, but let's go see what happens!" They both jumped down from the wall and raced down the street.

When they got to the plaza the sentinels had already arrived. The children tried to run from the sentinels, but they quickly caught up with children, dismounted, and restrained them. Each child had their right arm presented to the sentinel captain who inspected the back of the child's wrist. Rissyl guessed that none of the children had a tattoo on the back of their wrist. The Dregs all had a tattoo to indicate that they were a Dreg. It looked like these children had no tattoo, so they were Denizens. Perhaps they were unloved, poorly dressed, and smelly Gentry. However, that was unlikely.

The sentinel captain said, "What are you doing here, children?"

The oldest looking kid, a girl who was probably not yet a teen, looked up at him. She said, "Nothing. Walking around. Not bugging no one."

"Oh really? Well, someone tells me that four kids, who look an awful lot like you four, were in the plaza picking pockets. Where are you from? Where are your parents?"

The girl yelled, "RUN!" and all of the kids took off in different directions. The sentinel captain grabbed her arm before she even got a step away. The other sentinels took off after sprinting children, and before long each one had been captured and brought back to the captain.

"In the name of the chancellor, I am taking all four of you into custody on charges of pick pocketing."

One at a time, the sentinels chained the children's hands together in front of them. The end of the chain was then attached to one of the horses. Several people gathered around, but no one dared naysay the sentinels. Within moments of arriving the sentinels began to ride off with their prisoners. The children trailed behind the horses trying to keep up.

After the sentinels left the plaza with the children, Burga said, "Well that sucked! I wanted to see them being sold!"

Rissyl shrugged, "It's not like they're going to sell them right away. They get a trial or something don't they?"

"Dunno? Wanna have lunch?"

"Yeah, I suppose."

Later that night, Rissyl sat down to enjoy dinner with his family. His mother, Amalia, sat to his left at one end of the large table. Her golden blonde hair was just starting to show streaks of grey, and she had it pulled back into a loose pony tail at the back of her neck. She straightened the napkin beneath her silverware as she waited for the food to be brought to the table. "How was your day, Riz?"

"It was okay, I guess. Urg and I went down to the Commons for lunch. We stopped by the bazaar to see if they had any blue or green wool cloth for his mother. We must have gone through bolts of cloth at ten different merchants and none of them had blue or green. But if you want some brown wool cloth, that stuff is everywhere."

To his right, at the other end of the table was his father, Tuknor. He was tall and skinny, with his brown hair cropped short and a well-kept beard and mustache. His skin was light from working indoors for so many years. He replied, "Well, that's because the plants used for blue and green dye are hard to find, and the only places where they grow are not very safe. We've had to cut down on Dreg expeditions to those regions because the Dregs were needed for other things."

His mother said, "Well, the Dregs certainly weren't reallocated to the farms! The alms farmers are desperate for Dregs to work the fields to get the crops planted in time, and for some reason we just can't get enough Dregs to do the work."

Tuknor replied, "We have several new roads projects right now, and the chancellor insists that the roads be finished before Early-Fall. Every available Dreg has been reassigned to the stone quarries, to transport stones, and to build the roads. We've allocated as many as we can to other needs, including farming."

Rissyl had heard this discussion many times. His mother was a magistrate who oversaw alms distribution, to make sure that all citizens of Sorgo had some food to eat if they couldn't buy their own. It was her job to coordinate which farms grew food for alms, oversee the delivery and distribution of the food, and that sort of thing. From what he could tell it was an exhausting and thankless job that frequently kept her away from home late into the night.

His father was a magistrate who oversaw the allocation of Dreg labor. Magistrate of Live Property was his official title but most people just called him the Dreg Dealer. From what Rissyl understood, his father's job included everything from assigning which Dregs would do which job, to handling the buying, selling, and trading of individual Dregs.

With their jobs so closely tied to each other, his parents often brought their work disagreements home with them.

The mention of the Dregs reminded him of the incident with the children in the plaza. He said, "Urg and I saw some Denizen children in the Gardens market today. They were pick-pocketing! The sentinels showed up and dragged them away in chains."

Across the table from him, his little sister slammed her fist on the table causing tableware to jump and creating quite the clatter. She was two years younger than he was, but she looked even younger than that. Her long blond hair was tied into eight pony tails, the bases of which formed a ring from one side of the crown of her head around the back and over to the other side.

This was the fashion these days, but Rissyl frequently teased her about it. She folded her arms in front of her and leaned back into her chair, huffing, "I never get to see nothing fun! Did they sell any of the kid Dregs before they dragged them away? I wish I could've seen it!"

Tuknor hid his grin in his hand and tried not to laugh out loud. Amalia looked shocked and said, "Brielle Ezmorelda Fransisca Sokigo! What an awful thing to say! Dreg children are people too!" Amalia had noticed their Dreg servants walking into the room as Rissyl finished his story. She also noticed the look of shock and alarm on the servants' faces at Rissyl's story.

Brielle rolled her eyes, "They're not people when they become Dregs! They're just things to own! Like farm animals, but not as smelly!"

Rissyl faked surprise, and looked to his father, "Is that true, Father? I always thought Dregs were much smellier than farm animals?"

Brielle, Rissyl, and their father burst into laughter. Amalia was not amused. "Stop it this instance!" She motioned towards the servants standing at the entrance to the dining room. All eyes turned in that direction and an awkward silence fell over the room.

After a long moment, Tuknor said, "I apologize. We were simply joking around. No offense intended." His words were apologetic, but his tone was dismissive.

Rissyl felt dreadful. The servants were Dregs, but he was sure that his joking was probably hurtful to them. He had been raised, as were all citizens of the empire, to look at the Dregs with contempt. At times like this he felt that maybe they deserved to be treated with a little more courtesy.

The older of the two servants was an elderly woman named Marisul. She walked into the room carrying a large platter of beef. She smiled at Tuknor as she walked over to serve his dinner, "Of course, milord! All in good fun." Rissyl found himself wondering if she was really that happy and forgiving, or if she was just acting as expected to avoid problems. He guessed it was just a very good act. He didn't know how someone could take such a blatant insult and laugh it off like that. He was certain that he couldn't do it.

The younger servant, Cynia, stood behind her. She was a year younger than Rissyl and had only been in the Sokigo household for a few months. Marisul was getting close to the end of her term as a Dreg, so his father had bought the new Dreg to replace her. Cynia was slender and, as Burga had pointed out, she was well-rounded in the bosom. Her hair was strawberry blond, roughly cut about shoulder length and her long bangs were tucked behind her ears. Her facial expression revealed that she was annoyed, but she remained silent.

Once Marisul moved to Brielle, Cynia walked over to Tuknor and offered him beans and bread from her serving tray. The two housemaids continued around the table until everyone had been served. On their way out of the dining room Cynia stopped and turned around, "I wash your clothes. Trust me, Dregs ain't the only smelly folks in this house." She smiled sweetly.

Rissyl was shocked. Never before had he heard a Dreg talk back like that. He had no idea how his father would react. He looked at his little sister and she looked like she had just seen a three-headed horse, as she sat with her mouth agape and stared at the servant.

His father slowly wiped his chin and then looked to the older servant, "Remove her this instant before she further spoils our meal. I will deal with her later. Off you go!"

Both of the servants rushed out of the room. Rissyl saw the older housemaid smack the younger up against the back of the head as they moved out of the dining room.

Later that evening, after Rissyl had cleaned up and changed for bed, he found himself walking past the servants' room. His family's house was large, but it was average size for a home in the Garden District, and like most houses in this district it included a small bedroom for a servant to stay in. This room was always located on the back side of the kitchen area near the storage and utility areas of the house, and far away from the sleeping rooms of the rest of the family. Some houses had a separate building altogether for their servants, especially if they owned several of them.

Since his family was in transition between servants they both stayed in the one little room. There was only room for one bed in there, so he assumed that the younger servant slept on the floor. He could hear the servants talking as he walked past, so he paused for a moment to listen.

"I don't care, Cynia! You can't talk like that to the lord of our house!"

"They don't gotta be mean with us standing right there!"

The older housemaid laughed in a short abrasive burst, "That was mean? Are you dense? Most Gentry would've had you beaten for that little stunt! Now shut up about it, and get to sleep!"

"Someone needs to stand up for Dregs."

Something slammed against a large wooden object, "Now you've lost your sarding mind, haven't you? You know what'd happen if anyone heard you say that? After a fortnight of beatings and worse to make you regret your stupidity, you would be sold! No more easy housemaid job living the good life in a nice house! No, you stupid girl, you'd get a new owner. And mark my words the new one wouldn't be as nice as this one. Is that what you want, you thankless wench?"

There was silence for a moment, and Rissyl could only hear faint sounds of someone moving around in the room. Then Marisul said, "You're lucky to have this family. Don't squander it away, your next lord could be so much worse. Mr. Sokigo is a gentle and patient man, but even he has his limits. You might've just past those limits tonight. No one wants a mouthy Dreg!"

Rissyl couldn't stand to listen to any more. He turned around and returned to his room. Now more than ever he was thankful that he wasn't born to a Dreg mother.

The next morning Rissyl woke with the sunrise. He woke up feeling bad that his joking had caused problems for the young Dreg, and he wanted to talk to his father to make sure he wasn't planning to do anything drastic. He certainly couldn't stand watching the girl beaten because of him. When he got downstairs he was surprised to see his neighbor, Belro, in the family room talking to his father.

"Why don't you just offer her up in the bazaar at the next Dreg Day?" Belro sipped a cup of coffee and lounged on one of the comfortable couches on the east side of the room, near the windows.

His father sat in his usual chair, partially facing the window but also looking upon the other chairs and couches in the room. It was Rissyl's favorite chair when his father wasn't home, because it was the most comfortable in the house. When Father was home that chair was off limits.

"I've thought about it. I'd certainly get the most money for her that way. But it seems like a waste. It's rare to find a Dreg her age that hasn't gone at least partially crazy. Especially if they were born to a Dreg. There is such a shortage of young female Dregs who can be a servant in a respectable house these days. She's a comely lass, so the more unscrupulous buyers would run her price way beyond what anyone would pay for a simple servant because she'd be a good commodity for their unseemly establishments. After a few months in that environment she'd no longer be a viable option to work in anyone's home, that's for certain."

"You're the Dreg Dealer for the entire city; don't you have a dozen buyers lined up to buy someone like her? Why not sell her to one of them?"

Rissyl sat down on a chair next to his father. Neither man seemed to notice that he joined them. His father took a sip of coffee, "Actually I have thirty-six petitions on my desk requesting an in-home servant, thirty-two of them are specifically looking for a female, and twenty-eight of those are looking for a female under twenty-five. I could surely sell her to any of them, but I don't feel right mixing business and personal profits. Plus, if she goes crazy and hurts someone then I've got angry people banging on my door. I really don't have time for that."

"You could sell her back to the city, couldn't you? That wouldn't be nearly as much money as selling her on Dreg Day in the bazaar, but it should be a fair price."

"Oh yes, I'd get a fair price. But then she'd be put back in the Dross. She's not really cut out for farm labor, or working in the mines. She's full grown now so within days she'd be sent off to serve in the imperial amity corps and assigned to one of the military regiments. That would be a waste. I'd really rather find a good Gentry family to buy her directly."

"Well, I have a friend who mentioned that he was either going to get another dog or get a Dreg to help around the house and yard. I could see if he has made up his mind yet. He doesn't have a lot of extra money right now, but he does have a nice spice garden. Would you take part of the payment in barter?"

"Talk to him, and see if he is interested in a comely but mouthy Dreg." Tuknor took another sip of coffee. "I'm sure we can work out some barter arrangement, especially for spices."

Rissyl listened with a growing pit in his stomach. On one hand, it was intriguing to hear his father talk about the business of owning Dregs. That wasn't a topic that he heard very often, and it was probably something he'd need to understand better as he rushed quickly towards manhood. On the other hand, he felt bad that his joke was going to make the poor Dreg girl be sold to someone else.

After a moment he said, "Couldn't we just keep her? It was my fault that she spoke back like that."

"No, son. If I tolerate back talk from her it will just continue to spiral out of control. Pretty soon I would have no choice but physical punishment to put her in line. And I'll not allow a lowly Dreg to cause me to stoop to that level. She's got to go."

Three hours later Belro, his friend Tommis, and Rissyl's father stood in the family room. Cynia stood off to one side of the room quietly. She looked

18

nervous, but she didn't make a sound. Rissyl kept looking to her, hoping that she would look his way so that he could apologize, or give her a reassuring look, or something. She just stared at the opposite wall. His father and Tommis signed a parchment with a bunch of formal looking writing on it. Then they both shook hands.

Without any further pleasantries, Tommis motioned for her to follow him and they left. She took nothing with her except what she was wearing.

Tuknor and Belro walked to another room and Rissyl decided to follow Tommis and his new Dreg. He just wanted to see how the man treated her.

He followed them discreetly, and was surprised to see that the man lived just down the street from them because he didn't remember ever seeing the man before. As Gentry went, Tommis was not the best example. Most folks from the Gardens district tried to dress presentably when they went out. However, Tommis wore clothes that made him look more like a Denizen than a respectable member of the nice side of town. Rissyl watched the man lead her into his back yard, and shut the gate behind them. Without climbing the man's wall he wouldn't be able to see any more, so after a few moments he headed back home.

As he walked he started to wonder if he could see that yard from his favorite spot on his wall. Curious, he hurried home and climbed up onto his favorite spot. When he looked down the street to Tommis's home he was able to see into his yard fairly well. At first he didn't see the girl, but then he realized that she was within one of the dog cages along the back fence of the home. Tommis was nowhere around. Rissyl wasn't sure what the girl could have done in the two minutes that it took him to get back home that would cause the man to put her into a cage.

Rissyl sat on his spot and watched down the street for quite a while. Every half hour or so Tommis came outside and spent several minutes tormenting the girl. The first time he poured water on her and the next time he brought a mean dog out and put it into the cage with her. Rissyl was afraid the dog might really attack her, and from her reaction of cowering in the corner, the girl believed so as well.

The next time Tommis went outside he unlocked the cage and called the girl out. He held a stick in front of the girl's face and then threw it across the yard. After a good amount of prompting the girl crawled on her hands and knees after the stick, and carried it back to Tommis in her mouth. The man repeated the game several times before putting the girl back in the cage and returning to his house.

Almost an hour later the man came out of his house with a big bucket of slop. He poured some of it into each of the cages, and the dogs within ran over and devoured the food. Then he poured some into a pan in the girl's cage. He shouted at the girl to eat it. When she refused, he unlocked the cage and motioned for her to come out. When she refused to do that as well, he reached in and dragged her out of the cage. Tommis grabbed the stick and began to whack the girl on the back and backside with it.

That was all that Rissyl could take. The whole mess had gotten completely out of hand. It was his fault and he was going to fix it. He jumped down from the wall and sprinted down the street. Slightly out of breath, he arrived at the gate to Tommis's back yard. He paused for a moment to breathe, and then he pounded on the gate. He could hear the girl demand that the man stop hitting her. When the gate wasn't opened right away Rissyl threw open the gate and stomped into the back yard. He was not someone who was accustomed to fighting, or even to making strong demands of people. None of that mattered now. It was time to fix the damage he caused.

"Sir, my father has changed his mind. We cannot sell this Dreg right now. He has sent me to retrieve her. You will stop hitting her immediately and allow me to return her to my father's home."

"How dare you presume to tell me what to do with my Dreg? I bought her fair and square, and I won't give her back!"

"My father is the Magistrate of Live Property, ownership disputes are handled by the petty clerks who report to him. Do you really wish to challenge him on this?"

The man gave him an angry stare, and then tossed the stick on the ground. He pushed her away from him with his foot, roughly, as she tried to stand up and walk. Rissyl flung out his hand and caught her, and led her out of that yard and back up the street.

He was dreading what he would say to his father when they got in the house. He was sure that his father would be extremely angry. Especially when Rissyl told him that he had threatened the man using his father's position in the city's government.

When they walked into the house, his mother was walking out of the family room. She said, "Why have you brought the girl back here and what in Khalius happened to her?"

Cynia was still wet from head to foot, and she was covered with dirt, mud, and dog feces. Water, and other gunk, was dripping from her clothes onto the floor as she clung to Rissyl's arm. She smelled awful of dog urine and worse from the filthy cage where she had spent the last several hours.

Rissyl wasn't sure what to say and before he could answer, his mother said, "Riz, run along and find Marisul. Tell her to draw up a bath for the girl." As he rushed out to find the older servant he heard his mother say, "Hurry up, girl. Take off those awful clothes."

Half an hour later Rissyl sat on the couch and looked at his parents. Brielle sat on the other end of the couch, crocheting something and not really paying attention to them. He had explained what happened. Actually, he had explained it a couple of times, each time emphasizing different aspects of what angered him. Neither of his parents had said anything yet, and he wasn't sure how much trouble he was in, but he didn't regret his actions. His blood was still boiling from what the man was doing, and he spoke passionately and angrily when he explained things to his parents.

Finally his father said, "Did you berate the man for hitting the girl?"

"I told him to stop hitting her, because you decided that you couldn't sell her and you wanted me to bring her home immediately."

His father let out a deep sigh. "Okay, I think I can salvage this without too much drama. I'll go talk to Tommis now." He stood up to leave.

"You're not taking her back to him."

His father stopped in mid stride, and even Brielle looked up from her crocheting to look at him in surprise. His father looked to him and said, "Excuse me? Was that a question, or a statement?"

"I am sorry. It is not my place to make demands in our family, but if you take her back there I couldn't live with myself! She's a Dreg, I get it, but if I have to look into that yard every day and see what's happening to her, it would be almost as much punishment to me as it is to her. Besides, it is so difficult to find a decent Dreg for the home these days. You said so yourself!"

"Whoa your horse, young man. I will not return the girl to Tommis. If she can control her mouthy tongue, she can remain here. Perhaps this incident will teach her a lesson to appreciate how good her life is, but I must smooth things over with Tommis. I'll not have a neighbor cross with us because he was robbed of amusement."

Rissyl breathed a sigh of relief. "Thank you."

"We're not finished talking about this. We have a long discussion ahead of us about not using my position as leverage over people. A very long discussion."

Chapter 3

Rissyl

He was sitting in his favorite spot, looking out over the city. His head felt odd, he couldn't actually remember climbing up onto the wall, and he wasn't exactly sure why he was on the wall late at night. Well, at least he thought it was night. Just a few minutes ago he had climbed into bed. Was it morning already? Rissyl wasn't sure. He looked around and everything was covered in a haze.

He heard something that sounded an awful lot like "Darp! Darp! Darp!" Looking down at the top of the wall by his feet he noticed a little glowing... thing. It was about the size of his fist, and it almost looked like a fuzzy little floppy-eared puppy made out of pure light. He was a little afraid to move, until the little thing started barking at his foot again. "Darp! Darp!" It turned in circles a few times, and then it got close enough to sniff his shoe.

Rissyl reached down to touch the tiny light puppy-thing. It jumped back, put its head low to the ground, and stuck its little fuzzy light-puppy butt up in the air. Its long tail wagged quickly. He wondered if the thing really was some sort of puppy, or if it was just in his imagination.

Something off to his left caught his attention. He looked over and saw an unbelievable sight. There was a man made out of light walking in his back yard! The man was probably four feet tall, but he was incredibly skinny, even his head was elongated. He had long narrow arms and legs, and a long narrow body. His hair was long and flowing, and each hair looked like a single strand of sunlight. Even though the man was made of light he didn't glow brightly, and he wasn't transparent. The light seemed to draw the outlines of his features. The man was carrying one end of a long golden log of some sort.

"Hey there, why are you bringing a long golden log thing into my yard?" It seemed like a logical question.

"No time to talk, she comes!"

Rissyl felt bad for interrupting the man when he was clearly busy doing whatever it was he was doing. Not wanting to bother the man further, he pulled a lute down from the roof of his house and started playing a song. As the light-man walked further into his yard the long golden log just kept growing. Eventually the other end appeared and another light-man was carrying that end.

After a while there were several light-men throughout his back yard. They had all dragged in several long golden logs. He wasn't sure what they were going to do with them, but he was pretty sure that his father would be annoyed. Especially since several of the light-men smashed the vegetable garden as they tromped around the yard.

He was pretty impressed with the song he was playing on the lute. He smiled to himself as he strummed the catchy tune. It wasn't too shabby for someone who had never played an instrument before. He looked down at his feet and noticed the little light puppy-thing standing on its back legs, dancing to the song. He was impressed. He had never seen a creature like that who could dance on its back legs.

A couple of the light-men started rolling one of the golden logs around his back yard. As they did the yard was covered in gold. It was as if a massive roll of golden fabric was being rolled out across his back yard.

He really needed to say something before one of his parents arrived. His mother would not approve of such an ostentatious display of having a golden back yard. What would the neighbors think? "You there, you really shouldn't be doing that. Perhaps you could roll out your golden stuff somewhere else?"

Several of the light-men made "Shhh!" sounds and hand motions. One of them said, "Hush, she's almost here!"

He couldn't help but wonder who was coming. He watched as the light-men started rolling their golden fabric up to the sky. It was the most unusual sight, as his back yard was slowly transformed into a massive golden room with four golden walls, a golden ceiling, and a golden floor. He figured that he should get out of the way so he placed the lute on top of the wall and jumped down. He was happy to see the little light puppy-thing jump down also, and they both floated slowly to the ground together.

One by one, the light-men lined up along two sides of the golden room, and the little light puppy-thing crawled into the floor and vanished.

A moment later all of the light-men knelt to the ground, leaned forward, and bowed so deeply that their arms were laid out on the floor before them and their faces were planted right onto the floor. He wondered if he should bow or curtsy or something, but he thought he would feel silly doing such a thing.

Suddenly the room was filled with an unimaginable brightness directly in front of him. He was filled with an uncontrollable wave of reverence and adoration. Without thinking he dropped to the ground on his knees, with his arms outstretched before him. He tried desperately to bury his face into the ground because he knew that he was not worthy to gaze upon the incredible power and beauty that stood before him. He sobbed with joy and fear.

In his mind he heard the being say, "Arise, my child!"

He instantly stood up. He desperately wished that he could have stood up faster, because this being deserved immediate obedience, not the sluggish movements of his feeble legs.

He didn't feel worthy to speak to the being before him, but he had to know, "Who are you?"

The answer resonated through his mind, piercing, and almost painful in its glory. "I am known by many names. Your people call me Nalria"

"Nalria? The goddess of magic? You're a goddess?" He felt even less worthy than he had earlier. He wanted to bow down again, but he could not bring himself to violate her wish since she had earlier told him to stand.

"Yes, my child, I am one of many. Your actions for my child Cynia Dodisen were seen and noted. You have proven yourself worthy of my gift, if you choose to accept it."

He was overwhelmed, "Gift? What gift? How could I possibly refuse your gift?"

"You must not answer in haste. My gift comes with a great burden and often with profound consequences. Great evil is spreading in these lands, and much worse is to come. It is time for magic to once again stand against the evil. You have been chosen as one of the four to bring the light of magic back to these lands. You cannot begin to comprehend the importance of the choice that you will be asked to make."

"But, if it is that important, couldn't you simply command me? Why ask, if so much is at stake?"

"I cannot violate the free will of one mortal in order to save others. The choice will be yours to freely make."

"How do I make the choice? I don't understand!"

"Speak with Cynia Dodisen. She and the others were chosen long ago. She will know what to do."

He could feel that Nalria was leaving. He still hadn't looked upon her; he could only gaze at the golden walls to either side of her. He desperately wanted her to stay, he had so many questions, and he longed to be in her presence for just a while longer!

Rissyl woke up in his own bed, and sat up with a jolt. He looked around his room, and it was completely dark. His heart was racing, and he was sweating like crazy even though the room was cold. He lay back down and pulled the covers up to his nose. For a very long time he lay there staring at the ceiling, and saw only darkness. He felt vaguely empty and uneasy. That was certainly the most intense and bizarre dream he had ever had.

Chapter 4

Vendino

Minister Vendino straightened the parchments before him. He was seated at a large table in the Royal Hall, waiting for the regular audience with the emperor to begin. It was early in the morning, well before the sun had even come up, but such was the way of things for busy people. As the Minister of Affairs he was the top official in the Council of Ministers and he frequently met with the emperor to discuss all aspects of governing such a large and prosperous empire. The emperor liked to get meetings out of the way early, which meant many early mornings for Vendino.

He was a small, skinny man, with thinning white hair and a pointy nose. He wore the customary white and yellow robes of a member of the Council of Ministers. Eleven other men and women were seated at the table with him, and the seat on the end of the table was left open for the emperor. Being the highest ranking minister on the council, Vendino occupied the seat immediately to the right of the emperor.

One of the guards posted beside the door to the emperor's offices announced, "The emperor approaches!" The people at the table stood up, and everyone in the room assumed the Royal Reverence Bow. They placed the pads of their fingers of one hand against the pads of the fingers of the other hand, fingers apart, arms and hands pointed in a forty-five degree angle from the body and elbows pressed tight against their sides. They bowed their heads slightly, and maintained this posture until the emperor entered the room. Once he got to his chair, he mimicked their bow quickly but did not maintain it. As soon as the emperor finished his bow, the remainder of the room finished theirs. Only once the emperor was seated did the others take their seats.

The emperor said, "Greetings ministers. I hope you've had a pleasant and successful fortnight." A chorus of greetings came from around the table. After a moment the emperor continued, "What issues do we have to discuss today?"

The room was silent briefly, and then Vendino said, "Your Majesty, we must address the problem of excessive population in several of the cities.

Chancellors from more than half of our cities report that the problem is becoming critical."

A woman on the far end of the table named Aribeth, the Minister of the Treasury, sounded annoyed as she said, "Your Majesty, couldn't we just exterminate a bunch of the Denizens and get the numbers down to a more manageable level?"

Across from Vendino, Minister Thorli sat in the chair to the emperor's immediate left. As the Minister of War, Thorli commanded the vast armies of the empire. He had been a watchman and then a marshal in charge of units for decades before being appointed to the minister's chair. He was one of the few ministers who had actually been a Denizen. He rose in social status to Gentry and then again to an Aristocrat. Most of the other ministers were born into the Aristocracy. In a loud and firm voice he said, "You can't just kill large groups of people."

Someone else at the other side of the table said, "Why not? If it is the will of the Council of Ministers, the people should be happy to comply!"

Without raising his voice, the emperor said, "Thorli is right. Next suggestion?"

Vendino only half listened to the proposals. These things typically digressed into arguing and bickering, and he tried not to get involved with it.

After a moment a minister about halfway down the table said, "Why not take several Denizens and make them Dregs in these cities? We'd solve the overpopulation problem and provide more Dreg labor to the city. There are many projects that have been clamoring for more Dregs. It's a win-win solution."

There was great consensus around the table, with the majority of the council nodding their heads in agreement, or muttering their approval at the idea. Then someone asked, "How do we decide which ones become Dregs?"

Someone suggested, "We could draw names at random, perhaps at a festival or celebration?" This was met with negative comments and body language from the other council members.

Someone else said, "Why not go around to the various whore houses and gambling halls and start rounding up some of the cretins that frequent those places and make them Dregs?" This received some positive responses, but the reaction was clearly mixed.

Aribeth cleared her throat and said, "No, let's raise the taxes. Those who can't pay would become Dregs. That would solve the problem on its own, and raise more coin for the treasury." Again there was general agreement.

Minister Thorli pushed some parchments away from him and let his hand fall heavily. It made a loud thud as it struck the table. "You're not thinking clearly. The people need to believe that the Dregs are scum. They need to look down on them and not feel bad about it. You can't expect the majority of folks to enslave a huge group of people if they don't genuinely believe that the enslaved deserve what they get! No one cares when rapists and murders become Dregs. But if you suddenly take a large number of honest hard-working folks and make them slaves you risk unraveling the peace and order of our empire!"

Everyone started talking at once. The man who suggested raiding the whore houses added, "That's why I said to raid the gambling dens and whore houses. Clearly, these people are degenerates and deserve to be Dregs." Whether everyone at the table heard him was unlikely because there was so much chatter and heated debate going on.

The emperor looked to his left and said, "What do you propose, Minister Thorli?" The room quickly became quiet and everyone looked to the warrior, who looked rather out of place in his minister's robes instead of armor.

"It seems simple, Majesty. We just need to open Misi for population."

The room instantly erupted in shouting and heated arguments. Several ministers stood up to more adamantly make their point. The debates raged on for several minutes before the emperor called for silence.

"Minister Crawley, what are your concerns?" The emperor looked across the table to a short and round man standing and gesturing wildly as he tried to make his point to someone next to him.

The Minister of Records sat down and paused for a moment to compose himself. Then he replied, "Your Majesty, populating a new city is nightmare for the ministers and all of the magistrates below us. It is nothing but endless documents and planning. I'm just now getting caught up from the last city that we populated several years ago!"

Of all of the ministers in the council, Vendino knew that Crawley would be one of the most affected by the decree.

Minister Aribeth added, "Your Majesty, Minister Crawley has a very good point. Additionally, there would be no end to the complaints from the Denizens. Some Denizens will want to relocate, and others won't. We can expect countless requests for financial assistance with moving costs."

Thorli said, "Majesty, Misi was reclaimed almost eight years ago. It's been purged, and the builders were done renovating it a year ago. Plus, Wolverine Regiment has been garrisoned in Misi for way too long. They'll

28

lose their edge if we don't use them soon. Training is good, but only real battle can keep a force at its best. I suggest we deploy Wolverine Regiment to capture another barbarian city, and you can begin populating Misi."

The emperor looked to Vendino and said, "I need a map." Vendino looked quickly through the pile of parchments before him. When he found a map of the empire and surrounding lands he placed it before the emperor. The emperor studied it carefully, "Our last three expansions have been to the east, and the capture of Misi was the most problematic yet. The barbarians in that region seem to resent our steady approach. Perhaps we should turn our attention to the west this time?" He paused and looked at the map for a while. "This place called Grum'Glin is the closest to the western gate of our border wall. How about that one?"

After some discussion, the room seemed to be in agreement with the choice of Grum'Glin. Aribeth spoke up, "That city is on the banks of a large river. Extending the western wall to claim that portion of the river will disrupt river trade for the barbarian cities upriver from Grum'Glin. They're likely to be unhappy about this."

Vendino heard Thorli whisper something to the emperor, and he pointed to something written on a piece of parchment before him.

The emperor responded, "I'm not worried about barbarian cities and their trade woes. If needed we'll move Wolf Pack Regiment over there from the eastern regions. If we need to capture three cities instead of one then we'll do that. Ladies and gentlemen, begin your arrangements. I want the Misi population project to begin by this coming Summer Solstice."

Vendino said, "For the documents, Majesty, what shall we call Grum'Glin once it's been reclaimed?"

There was a long pause as the emperor thought. "Let's call it, Grulin."

The rest of the meeting carried on much the same as the first part. Vendino only paid partial attention to what was being said. He was too busy running through things in his mind, trying to organize all of the things he was going to have to put in motion to start a smooth population of Misi.

When the meeting ended the emperor excused all of the ministers except Vendino. When they were alone the emperor asked, "Is there anything else that we need to discuss?"

"Yes, Your Majesty. A merchant has arrived from the dwarven kingdom. He has setup shop in the Gardens market selling jewelry and such. He sent word to me discreetly that he has some of the garroliron that we requested."

"Some? Why not all?"

"He didn't say, but it is reportedly very rare and dangerous to mine, which is probably why they feel that they can demand twice what you were offering. They brought four pounds of the garroliron."

"Twice?" The emperor slammed a fist on the table. There was a long pause and then eventually he said, "Absolutely not! Let the merchant know that I will pay exactly as we agreed! And inform him that when he returns I expect at least sixty pounds of garroliron!"

"Begging your pardon, Majesty. But we're not really in a position to demand anything. They live deep in the Rukthor Mountains far from our reach. They have the only known supply of garroliron, and we have very little that they need. What we do have they can get more easily from the barbarian cities."

He sat and pondered the situation for a few moments. "That is very true. We do have very little that they desire. Perhaps we should change that? How many dwarves accompanied the merchant?"

Looking down at his notes, Vendino replied, "My sources reported that the merchant arrived with twelve guards and three others. The other three dwarves are the merchant's wife, son, and daughter."

The emperor smiled, "Perfect! Inform the guards that the entire dwarven merchant troupe is to be arrested immediately for attempting to swindle the empire! Have the merchant's son brought to me in my audience chamber so I can inform him of his father's crimes and my demands for sixty pounds of garroliron in retribution payments for insults to the crown!"

"Yes, Your Majesty. What shall I have done with the others?"

"All of them, including the merchant, shall become Dregs for life. All of their supplies and merchandise will be claimed by the empire."

He bowed his head to acknowledge his instructions. "Yes, Your Majesty. The son is to be sent back to the dwarven lands with our demands?"

"Yes."

"If I may suggest. The roads are dangerous; perhaps we should allow the son to take a couple of his guards with him? We're not going to get the garroliron we want if the son never makes it back to the dwarven lands. I might also point out that if we don't intend to release the merchant and his family, the dwarves are unlikely to trade with us again."

"Yes, I am aware of that, minister. But sixty pounds should be all that we need." Without warning the emperor stood up and left the room.

Vendino picked up his parchments and left the meeting room as well. He stopped in his office briefly to drop off his things. He passed a page along the way and asked the boy to take word to Minister Thorli asking him to come to the atrium. He watched the boy run off and then he made his way to the atrium.

He walked out into the beautiful flower garden and sat down on a bench. The atrium was on the top of the emperor's palace and looked out over Clornoss, the capital city. He enjoyed watching the sun rise from this spot in the atrium when he could. Vendino had traveled to many of the empire's cities, and they all basically looked the same. Each city featured four districts. The Chancery District was the seat of government of each city. The Chancery District in Clornoss was the most elaborate and impressive of all of the cities in the empire. Each of the other cities had an impressive Chancellor's Palace, and of course all of the cities had a vast array of office buildings for the various branches and departments.

Soon, countless bureaucrats from the cities all across the empire would be relocated to Misi to build a new government there. The next few weeks would feature an endless array of high level bureaucrats vying for a chance at becoming the chancellor of Misi, and then the scramble would set in for all of the lower seats in line as everyone attempted to gain power and influence. There would be vacancies in the bureaucracies in each city, which meant a good number of Gentry moving up in social status to the coveted status of Aristocrat as they are promoted from magistrate to minister. In turn, a good number of Denizens will be climbing the social ladder to Gentry, those low level Denizen clerks within the bureaucracy moving up to magistrate. That would be the beginning of a completely new slate of hassles and problems that Vendino would end up having to deal with.

Populating a new city was a planning nightmare. Vendino was not looking forward to starting it. Instead, he sat in the atrium and watched the flowers blow in the breeze for a while. It will be a headache for him and the other ministers, but the Denizens will be dancing in the streets. It had been almost a decade since the emperor called for a new city to be populated. It was certainly great for the morale of the people. Somehow he doubted that the current residents of the Grum'Glin place would be quite as excited when they were exterminated to make way for Grulin

Then his thoughts turned to the dwarves. A nagging voice told him that it was a mistake to move against the merchant. That wasn't his call to make. His job was just to communicate the emperor's orders to Minister Thorli.

Minister Thorli walked into the atrium and Vendino motioned for the general to have a seat next to him.

31

Chapter 5

Rissyl

Rissyl felt anxious and uncomfortable. After waking up from his dream he spent most of the rest of the night lying in bed, unable to sleep. When the sun finally started making its slow march into the morning sky he decided that he'd been lying there long enough.

He started his morning routine, and then made his way down the stairs and out to the workshop behind his home. He picked up a partially finished wooden carving of an ogre. When he had free time he enjoyed wood carving and his room was filled with wooden statues of goblins, dwarves, elves, and many varieties of forest monsters. Some of them weren't very good. He was getting quite a bit better, and this one was his favorite so far. He had been working on it for weeks. He still only had the basic form worked out, and the details of the top third.

He couldn't stop thinking about the events of the day before. His father hadn't been as mad as he expected, so that was good. He wondered if most people treated their Dregs like his father treated theirs, or if more people were like Tommis. He found it hard to believe that there could be many people quite as bad as Tommis.

He placed his carving on the workbench and looked around the shop. He wasn't really in the mood to work on his ogre at the moment. He decided to find out how the servant girl was feeling.

He went into the house and saw his little sister walking down the hallway towards him. He asked her, "Where is the servant girl?"

She gave him a dirty look, "I don't sarding know where the servant is. I ain't her nursemaid!"

"If Mum heard you talking like that," he started to say as he passed her, but he left the statement unfinished and walked on. After looking through the house, he went back out into the back yard and looked in the garden. He found the Dreg girl tending the vegetables there.

He walked towards her. He wasn't sure what to say, but he wanted to make sure that she was okay after the ordeal at Tommis's place. He hadn't even seen her after his mother had sent her to the bath. He walked over and knelt down next to her.

She smiled when she saw him, but then seemed to remember her place and looked back to her work. She said, "Greetings, milord. Do you need me for something?"

"No, I just came out to see how you are. That was an awful mess yesterday."

Before she could answer he heard something that sounded like, "Darp darp! Darp darp!" The sound was vaguely familiar, but he couldn't place where he had heard it before.

She smiled and looked down at her knees, "Thanks for coming for me. Sorry if I caused problems with your folks."

He saw movement on the far side of her legs and he leaned over so he could see what it was. Playing in the dirt next to her was a small puppy-like creature, made entirely of soft white light. The creature saw him looking and barked, "Darp! Darp!"

He jumped back, falling onto his backside in the grass beside the garden. He gasped, "Mother of all the gods!"

She looked down at the creature and then looked over at him. She looked almost as surprised as he was. "Can you see my Rolimi pup?" Her eyes were wide, and her mouth was slightly agape with disbelief.

He moved closer to get a better look at the creature. "Of course I can see it. It's right there!" He thought about the light-puppy creature he had seen in his dream. This one was shaped differently, and its ears were much smaller, like it was a different breed.

She held out her hand and the little pup crawled up onto her hand and then climbed up her arm. Then it sat down on her shoulder and started chewing on the edge of the collar of her dress. "Aye, but ain't many that can see them. Most folks don't even know about them."

Then, from behind him, came a soft bark. "Darp!"

The little light-puppy from his dream ran in little circles next to him, it was no bigger than his fist. The one on her shoulder started barking excitedly, and then it ran down her arm. The two little light-puppies nipped at each other and rolled in the dirt playfully.

She stared at him in complete shock.

He pointed at the little puppy, "That was in my dream last night." He sat down fully on his backside, and watched the two Rolimi pups playing with each other.

"And Nalria?" She asked him, quietly.

33

It was his turn to be shocked at her. "How could you know that? I haven't mentioned that dream to anyone!"

"Wasn't really a dream. You were visited by the goddess of magic! What'd she say?"

He was in a haze. He started to wonder if he was still dreaming. "Ah…" He stammered, not knowing what to say, "I don't really remember, exactly. Something about being found worthy, a gift, a choice, and-"

She flung herself at him, engulfing him in a tight hug! She held him for a long time, and he just sat there hugging her back. He wasn't experienced at hugging girls who weren't his mother. He felt he should probably break the hug before she did, but he put it off too long and she released him on her own. She sat next to him in the dirt.

The little Rolimi pups were teaming up to try to rip down a leaf from the garden.

"We've waited so long for this. Years!"

Rissyl groaned in frustration, "What does it mean?"

She looked down and said, "You should go see Dalen, my cousin. He could tell you better than me."

"No, I need you to tell me. Now."

She straightened up and turned to face him. "She's gonna give you the gift of magic! Nalria, the goddess of magic, wants to make you a Magi!"

He laughed a single humorless laugh. "Magi?"

"Yes, milord."

He yanked a clump of weeds from the dirt with much more force than was necessary, spraying dirt on them both. "That's crazy. If you don't want to tell me what she meant then just say so. But making up stories doesn't help!" He shook his head, and tossed the weeds to the ground.

"It ain't crazy and I ain't making it up."

"Magic is dead, you are aware of this. Yes?"

She brushed some dirt from her dress and then replied, "It was outlawed and the Magi were killed. But Nalria lives and plans to bring magic back to the world. She musta told you?"

He laughed again, "Exactly! It's illegal! And it is dead! And that dream was just a dream! It had to have been."

She pointed at the Rolimi pups, "Do Rolimi pups from your dreams often try to eat your carrots, milord?"

He looked at them, and then he looked at Cynia, "But magic is illegal."

She nodded, "And you'll be killed if they find out you can use it."

They heard the back door of the house open and Marisul walked out into the back yard. She walked over to the garden and started to speak. She paused before saying, "Milord Rissyl, I didn't expect to see you here. If you don't need Cynia, I need her in the kitchen."

He nodded, "Yes, of course. I was just inspecting the garden. Carry on." The servants walked inside, and he was left alone in the garden, reeling from the events of the last few minutes. Somehow, in a single morning, everything he understood about the world and his place in it was turned upside down.

Later that morning at breakfast Rissyl felt anxious to have the meeting with Dalen finished. He thought about asking Cynia for directions on how to find the guy, and then he could travel to meet Dalen alone. However, then he'd have to explain everything to Dalen, who he had never met before, and he wasn't sure how comfortable he felt about that. On top of that, he had never done anything before that might make people want to kill him. This newfound magical gift was more than a little frightening, and he wasn't sure who he could trust with the knowledge of it. Whether he wanted to or not he would have to trust Cynia. As he sat there eating his poddidge, he realized that it was probably unwise to trust a Dreg with a secret that could cost a person their life. At this point he had no choice.

He decided that he should probably bring Cynia along when he looked for Dalen. She sounded like she knew how to find him, and the guy might be more inclined to be helpful if Cynia was there. He just needed a cover story to get her out of the house without raising suspicions. "Hey dad, after breakfast I was going to run to the Commons to pick up some supplies for my next wood carvings. Do you care if I take the new Dreg along to help carry things?"

His father finished chewing his poddidge and wiped his chin, "A strapping young lad such as yourself can't carry his own wood crafts?"

Brielle said, "Well look at that. Making the Dreg tag along to lug your crap? You just might be a Gentry after all. I'm proud that you're my big brother!" She laughed at her own joke as she scraped the bottom of her bowl to get the last of her food.

The little Rolimi pup climbed up his body as he sat at the table. He tried to push it back down into his lap, but the pup clawed his way up Rissyl's arm and onto his hand. Then it jumped onto the table. Rissyl looked around, afraid that his family would notice the creature. However, even as they looked at him they didn't seem to notice it.

The little pup moved over to his bowl. It put both front paws on his bowl and started licking the poddidge. Rissyl tried to push the little pup away, but it kept running around his hand and back to the bowl.

Tuknor laughed quietly at his daughter's joking, "I don't care, Riz, as long as your mother doesn't have anything planned for her this morning."

She shook her head no. "As long as she is back in time to help with dinner, I don't care."

He continued to try to push the tiny pup away from his food. His mother gave him a quizzical expression. "What are you doing?"

He realized that they couldn't see the Rolimi pup, but they could see his actions. He stopped blocking the pup from his food, and replied, "Oh! Nothing. Just messing around." The pup resumed licking the poddidge.

After breakfast he stopped by the kitchen to talk to Cynia. He found her and Marisul washing dishes. "When you're done, I need you to run into the Commons with me to help with some shopping and carrying some things back."

Cynia looked at him and said, "Yes, milord. I'll be done soon."

Marisul tossed a towel at her to dry off. "You'll be done right now. Off with you, girl. I'll finish up these dishes, there's not much left."

She wiped her hands and took off her apron. "I'll grab my shoes."

A few minutes, later they were walking down the street. The north gate to the Commons District wasn't too far from his home. The sentinels at the gate didn't even seem to pay them any attention as they walked through to the land of the Denizens. "So, where does this Dalen live?"

"In a pod by the west wall. But he's usually at grandpa's apothecary shop, or out hunting for rare herbs and plants for the shop."

Once on the other side, as always, he noticed how different this section of the city seemed from what he was used to seeing in The Gardens. His side of the wall was filled with large homes, wide streets, plazas, statues, and a few small merchant stands. There were more grassy areas than stone-covered walkways and such, and there were many trees and bushes throughout the Garden District.

The Commons District was mostly covered with stone. Grass peeked out between stones in spots, but the grass looked like an unwelcomed pest instead of an inviting place to sit. The most striking difference was the homes. Instead of nice looking villas and large houses, the Commons District streets were lined with small homes packed closely together. Street after street, the houses all looked the same and they were all close together.

He was happy that his family had such a spacious lawn with a couple of gardens, a fountain, and other nice places to sit and relax. The people who lived in the small houses in the Commons would have to walk to a public plaza to find somewhere like that. They walked past a small plaza with some benches where people could sit. There was a fountain with a large statue of Emperor Ryal I. It was nice, but not nearly as splendid as the simplest plazas in his district.

The next most striking difference in the Commons was the people. In The Gardens the streets never seemed very busy. Sure there were people walking and horses pulling wagons. Everything felt so spacious and open, never crowded. Here in the Commons there were people everywhere, and it was almost impossible to walk down the street for very long without bumping into someone, or having people bump into you as they try to get wherever they were going.

"Ain't far now, by the bazaar. Follow me, this way's faster." She pointed down a narrow alleyway between buildings. After a while they arrived at the bazaar, a large cluster of merchant carts scattered around a massive plaza. There were also merchant shops set up in buildings around the perimeter of the plaza. It was set up in the heart of the Commons, and it was always a chaotic scene. Hawkers were everywhere shouting out the latest bargains and trying to lure people to their stand. A person could not pass through the bazaar without several dozen people aggressively trying to persuade them to take a peek at the fabulous wares in this stand or that. Sometimes merchants grabbed passers-by and physically pulled one way or another. The noise was unbelievable, and at times he had several merchants pulling him in different directions at the same time.

He had been to the bazaar many times since he was a small boy. He preferred the shops and friendly merchant stands in the Garden District, because there was so much less pressure and he could actually browse around without being shoved this way and that. However, many things that he needed or wanted to buy simply weren't for sale in The Gardens, and then he had to brave the bazaar. Today he found that just trying to walk through the bazaar without buying anything was surprisingly challenging.

Eventually, they got to the other side, and walking got easier. "Have you always been a Dreg?" As soon as he asked it, he regretted the question. He wasn't sure what was socially acceptable to say to a Dreg about their servitude.

She held out her right wrist so he could see the tattoos there. He knew that she was marked, but he had never really paid much attention to what the tattoo looked like. She had "117 RY" tattooed on her wrist. He knew that 117 RY meant the 117th Ryallic Year, which was another nine years away. Above that was a roughly drawn black rectangle tattoo about the same size as the date below it. He pointed to the rectangle tattoo. "What does it mean?"

Pointing at the year, she said, "I'll be a Dreg until the end of 117." Then she pointed at the rectangle, "That used to say 106 RY. I was freed at the end of 106 and they covered the 106 with a black rectangle to show I wasn't a Dreg no more. It's called a Denizen Box, because it means we're free."

"Unless a new date is tattooed above it?"

"Yep."

"You didn't stay free very long."

She looked down at her feet as they walked, "Thanks for that. Lots of freed Dregs get made Dregs again. I've seen bunches of Dregs with three or four Denizen Boxes." She looked like she wanted to say more, but she bit her tongue.

He figured she must be biting her tongue so she didn't upset the son of her owner.

Before long she pointed down the road. "The shop's over there."

The building looked very old, and the sign out front was nearly unreadable. The shelves near the window filled with vials, jars, baskets of herbs, and plants of all sorts were a strong indication of what kind of shop it was. They stepped inside and he was overwhelmed by the potent blend of odors, as if each plant was competing to see which one could be the most effluvious. Inside was a dark haired young man around Rissyl's age, pulling dried plants from a basket. He looked up briefly and saw Rissyl looking at him, and then he looked over at Cynia. He threw down the plants and stood up quickly. He rushed over to her and engulfed her in a huge hug, lifting her feet off the ground and rocking her back and forth. Rissyl stood and watched, feeling a little out of place invading in their reunion.

The large man put her down and held her at arm's length, examining her. "How are you? Grandmum said some magistrate bought you. They got you living in the Gardens now?"

"Yeah. Dalen, this here is Lord Rissyl. His dad is Lord Magistrate Sokigo, my owner." She pointed to Rissyl, who gave a half-smile.

Dalen looked at Rissyl with cold eyes. "I ain't gonna bow. Lord Rissyl."

He emphasized the word lord, and the way he said it was more of a curse word than a term of honor.

Rissyl felt even more uncomfortable and was starting to regret coming. "Just Rissyl, is fine."

Looking back to his cousin, Dalen ignored Rissyl's statement and instead said, "They better be treating you good." It was a statement, and Rissyl felt that it was probably a thinly veiled threat pointed at him instead of a question to her. He had a bad feeling in the pit of his stomach that she was going to tell him about the events at Tommis's house.

She shrugged her shoulders away from his hands. "Dalen, don't be a creep. It ain't his fault I'm a Dreg. His family's been good to me." She paused for a moment and then added, "It could be much worse." She looked over at Rissyl with a little smile.

Dalen turned and looked directly at Rissyl. "That don't change nothing. It ain't right for folks to own other folks!"

Rissyl threw his hands out in exasperation, "She's not a person. She's a Dreg!" He looked at Dalen with disbelief and indignation.

Dalen rushed forward, grabbed Rissyl by the tunic with both hands, and shoved him backwards into the wall. Hard! Jars and baskets of dried plants crashed to the ground, and Rissyl groaned loudly as the air rushed from his lungs. Dalen held his tunic tightly, and curled his hands up shoving him tightly up against the wall. Rissyl looked at his attacker's hands as he grabbed them with his own, trying to get them off him. He saw Dalen's Denizen Box tattooed on his right wrist. He hadn't considered that the young man might have once been a Dreg.

"Dammit Dal! Let go of him, now!" Cynia grabbed Dalen's shoulder and tried to pull him away.

He stopped shoving Rissyl as hard, and Rissyl stopped squirming. However, both young men stared at each other angrily.

She pulled on his shoulder again, more firmly this time. "Nalria chose him as the fourth."

Dalen instantly backed up several steps, and held up his hands in front of himself to show that he no longer intended to be a threat. "By all the gods, Cynia! Are you sure?" He dropped his hands to his sides and looked away. "Why him?"

Rissyl pushed himself away from the wall with his elbows and tried to straighten his tunic. He laughed a humorless laugh and said, "I have thought the same thing, frequently, over the last several hours!"

"He can see my pup." She stated it as if that should be proof enough. When Dalen started to counter her statement, she added. "I saw his Rolimi pup."

His jaw dropped in surprise, "He's got a pup?"

"It's got floppy ears."

"After all this time, could it really be happening?"

She nodded. "Yes, finally. The Society will be reborn."

He sat down on a stool. His demeanor changed to one that was much less confrontational, and he lowered his voice. "We're the Society now. How often has Grandpap said it's our destiny? Dammit, it's crazy that it's really time to start."

"What society are you talking about?" Rissyl was confused, and trying to catch up. He felt like he had walked into the middle of a complex conversation and missed the important first several minutes of the talk. "Are you talking about the Magi Society? Do you mean to say that was a real thing? My father says that those tales are exaggerated myths."

"Aye, the Sovereign Magi Society. Of course your dad says it's all a myth. He's a pawn of the emperor! The emperor's granddad betrayed and slaughtered the Magi, and slaughtered tons of common folks at the same time. The emperors have tried to ruin even the memory of the Society ever since!"

He shook his head, "It all seems very farfetched. Magical societies, imperial conspiracies, mass slaughter of powerful Magi? It's the stuff of fire-side stories!"

Dalen slammed his fist into his own leg, "I don't give a sard if you believe! It's best you don't, because I wouldn't let a Dreg-owning Gentry like you into the Society anyway!"

"You don't mean that, Dalen." Cynia stepped closer to her cousin.

"Yes, Cynia, I do. I don't trust him! The first emperor slaughtered the whole Society by turning one Magi into a betrayer! And now you wanna let a Gentry, the brat of a magistrate, into our society before we even get started? He will betray us! You shouldn't have brought him here."

"It ain't our choice, Dalen! I didn't choose him, the goddess of magic did! Send your anger at her!" She stepped closer to him and poked him in the chest with her finger. "How long have we waited? Years, dammit! Honestly, I kinda thought we'd never even get started! I thought maybe it'd be my kids, or their kids, that finally rebuilds it! But there he is." She pointed at Rissyl. "He is the sarding key we need! And you wanna push him away?

You're an idiot!"

He looked down, and his determination left his voice. "I don't trust him."

"You don't like him, that's different. You don't know him enough to trust him or not trust him. His family owns Dregs. He's a Gentry and you're jealous, or scared, or worried his snake might be longer than yours? Maybe you're just afraid to begin the destiny that was dropped on us? I dunno what your real problem is, Dalen. But Nalria chose him! I trust him. And if you trust me, then you'll give him a chance."

Dalen stood up without looking at either of them and walked into the back room. Cynia motioned for Rissyl to follow, and she fell in behind them both. They walked into a small room with a desk, a few candles, and a large amount of baskets, boxes, and bags of dried plants of every shape and size. Dalen walked around behind the desk and sat down on a chair. He pulled something out of a box, which was on the bottom of a stack of other boxes. He sat it on the desk in front of him and Rissyl saw that it was a short, squat wooden box with fancy lettering. It also had a number of oddly shaped symbols that he didn't recognize. On the top of the box were words written in a fancy script that he couldn't read without getting closer. He stepped in and read:

Sovereign Magi Society

Initiation and Indoctrination

May the Unworthy Beware

"Well, that's a bit ominous." Rissyl looked at the box for a long moment. It was old, probably at least a few hundred years old, he guessed. He had never seen anything like it. He stood there for a while in silence. Finally, assuming that they were waiting for him to take it and look through it, he reached out to grab it.

Dalen pushed two fingers against Rissyl's collar bone to keep him from grabbing the book. "You willing to take the Covenants?"

"What are the Covenants?"

Dalen responded first, "Your sworn promises to the Society."

Cynia added, "And your answer to Nalria, that you'll accept her Gift."

"Would we do it here? Now?"

Dalen shook his head, "No, we'll need my sister too. And we got lots of things to get ready first. How about one month from today? You've gotta decide by then."

After thinking for a while, Rissyl said, "You mentioned your grandfather saying that it was your destiny. How can he be so sure?"

Dalen started to answer and Cynia put her hand on his arm. "Almost ten years ago me, Dalen, his sister Sarasa, and my older brother Vinn all had a vision of Nalria on the same night. She came to us to say that evil was coming to the empire. She told us our great grandpa was a Magi hero, and to honor him she chose his great grandkids to rebuild the Magi Society. She said that one day we would each lead one of the four Magi Orders."

She paused, and dried her eyes on the sleeve of her dress. He hadn't noticed that she had started crying before then, but she continued to cover her eyes for a moment.

Dalen asked, "You want me to finish it?"

She put up her hand and shook her head. After a moment she dried her eyes again and continued, "Vinn told Nalria that he wanted to rule all of the Magi Orders, and he didn't wanna have to share power with us. The goddess tried to tell him it didn't work like that, but he insisted. He asked if he would be the all-powerful Magi if he killed me, Dalen, and Sarasa. She said she'd consider it if he proved right then that he'd kill his own sister for that power." She paused for a moment and cleared her throat. "He walked over to me in the vision and tried to strangle me to death. He was a teen, and I was smaller. I could only just look at him as I felt the vision grow dark."

Again she paused to wipe her eyes. Her voice broke a little as she finished, "Nalria smited Vinn inside the vision. She said he was unworthy, and we couldn't claim our gifts until she found someone worthy of the gift she'd offered him."

Dalen said, "When we woke up in the morning we found that Vinn had died in his sleep. We told the adults about the vision. Vinn's death was devastating to his mom. She never got over it."

Chapter 6

Gordo

The streets of Sorgo's Commons District were always fairly empty at this time of the night, and Gordo liked it that way. He had just stepped out of the *Rat Bastard* tavern and the cool night air felt great. He was in a fabulous mood since he had just won a fortune in cards. A little voice in the back of his head kept pleading with him to head straight home, but he was simply too excited about his winnings. Well that, and about three too many bad ales had his head spinning a bit. He decided to sit down on the steps outside the tavern for a while to clear his head.

Gordo was shorter than average, but he was muscular and built like a sailor. He kept his hair cut so short that he looked almost bald. His tunic and breeches were clean and well made, and he wore his favorite floppy hat with a small blue feather on one side.

After sitting for a few minutes, when he was just about to stand up and head home, he heard a loud commotion inside the tavern. He heard crashing and a man screaming terribly. A moment later the tavern door burst open and he saw the tavern owner's son rushing out of the door. The young man tossed a large dagger on the ground as he ran, and Gordo watched him run north up the road. His heart was racing, and suddenly he was very sober. He felt fortunate that the man who ran past had thrown the dagger instead of attacking him with it. Gordo had beaten him badly in cards, and much of the man's money was now sitting in Gordo's coin purse. There's no telling what some people might do to get their coins back.

He stood up and thought about going into the tavern, but he was apprehensive about what he might find in there. Then it was too late, the turmoil inside stumbled out of the door and found him. The man was covered in blood, and he could barely walk. Gordo realized that the badly bleeding man was the other person from his card game. For a brief moment he felt bad for doing so well at cards and winning all of the man's money because clearly the guy was not having a very good night. The man stumbled to the edge of the tavern steps and then started to fall down the stairs. Gordo caught him and helped him to lay on the ground. Looking down,

Gordo was certain the man had died in his arms before he even got him fully to the ground.

Then the tavern owner rushed out the door screaming. "Help! Help! Someone get the sentinels! Help!" Within seconds people started coming out of various buildings to see what was going on. The tavern owner yelled, "Someone stop him, he attacked Oolar!"

Gordo looked around for the tavern owner's son, although he was sure he was long gone by this point. He was surprised that the tavern owner would be so quick to point out his own son as a murderer. It wasn't until people started rushing over and roughly knocking Gordo to the ground that he realized that the tavern owner had pointed to him as the attacker.

He tried to plead with the people and assure them that he was just minding his own business and really had no idea what even happened. Nevertheless, they wouldn't listen. Before long a squad of sentinels arrived.

Gordo was immensely relieved when the sentinels arrived. He was seriously starting to fear that the growing mob might harm him. One of the sentinels helped him up as the mob slowly released him, and the sentinel captain demanded, "What's going on here?"

One of the other sentinels knelt down next to Oolar. He looked up and said, "This one is dead."

Gordo started to reply to the captain's question but the man said, "Shut up! You'll get your turn!" The captain looked at the tavern owner and asked again, "What's going on here?"

The tavern owner made his way down the blood covered stairs carefully, and walked over to the captain. He pointed at Gordo, and said, "I saw that man, Gordo, playing cards with that dead guy. Dead guy's name was Oolar. Gordo lost a fortune in cards to Oolar." He pointed at Gordo again. "Gordo pulled out a dagger and grabbed Oolar's coin purse! Oolar tried to get his coins back and Gordo started stabbing him! He followed him right out the door, he did, stabbing him the whole time!"

Someone in the crowd said, "Yeah, I saw him kneeling over the body!"

Someone else said, "And look, he's covered in blood!"

Gordo tried to explain, but the sentinel barked at him to shut up. One of the other sentinels held up the dagger, "Capt'n, the dagger he used was laying right over there near the body."

Another sentinel pulled a pair of manacles from his saddle bags and walked over to Gordo. He roughly closed and locked the irons onto Gordo's wrists and ankles, and then attached the end of the chain to one of the horses. The sentinels then started going through his waistband and pockets and took all of Gordo's possessions, including his wondrously full bag of coins.

The whole thing seemed surreal, like some kind of dream that he was watching. The cold iron on his wrists drove home the reality of the situation. "Wait. No! You got the wrong guy! I was just sitting there on the steps!" Gordo motioned towards the tavern owner. "The killer was that guy's son, I saw him run off a second ago! We were all playing cards, and I WON! The son musta stabbed him and took off! Honest, I was just sitting there!"

The tavern owner smacked Gordo up against the head, "How dare you accuse my son! He wasn't playing cards with a low-life like you! You make me puke!"

"No! I was just sitting there!"

The captain walked up to him and said, "Now you're just making enemies. I suggest you shut up and don't make it harder than it needs to be. Being a Dreg is much better than being dead, now ain't it? If you play nice the magistrate just might let you live out your days as a Dreg instead of giving these people the satisfaction of watching you hang."

Panic was starting to settle in, and much too late he felt the urge to run. "Hang? Dreg? You gotta be joking! I was just SITTING there!" His head was reeling, his knees felt weak, and he wasn't entirely sure that he was going to keep his dinner down. It had started out as such a wonderful night.

The next several days were a terrible nightmarish blur for Gordo. Once again he woke up from his nap to the dreaded view of stone walls. He sat up and looked around, he had no idea what time of day it was. He was in a little cell below one of the gate towers along the western wall in Sorgo. It was the same cell in which he had spent the majority of the past six days since his life had taken a sudden unfair turn for the much worse.

Ordinarily he was a positive and happy-go-lucky guy, and that attitude served him well as a street performer. The past several days had been awful, and what he missed most was performing on the streets and making people happy. When he performed he would dance a little and he did various feats of strength like holding his entire body horizontal a foot above the ground supported only by one hand. Sometimes he would bring heavy weights and juggle them, or stand on his hands and do pushups with his feet straight up in the air with the weights strapped to his ankles. Sometimes, he would run a rope from a tree to another tree or pole and do tricks while standing on a tight rope. He was always thinking of new, impressive stunts that would excite the crowd and encourage them to drop a coin or two in his box. When he wasn't performing, he was practicing for his next performance. It was his life, and he couldn't imagine doing anything else.

Now this was his life. He looked down at the new tattoo on the back of his wrist. It said, "999 RY." He highly doubted that he would live 1000 years. He realized that this must be the empire's not-so-subtle way of saying that he was going to be a Dreg until he was buried.

The whole thing was unfair, and he just wanted to roll up into a ball and cry for a few fortnights. He had gone through the angry phase, and now he was mostly numb. He met with the magistrate yesterday, and that had gone about as well as he expected it would. The tavern owner was there to speak against him, and the son had come just to taunt him. Gordo had tried to explain to anyone who would listen that he was just minding his own business, but no one would listen. The magistrate listened to what the tavern owner said. Then he listened to the sentinel captain explain that Gordo had been drinking, was covered with blood, and was holding a large bag of coins. The magistrate didn't even need to hear the statements from the people who saw him kneeling over Oolar's body. The magistrate decided he was a threat to the city and declared him to be a Dreg for the remainder of his days.

He heard someone walking down the stone hallway and eventually one of the Dross Lions walked up to the cell door. Technically, the soldier was a member of the Sorgo Lion Battalion, the imperial unit responsible for guarding the Dross District, but no one called them that. They were usually just referred to as Lions. He wore full plate combat armor with an open face metal helm, and his tabard was solid blue with a black lion silhouette in the middle. Gordo looked at the man in awe and fear. Until then, he had only been escorted by sentinels. If this was a bad dream, it had just gotten much scarier.

"Let's go buddy, time to go to the barracks. Put these on." The Lion threw a bundle on the ground at his feet.

Gordo stood up and held out his hands to plead with the soldier. "Please, sir! You gotta believe me! I didn't do nothing. I was just sitting there!"

The Lion opened the door, "It's too late for all that. You're a Dreg now. Even if I believed you, which I don't, ain't no way I could change things. You've gotta quit whining. If folks in here think you killed some guy over a card game they'll respect you. That might keep you alive for a while. In here,

46

that '999' means you're dangerous. Now, take those clothes off and put these on."

He stood up and stripped off the meager clothing that the sentinel had given him. He picked up the pair of breeches that the Lion had thrown on the ground. They were wool, scratchy, and extremely uncomfortable. They were also dirty and tattered. He didn't think it would have been possible to be disappointed to give up the clothing he had gotten from the sentinel. He looked at the Lion and asked, "Where's the shirt? Should I put this one back on?"

"Dregs don't need shirts. Let's go."

Gordo let the Lion lead him down the hall. They went in a direction that he hadn't gone before. After a maze of twists, turns, and treks up long stairways they came to a large room with several Lions. One of them had silver and gold trim around the edges of his blue tabard, and Gordo assumed he must be the leader.

The Lion who brought him in said, "Colonel, where's this one assigned?"

The Colonel, who was indeed the one in the fancy tabard, said, "What is it called?"

"Gordo Swann."

The Colonel looked in a ledger and then said, "Firehound seventy-three"

"Yes, Sir." The Lion saluted his Colonel with his right fist over his left chest and inclining his head slightly. The Colonel returned the salute and the Lion escorted Gordo out the door, into the Dross.

Once outside, the light rain threatened to have them both drenched before they reached wherever they were going, and the cool evening air chilled Gordo's skin. The Lion led him down wide corridors between large wooden buildings with no windows. He didn't think of the spaces between the buildings as roads because they were just large gravel covered spaces. Wherever he looked there was either a building or an open area covered with loose gravel. There was no grass and no trees. He didn't see any merchant carts or vendor signs. Nothing but gravel and non-descript windowless wooden buildings as far as he could see. Well, that and a wall. A tall stone wall surrounded the Dross, separating it from the rest of the city and the outside world. There were tall stone walls around the entire area. So, this was the Dross District. He regretted ever wondering what the place looked like.

A squad of Lions marched past them, and looking down one of the corridors he saw a long line of men wearing only brown breeches. They were five wide, walking in long straight columns, and four Lions walked along with them.

Gordo and his Lion escort turned right once, and then turned left. They passed a group of about thirty women marching five wide with four Lions escorting them wherever they were going. Gordo was disappointed to see that, unlike male Dregs, apparently female Dregs do indeed need shirts after all, because each of them had a long tunic to match their breeches.

He asked, "What's Firehound seventy-three mean?"

The Lion didn't look at him as he replied, "Firehound is the soldier's way of saying the letter 'F'. You're assigned to building 'F', bed seventy-three. So from now on you'll be called Firehound seventy-three."

"How many folks live here?"

"None."

"Yeah, thanks. Okay, how many Dregs live here?"

The Lion stopped walking and faced Gordo. The rain was picking up and splashed against his face. "Dregs don't LIVE anywhere! They're not people, they're property! They're the useless problematic property that the empire must feed and house! The sooner you get that the better off you'll be. You gotta stop thinking of yourself as a person. You're now a Dreg!"

After a moment they started walking again. After a few steps Gordo said, "Fine. How many Dregs are housed here?"

"Two thousand three hundred and twelve, counting you. Those are just the Dregs owned by Sorgo. Another six hundred or so are owned by folks around the city, and they don't reside in the Dross they reside with their owners."

They arrived at a building with a large 'F' on the wall next to the door. The Lion motioned for Gordo to enter, and he followed him. They tried to shake off some of the water, but it didn't help much. They walked down a long room with crude beds lining both walls. Eventually they came to one with the number seventy-three carved into the wall behind it.

Gordo looked at the bed and then looked around the room. "Where's the dresser? Is there a chest or something where I can put my things?"

The Lion shook his head in disbelief. "What things? You are property! Property doesn't own property! That's stupid! You have nothing. You own nothing! What would you even put in a chest? Your only possession is that pair of breeches, and I suggest you guard them or you won't even have those!" He motioned at the bed. "Sit there. Don't talk, and don't move. The rest of the Firehounds will be back soon. Then I can release you to your

Sergeant."

"Where are they?"

"Firehounds are on road duty, so they're probably walking back. You're fortunate, I hear road duty is hard work, but not as bad as most other duties around here. Now shut up and leave me alone." The Lion walked a short distance away to discourage further conversation.

Gordo was feeling many things at the moment, but 'fortunate' was not one of them.

Chapter 7

Rissyl

It had been raining for four days straight. It was Early-Spring and that was to be expected, but Rissyl felt annoyed anyway. The past fortnight had gone by quickly, and he felt no more at ease with the thought of accepting this magical gift. He spent most of his time in the workshop carving his ogre. He did get some satisfaction yesterday when the ogre was finished and he added it to his collection. When he wasn't carving he was trying to figure out what to do about the business with the Covenants. He also spent a good amount of time worrying about someone finding out about his gift and turning him in to the chancellor.

He looked down at the chunk of wood that he'd been holding for half an hour or so. He wasn't sure what he wanted to carve next. He thought about carving a Magi, but then thought that might be a bad idea. He decided that he would carve another dwarf to add to his collection of ogre hunters. He wasn't exactly sure what a dwarf looked like, but from stories he imagined them to be short and stocky with bushy beards and strong muscles.

The door to the shop opened, and his father walked in. He was surprised to see his father in the middle of the day, because he was always at work by this time. Tuknor did his best to shake the rain off his overcoat and then he took it off. Rissyl was even more surprised to see his father wearing his magistrate robes. He rarely saw him dressed in his official regalia. He was starting to worry that something was wrong.

Tuknor walked over to the table, pulled a stool over and sat down. "Riz, the chancellor is going to announce tomorrow that the emperor has ordered that a new city be populated."

Rissyl breathed a sigh of relief. He wasn't sure what he was expecting to hear, but he was afraid it would be bad news. "That's good news, right? It's been a very long time since the last city was populated. I was just a boy. But I remember festivals and celebrations. The people will rejoice, right?"

"Oh yes, most of the people will be overjoyed! Some will not, but that is the way of things. I have been asked to be a minister."

For as long as Rissyl could remember his father had talked about his dream of one day becoming a minister. Rissyl often dreamed of the elevation in social standing, not to mention the wonderfully large manor house or villa that came along with such an honor. "Father, this is great news! A minister? That means that we'll become Aristocrats? Live in a villa outside of the city?"

"They want me to be a minister in Misi, the new city."

"Wait. What? We won't live in Sorgo anymore? But everyone I know is in Sorgo. I don't want to move to the other side of the empire."

"That choice is yours. Your mother and I have already discussed it. We are moving to Misi, and yes we will be elevated to Aristocrats. You are welcome to come with us, of course, and you would enjoy the villa and the status of my new position. Brielle will be coming with us, but you are on the cusp of being an adult and you must make that decision on your own. If you choose to stay in Sorgo I will arrange for you to take a position as a minor magistrate here once you are old enough. You would keep this house, and the status of Gentry. I know that this is a difficult position to put you in but I have to do what I feel is best, and so must you."

"They would make me a magistrate? Doesn't someone need to put in years as a clerk before they can become a magistrate?"

"There are a few low level magistrate positions that don't require prior work as a clerk, and I would pull some strings to arrange that for you."

"When do you need to know?"

"The chancellor expects all of these details to be worked out within a fortnight of the announcement. So you still have sixteen days to decide."

Tuknor stood up to leave. Rissyl said, "I have a question, about something else. Is magic dead? I mean, do you think there is any chance that it might come back?"

He laughed, "You and your vivid imagination. All of these elves and goblins that you carve and place around your room. Of course magic is dead; Emperor Ryal I freed us from the claws of magic long ago. It's just the stuff of legends and wild tales now."

"Well, if it's forever dead, why is it still illegal? How could anyone ever break that law?"

His expression grew more serious, "It is illegal because it's dangerous. It is highly unlikely to happen, but if it did return then the perpetrators could be dealt with quickly. Yes, I have heard of a few instances where someone was brought before a magistrate accused of practicing magic."

Rissyl hesitated, unsure that he wanted the answer to his next question.

Finally, he asked it anyway, "What happened to those people?"

"Nothing, of course. There was no evidence or credible information to prove that magic had been performed. Because it's dead, and that is that."

"Oh, good. That's a relief." That was as far as he was willing to take the discussion. He desperately wanted to confide in his father. He wanted his advice and wisdom. He needed his guidance now more than ever. However, he couldn't do that to his own father, especially now. How could he expect his own father to possess the knowledge that his son was a Magi, when his father would have to work closely with the chancellor of Misi? If magic was as forbidden as it seemed to be, then certainly a minister would have the obligation to tell the chancellor if he had knowledge of it being performed, even if it meant turning in his own son.

He looked over to his father and realized that he hadn't addressed his original question. "Okay, well, I will consider what you said, and congratulations on being offered the role of minister! I know how long you've wanted that! I am very proud."

Tuknor hugged him tightly and then put on his overcoat and left the shop. Rissyl dropped his head onto his folded arms on the table. *"Why does life have to be so complicated?"* he thought to himself bitterly.

Later that afternoon Rissyl walked into the house, tired and ready for a nap. On his way through the kitchen Cynia stopped him. "Milord, can we talk?"

He led her to the study and closed the door behind them. They hadn't spoken more than a dozen words since the two of them had gone to see Dalen.

"Milord, it has been a fortnight. Dalen is getting the ceremonies ready. He wants to do them a fortnight from tonight when the moon's full. Did you make up your mind yet? Will you take the Covenants?"

He was frustrated, and the news from his father was making the decision much worse. He struggled to keep his voice low, "No. I don't know what I'm going to do. My father has been offered the honor of serving as minister in a new city, on the other side of the empire. He is taking the family there. He wants me to go with them."

She stared at him in disbelief. "You can't go. What about me? I can't leave Sorgo. Rissyl, no please! You can't let them take me there! We have so much to do!"

He made a gesture to tell her to be quiet, "Listen! I don't know what is going to happen, and I don't know what I'm going to do yet. I just found out!"

She composed herself and took a deep breath. After letting it out slowly she said, "Let's go talk to Grandpa. He can help. I assume you can't tell your parents. Maybe my Grandpa has some advice for you?"

He huffed, "Fine, let's go and talk to your grandfather." They left the study and walked through the house to the living room where Marisul was dusting. "I'm headed to the Commons to get some things, and I'm taking the girl with me."

"Yes milord. Will she be back to help with dinner?"

He thought about it for a moment, and then replied, "Not likely. And we probably won't be back in time for me to eat with the family either, so don't set a place for me. I will pick something up at the bazaar."

"Yes milord."

They walked without talking much. The streets of the Commons were crowded, like normal. He was thankful that the rain had finally stopped, but he suspected they would probably be soggy by the time they returned home.

Before too long they arrived at the apothecary shop. The smell was about the same as last time. When they entered they were greeted by a frail looking old man in dirt covered grass stained clothing. The old man stood up and greeted Cynia warmly. Then he turned his attention to Rissyl

"Grandpa, this is Lord Rissyl, my owner's son. He's the one chosen by Nalria."

The old man grabbed Rissyl's shoulder and pushed him this way and that, "Lemme look at you, boy. You've a sturdy frame, but a Gentry's physique. You don't look like the most deadly weapon in the last century."

A young lady stepped out of the back room. When she saw Cynia she ran over and gave her a long hug. The girl was noticeably shorter than Cynia and had long bright-red hair. She resembled Cynia with the same sort of round face and pointy chin. When she released her, Cynia said, "Sarasa, this is Lord Rissyl. Milord, this is my cousin Sarasa."

Rissyl's could feel his heart start to race. Sarasa was the most gorgeous girl he had ever seen, and he was not entirely sure that he would be able to form words. He stood there, feeling like an idiot, staring at her. She glanced at him but then quickly looked away to something on one of the shelves.

Cynia elbowed him slightly, "Milord?"

He had never minded having the Dregs call him lord or milord. However, in front of Sarasa he thought it sounded arrogant and made him look bad.

He had been lost in inappropriate thoughts as he gazed upon the adorable redhead, and Cynia addressing him as milord suddenly struck him badly. "For the love of all of the gods, Cynia. Stop with the 'milord' crap! At least when it is just us like this. It makes me feel pompous."

She gave him a playful smile and said, "Yes, milord."

They all broke out into laughter, and the mood seemed to lighten slightly within the room. After a moment the old man said, "So will you accept your gift from Nalria? It's your destiny, you know."

He didn't answer right away. Sarasa said, "I don't understand what there is to decide? Are you sure that Nalria chose you?"

He looked down at the Rolimi pups playing together on the floor. There were three of them now. He said, "Oh yes." Then he pointed down at one of the pups. He asked, "Is that one yours?"

The little redhead shrugged, "Yep, the tiny one." She paused and then said, "If Nalria offered you a powerful gift, then you are to be a Magi. There is no choice to be made. The gods have chosen you, and it is an undeniable responsibility. For nearly a thousand years the Magi stood as the vanguards for justice and morality. We have the power to bring that back to the world. You have that power. We cannot do it without you."

He looked into her beautiful green eyes and knew what his answer would be. How could he deny her, and all of them, the chance to pursue their destiny? His own destiny?

He said, "Then let's do this."

The next morning Rissyl woke to his sister yelling, slamming doors, and stomping down the hallway crying. He guessed that his parents must have broken the news to her that they were moving to Misi. He figured this would be as good a time as any to give them his answer, so he made his way downstairs and found them sitting in the main family room. He was surprised to see a fire blazing in the fireplace, since it was spring and starting to get fairly warm. However, his sister loved fires so their father must have started one to ease her into the discussion.

Rissyl must have gotten lost in that thought because his father said, "Yes, son? Did you come down to stare at the fire, or did you want to join us?"

He figured there was no sense beating around the bush, so he led off with, "Mom, Dad, I've decided that I am going to stay in Sorgo. I don't want to disappoint you, and I will miss you terribly, but my life is here."

His mother wiped a tear from her eye, and his father walked over and clapped him on the shoulder, "It takes a lot of bravery and maturity to make a decision like that. The easy route would have been just to tag along. I am proud, son. I'm going to miss you, it will be difficult to travel back here more than once a year or so."

"I understand. So, you mentioned the prospect of a job. Do I need to talk to someone?"

"It will be almost two years before you're old enough for that job. I will leave enough coin here for you to live on until then."

Rissyl choked back tears and took a moment to compose himself. "I would like to buy the new Dreg from you. So I have a Dreg to take care of meals, and things."

Tuknor laughed, "Buy her? With what money? You don't have any of your own yet. You want to use my money to pay me for my Dreg? That's the funniest thing I've heard!" Both of his parents enjoyed a good laugh at his joke, but Rissyl still looked serious. Tuknor added, "I was planning to give you Marisul."

He was beginning to panic. Everything would be wrecked if his parents took Cynia with them, but he had to play it cool. He thought for a moment and said, "Isn't Marisul due to lose her Dreg status at the end of the year? Then I'd just have to buy a new one. You remember how hard it was to find a decent Dreg when we were looking for Marisul's replacement before you bought the new one. How many did you bring home that month? Eight? Nine?"

Amalia answered, "Eleven, and most of them were awful. I think two of them actually weren't even house-broken."

Tuknor said, "And one of them woke up every single night screaming at the top of her lungs."

Rissyl nodded, "Oh, I forgot about that one, and there was the one who kept sneaking into Brielle's room and trying on her clothes."

"Oh, Tuk, let's just give him both of the Dregs. We can buy a new one when we get to Misi."

"That might be difficult. Misi will have very few Dregs available at first, and a lot of new people will be arriving each day who will want to buy some." He thought for a moment, and then continued, "Fine, we'll give him both of the Dregs and we'll buy a new one here to take with us to Misi. You won't be old enough to own a Dreg for a couple of years now, so they'll need to stay in my name for now. I'll sign the new one over to you when you're old enough to own her."

Chapter 8

Rissyl

The next few days went by very quickly for Rissyl. There had been some tension about where to actually perform the ceremonies. Dalen knew of an abandoned warehouse in the Commons, but Rissyl didn't like the idea of breaking into somewhere where they weren't welcomed. However, when it came down to borrowing an abandoned warehouse, or squeezing several people into some room in Rissyl's home, he gave up his arguments.

When Sarasa and Dalen arrived at the warehouse, Rissyl and Cynia were already there. They walked in and everyone exchanged greetings.

Dalen opened up a large bag he brought with him. Rissyl stepped over to check out the things Dalen was pulling from the bag. The first was the elaborate box that Rissyl had seen back at the shop.

Sarasa said, "We have had this box since the night of the visions, all those years ago. It holds the secrets to our magical gifts, or so we were led to believe."

Cynia placed her hand lightly on Rissyl's shoulder, "And you're the key to that box."

"Me? Why?"

"There's a magic seal on it, gotta have the four chosen Magi to break it." Dalen placed the box on the floor gently.

As Rissyl looked at the box he felt a tightening in the pit of his stomach. He knew that his whole life was about to change and the flame to light the fire of change was on the floor before him.

His attention was drawn away from the box as Dalen rummaged around in the bag again. He pulled out some candles, snacks, and a water jug.

Cynia moved a large crate into the center of the room and Sarasa carried the elaborate box labeled *Sovereign Magi Society - Initiation and Indoctrination* from the floor next to Dalen's bag and placed it upon the crate. She looked at the box for a moment, and then she walked up to Rissyl and said, "How well do you know the Pre-Ryallic History of this region?"

"Ah, I don't know, about as well as anyone I guess. Next to nothing? I never really thought about it before."

She sighed, "Before the Ryallic Empire, there were six kingdoms in the known lands."

He was anxious to show her that he wasn't stupid, and eagerly interjected, "Oh, I've heard of the Six Kingdoms!"

She didn't look impressed. She said, "Yes, the Six Kingdoms existed in relative peace for centuries. King Ryal VI reigned over a land called Clornovia, one of the six kingdoms. In the fifth year of his rule he betrayed, hunted, and began the ruthless slaughter of all magic users. At the same time, in the name of making the region safe from magic, he also began conquering the other five kingdoms one at a time. In the process of hunting the magic users, the newly self-proclaimed Emperor Ryal I also murdered thousands of innocent people. All citizens of the new empire were encouraged to turn over the names of any suspected magic users, and those people were killed. More often than not the people turned over the names of foes, rivals, and anyone else who wronged them. It was a bloodbath, and some stories claim that for every magic user killed there were ten to twenty non-magic commoners killed."

Rissyl cringed at the bleak history that Sarasa painted of their empire. He had gone to Ryallic Victory Festivals every year since he was a boy and they were filled with stories of valiant knights and glorious battles bringing the birth of an empire. The festival games and events never talked about mass slaughter of innocent commoners. A chill went down his spine as he let the numbers sink in. He had no doubt that Sarasa believed she was giving an accurate account of the history, but in his heart he had to believe that she was mistaken.

Dalen cleared his throat and said, "Focus, Sarasa, or we'll never get done."

She replied, "I'm sorry. Now isn't the time for stories about the evils of the first emperor, we can discuss that another time. Where was I?"

Dalen said, "King Ryal conquered the other five kingdoms."

"Oh yes, so the southern kingdoms were the first to fall. Then, as King Ryal's forces took control of the northern kingdoms, they met more resistance. Although the final three kingdoms and their capital cities fell quickly, resistance fighters retreated north and established a foothold in the cities along the southern edge of the mountains."

She paused for a moment, and then said, "King Ryal declared that the Ryallic Empire was forged by the divine will of Zortha, the matron goddess of war. He crowned himself Emperor Ryal I at a lavish celebration in Clornoss and decreed that the day of that coronation, the 24th of Late-Fall, be established thereafter for an annual Ryallic Victory Festival throughout the empire. At the coronation he also called for a massive wall to be erected between the empire and what he referred to as the Barbarian Lands to the north."

Sarasa paused again and took a drink from her waterskin. Rissyl had wondered why there were a bunch of independent cities between the empire and the mountains. Her description of the history did give a plausible explanation for them, even if he doubted the complete accuracy of the story overall.

She continued, "It was widely rumored that the emperor was furious that his armies could not defeat the resistance fighters and capture the cities throughout the north. But they had suffered staggering losses in the Betrayal against the Magi and the battles to establish the empire. So he was left with little choice but to build the wall and focus on stabilizing his new empire."

Dalen gave her an impatient look and she held up her finger to him. "One last thing to note. The first year of life in the new empire was dreadful. Lawlessness was rampant throughout the empire, as most of the soldiers had yet to return from their campaigns and there were few people empowered to enforce laws or ensure the safety of the citizens. The nobles who could afford private guards were generally safe but everyone else was left to protect themselves. On 24 Late-Fall 1 RY, at the first Ryallic Victory Festival, Emperor Ryal I issued two key edicts. The first did away with the noble class and established the three social classes that we are familiar with. Most of the nobles became Aristocrats. The petty nobles became Gentry and the commoners became Denizens. Although it didn't change much, it did remove the birthright of the old noble class and established a path for Denizens to raise in status. The second edict established the Dregs, and it began a time of forced servitude for criminals and anyone else who was deemed a threat or nuisance to the empire or the individual cities of the empire."

After another quick drink of water she continued, "I could talk for hours about-"

Cynia leaned over to Rissyl and said, "Yes she can!"

That comment got him thinking about how Sarasa spoke. She spoke more like a Gentry than a Denizen. She even spoke without the usual Denizen accent that he was growing used to as he talked with Cynia more often. He was curious why she spoke differently than her brother and her cousin. He assumed they were all raised together. He decided not to ask, so he didn't sound rude.

Sarasa gave Cynia a sour look and repeated, "I could talk for hours about the social and economic impact of the edict establishing the Dregs. But as it relates to our magical studies and the Sovereign Magi Society, I will just say this. The Society stood for hundreds of years with the primary goal of protecting the common people. In a few short years, Emperor Ryal I destroyed the Society and then threw thousands of people into the chains of slavery, thus undoing the most basic ideals that the Society had works so hard to protect."

"Okay, thanks Rasa. Now, let's get started!" Dalen gave the order and walked over to the elaborate box that Sarasa had placed on the crate. "Everyone ready?"

Rissyl's heart began beating so hard that he thought it just might jump right out of his chest. He nodded.

Dalen reached towards the elaborate box, "Okay, everyone touch the box together." He waited for everyone to grab a hold of the box, and then he said, "Sovereign Magi Society. Class is in session."

One at a time, all four Rolimi pups seemed to climb out of the top of the crate. They stood side-by-side in front of the old box, and then all at once they reached out a light-paw and touched the box. It popped open, and all four Magi pupils jumped back away from it!

A light-man, like those that Rissyl had seen in his dream, crawled out of the box. The box was just a foot wide, two feet long, and half a foot tall. It was much too small for someone to climb out from inside. Nevertheless, the light man squeezed his way out of it with no problem. He jumped down from the crate and then pointed a long thin arm at the box. The box smoothly floated off the crate and onto the floor. Then a large arched doorway popped up from the center of the box. Several other light-men started coming through the doorway. They carried desks and chairs with them.

Four wooden student's desks were arranged, two by two, in the middle of the room facing the light-man who first climbed from the box. He motioned for the youths to sit at the desks. Then he said, "I am Mr. Pyllistacaillian. You may call me Mr. Pyllis." Other light-men pulled a chalkboard beside Mr. Pyllis, and he arranged it so the students could see it. He wrote his name in the top left corner of the board. "Under no circumstances may you call me Mr. P." He looked at each student to make

59

sure that they were paying attention.

"In case you don't know, I am a Rolimi. We are a race of gods-blessed beings from far from here. The Sovereign Magi Society was a friend to the Rolimi and over the centuries we agreed to teach their new members in the basics of magic use. When Nalria asked us to assist in the rebuilding of the Society it was our honor to say yes. We have agreed to serve you, as we served your forefathers, for a limited time. You must earn our respect and trust if you are to earn our loyalty on your own merit, as your forefathers did before you."

Rissyl hadn't noticed it in his vision, but the Rolimi before him talked faster than most people. At times it was difficult to understand what the light-man was saying. To make it more difficult to listen to, the Rolimi also spoke with no voice inflections what-so-ever. The entire statement was at the same pace, tone, and inflection. To further complicate the understanding, the little man seemed to have little to no use for pausing for things like commas and periods that one might find in a sentence. Another thing that Rissyl noticed was that the Rolimi's voice had an almost inaudible buzzing sound to it.

"Before we begin you must each take the Magi Covenant. This is a binding agreement between you and our beloved Nalria. Taking this Covenant makes you a member of the Sovereign Magi Society, and by taking this Covenant you agree to receive and accept the treasured gift offered to you by the goddess."

A complex magical symbol appeared, inscribed in the desk before each of them. The teacher continued, "Place both palms, and your forehead, upon Nalria's symbol before you, and repeat after me."

"I swear, to the goddess Nalria, that I will always remain loyal to the Society and all of its fellow members, and that I will always strive for the preservation of life and the freedom of all people. I will use my magical gifts for the enrichment of mankind, and never for evil or nefarious motives. I will not allow the secrets of magic use, nor any of the spells, rituals, or powers that I learn as a Magi to be revealed or taught to anyone who is not a worthy member of the Society."

Rissyl was hesitant to start, because he was still waging an internal war about whether he was ready to turn his entire life upside down. Hearing the others say the Covenant with such vigor and commitment, he had no choice but to do so as well. Besides, he was here and he was extremely curious about what would happen next.

Before he knew it, the Covenant was finished and the teacher said, "You may raise your head and release your hands. You are now members of the Sovereign Magi Society." The little Rolimi pup appeared on his desk top. Looking at the other desks, Rissyl noticed that all of the pups had climbed up on a desk also.

The teacher continued, "The Rolimi pup on your desk is bonded to you, a gift to you from the Rolimi because you four are the chosen of the goddess of magic. As you grow in power, your pup will grow in size and power as well. It will become your companion and your fiercest protector, if you allow it to. It may not always be nearby, but it will come to you when you call it and it will come to you when it wants to. Most importantly, it will be at your side when you need it throughout your lifespan, as long as you stay in good favor with the Rolimi."

Rissyl reached out to pet his little pup, and it ran up his arm. It climbed up his shoulder and plopped down to snuggle up next to his neck. He was surprised to be able to feel the individual light strands of the pup's 'fur' tickling his neck slightly.

The teacher continued talking, "For the first discussion, who can tell me the name of magical essence, or the magical power, within your body?"

Cynia raised her hand, "magewel."

"Very good, yes! Each of you has magic essence pooled up within your body. That essence is referred to as your magewel. The term is a combination of the words Magic and Well, and for centuries it was pronounced magicwell (mag-'E-quell). But over the centuries that gradually changed, and around five centuries ago, at the urging of the Magi, we began teaching that the term was pronounced magewel (ma-'JEWEL)."

Rissyl raised his hand. When the teacher acknowledged him, he asked, "That brings to mind a question that I've been thinking about. My mother has mentioned that the term Magi is actually plural, and that when people talk about a single Magi, they should actually say Magus instead of Magi. I don't know how many times I've heard someone say 'a Magi' in front of my mother and she responded 'No, it's a Magus or many Magi, it's never a Magi'."

Dalen rolled his eyes, Cynia smirked, and Sarasa plopped her face into her palm. The teacher said, "While I am not an expert on your land's language rules, I can tell you that within the Society it was a bit of a controversial issue for many years. About seven centuries ago, the Exalted Grand Evoker declared that no Evoker was permitted to refer to any Magi as a Magus. He also strongly implored the other orders not to refer to any Evoker as a Magus. Over the next few decades there was some ambiguity about what term to use. Before long the term Magi was adopted as the singular and the plural title for all Magi.

"But, we digress. Let us continue. Magic flows throughout the world in ley lines, you can think of them as rivers of magic that your kind can not see. Rolimi can see and ride upon ley lines as easily as your people can navigate rivers of water. The magic essence in your body is gradually replenished from the world around you, and it most rapidly replenishes as you sleep. Unless you are very powerful, your magewel will be fully replenished after a few hours of good sleep."

He looked at the students to see if there were any questions, "You must learn to sense your magewel. Being able to gauge how much magic essence you have available for your use is vital. You must also remember that all living beings have magic in their blood. If you completely empty your magewel you will be greatly weakened, and will experience difficulty standing and possibly even fall unconscious. It is even possible to die because of a lack of magic in your body. For your first lessons we will practice skills to get you accustomed to sensing your magewel."

Rissyl raised his hand again, "If everyone has magic in their blood, does that mean that everyone could be a Magi?"

Mr. Pyllis said, "Not all oysters have a pearl. And not all people have a magewel. Although everyone has a little magic in their blood, if they have not been blessed by the gods then they will not have a magewel and without that pool of magic they will not have the ability to summon or cast spells. You'll find that the vast majority of people do not have the potential to be Magi. And most people who do have the gift of a magewel only have a very small one, and thus will never truly be very powerful. Later I will show you how to gaze into someone's eyes and see the magewel for yourself."

Thirty minutes later the magewel lessons were still ongoing. Rissyl could certainly feel the magewel within himself. Now that he understood what to sense for, he was surprised that he had never noticed it before.

The teacher called their attention to him, "Okay, we'll work on that more at another time. Next topic is Society Orders, who can list and describe them?"

Sarasa raised her hand. "There are eight schools of magic spread out among the four Magic Orders. The Order of Evokers specializes in the

Conjuration and Evocation schools of magic. Primarily a spell casting order, the Evokers are known for powerful spells of destruction as well as for their skills in teleportation and summoning.

"The Order of Diviners specializes in the Divination and Transmutation schools of magic. It is also focuses on spell casting when forced into combat. But Diviners are mainly known for the ability to see glimpses of the future as well as spells that alter or enhance people. They're said to have been skilled at causing someone to gain significant strength for a brief period of time, or even change their own shape."

She was counting on her hand by this point. She held up a third finger and said, "The Order of Shadows specializes in the Illusion and Enchantment schools. When forced into combat this order favors subtlety, quick movements, and short blades. They are known for their invisibility, charm, and compulsion spells."

"Very good!" Mr. Pyllis clapped his hands twice, "And the last one?"

Sarasa held up her fourth finger, "The Order of Champions specializes in the Abjuration and Artificing schools. This is an order of Warrior Magi who spend as much time working on physical combat as they do magic use. Their Artificer skills allow them to craft magic weapons, and imbue standard weapons with magical powers. They use Abjuration spells in place of armor to keep themselves and others safe from harm."

"Excellent, Sarasa! Someone has been paying attention to stories passed down from loved ones?"

"Yes, my grandfather has talked about some of this since I was little."

Mr. Pyllis wrote the word 'spells' on the chalkboard, "Alright! Now for the fun part. Spells! You'll learn a couple of spells from each of the eight schools of magic. Conserve your magewel, you will be casting several spells tonight, and if you're not careful you'll end up with an empty magewel before the lessons are over. The first spell you'll learn is called Fire Orb, from the Evocation school. Rissyl, come on down here."

Rissyl walked to the teacher. Mr. Pyllis said, "Place your right hand out, palm up. Good, now close your eyes."

He did what he was told.

"Now visualize your right hand in your mind. See it as it is now, palm up between us. Focus on the image of your hand."

He did so. He visualized his hand floating in an endless sea of black. Then he heard a Rolimi pup barking off in the background and it distracted him. He pushed those thoughts away, and once again he visualized the hand.

"Now focus on all of the energy scattered around in your body. You have some in your feet. Use your mind to bring that up. Move that energy up to your legs. Let the energy in your calves merge with the energy from your feet. Feel it building as it merges."

He felt silly, but he did as the teacher said. He could feel the energy in his feet. He felt it building as it merged with the energy in his legs. His legs were warm, as if he could really feel some sort of energy building there.

"Good, very good!" The teacher sounded pleased, "Now send that energy to your right hand! Twist it and shape it into a ball with your mind. Will it to manifest itself as energy outside of your body, in your right palm! As you do, speak the word Krol'Tu!"

He did what the teacher said. He could feel the warmth flow through his abdomen and down his right arm. He said, "Krol'Tu!" Suddenly a large globe of fire erupted in the palm of his hand! It was the size of a watermelon, and it was incredibly bright. And hot!

He screamed and pulled his hand away. There were several gasps from the other new Magi in the room. The globe of fire fell to the ground and spilled across the dirt. Rissyl jumped back and Mr. Pyllis reached out his hand. A stream of water sprayed from the Rolimi's hand and quickly extinguished the flames.

Once the fire was out he looked at his right palm to see how badly he was burned. However, the skin on his hand was unharmed.

The teacher placed his light-hands on his skinny hips, "That was too much power! I said feet and calves! How much of your magewel did you just use?"

He turned his senses inward for a moment. It was difficult to get a good feel for how much was used. "I don't know! I only tried to pull from my feet and calves! Did I do it wrong?"

The teacher stepped forward and motioned for Rissyl to squat down. He looked into Rissyl's eyes. After a moment he exclaimed, "By the goddess! No, young Magi, you didn't do anything wrong. The goddess has truly blessed you, your magewel is significantly more powerful than I would have expected for a new Magi."

He dismissed Rissyl back to his chair and went one by one to the other pupils. He looked into their eyes for a moment, and then walked back to the front. "It seems the goddess has truly blessed you all. You are each gifted with a magewel that is much more powerful than a novice Magi normally has. You will just continue to gain power from this point. Let us continue, Sarasa, you are next."

Rissyl sat down on a crate out of the way. He felt completely spent. For several hours they had been learning and practicing spells. He was overwhelmed by all of the knowledge and all of the new questions that he now had. Cynia sat on the crate next to him, and she looked about as worn-out as he felt. Sarasa and Dalen were on the other side of the warehouse, munching on some bread.

Other than being extremely tired, he felt pretty good about himself. He was amazed at some of the fantastic spells that he had learned, and he was anxious to practice them and become even better. The teacher had passed out small booklets to each of them, each with a magical seal. They were to practice the spells and drills that they had learned, and then the next lesson would be ready after four days.

He watched as the Rolimi cleaned up the tables, chalkboard, and other items. Then one by one, each of the Rolimi climbed back into the arched doorway that was sticking out over the ancient box. Once they were all back to wherever they had come from, the arched doorway sprung back into the box.

Mr. Pyllis said, "Practice! Learn which of the orders most suit you, because when we meet next, you must choose your order. Consider carefully, because your choice now will form the foundation for your entire lifetime as a Magi." Without a farewell, he jumped into the box, and closed the lid.

The four of them sat in silence for a while. Cynia looked at Rissyl and said, "Well, that was fun."

"Fun. Like drinking from a waterfall. Think anyone would notice if I just slept here?"

She laughed, "We gotta get back soon or they're gonna assume we ran off together."

He chuckled at her joke, but didn't reply. Sarasa walked over to them, carrying a large chunk of bread. She said, "You two should have some, you'll feel better."

He had no interest in food. He just wanted a bed. "Yes, I would love some. Thank you!" He decided to accept a little bit, since it was the cute redhead offering it, and he didn't want to appear ungrateful.

She handed them both a chunk of bread and then sat next to Cynia. "Have you guys started thinking about what order you're going to choose?"

"We each probably gotta pick a different one, if we're gonna lead them

65

someday." Cynia took a small bite, and then added, "So I was gonna see which ones you guys want before I pick one."

From the other side of the room Dalen said, "I'm choosing Champion. You all fight over the rest."

Sarasa rolled her eyes, "I didn't want Champion anyway. I've always pictured myself as a Shadow; I think it fits my personality. And those were the spells that I enjoyed the most today." She paused, and then turned to look at Cynia, "Do you have a preference between Diviner and Evoker?"

"It's up to you, milord." She winked at Rissyl as she stressed the word milord.

He ignored her teasing, "I enjoyed the Evocation spells the most. I was sort of thinking of Evoker."

Sarasa said, "Traditionally the Order of Evokers was looked at as the leaders. They were surely the most powerful. Think you could handle that one?"

He shrugged. He had never really imagined himself as a powerful person. "I haven't really had much time to think about it." He hopped down from the crate. "But Cynia's right, we should get back before it gets too late."

Chapter 9

Sarasa

"Don't look at your opponent's eyes!" Guild Master Thon stood beside two of his students. They were sparring with each other. Both had their hands up to guard their face, their elbows were tucked in to guard their bellies, and their knees were bent to keep their movements quick. One threw a punch at his opponent's head, and the opponent moved and blocked to avoid being hit. Guild Master Thon poked one of the students in the middle of the chest. "Always look at the center of his chest! He will try to lie to you with his eyes!"

One student looked to his opponent's left but then shifted and attacked him from the right, punching his opponent solid in the side of the head! Guild Master Thon said, "Right there! Break! Did you see that?"

The two students stopped fighting when Thon said break. He pointed to a spot off to his left, and both students went to that spot and knelt down to listen to their instructor speak. The three of them had been standing in the middle of about a dozen other students. Those students were arranged in a circle, kneeling, watching the instruction.

"Did you notice how Bailen looked left, and moved like he was gonna go left, but then he changed his motion and attacked from the right?"

Several of the students nodded.

"I was just telling Ralff not to look at Bailen's eyes because they lie. Thank you for proving me right, Bailen. Now, what part of the body can't lie when it comes to movement like that?"

When no one else answered, Sarasa said, "His hips." She had been training with Guild Master Thon since she was a tiny girl, and she had heard this lecture many times. After two of her long time training partners left to serve in the emperor's army a few months ago, she was left as the most experienced student in the guild. She had been the assistant instructor of the guild since then, and it was an honor that she took very seriously.

"Exactly right, Miss Dodisen. And few are as wily as you are when it comes to this. Please show the class." He motioned for her to join him.

She instantly jumped up and rushed to the spot where he pointed, "Ralff,

I'll need a partner."

Ralff groaned softly as he hurried over to face her. The rest of the class giggled softly and Sarasa knew that most of them were relieved that she didn't call on them. She wasn't offended; she was in their place for a long time and knew that being called to be the instructor's assistant usually meant that something would be in pain soon.

She got into a fighting posture, and Ralff squared off with her. Talking to the class she said, "Watch my hips. As I feign left, my left foot and my body weight shift slightly to the left. I might even look to the left. But my hips go to the right in anticipation of the movement that I'm about to make in that direction. If you look squarely in the center of the opponent's chest as Guild Master Thon says, then you'll notice that hip motion."

With her partner, she demonstrated several different variations of that sort of deceptive motion. When she was finished she bowed to Guild Master Thon and took her place with the students, kneeling and watching him.

He walked back to the middle. "Another reason not to look at your opponent's eyes is because they can distract you from the main danger... their hands or what they've got in their hands. People ain't gonna attack you with their eyes, they're gonna attack you with their hands. If you're looking at their chest you can see sneaky body movements. Now grab a partner and spread out. Time to practice these concepts."

As Sarasa stood up, she reached out and grabbed one of the new students. He was trying to partner up with someone else, but she had wanted to work with him for a while and, since she out ranked him, he didn't have any choice. This guy had an attitude. He was big and strong, older than she was, and thought that he was tough. It was important to put these people in their place before they gained too much skill. She hadn't worked with him yet, but she saw how he looked at her. She'd dealt with countless guys like this before. They see a young woman of small stature and assume that they can push her around. It was time to bring him down a notch or two.

The guy put up his hands and looked at her as they squared off. Then he made kissing motions with his lips and winked at her. He whispered, "Don't worry babe, I'll be gentle."

She was too experienced to allow stupid verbal games to alter her attack plans. Thon shouted, "Begin!" and she quickly closed the distance between them. She looked at the top of his head, and threw a quick jab at the top of his head to make him think high. He had been watching her eyes, and he brought both hands up to guard his head. She followed that motion immediately with a shift to the left and a solid punch with her back hand to his stomach. That motion carried naturally into a flurry of about eight to ten strong punches to his ribs and side, alternating her attacks between her left and right hands. Just as quickly as she moved in, she darted back out.

The cocky partner held his stomach with one hand and stepped back to catch his breath. He looked at her with anger in his eyes and lunged forward. He tried to tackle her to the ground where he could use the advantage of his weight and strength. She stepped back and put her hands on the back of his head as he lunged forward. Then she rammed her back knee into his face as he got close to her. Finally, she stepped to the side and tossed him face first to the ground.

He jumped back up and the match continued. He got in some good shots, but more often than not, every clash left him with a new bruise. She was fast and agile, and he always seemed to be one step behind her.

Then he finally got a hand on her shoulder and he pulled her to him. Her back was against his chest and his long arms held her tightly against him. He was bleeding from a small cut on his cheek, and he looked like he would end up with a black eye. He was angry, and he finally had a hold of her. He squeezed tightly, turned, and slammed them both to the ground.

He whispered in her ear, "I shouldn't have gone gentle on you, you little wench!"

She was extremely frustrated with herself for letting him get a hold of her. To make it more annoying, he was squeezing her left breast with his hand as he lay on top of her with his massive arms wrapped all around her. She assumed that he wanted her to know that he was stronger and would do what he pleased. She walked into his trap. She knew better and it bugged her. She knew that Guild Master Thon would not stop the match now, because she needed to work out of this situation on her own, partially to put this young student in his place, and partially to teach her how to get out of this situation if it happened outside of the class.

She was laying mostly on her right side, face down. He was behind her with much of his weight on her, trapping her against him with is big arms. With a scream of frustration she slammed her head backwards, and the loud thud echoed in her ears as the back of her head found her opponent's nose. That caused him to loosen his grip slightly. She brought her left arm forward, and then drove it backwards hard, slamming her elbow into his ribs with all of her strength. That gave her enough wiggle-room to spin around so she was facing him. They were both laying on their sides and she started elbowing him in the head over and over.

He brought his arms up to block his head, as he lifted his leg over her to try to roll on top of her. As he rolled on top to straddle her, she punched him in the side of the abdomen as hard as she could. With his hands occupied at his head, her hook punch to the side was completely unblocked.

To her satisfaction he cried out in pain and rolled off of her. She didn't even pause. Following his motion away from her, she rolled onto him and grabbed the hair on the top of his head with her left hand. Then she punched him in the face with a palm-heel strike. As she struck him she let out a shout of rage. She didn't hit him full force, but she did use enough force to let him know he lost.

"Break! Break! Break!" Guild Master Thon stopped all of the matches.

She looked down at her opponent with a steely gaze. He looked up at her, and then closed his eyes. She released his hair and stood up slowly.

As Sarasa looked around she noticed that most of the matches had already stopped as many of the students had gathered around to see the conclusion of her match with the new student.

Thon said, "Miss Dodisen, please lead the class through the final round of sparring."

She looked around the room. "Grab new partners!" The thrill of combat was still hot in her blood. She paced around the room watching the students break into pairs. She squeezed her hands into fists and then released them as she paced. Like a panther on the prowl, she looked around. When everyone seemed ready, in a loud voice she said, "Begin!" She was disappointed that she had to oversee this round of matches and didn't have an opponent to fight.

She watched as Guild Master Thon took her previous opponent and led him off to the side of the room to talk. A few minutes later the student gathered his things and left the room.

As Thon walked back he said, "Light contact, Ralff. Light! We ain't here to beat each other stupid. We're here to learn something and maybe have a little fun." Thon and Sarasa stood together and watched the rest of the students sparring each other.

A few hours later she sat on a bench at Dalen's fighting guild. They had trained together in Thon's guild when they were little, but several years ago Dalen decided that he wanted something different. Guild Master Thon only cared about teaching people combat, he didn't get involved with competitions, and Sarasa loved that. However, Dalen was driven to compete. He loved the challenge. Mostly, Sarasa felt, he loved the attention.

The fighting guild in which Dalen had been training for the last several years was taught by Guild Master Xanor. The guild competed against other guilds each year in a large full-contact sparring festival called Blood Night. Many of the fighting guilds from Sorgo, and some of the nearby cities, met at a hidden location to hold the festival. The whole thing was illegal, but the sentinels ignored it as long as the guilds pretended to keep the festival hidden. Sarasa assumed some of the money from the lucrative event probably ended up in the purse of someone influential within the sentinels to encourage their inattention. Somehow the fact that the event was illegal increased its popularity, and every year Blood Night was extremely popular with fighters, people who liked to watch fights, and anyone who had money to bet.

Sarasa hated to see her brother competing in those events, but he loved it, and simply would not listen to her protests about it. Over the years, he had competed six times, and every year he improved. He was never one of the finalists, but he was making a name for himself, and each year he got tougher.

Today they were fighting with daggers. Actually, they were fighting with pointy wooden sticks carved to look sort of like daggers. Dalen fought against three other students, and they all had daggers. Even though their sparring match lasted for well over a minute, she was sure that most of the students would have been lying on the floor dying within about four seconds.

There was a lot of yelling and cursing, and even some crying. As it turned out, pointy wooden sticks could actually cause some wicked cuts when jammed hard enough into someone's arm or chest.

Guild Master Xanor stood off to the side as his class trained. There were at least fifty people in the large room, and Xanor had a dozen assistants who did almost all of his teaching for him. He did take the time, however, to walk around the room criticizing everyone about one thing or another. Everyone was too slow, too fat, or too stupid and if they wanted to live up to the potential that his superior guild could provide, they were going to have to work much harder.

Xanor had been an officer within the Imperial Lions, the troops that guard the Dross and rule over the Dregs. He was arrogant and mean, but he was tough, and he did create some extremely mean and tough fighters. That was the reason that Dalen stuck with it for so long. He wanted to be the best, and he felt that Xanor could help with that. No matter how hard he trained, however, there were always several guys above him in competition for guild fighting leaders when it got close to Blood Night.

She had watched Dalen train many times, and something was different tonight. It was as if everyone was struggling to get a solid attack in against him. A few got in and hit him solidly, but anything that wasn't a solid hit just missed him entirely. At first she just thought he was just having a good night, or some of the other fighters were having a bad night, but then it dawned on her.

She realized that he was using magic. She thought back to the day before, when they were learning spells from the Rolimi. One of the Abjuration spells they learned was called *Glancing Blows*. She and Dalen had practiced that one quite a bit and he insisted on practicing it again this morning. As she watched she could see that the spell was keeping strikes from hitting him, unless they were excellent strikes that were right on target.

After the class finished, as she and Dalen walked home, she confronted him about it. "Do you think it's fair to summon *Glancing Blows* to aid you in sparring?"

He looked like he might deny it, and then he smirked, "Noticed that, did you? Couldn't believe that I'm getting' better?"

"Do you think it's fair?"

"What? Course it's fair! Is it fair that these ogres were born with huge muscles and an iron skull? They use what the gods gave them, why can't I use what the gods gave me?"

"Fair enough, but you know what I mean. Would your competitors think it was fair?"

"I don't sarding care what they think. Besides, we gotta learn to blend our new magic skills with our other skills right?"

"I guess so, but be careful. If anyone catches on it could make things difficult."

He shrugged, "I will, but those losers are too stupid to catch on."

She said, "Let's hope so."

"Speaking of making things difficult, I saw how Rissyl can't keep his eyes off you."

She forced herself not to smile, "Oh? I guess I haven't noticed. Maybe you're just imagining it since you're my over-protective brother and you assume every male can't keep his eyes off of me?" She actually knew exactly what he was talking about it. She had noticed it too.

Her first priority was learning magic. She thought that Rissyl was good looking, and she was flattered by his attention. However, she was afraid of letting relationship things get in the way of her dream of becoming a Magi. She had waited for so long, and the dream was finally starting to come true. She was determined to keep her focus entirely on her training, both physical and magical. Relationship things would have to wait.

"I'm a man, Rasa. I can tell when another man is undressing my little sister with his eyes. Especially when that man is a Dreg-owning Gentry! He may be a Magi, but he'll always be Gentry first. Don't forget that."

She sighed, "Don't worry, Dalen. If I start to forget, I'm sure you'll be there to remind me."

He gave her a dirty look, "I'm just trying to look out for you."

"Well, don't. I can look out for myself. Besides, you have nothing to fear, he is not my type." She didn't like lying to him, but she wanted to put the conversation to rest.

"Okay, everyone, focus. Let's do another one." She opened the booklet that Mr. Pyllis had given her. She turned through the pages, trying to decide which spell to work on next.

"This is the last one, Rasa. We've been going for hours, and it's getting late." Dalen picked up his booklet also. He stood up and moved closer to her.

She looked over at Cynia and Rissyl. They were both sitting on a crate talking about something. The four of them had come back to the abandoned warehouse because they didn't have any place better to practice their spells. Mr. Pyllis wanted them to practice some before their next lesson, and this was their first opportunity to get everyone together.

"Cynia, Rissyl? Do you guys want to come over for one more? Are you done studying that last spell?"

"I'm going to need a lot more time to master the *Cause Sleep* spell; I'm struggling with this one." Rissyl closed his booklet and stood up.

"I think we're pretty good for tonight, Rasa." Cynia stretched her legs and leaned back against the wall.

Sarasa picked up a small piece of discarded wood from the floor and tossed it at Cynia. It missed, and smacked into the crate below her. "Come on, how are you going to become a powerful Magi without practice?"

Sarasa took the stopper from her waterskin for a drink.

Cynia climbed down from her crate and walked towards her. She held out her hand as she walked towards Sarasa. As she walked she whispered something under her breath.

One moment Sarasa was taking a big drink from her waterskin, and the next moment the waterskin shook and fell to the ground, splashing water down her neck and shirt and all over her pants on the way to the ground. The water was surprisingly cold against her skin and she jumped back. "Dammit, Cynia!"

"What?" Cynia faked an innocent expression, but Sarasa could tell that she was trying to suppress laughter, "I was just practicing the *Disarm* spell. You said you wanted to practice!"

Rissyl and Cynia laughed loudly, and even Dalen giggled.

She was not amused, and she tried to wipe the extra water from her clothes. She turned to Rissyl and waved him closer. "Alright, Rissyl, you need to practice the *Cause Sleep* spell?" He nodded, and she said, "I'll lay down, come here and try your spell on me."

She heard Cynia start to snicker, and Rissyl looked like he just swallowed something that was still alive. Then Cynia exploded into laughter. That brought both of them into belly-laughter so hard that it brought tears to their eyes.

Sarasa was starting to get annoyed. She was typically amused by crass jokes as much as the next person but she really wanted to take her magical studies seriously and the behavior of her fellow Magi was starting to get old. Dalen looked as annoyed as she felt.

Rissyl leaned against a barrel, and Cynia was on the ground, holding her stomach, laughing loudly. Both of them slowly started to regain their composure.

Cynia took a deep breath and let it out slowly. Then she said, "Well, go on then. She's gonna lay down for you. Let's see your magic."

That brought about another wave of uncontrolled laughter. Sarasa noticed that Rissyl's face was beat red. She couldn't help but be caught-up in the amusement, and soon she was laughing along with the others. Dalen even cracked a smile.

Chapter 10

Kimly

Up on the roof of the warehouse, Kimly moved her face away from the window and rested her head against the roof. She was pretty sure that her left leg would fall off at any moment because it was folded up like parchment and had been the only thing holding her from falling from the roof for the last several hours. She sat motionless for another half an hour or more while the people in the warehouse talked and joked and packed up their things.

Finally, after what seemed like an eternity, she watched them leave the warehouse and head down the road. She waited several more painful minutes to make sure that they weren't going to reappear to come back for something they had forgotten. Finally she risked moving, grabbed hold of a ledge and allowed her left leg to stretch for the first time in at least five hours. She knew it was asleep, and it wasn't long before the numbness turned into the expected throbbing. She braced herself and then intentionally tried wiggling some toes. She almost cried out. The pain was so quick and sharp; it felt like a thousand little needles jammed into her foot all at once. It was probably a little masochistic, but she just loved the feeling of waking up a sleepy foot. Eventually the feeling came back completely and she finally trusted that she could climb down from the roof.

She was an average size person, not abnormally tall or short and she liked it that way. It was much easier to slip way in a crowd if you didn't stand out much. She also thought of herself as a fairly average looking girl, although her mother was quick to insist that she was heinously ugly. Her dark hair was long and she usually pulled it back into a loose bun at the base of her neck.

Her head was spinning at the things she had just witnessed. Real Magi, right here in Sorgo? Her mother would be so jealous. The things that she had witnessed, from balls of fire to people moving things with their minds, were almost impossible to comprehend.

Kimly hurried through the streets, twisting and turning through back allies and cutting between buildings, until she finally arrived at the cemetery. She took four steps into the familiar place and breathed a sigh of relief. She loved the peace and serenity of the cemetery. Most people avoided it when they could, especially at night. That was a large part of the appeal for her, because it was one of the few places she could go to get away from all of the people. She hurried down the paths, stepping between tombstones here and there, until she got to one of the larger mausoleums. The stone next to the door said:

Leomal Cylett
Born: 29 Mid-Summer 42 BRE
Died: 5 Mid-Summer 3 RY
Ezmorelda Cylett
Born: 20 Late-Spring 39 BRE
Died: 5 Mid-Summer 3 RY

She looked around to make sure that no one was looking, and then she pulled open the door and slipped into the mausoleum, carefully closing the door behind her. She could hardly control her excitement any longer, and she said, "Leo! Ez! You're not gonna believe what wondrous things I saw tonight! Magi! Living breathing Magi right here in Sorgo!" She paused for a moment to hear her great, great grandma and grandpa's reaction to the exciting news. The skeletal remains within the stone sarcophagus did not respond, but in Kimly's mind she could almost hear what she thought they might want to say to her.

They would be excited and proud of her, she was certain. "I could hear it all, every word!"

Again she paused and listened. "Yes, even the spells!"

Her heart was racing. "I dunno? I ain't tried no spells yet. Had to rush back here. There was so much, most of it's already garbled up. But I think I remember a few of them!"

She took some deep breaths and blew them out slowly to try to calm herself. Then she thought about what she had learned while watching the Magi in the warehouse. She visualized her upturned palm and then felt deep down inside herself to try to tap into something called the magewel. She could feel it, and it felt wondrous! She carefully directed a little sliver of that essence through her body and willed it to manifest itself in her hand as a sticky ball of light. She said, "Mayl'Hok" and a little ball of light appeared in her hand! She squeezed it with her other hand and then played with it, rolling it around between her hands. It was a bit brighter than a candle, but it gave off no heat. It felt like rolling a little ball of wet mud between her hands, but it left no trail of dirt. She grabbed the light orb in her right hand

and tossed it against the wall, and it just stuck there. It was the most amazing feeling. She had never felt as happy as she did in that moment.

She sat down and leaned her back against the wall, staring at the magical light orb that she had created with her own magic. All her life she had heard stories about her great, great grandparents who were powerful Magi. She didn't know too much about them. However, she knew that they worshiped Viator. Most people referred to him as the god of death, but her mom insisted that he was the god of the deep mind. Sometimes she called him the god of the dark mind.

Kimly closed her eyes and thought about all of the times when she had been going about daily life and suddenly she felt Viator plant a thought in her head. Just the other day she was sitting in the plaza near the market, eating her dinner and watching some children playing on a fountain. Several of the children were climbing up the side of the fountain and Kimly suddenly envisioned one of the children toppling off the fountain and landing upside down in the water on his head. She giggled out loud at the memory of how goofy-looking the image was. She must have sat there for over an hour watching those children playing on that fountain. The wicked Kimly inside her secretly wanted to see the funny scene from her head play out on the fountain. If she would have told her mom about that incident her mom would have told her confidently that it was an example of Viator planting wicked ideas in her mind.

She wondered what it must have been like being powerful Magi like her Grandpa Leo and Grandma Ez. She was certain that no one dared make fun of them. She imagined that they never cried themselves to sleep because there was no food to eat for days. It was unlikely that anyone ever stopped them in a dark alleyway at night and took what little coins they had with them. She thought about some of the things that had happened in her life, the things that she usually kept hidden away even from herself, and she knew that Grandma Ez would never have tolerated such things.

All her life, at least the parts since she was old enough to remember things, she swore that one day she would be a powerful Magi like her great, great grandparents. Tonight, for the first time, she really believed that it could happen. She did have magical power inside her. She was looking at an example of it glowing on the wall in front of her.

When she saw the people breaking into the abandoned warehouse a couple of nights ago, she never dreamed that her curiosity about what was going on would be the event that would lead her to her dreams. She thought that maybe those people were planning to steal things from the warehouse, and she was going to try to blackmail them into giving her some of the profits. However, this was so much better!

Kimly woke up the next morning cold and shivering. She had fallen asleep in the mausoleum, on the floor. She said goodbye to her grandparents and slipped quickly out of the mausoleum. As she feared there were some people walking through the cemetery already, but they were looking the other way so they didn't see her come from within the mausoleum. She didn't know the consequences if she was caught inside the mausoleum, but she assumed that she would get in trouble. Everything that she enjoyed seemed to be against one rule or another.

Her stomach was growling, so she headed to the bazaar to find something to eat. Once there, she climbed up on a stone wall to watch the people and get a feel for the day. She didn't have any coins, so she would have to be creative. She thought that the magical spells that she learned last night might be able to help her with that problem. After a while she saw some Gentry fellow walking down the road. The wind blew his cloak back enough that she could see his coin pouch hanging from his belt. Last night, she watched the guy called Rissyl practicing a spell where he picked up things with his powers and moved them around. At one point, he even moved a heavy looking crate. It didn't move far. However, if the *Invisible Helper* spell could pick up a crate, she should be able to use it to bring a little coin pouch from some Gentry's belt to her own grubby little hands.

As the man got closer she started to summon the magic. She pointed her palm at the coin pouch and whispered the trigger word. The pouch jerked away from the man's belt, but the straps caught on the belt and the spell lost its hold. The pouch fell to the ground and some of the coins spilled out. The Gentry man looked at some guy who was walking beside him, and he shoved the man and accused him of trying to steal his coin pouch. Soon there was shouting and all sorts of unpleasantness. Kimly watched with her head rested in both of her hands. This isn't what she wanted at all. She needed the coins, and she was certain that the Gentry man wouldn't really miss them. However, she didn't want to get some Denizen guy to get in trouble over something he didn't do.

Her heart sank when she saw the squad of sentinels arrive. She had to do something or this fellow was going to get in a lot of trouble because of her. She jumped down from the wall and walked over to the middle of the mess. Perhaps if she told the sentinels that she saw the Gentry drop the pouch on his own that the Denizen fellow wouldn't get in trouble.

She approached one of the sentinels and said, "Excuse me, sir. I was sitting up there and I saw what happened."

The Denizen who was being accused looked at her and said, "Sard off, you filthy little liar! I don't need no ugly street urchin speaking against me too!"

She stood in stunned disbelief. She had jumped down to help this jerk and he had the nerve to call her names? This was exactly why she didn't like people, because they all sucked.

The sentinel said, "Well, don't just stand there girl. What'd you see?"

Looking back at the Denizen briefly, she looked up at the tall sentinel and said, "It's just like the respectable Gentry man said. He was walking along minding his own business, and this guy over here tried to swipe the Gentry man's purse. I was shocked to see it happen in the light of day!"

The Denizen man started cursing and yelling at her. The sentinel wrestled him to the ground and bound him in chains. She smiled to herself as she watched the men stand him up. As she walked past she winked at him. It served him right, he should learn to be nicer to people who were trying to help him. She climbed back up on top of the wall and enjoyed the rest of the show. She no longer felt any sort of remorse over that guy taking the blame for her attempted thievery. If he wasn't such a creep he probably wouldn't be in trouble, so whatever.

Once the sentinels left with the Denizen following behind in chains, she watched the Gentry man picking up coins that were still on the ground. They shined brightly, and she was astonished that no one had tried to make off with any of them in all of the confusion. Once he got them all stuffed into the pouch, he sat it on a nearby table. One of the straps was broken and he was trying to get the pouch to close properly. He turned and asked someone where he could find a leather smith. That's all the opening she needed. She reached out with her hand again, and summoned the magic one more time. When she whispered the trigger word the *Invisible Helper* grabbed the coin pouch and carried it directly to her outstretched hand quickly! She grabbed it and jumped down the backside of the wall. She didn't stick around long enough to see what the Gentry did when he realized that his pouch was gone!

She sprinted down back alleys and darted across streets until she was out of breath. She didn't hear any shouting, so she was pretty sure that no one was following her.

Her first thought was to be happy with the pouch that she had, but a little voice in the back of her mind said since the first one had been so easy, she should get out there and try it again. She made her way slowly back to the bazaar and started staking the place out for an easy mark. It took almost half an hour to find someone who gave her an easy opening. Her second mark was an elderly Gentry woman. The woman took a large coin purse from her bags and sat it on the table next to her. When she looked away Kimly summoned the magic to bring forth an *Invisible Helper*. She directed the helper to grab the coin bag and set it gently on the ground. After quite a while, when she was confident that no one would notice, she directed a new *Invisible Helper* to quietly carry the bag from the ground next to the old lady and place it quietly in a group of bushes. Eventually the old woman noticed that the coin purse was missing, but everyone assumed the absent minded old woman must have just misplaced it on her own. Kimly giggled softly at her own cleverness. An hour or so later, after all of the hubbub subsided and everyone had completely forgotten about the obnoxious old woman, Kimly slipped over to the bushes and casually picked up her little trophy.

This game carried on throughout the day. She was extremely patient and careful to only target the pretentious looking Gentry who probably had mountains of coins piled up in the spare bedrooms of their large homes. With the blessing of the miraculous *Invisible Helper* spell, she could make the whole thing happen while not being near the drama. It was a dream come true. By dinner time she had nine coin purses weighing down her many pockets. She headed back to the cemetery and snuck back into the mausoleum where her great, great grandparents rested.

She had been anxiously awaiting this part all day and she was so excited, she could hardly stand it. She started removing the coins from one of the coin purses and placing them in little stacks on the stone floor beside her. Her first handful was mainly a bunch of large copper falcons, with a few smaller silver doves. She emptied the rest into her hand and found a couple of golden cardinals! She was so excited! Her mother was happy when she earned a whole cardinal in a fortnight of work. Kimly had just scored two of them in a single day, and there were still a lot of bags left to open. She grabbed the next one and dumped the few coins into her hand. Not too bad, a bunch of falcons and doves.

She emptied purse after purse, and the piles of copper and silver coins were getting bigger! She had even scored a few more golden cardinals.

She had four purses left and she grabbed the next one. It was pretty full so she grabbed a handful of coins from within. Looking down at her palm she almost fell over. In her palm, among the doves, falcons, and cardinals was a platinum raptor! She was so excited that she almost peed herself, right there on the floor!

One hundred copper falcons were worth a dove. One hundred silver doves were worth a cardinal. One hundred gold cardinals were worth a platinum raptor! She held the small grey coin up and looked at the details on both sides. In her whole life she had never even seen a raptor coin. Her mom would have to work for a long time. She tried to work the math out in her head. There were fifteen days in a fortnight, two fortnights a month, twelve months a year. Her mom made about twenty-four cardinals a year, so it would take her mom over four years to earn a single raptor!

She looked at the wonderful raptor-giving purse and smiled. A few at a time, she poured coins from the purse into her little hand. Every time she dumped another raptor from the purse she giggled. They were the smallest, so most of the last coins she dumped from the pouch were raptors. When the purse was empty, she moved onto the final coin purse.

Once they were all emptied, she piled all of the coins into organized stacks. There were a whole bunch of falcons, doves, and cardinals and there were sixty-one raptors! Almost all of the raptors came from that one purse. She couldn't remember which mark gave her that wonderful purse, but she was very thankful to that person for carrying so many coins with them to the bazaar! Looking down, she realized she had a small fortune on the floor beside her. She could buy a nice home in The Commons for two or three raptors, so it was difficult to even wrap her mind around how much wealth sat next to her.

Her small hand was shaking noticeably as she carefully put all of the coins back in the pouches. She put all of the raptors into one pouch, and all of the cardinals into two other pouches. The rest of the coins filled up several more purses. The she loaded a purse to carry with her, with an array of each type of coin. Leaning back against the wall, she dreamed about all of the things that she could do with her new fortune. This would change her life forever! Somehow she would have to explain having so much money, or people would suspect that she acquired it in a slightly less than legitimate manner. She would have to be very careful about spending too much at once, or people would get suspicious. Her mother would get suspicious first, and she would expect her to share it with her. Her mother was the last person who would get any of these coins.

She grabbed all of the full coin pouches, except the one she would keep with her, and hid them carefully in an urn up on a shelf in the mausoleum.

With a tear in her eye she said, "I'm really doing it Leo! I'm gonna be rich and powerful!"

Kimly had been a Magi for less than a day, and already her dreams were coming true! Truly, Viator was smiling upon her. She made a mental note to say her exhortation to Viator tonight before bed.

The next morning Kimly was lying in a hot bath, with one foot dangling over the side of the metal basin. She had taken several baths in her life, but she had never actually had a hot bath. It was the most amazing feeling she had ever experienced in her entire life. The sting of the hot water touched every inch of her body below her neck, other than the right leg that was dripping water onto the floor. The sting was exquisite. If this was a taste of how the rich folks lived, then she was going to be a very happy young lady indeed.

She told herself repeatedly that she needed to keep a low profile, especially in the days immediately following her little acts of thievery. Even Gentry were likely to miss a bunch of raptors, so she had to be careful. Nevertheless, she couldn't resist buying a single night at one of the nicer inns in The Commons. It cost her nearly ten doves for dinner, a hot bath, and the Emperor Suite for the night. Her mom just might fall over dead to know that her daughter spent so much on a single night at an inn. She took incredible pleasure thinking about the look on her mom's face if she knew.

Kimly enjoyed lounging in the water until it started to get cold, and then she got out and dried herself off. She dried her hair, combed it out, and left it loose instead of tying it into a bun. Then she put her new dress back on and put her new shawl back around her shoulders. When she was looking at the new clothes in the bazaar she debated whether or not to buy them. However, once she had made up her mind to splurge and enjoy a wonderful night at the inn, she was afraid that she would look too out of place there wearing her old grubby and tattered clothing. The new dress was much more colorful than she would normally wear. It was the current style, and much fancier than anything that she had ever worn before. It was the style that Denizen women wore when trying to look like Gentry, or something a Gentry woman might wear if she was going to spend the day in The

Commons and didn't want to soil anything too nice.

She giggled to herself as she turned in a circle, looking at herself in the mirror. She almost looked like a respectable young lady. She wasn't sure if her mother would even recognize her. As much as she wanted to go home and rub it in her mother's face that she was now a real Magi, and fabulously rich, she would have to resist that urge. There were just too many questions she wasn't willing to answer, and she was certain that she didn't want to share the money or the knowledge of how to summon real magic.

Besides, she wanted to try to get to know one of the four Magi. Those people had talked about many more spells to be learned. It was dangerous for many reasons, but if she could make friends with one of them maybe they would invite her to be a part of their little society. Clearly, she would have to hide the fact that she worshiped Viator. From their comments she supposed they had some hang-up about that type of thing. She had followed the guy named Dalen back to an old apothecary shop near the bazaar the other day. That was probably her best bet to meet them without looking suspicious.

Later that morning, she made her way to the apothecary shop. She felt uncomfortable in the fancy shoes and dress, but she rather liked the shawl. It felt like everyone was looking at her when she walked down the street. She couldn't exactly climb a wall and run along the edges of the bazaar while wearing a dress, at least not without standing out like a bear in a fishing boat. So she walked down the road and tried to pretend to be a respectable lady.

She opened the door to the shop and walked in like a regular customer. She saw the guy named Dalen sitting behind the counter. He stood up and walked towards her when she came in. She pretended not to notice him, and she looked at some dried weeds on a shelf like she knew what they were.

"Morning Miss. What are you looking for?"

"I'm looking for something that might lighten my monthly cramps. Got a mix that would help with that?" He blushed brightly at the mention of something of such a private female nature, which was exactly the affect she had hoped to have on him. She wanted him to remember her.

He said, "Ah yes, Miss! I know of a mixture of herbs that would help. I can fix some up. It'll be three falcons for a vial."

"Yes, please. I want one."

He smiled at her and headed into the back room to mix the various herbs together. Several minutes later he returned and set a vial on the table between them. She pulled out her new coin pouch and bent over the table a bit, to slowly count out the three falcons. She glanced at him and his eyebrows were raised in surprise as he stared down the low neckline of her dress. She realized that most respectable ladies probably wore a fancy brassiere or something under a dress like this, and her lack of such things was providing him with a full view of her small breasts as she leaned forward. He blushed furiously and looked at something else when he realized that she saw him looking. She stood up straight and pushed the coins towards him. "Three falcons?"

She smiled at him when he handed her the vial and he gave her a huge grin in return. His face was still red when he said, "I hope you have a wonderful day!"

As she walked out of the shop, she replied, "I hope I do too!" She thought that he must think she's a pretty lady, or at least he admired her breasts. That was okay too, as long as he remembered her when she stopped by the shop next time.

Chapter 11

Gordo

The sound of metal slamming against rock echoed throughout the chamber. Gordo was in the rhythm of hammering away at a spike he was driving into the limestone rock. There was something somewhat relaxing about the endless hammering. It was predictable and he was in control. There was little that he was able to control these days, so he enjoyed little victories where he found them.

Earlier there had been a dozen or more people in this chamber hammering away at the stone they were cutting away from the wall, plus the Lions who walked through on guard duty. A while ago several men finished cutting free the stone they were working on and had pushed it down the corridor.

As slave work went, working in the limestone mine wasn't too bad. For the first fortnight after he became a Dreg the Firehounds were assigned to road duty. That was back breaking work. After that the emperor ordered several Dreg companies to the limestone mines to cut new stones for the expansion of the border wall. He thought that the wall already extended from one sea to the other, so he wasn't too sure where the wall would be expanded. However, the Lions say to cut four foot cubes of limestone, so now they were cutting four foot cubes of limestone.

His time as a Dreg had been so much more awful than he could have ever imagined. Even if he didn't count the waking up at 4am, working from sun up until sun down every single day, never having a bath, only two meals a day, the fact that Dregs are property, the lack of clean clothes, the inability to do anything fun or enjoyable, or never being able to see anyone that he loved or cared about. Even without considering any of those hardships, being a Dreg was so much worse than he could have imagined. The most frustrating part was the constant beatings and abuse. A Dreg in the Dross could hardly walk more than ten steps without being pushed, poked, hit, smacked, whacked, or slammed into something. Sometimes it was from one of the Lions, but more often it was from another Dreg.

Things had been a little better since they had come to the limestone mines. They didn't have to walk to and from the Dross each day, and that helped because many of the problems happened during long walks. The limestone mines were several days walk from Sorgo, far to the west near the wall that separated the empire from the Barbarian Lands. Since they were so far from Sorgo, they had been sleeping in the mines each night. After going underground, they continued to walk several miles to the northwest. Some of the Dregs talked about how far west they had traveled underground, and how they might be digging in mines directly under the Barbarian Lands.

This room had been his home and workplace since he arrived a few days ago. He spent a lot of time looking at the walls of the underground chamber as he worked, and considering how it had come to look like it does now. The room was about fifty feet wide by fifty feet long and at least one hundred feet deep. Judging from the cut patterns in the walls, he could tell that the room was originally fifty feet wide by fifty feet long and eight feet deep. Then they cut down eight feet and stripped away another eight foot swath out of the floor making the whole chamber sixteen feet deep. Then, over the years, they continued to cut deeper and deeper into the floor. The ceiling, which workers used to be able to reach up and touch, was now very high above him, and the corridor leading out of the room was a steep ramp back up to the level where the first row of stones was originally cut from the room.

He finished driving another spike into the stone that he was working on, so he grabbed another spike and put it in position. Then he heard something above him and looked up in time to see a large section of rocks falling towards him! He dove to the side, and rolled gracefully to his feet. That actually felt great! It had been too long since he had done anything physical that he enjoyed, and rolling like that brought back memories of his life before becoming a Dreg.

Then, yelling from above rattled him out of his memories of the past. There were men about sixty feet up, almost directly above him, holding chisels and hammers. One of them yelled, "Sorry about that! You alright down there? Didn't expect to find another crew working here!"

He hollered up at them, "Are you Dregs? What unit are you with? I'm from Sorgo, Firehounds!"

The men looked at each other, "We're with the Stonecutter's Guild. What's a Sorgo?"

All of a sudden it dawned on Gordo that these people were not Dregs and that they were probably not guards. He was surprised that they didn't know what Sorgo was? Perhaps they were people from the Barbarian Lands? He knew that they had been travelling far west, perhaps they really were under the Barbarian Lands. He just might be looking at his ticket out of this life of nightmares! He looked around the room and realized that he was alone, but he knew it wouldn't last long. He could already hear the sounds of metal boots on stone echoing down the hall, so he didn't have much time!

He ran at the wall and started climbing! The hand and foot holds were small, and it was going to be a tricky and dangerous climb, but this was probably his only chance at escape. He made the first few feet really quickly. Then one of his handholds gave way, sending him falling back to the ground with a thud. He jumped up and started climbing again. He could tell that the guards were getting close.

Above him the men were shouting down, "Hey man, are you crazy? What are you trying to do?"

From down the hall he could hear one of the Lions shouting, "What's going on in there?"

He climbed as quickly as he could. He couldn't afford another failed hand hold like the last time. He was almost halfway to the new hole above, where the men stood, and if he fell now it was unlikely that he'd get another chance before the Lions arrived. He shouted, "Help me! Throw a rope or something!"

He heard one of the Lions say, "Get down from there now, Dreg!"

One of the men above him said, "Dammit, those are Ryallic soldiers! Let's get outta here!" They ran down the hall.

Gordo kept climbing. The Lions had reached the room, and several of them were shouting at him to get down. They were in full combat armor, so he knew that they couldn't follow him. He hadn't seen any of them with crossbows, so as long as he was careful he would probably make it.

Suddenly there was a loud crashing sound directly to his right! Bits of rock slammed into him from that direction, and it took him a moment to realize that someone had thrown a sword at him. They were throwing swords! A few moments later, another slammed into the wall to his left! He was almost to the new exit above him, just a few more feet.

The next sword slammed into his back, and then flipped up and smacked him in the back of the head, which in turn, slammed his face into the limestone wall in front of him. The wall, being jagged and made of stone, cut a large gash in his forehead. The force of the sword hitting him in the back had knocked the wind out of him. He struggled to catch his breath, and blood ran into his eyes. He tried to wipe the blood from his eyes but it just kept dripping from the gouge in his head. He finally got a breath, and then another one. He winced as another sword landed just to his right.

He found a hand hold and pulled himself up some. The shouts from below grew louder as more people entered the room. He even heard people placing bets on whether he would die when he fell. He found another hand hold and gained another few inches.

The next sword hit tip first, right next to his head, and the handle then slammed against the stone on the other side of his head. He was pretty sure the blade rode across his back as it fell to the ground. He would have to worry about that when he reached the top, if he reached the top.

Two more hand holds came in rapid succession, and then he found what he was looking for. The tips of his right hand found the ledge! He repositioned his left hand, took another push with his right foot and was able to get both hands on the ledge. He heaved with all of his might, and got his torso onto the rough floor of the tunnel sixty feet above the floor of his chamber!

The final sword thrown hit almost directly between his still-exposed legs! Something hit the back of his leg and it was cold and hard. Whether it was the edge or the flat side of the blade, he didn't know. He clawed forward and pulled himself the rest of the way into the tunnel, and then crawled several feet to get away from the edge. Then he stood up and started running! He knew that the Lions wouldn't be content to let him get away this easy. They would build a ladder or something and come after him before very long. He intended to be as far away from that tunnel as possible when they did.

He was cut on more than just his forehead, and he was sure about that. He hadn't run very far before he started to feel light headed. He couldn't afford to stop and assess the damage to his back and legs, but he was able to run without too much difficulty, so his legs couldn't be injured too badly. The light headedness worried him. If he lost too much blood he wouldn't be able to flee very far. If he passed out before putting more space between him and the Lions then it was all for nothing. They would catch him and kill him; there was no other punishment available to make things any worse for a Dreg.

The tunnels were rough and there were a lot of twists and turns. He tried to keep track of how many times he turned left and right, to try to keep his bearings, but it was no use. Before long, he had no idea if he was running towards or away from the Lions. He had passed so many three and four way intersections that he was just as likely to run right back into the room where he started as he was to find the exit.

Soon, his run had become more of a determined walk, and then he leaned against the walls and half walked half slid along the wall. He came across a group of miners who helped him to the ground. They wheeled over some sort of cart and lifted him into it. Everything went black after that.

Chapter 12

Rissyl

Rissyl walked downstairs and was surprised to see both of his parents packing things into bags. He expected to find everyone in the dining room getting ready for breakfast. When he walked into the room, his father said, "The new chancellor of Misi sent word. He would like me in Misi immediately. Apparently the transition is not going as smoothly as he hoped, and I'm needed there right away. Your mother and sister will be leaving with me tomorrow morning. We'll pack vital things now and then have the rest sent later. We weren't able to buy a new Dreg; they're just in too short of supply these days. So we are going to take Marisul with us, we'll send her back to you once we can buy a new one."

Amalia rushed over to him and gave him a strong hug, "I am going to miss you so much!"

"I'm going to miss you too! But we'll see each other soon."

Then Brielle walked in the room. The four of them spent several long minutes expressing their love, and expressing how much they'd miss one another. He dried his eyes on his sleeve and tried to act brave. Things were changing too quickly and he was reminded how much he didn't care for change.

"After breakfast we should all walk down to the East Plaza. Lately there has been a bard there playing music during the late mornings. We could listen and have a quiet morning with all of us together."

Everyone ate breakfast silently, and then the four of them headed out to the plaza. It was a beautiful morning. The breeze was blowing softly and the temperature was perfect.

A few blocks down the street they passed a Decree Caller, a young boy who stood on the corner and shouted out news, events, and decrees handed down by the chancellor.

The boy cupped his hands beside his mouth so his words carried further, **"Imperial Armies now recruiting strong lads and lasses looking for adventure, travel, excitement, riches, and glory! Sign up today to ensure a stronger empire tomorrow!"**

"When did they start letting the stupid shouting boys into the Gardens?" Brielle covered her ears.

"Assisting escaped Dregs is a crime! Don't let it happen in your neighborhood! Report it, and earn a big reward!"

Rissyl shrugged, "I've seen a couple of them in the Gardens over the last few fortnights."

"Remember, pick pockets are constantly on the prowl. Keep your purse secure and report pick pocketing immediately!"

"Yes, it's been over a month now." Tuknor responded, "The chancellor wants a caller somewhere in the Gardens at least three days out of every fortnight so the Gentry doesn't have to travel to the Commons to hear current decrees."

Rissyl heard a soft "Darp!" and looked down to see his little Rolimi pup bouncing along beside him. It nipped at the hem of Brielle's dress as she walked in front of him. Each time the little pup almost got the edge of the dress in its mouth she took another step with that foot and the dress moved just out of the pup's reach again. It let out a string of barks and then moved into a full run to chase the edge of the dress, running head first into her heel and knocking the little translucent pup into a roll across the street.

Rissyl couldn't help but laugh at the sight.

They were finally starting to get far enough away that they could walk and talk without being drowned out by the noisy boy. Amalia added, "I agree with Brielle. It's obnoxious and spoils the atmosphere. It's fine for the Commons, but I don't like seeing them in the Gardens. Something should be done about it."

His father grabbed her hand, "Well, we won't have to worry about that after tonight. There will be no callers near our new Villa in Misi."

Amalia looked over at Rissyl, "What's so amusing, dear?"

He shook his head, "Nothing. I was just thinking about something funny that Urg did the other day."

Before long they arrived at the east plaza. The bard was already playing when they walked up, and several people were sitting in the grass listening to him as he strummed his mandolin and sang a song. He was younger than many bards Rissyl had seen. He was short and skinny, with dark hair cut in a straight line about even with the bottoms of his ears. His grey robes were clean and well made.

The song ended as Amalia and Brielle laid out a large blanket to sit on. Everyone got settled as the bard prepared for his next song.

The bard began to strum his instrument in a lively tune and soon everyone tapped a foot or bobbed their head to the rhythm. It was a song that Rissyl didn't know and it was sung in a language he had never heard. Nevertheless, he enjoyed the song quite a bit.

That song was followed by several others, and Rissyl knew most of them. The whole family, and several other spectators, sang along to several of the songs. It was a fun and relaxing morning, and Rissyl was happy to have such a nice time with the family before they headed off to Misi.

When the bard was finished, Tuknor handed Rissyl some coins. "You should drop these in the bard's cap."

He walked up to the bard and waited in line as several other people placed some coins in the cap at the bard's feet. When he got up to the bard he placed the coins in the cap and said, "I really enjoyed your songs. Thank you for playing."

The bard looked him in the eyes for a long moment, and then he raised an eyebrow. After a long pause the bard said, "You're most welcome, my lord."

"I didn't understand the words to one of the songs. What language was that?"

"It was an ancient song, my lord. One that was sung even before the days of the Six Kingdoms in a realm called Menelia. Few bards today know songs from back then, but it's one of my favorites. Sadly, I only know how to sing it, I don't know what the words mean. Maybe someday I'll meet someone who can translate it."

Rissyl didn't mean to get into a long conversation about some ancient song, he was only a little curious what language it was. He said, "Okay, well thanks again. The songs were wonderful."

The bard started to say something else as Rissyl turned to leave. He pretended not to hear as he walked back to his family. The last thing he wanted was to get pulled into a dreadfully long conversation about some boring topic.

When he got back to his family, his father asked, "What was that about?"

"Nothing, he was saying something about one of the songs."

Amalia said, "If you're not careful, bards will talk your ears off."

After dinner, his parents and sister all went to visit friends that they wouldn't see for a long time. Rissyl and Cynia walked down to the abandoned warehouse to meet with the other Magi.

When they walked in they found that Dalen and Sarasa were already there, and they had the box sitting on the floor near them. Sarasa hopped down from the crate and said, "Great, let's get started!"

Dalen jumped down from the crate and knelt next to the box. "Okay, now that the magic seal has been broken, any of us can activate the box on our own." He reached out and grabbed the box, and then he said, "Sovereign Magi Society. Class is in session."

It popped open on its own. Mr. Pyllis crawled out of the box and pointed at it, bringing the large arched doorway up out of the little box. Quickly, the other light-men started coming through the doorway carrying the desks and things with them. This time they also brought out a tall irregularly shaped table with four sides. It was placed in the front of the class area, near the teacher.

He waved them over near him, and pointed to the tall table. The table top was divided into four quadrants, and each quadrant was a different color. In the center of each quadrant was a small cup filled with some sort of liquid.

In his fast monotone voice he said, "The Order of Evokers specializes in the Conjuration and Evocation schools of magic. It is represented by the color red." He moved over to the green quadrant, "The Order of Diviners specializes in the Divination and Transmutation schools of magic. It is represented by the color green." Then he moved over next to the grey quadrant, "The Order of Shadows specializes in the Illusion and Enchantment schools. It is represented by the color grey." Finally he moved to the blue quadrant, "The Order of Champions specializes in the Abjuration and Artificing schools. As you can probably guess, it is represented by the color blue."

He gave them a moment to look at the detailed carvings and runes on the table top, and then he continued, "It is time to choose your order, and take the Covenant of the Orders. Have you all considered your choices carefully?"

There was a general murmur of affirmative answers so Mr. Pyllis pointed at Cynia, "Okay miss, you're first. Walk over to the table, grab the cup of the color of your choice, and state that you choose whichever order you are picking. Then drink the entire contents of the cup."

She walked over to the table. Rissyl was impressed that she didn't look nervous at all. If she was half as nervous as he was then she was hiding it very well. She walked around the table a few times, looking at each quadrant. Rissyl noticed Dalen start to tense up every time she got close to the blue quadrant. On her next time around the table, she stopped at green. She grabbed the green cup and said, "I choose the Order of Diviners!" In one swift gulp, she swallowed the contents of the cup. She placed the empty cup upside down where she found it, and headed back to her spot. She looked like she might get sick, but she didn't say anything.

Mr. Pyllis pointed at Sarasa, "You are next, my dear." As she walked over to the tall table, Rissyl was certain that she was getting more attractive. Her movement was graceful and fluid, even when she was just walking normally from place to place. As he watched her pick up the cup at the grey quadrant, he thought again about how gorgeous she was. He sighed, because she didn't show any interest in him what-so-ever. Maybe it was because his father owned her cousin? Maybe it was because she thought he was chubby and stupid looking. Whatever the reason, he was starting to think that she might be out of his league.

She said, "I choose the Order of Shadows!" After drinking from the cup she made a disgusted face, and returned to her place.

Dalen was almost hopping, trying to get the teacher's attention. Mr. Pyllis pointed at Rissyl, "You're up next."

He walked over to the table. All that was left was blue and red. The thought of taking red was scary, but Dalen wanted blue and Rissyl was sure that Dalen would make a much better Champion than he would. Even so, he couldn't resist the urge to scare him just a little. He stopped at the blue quadrant and reached for the cup, and smirked at Dalen. He drew an angry face until Rissyl kept walking around to the other side. Rissyl grabbed the red cup. "I choose the Order of Evokers!" He drank down the potent drink, and it was like swallowing fire! He desperately wanted to scream, and maybe roll around on the floor holding his neck and kicking his legs. Both of the girls walked away looking mostly composed. He gasped twice, and wiped his eyes as he walked back. The others giggled at him as he wiped his runny nose on his sleeve.

He whispered to Cynia, "For the love of the gods, what was in that cup?"

She smirked and pointed towards the table as Dalen grabbed his cup. With his chest puffed out and his chin held high he said, "I choose the Order of Champions!" He swallowed the drink with a big gulp, and then tipped the cup back to get the last drops. As he walked back he whispered, "Yum! Spearmint!"

Mr. Pyllis motioned for them to get closer, "Okay, time for the

Covenant." One by one they each took the Covenant.

"I swear before all of the gods that I will live as a champion of the principles of this society which are truth, morality, compassion, sovereignty, and justice. I will do all I can to uphold these principles and will encourage and guide my fellow Magi to always do the same."

"In the pursuit of truth, I will be true and loyal to myself, my fellow Magi, and to the Society. To a Magi, the principle of truth is not the absence of misinformation to the outside world, nor is it a requirement to speak without falsehood in all situations. It is a promise to remain ever loyal and true to the ideals of the Society and to her members."

"In the pursuit of morality, I will always strive to preserve the sanctity of human life. To a Magi, the principle of morality is not the judgment of the acceptability of vices or habits, nor is it a requirement to live without vice. It is a promise to value and preserve the lives of all people, except in the act of preserving the lives of myself or others."

"In the pursuit of compassion, I will strive to help those less fortunate who are worthy of such consideration. To a Magi, the principle of compassion is not a requirement to provide endless gifts to those who refuse to help themselves. It is the belief that all people deserve a helping hand in times of need, if they are willing to right the wrongs that brought about the misfortunes to begin with. It is a promise to provide aid when possible to allow a person to make their own life better."

"In the pursuit of sovereignty, I will strive to ensure that my Covenant to the Society extends beyond the petty and ever shifting political boundaries set forth by nations. The Society is a network and a system of ideals that transcend borders and nations. I shall not allow any person outside of the Society to impose rules or beliefs upon me that conflict with any of the principles of the Society, and shall always put the principles and ideals of the Society before the malleable rules of nations."

"In the pursuit of justice, I will strive to defend the fundamental right of all people to be treated equally and judged on their own actions and merit. To a Magi, the principles of justice extend beyond the boundaries of nations and apply equally to all people. Those guilty of the most grievous crimes must be punished appropriately, and those grievously wronged must be avenged or fairly compensated. I shall always be impartial, fair, and merciless when administering Society law."

"Finally, I will not allow the secrets of the Magi, nor any of the spells, rituals, or powers that I learn as a Magi to be revealed or taught to anyone who is not a worthy Magi of the Society. I swear this Covenant on my honor, and to all the gods, most especially Nalria, the goddess of magic."

When they were finished, Mr. Pyllis had them all stand in a line facing him. Other Rolimi brought a pile of items and set them next to the teacher.

He called Cynia forward. He grabbed an elaborate cloak from the pile and placed it around her shoulders. It was green on the top and hood, and the bottom was white. It had elaborate runes sewn into the edges down the front, and it was made from very thin fabric that seemed to flow as she moved. It adjusted to her body instantly, so it was the perfect length. Then the teacher handed her a beautifully crafted staff. It had runes carved up and down the length and at the top was a large green gemstone. He said, "I now present you with this cloak and staff of the Diviner. May they serve you well."

He then called Sarasa forward. He presented her with a grey and white cloak that was identical to Cynia's other than the top color. He put it around her shoulders, and it adjusted perfectly to fit her. Rissyl tried to hide his disappointment that the cloak now hid the curves of her posterior that he had been admiring, but he had to admit that she looked very impressive in the fine flowing cloak. Then the teacher handed her a pair of simple daggers with runes on the blade. She tested their balance and seemed satisfied with them. Then she put them, with their sheaths, into her belt. Mr. Pyllis said to her, "I now present you with this cloak and daggers of the Shadow. May they serve you well."

Next, it was Rissyl's turn. He was excited to see the brilliant red and white cloak as the teacher placed it around his shoulders. He could barely tell that he was even wearing it, and he was confident that it wouldn't restrict his movements at all. The teacher handed him a beautifully crafted staff. It also had runes carved up and down the length and at the top was a large red gemstone. He said, "I now present you with this cloak and staff of the Evoker. May they serve you well."

Finally it was Dalen's turn. Rissyl didn't pay much attention as Dalen accepted his items, because Rissyl was too busy admiring his own, and looking to see how impressive the girls looked in theirs. When he looked back at Dalen he was wearing a blue and white cloak and the teacher was handing him a long sword with runes up and down the blade. "I now present you with this cloak and long sword of the Champion. May they serve you well."

Mr. Pyllis said, "Magi, you must get in the habit of wearing your cloak most of the time. It will provide some protection from all sorts of attacks. The magical weapons that you have been given are designed for beginners. As you gain power you will want to replace them with something more appropriate when you can." He nodded towards Dalen, "Eventually your Artificer will be able to assist with that."

"Ain't we gonna stand out if we wander around the city dressed like Magi? Even the dullest sentinels will get suspicious." Dalen asked, while holding out the front of his cloak and admiring the runes that ran down the front seams.

"Not if you know how to use them." Mr. Pyllis began teaching them how to summon a tiny amount of magic to cause the weapon and cloak to vanish completely. Within a few minutes all four Magi were able to cause their cloaks and weapons to fade away with just a thought and a tiny, wordless, summoning. "Just keep in mind, when you do that you have sent them away to the plane of magic. They provide you with no protection until your bring them back."

Sarasa asked, "They go to the plane of magic? So they're not just invisible?"

"Oh no, they're not invisible." Mr. Pyllis shook his luminous transparent head, "They are sent away to the realm of Nalria, the plane of magic, where they are safely held until you call for them again."

She thought for a moment and then asked, "Could I send other things to the plane of magic in the same way?"

Again Mr. Pyllis shook his head, "No, not in most cases. Your cloaks and weapons have been enchanted with special runes to allow them to exist in that plane. If you try to send something that has not been properly enchanted then the spell will fizzle."

"Could someone else retrieve something that I sent to the plane of magic? If Dalen sends his cloak there, could I bring it back?"

"The simple answer is no. The most accurate answer is that it would be incredibly difficult and possibly dangerous, but it could be done by a powerful Magi who was skilled in that type of thing."

Mr. Pyllis waited to see if there were other questions. Then he said, "Speaking of the runes on your weapons and cloaks. Some of the runes make it so the item can be sent to the plane of magic. While some of them are protections against regular attacks and necromancer magic. Your weapons will also draw magic to you from the natural world, to help in your summonings."

Rissyl spun his staff in an arc, and pretended that he was going to smack Cynia in the head with it. She blocked his staff with her own staff and then thrust the end of her staff at Dalen, pretending to attack him. Dalen drew his sword, stepped to the side, and blocked Cynia's thrust with the side of his blade. This brought about a brief moment of chaos as all four Magi began play-battling with their weapons. The teacher gave them a couple of moments to enjoy some laughing and good-natured fun, before reigning things back on.

Then he said, "Okay, if you are all quite finished!" Then Mr. Pyllis said, "Next you will study individually with my assistant teachers." Four of the other Rolimi spread out to different corners of the warehouse. "It is time to learn some spells specific to your orders."

Rissyl raised his hand, "Mr. Pyllis, now that we have chosen an order to specialize in, will we still be able to summon magic for spells from the other orders? How does that work?" The others nodded, indicating that they were wondering that as well.

"Excellent question! The simplest spells from each order are called cantrips. Those spells can be cast by Society Magi as well as Order Magi from any order. However, the more potent spells can only be cast by Order Magi who are in the Order that specializes in that school of magic. Okay, now call your Rolimi pups to you."

Rissyl called out to his Rolimi Pup through his magic.

There was a bark from beside Cynia, "Darp!" Everyone looked over and there was her pup. It was noticeably bigger, and it was glowing green!

Mr. Pyllis said, "Excellent, Cynia! I knew you could do it!"

"Why is he green?"

"Well, because you've chosen your Order, of course! He's a little bigger and stronger now also."

Rissyl looked down to see that his pup was indeed glowing red, and it was larger! It sat down at Rissyl's feet and looked over to Cynia's pup. Its red glowing tail began to wag.

Soon there were four pups, each about the size of a large grapefruit, running around playing with each other. They were now the color of their Magi's Order. "Alright, enough playing. Time to get serious and learn more spells." He sent each Magi to a different assistant teacher.

A few hours later Mr. Pyllis called all of the students back over to him, and motioned for them to sit down at their desks. He gave them a motivational talk, and a brief lecture about what it meant to be a Magi. He also stressed the importance of growing the Society back into an influential society.

Dalen asked, "That brings up a good question. How do we wanna start adding people to the Society?"

The teacher stepped back. "This is your Society; I am simply a teacher of magic. The Society is yours to grow and build how you think it best."

Cynia said, "We should start slowly. I think we gotta have a solid group we can trust, maybe ten to twenty people. Then we can grow from there. We don't wanna just bring in bunches of strangers we can't trust until we get a solid core group."

"How do we know who to ask? If many people don't have the gift of a magewel, I guess the first step is to use magesight to see if they even have the gift to become a Magi?" Rissyl put his hands out to the side to add emphasis to his question.

Mr. Pyllis said, "That is valid. Since most people are magic-barren, you will need to look for the right candidates. Some people will always have a very small magewel, limiting them to the simplest spells. Remember that all Evokers are Magi, but not all Magi can become an Evoker. The same is true for the other orders as well. Back during its peak, many of the Magi were not a member of any order because they were not powerful enough. They were referred to as Society Magi, or simply as Magi, and they were given a brown cloak. A person with the gift of a magewel will continue to gain power over time, and eventually many Society Magi can become powerful enough to join one of the four Orders. But who is invited to join the Orders, and how powerful they must be before they're eligible, is something else you'll have to decide."

"It sounds like a lot of responsibility." Dalen looked a little intimidated.

Sarasa responded, "It won't be easy, but we can do this!"

Cynia added, "So, who has someone they're planning to invite?"

Rissyl said, "I can think of a couple of people, including my friend Burga."

Dalen said, "I gotta couple of folks in mind too."

Sarasa said, "So do I. Cynia, if you think of anyone, go ahead and talk to them. I realize it's difficult for you, since you don't really have any free time for socializing."

"That brings up a really good point." Dalen looked pointedly at Rissyl, and then continued. "Are you gonna continue to keep Cynia as a slave, now that you're both equals in the eyes of the Society?"

Rissyl shifted uncomfortably on his chair, "I've…" Rissyl stumbled over his words as he fought to put his thoughts together. "I've been thinking about this a lot, and to a large degree my hands are tied. She was declared a Dreg by the empire for the period of ten years. Nothing I can do will change that. She belongs to my father, but he could not set her free. He can keep her, sell her, or return her to the Dross to become the property of Sorgo once again. She will be a Dreg until 118 regardless of my wishes."

The tension around the room was almost palpable, and Dalen looked like he was going to start shouting. Even Sarasa looked upset, and that bothered Rissyl a lot. He looked at Cynia and found that she was staring at her shoes. He continued before someone else could start talking. "However, my entire family is moving to Misi, and they leave in the morning. Beginning as soon as my family leaves, Cynia will no longer be treated like a Dreg in my home or any other time when it's not absolutely necessary. She will be paid a wage to help me around the house, and she'll move into my sister's old bedroom-"

Cynia sprinted over to him and tackled him in a huge hug that caused them both to tumble onto the floor! They ended up with her on top of him still hugging him tightly, tears streaming down her face. She sat up, straddling him and rested both hands on his chest. Through sobs she said, "Do you mean it?"

His heart broke and he started crying too. He had never really stopped to think about how badly it must hurt her to live as a Dreg. Suddenly, he felt like an awful person and she leaned forward to hug him again. He clung to her tightly, both of them crying for quite a long while. Eventually, she sat up, still straddling him, and started to wipe her eyes.

As she sat on top of him, he realized that he was beginning to experience an uncontrollable physical response to her presence. Her eyes got wide with realization and she said, "Oh!" She stood up quickly. "So, ah, we should get you back in your chair. Sorry for flinging myself on you like that."

She grinned at him knowingly as she held out her hand to help him up. He was terribly embarrassed when he realized that she was able to feel exactly how much his subconscious mind appreciated having her on him. He felt like his blushing cheeks were on fire, and he was surprised that she didn't look angry, or offended, or whatever it was that a young lady might feel in that situation. He stood up and quickly sat in his chair and rearranged his tunic.

Before she went back to her chair she grabbed his hand and squeezed it, "Thank you so much, this means more than I can say! I'm so happy!"

The others were gathered around him as well. Sarasa went behind him, put her arms around him from behind, and gave him a big hug. She whispered, "Thank you! I knew you would do the right thing!" He put his hands on top of hers on his chest and squeezed them tight, not wanting her to let go.

Even Dalen patted him on the shoulder and said, "Thank you."

He didn't want to ruin the mood, or spoil the good will that he had earned, but as everyone returned to their seats he finished what he had been saying. "So, I'll make sure she is paid a fair wage for helping me around the house, and she can have my sister's room. She will live like a regular person so long as we're home and there are no strangers nor any of my family around. And I'll continue to treat her like an equal when it's just us, at these meetings, and that kind of thing. However, we still have to keep up appearances. There are certain expectations on Gentry, and how they treat their Dregs. When we're in public, or outside the house where strangers can see, we have to act 'normal' or it will cause problems. My father has told me many stories about the chancellor sending the sentinels to someone's home to reclaim Dregs. In the eyes of the city, becoming a Dreg is a punishment. And if the chancellor has reason to believe that a Dreg is not being punished or is living as a Denizen, then he can always reclaim the Dreg and send her someplace awful. That would be bad."

Everyone nodded their agreement that this would be bad. Even Dalen was reluctantly nodding in agreement.

Rissyl decided that they should change the subject while he was ahead, "What else do we need to talk about?"

Mr. Pyllis said, "I have a task for you, before our next lesson. You must travel to the Giliam Woods, not too far from here, to the south-east. There you will find Randol, an old Diviner and as far as we know he is the last living human who was a member of the Society before the Betrayal."

Dalen looked at the Rolimi with skepticism, "What? He'd be over 120 years old!"

"Just go to him, before it is too late. Open the box there and we will have your next lesson in the Giliam Woods."

"Alrighty, it looks like we're going on a little trip. When should we leave?" Dalen looked to Rissyl.

"Not tomorrow, my parents are leaving and I'll have things to do after they go. How about the next day?"

Dalen nodded, "Alrighty, looks like we'll leave at dawn on the twelfth. Meet here before dawn." He looked to everyone, and then said, "Make sure you pack smart. Bring food, waterskin, something to sleep on, and that kinda thing. Pack light because you'll be lugging this stuff for days."

The farewell, as his parents packed up the wagon and road away to live in the other side of the empire, was much harder than he expected it would be. Of course he would miss them, but the whole thing was much more emotional than expected. It didn't help that several of Brielle's friends were there, and a gaggle of friends of his parents. Even Burga came by to see them off, since he'd practically grown up in their house.

Finally, after everyone watched the wagon head off slowly down the road, people started to head home. Before long it was just Rissyl, Cynia and Burga sitting alone in Rissyl's family room. He looked around the room. It felt weird to think of this place as his.

After a few moments, Burga looked at Cynia, "Fiery Khalius, girl! Why aren't you cleaning or something? Run along and get me something to snack on."

She stood up instantly and apologized, and headed into the kitchen.

"Riz you've got to be firm with your Dreg! Now that your parents are gone she's going to try to challenge your authority. You've got to establish who is boss right away. Just like training a pup!"

"Knock it off, Urg. She's a Dreg, not a pup, and I'll decide how she is treated in my home." Rissyl spoke louder, "Cynia, please come back and sit with us."

"Whoa, what's gotten into you?"

"I don't know. I'm just messed up, with the family leaving and all."

"Yeah, that'd suck. Sorry, I wasn't thinking. Hey, do you want to run down to the Commons with me? I hear they're expecting a shipment of nuts and berries from the east. They might have some of those great little dark ones that we got last year. Remember those?"

"Those were great. But first we need to talk about something." Rissyl repositioned so that he could see Burga better. Cynia sat down beside him.

"Sure Riz, what's up?"

Rissyl looked into his friend's eyes, and opened his magesight to peer at his friend's soul for the first time. He had done it in practice with Cynia a few times, but it seemed odd doing it to someone who didn't understand what he was doing. After a moment, things came into focus and he quickly saw what he set out to see. He almost felt like he was violating his friend's trust in a way, and he quickly closed off his magesight and looked away.

"Whoa, that was weird. Why did you look at me all creepy like that? You're giving me the willies, what's up?"

Burga did indeed have a magewel. It wasn't nearly as large as Cynia's, but it was there. He looked at Cynia and nodded.

For the next half hour, together they gave him the simple version of his new reality. They discussed the existence of magic, their desire to rebuild the Society, and the fact that Burga had the potential to be a Magi.

Finally, they sat in silence, waiting for some reaction from him. He just sat and stared at them. Eventually, he smiled, "You two are so full of crap. Riz, I always knew you had a crazy imagination, but this is over the top!"

Rissyl and Cynia looked at each other and he nodded. As one, they summoned their cloaks back from the plane of magic, causing them to appear on their shoulders and back. They both stood up and summoned their staffs from the magic plane. Suddenly, they were holding the impressive and elaborate staffs that the Rolimi had given them.

Rissyl switched the staff to his left hand, held out his right hand and summoned a small orb of fire in his hand. He let the orb dance there, the flames burning and swirling without causing him discomfort.

Burga put his hand up and backed away. "Fiery Khalius, Riz! Is this for real? You can cast spells? Could I really learn them too?"

"Not without taking the Covenant."

"Ok, let's do it! I swear to the Covenant, are we good?"

Cynia laughed, and Rissyl said, "No, there is a lot more to it than that. There is a formal ceremony where you learn a lot of history, and after the Covenant you learn about spells. Four of us need to take a little trip and when we get back you can start your training."

They spent the next several hours talking about the Society, and their hopes and dreams of rebuilding it to its former size and status.

Chapter 13

Rissyl

They had been traveling for a couple of days, the sun was starting to get low in the western sky and their shadows were getting long. Sarasa rode in the wagon with the supplies reading her spell book. Dalen sat up front guiding the horse, and Rissyl and Cynia walked along side. Rissyl surprised them when he and Cynia showed up at the warehouse with a horse and wagon. He decided to buy the wagon so they weren't stuck carrying everything with them the whole trip. Plus, it was nice to have a wagon to ride in when the feet got tired. It wasn't the most comfortable ride, and he couldn't handle much more than an hour or so at a time, but it was a welcome break sometimes.

He had jumped out of the wagon about an hour before, and Cynia jumped out with him. They walked in silence most of the way, each of them lost in their own thoughts. After a while she said, "I still can't believe you bought that old warehouse."

Rissyl had used some of the coins that his father left him to buy the abandoned warehouse where they had been meeting. He was surprised and happy to see that the owner was anxious to get rid of it, so he picked it up cheap. "It was less than a raptor; I couldn't pass up such a good price for such a large building. Besides, we need a base of operations. And I couldn't stand sneaking into a place where we weren't welcome. Now we can use it whenever we want."

She shook her head, "I may never get used to your world. In my family a raptor would be treasured like a fortune, but in yours, you spend it like it ain't much at all."

He shrugged, "I guess in my world, it's not that much. I mean, my father had to work a fortnight to earn that raptor. But everything is expensive. I guess it's all relative."

"Still, it was very generous of you. You made Dalen jealous, but he'll get over it. He's just not used to having coins to spend. You're the Evoker and now you're buying us expensive stuff. That kinda sets you up as the guy in charge of the Society. Dalen is always the guy in charge."

"I don't want to be in charge. Dalen can be in charge."

"You don't really have much choice. Back in the day the Champions were the muscles, but the Evokers held much of the power. Traditionally, the Evoker Order was in charge."

They walked in silence for quite a while after that. Rissyl spent most of the time thinking about the challenges ahead of them. He also spent a good amount of time glancing over at Sarasa in the back of the wagon, and day dreaming about her.

In some ways, it was an enjoyable trip. Rissyl had never spent much time outside of the city, so the rolling meadows and occasional grove of trees made for some beautiful landscapes. Up ahead, they were coming upon another small grove of trees to the right of the road. Many of the groves they had already passed were far back away from the road, but this one was growing very close to the road.

As they approached the trees he commented to Cynia, "Hopefully there are no bears or other hungry beasts in those woods." He was trying to mess with her, but she wasn't falling for it.

"Wouldn't a bear want more than a few hundred trees in his woodland home?" They laughed together at her comment.

One at a time, each of the four Rolimi pups appeared near the horses and started running toward the trees ahead of them. Their little barks sounded less playful and more menacing than usual.

When they were almost past the grove of trees, a large tree branch crashed down in the road in front of the wagon. At the same time, several men stepped out of the trees behind them, and pushed a large branch into the road.

Rissyl and Cynia both let out a startled curse, and stopped walking.

Dalen turned to the others and said, "Alrighty, no magic in front of these people. We don't want them blabbing"

Cynia said, "Yes, let's talk our way outta this."

"Don't hurt any of them." Rissyl said before the men got close.

Dalen tried to guide the wagon around the fallen tree, but the men in front stepped in his way and put their hands up, "Whoa there stranger! You gotta pay the toll to use our road!"

All four Rolimi pups stood before the stranger, barking as fiercely as their little Rolimi barks could sound, but the men couldn't see them.

From the front of the wagon, Dalen said, "How much?"

"Ten cardinals!"

Rissyl reached for his coin pouch, "Fine, we'll pay your demands."

One of the other men up front said, "Each!"

Dalen jumped down from the front of the wagon, "Forty cardinals? That's a fortune. You're outta your sarding mind!"

"No, it's okay Dalen. Let's just pay it and be on our way." Rissyl grabbed his pouch to begin untying it.

The first thug said, "Well, if you got forty cardinals in that pouch then we're just gonna have to take it all!" He stepped towards Rissyl as he drew a dagger.

Dalen reached out and put his hand on the man's chest to keep him from advancing towards Rissyl and Cynia. They were badly outnumbered, with five bandits in front of the wagon and another four behind it.

From behind them, one of the bandits jumped up into the back of the wagon with Sarasa. He had a long dagger in his hand, and he stood in front of her. "And I'm taking this one home with me!" He reached out and grabbed the front of her tunic, trying to pull the fabric away.

With her right hand she trapped the wrist of the hand that had hold of her tunic. When the man brought his dagger closer to her face, she grabbed that wrist with her left hand. She slammed the back of his fist into one of the beams of the wagon's rail. The man let out an angry howl at the pain and dropped the dagger. In anger he tore at the fabric of her tunic, which was still in his other hand. She shouted "Get off me, you troll!"

The bandit who was being held back by Dalen shouted, "Kill them all, boys!" He shoved Dalen against the wagon bringing his dagger up to threaten him, and the others in front of the wagon rushed towards Rissyl and Cynia. Dalen quickly smashed the man's wrist and forearm with both of his hands, disarming the thug immediately. Then he grabbed the man by both lapels and pulled him closer, slamming the top of his head into the bandit's face! The man staggered backwards and Dalen stepped forward and punched him hard in the face.

Cynia swept her hand from left to right and said, "Raeln'Zad." The spell caused a section of grass before her to grow long instantly. Several vines appeared and began grabbing at the legs of the men who were rushing towards them. The men stumbled and slowed as the plants actively worked to hamper their movement.

A scream of anger from Sarasa focused Rissyl's attention back on what was happening in the wagon. He saw the man in the wagon ripping at Sarasa's tunic and trying to pin her down. Rissyl burned with fury as he saw the man trying to harm her.

The other three men behind the wagon rushed towards it with their swords drawn. One of the men shouted, "You ain't taken her home 'til I've had a go at the foxy lil wench!"

Rissyl reached inside and summoned almost all of the magic within his magewel. He shaped it and formed it into a spinning force of destruction in his mind. He looked at the three men advancing on Sarasa and held up his hand, palm up. He shouted, "Krol'Tu Nari!" A thin column of fire raced down from the sky! It was at ten feet around and extended high into the sky. The flames swirled wildly, like a thousand fiery snakes racing up a tree. The column landed right in the middle of the three men behind the wagon!

The men didn't even have time to scream. For a moment, there was the roar of a massive inferno column, and the next moment it was gone. All that was left was a black circular scorch mark in the ground, and a handful of little burning twigs and grass around the border of the black circle. The three men were simply gone, apparently incinerated to ash.

Rissyl staggered slightly and looked at the bandit still in the back of the wagon with Sarasa. He said, "Get away from her! Now!"

After a moment of shock and disbelief, the remaining bandits started shouting and screaming in fear. The men trapped in the entangling grass hacked wildly at the vines and plant life with their swords until they finally broke free. They took off down the road, running as fast as they could. The bandit who was in the back of the wagon jumped to the ground, stumbled, fell, and crawled across the ground for several feet in his mad scramble to get away.

Completely spent, Rissyl collapsed to the ground. Cynia caught him and helped him down gently. Sarasa jumped out of the wagon and hurried over to him also, while Dalen desperately tried to calm the horse that was just about ready to bolt. Nobody said anything for a long time.

"What happened to 'Don't hurt them'?" Sarasa said, stone faced, as she tried to cover herself as well as possible with her torn shirt.

Cynia said, "They wanted to kill us, there was no choice."

"They were going to hurt you. Are you okay?" Rissyl felt completely drained. He had never actually seen someone die, let alone cause it to happen. He felt numb inside.

"Dammit Rissyl, I don't need saved. I can handle myself! I grew up training in a fighting guild." She looked annoyed as she paused for a moment and then added, "But that was an impressive display of power. I think you singed my hair." Sarasa held out the ends of her hair, looking to see if it was damaged.

With the horse finally calmed down some, Dalen stepped over, "It was stupid to let any of them get away. We should've killed them all."

"Why? They were running away, they were no longer a threat." Rissyl didn't have the energy to argue. "What is the first part of the Principles of Morality?"

Dalen replied, "In the pursuit of morality I will always strive to preserve the sanctity of human life."

"And killing people who are fleeing for their lives? How does that mesh with what you just stated?"

"Alrighty, how about 'I shall always be impartial, fair, and merciless when administering Society law.' They tried to kill us, and they all deserved to be punished. Now people are gonna know that Magi are back."

Cynia replied, "Good. Let them know."

"It is time for people to know that the Society is back, and we're willing to stand up for what's right!" Sarasa stopped trying to keep her ruined tunic closed and just stood there with her hands on her hips.

"Well," Dalen pointed towards the blackened circle behind the wagon, "Cynia, can you hide that scorch mark?"

She nodded as she started walking towards it, "Lemme see what I can do."

If Rissyl wasn't so drained, he would have been more upset at his friends' lack of compassion for the men he had to kill, "Don't any of you care about those three men that I killed? Aren't you at all shocked or disgusted at what I did?" He looked at the ground, "Or is it just me?"

Sarasa shook her head no, "Those men threatened our lives. We had every right to believe that they intended to carry out that threat. I feel bad that three people lost their lives, but I'm glad it was them and not us. The reality is that as Magi this is something we will sometimes be forced to do."

"What she means is grow some balls and be a man." Dalen tossed a stick onto the ground. "You did what you had to do."

She tried to suppress a smile, "But you might want to work on control. Dumping everything you've got into one summoning leaves you vulnerable."

"Four of them were coming after you." He tried to stand up, but he was still too drained.

"Yes, I noticed that. Come on, Dalen. Let's help him into the wagon. We should put some distance between us and them before we make camp for the night." Sarasa and Dalen half carried Rissyl and pushed him up into the back of the wagon. She jumped up into the wagon with him.

Two of the little Rolimi pups pulled at his tunic to try to assist in pulling him further onto the wagon, but then they gave up, and contented themselves with just chewing on his clothes.

Sarasa straightened Rissyl's legs, and put a bedroll under his head. While she caressed some hair out of his face her tunic fell completely open, and he couldn't help but look at what was underneath. The brassiere looked complicated, but he admired it anyway. She noticed him staring at her breasts and smacked him lightly on the forehead.

"Stop playing around, you degenerate." She summoned her cloak, and she pulled it closed around her as well as she could. Then she pushed his hair out of his face again. "Here, this might make you feel better." She took a pinch of herbs from one of her pouches and placed it on his tongue. After a moment his head started to feel a little better.

The wagon bounced them roughly as they started moving again. Cynia jumped in the back with the others, and said, "Hey, Rasa, let me fix that shirt for you."

Dalen drove them down the road towards Randol's place.

- = - = -

The next morning Rissyl woke feeling pretty good. He started to roll over and felt Cynia's foot resting on his leg. He had forgotten that she was sharing his tent. They only had two tents, and Cynia insisted that Dalen and Sarasa bunk together since they're siblings and used to bunking together. She had pointed out that she and Rissyl were basically roommates anyway. Things had changed between him and Cynia since his parents had moved, especially since the beginning of the trip to Randol's. He didn't consider it a romantic thing; he still had his heart set on dating Sarasa. However, it was a different kind of situation that he couldn't quite describe. He had to admit that he enjoyed having Cynia next to him to talk to before they fell asleep. It felt nice how she played with his hair while he was trying to fall asleep. He thought he might miss that when the journey was done, because he found that he was able to fall asleep faster when they were both quiet and she started fiddling with his hair.

He was ready to start his morning, but he didn't want to disturb her yet, so he stayed there a while longer. After a few minutes, he could hear Sarasa humming to herself as she tended the fire. He carefully slipped his leg out from under Cynia's, and let himself out of the tent. He sat down at the fire with Sarasa.

She said, "The alarm spell that we cast around the campsite sure worked well, didn't it?"

"Ah, I guess so."

"You didn't hear it go off in the middle of the night when the raccoon came through it? Dalen almost leapt out of his skin!" She laughed at the memory. She had a long stick that she was using to play with the campfire.

As he sat there looking at her, he couldn't get over how pretty she was. Without realizing that he was going to say it, he said, "You look pretty this morning." As soon as he said it, he regretted it.

She tossed the stick at him like a lance, "Don't be mean! I get it, I look like crap and my hair is messy. Give me a break, I just woke up."

"Yeah, no... I... Never mind. Sorry." He stood up and walked away from the fire. He walked for quite a ways, and then sat down in the grass. He could never find the right thing to say around Sarasa, and he was starting to get frustrated. He figured that he would give her some space. It gave him a chance to think about their journey anyway. The woods were supposed to be just south east of their camp, so, he expected that they would reach them by midday. He wondered what the Diviner would be like, and what he would think about the four of them attempting to rejuvenate the old society.

After a half an hour or so he walked back to camp. Dalen was awake and taking down his tent, and Sarasa got up to help him. Rissyl stepped into his tent to put on a clean tunic and realized that Cynia was still changing. She said, "Good morning, how do you feel?" in a chipper way.

He had been surprised at her lack of modesty around him on this trip. She stood with her back to him, wearing just a tunic and no breeches, and she made no move to cover or shoo him out. The other day, she had changed tunics in front of him without so much as a warning. He didn't mind so much, but he was pretty sure his mother would fall over dead if she knew.

"Good morning. Did you know your butt's hanging out?"

She laughed out loud, "Is it really?" She lifted up her tunic and wiggled her butt back and forth. "I grew up with eight folks living in a single small room. Modesty dies quickly when you live like that. You know where the door is if my naked butt bothers you."

"No not so much. It's a rather well-formed butt." He grabbed his new tunic, swapped it for the one he was wearing, and stuffed his old one in a bag. Then he started packing up things to get underway.

Before long, they had packed up camp, ate some dried muffins for breakfast, and continued south east on the open prairie. The ride through the long grass was bumpy, but uneventful, and by the time that the sun was high in the spring sky, they saw the trees coming into view.

Sarasa was sitting in the wagon, reading an ancient book. She looked up said, "Oh good! We're getting close!"

"I don't see how you read that thing in the back of this bouncy wagon. That'd murder my head." Cynia rubbed her forehead for emphasis.

"I don't see how you read it at all. What language is it written in?" Rissyl really wasn't very curious about it, but it was an excuse to get her talking to him. She'd been distant all morning.

She held it up so he could see the writing, as if that might help him identify it. He shrugged and she said, "It's a form of early Meneli." She waited for him to show some recognition, when he didn't she continued, "Meneli, the language of the ancient Menelian civilization." When he still showed no recognition she said, "Seriously?   I thought Gentry were supposed to be the learned folk of the city. The Menelian civilization existed before the Six Kingdoms. Well, actually the Kingdom of Menelica, one of the Six Kingdoms, was made up of the remaining Menelian people. The Society adopted their script as its official script, so you might want to think about learning it. Dalen is learning it. All of the old Society books and manuscripts are written in it."

"Yes, I would like that a lot. Would you teach me sometime?" He groaned on the inside as he said it. He really had no interest in learning a long dead language, but it could buy him a lot of one-on-one time with Sarasa, so it might be worth it.

"Of course! You can sit in when Dalen and I study it. I still have a lot of learning to do also."

"Great." Which actually meant, 'dammit.'

Then he remembered the bard he had seen in the plaza with his family. He said, "The other day I saw a bard singing songs in the plaza. He sang a song in a language that I didn't understand. When I asked him about it later he said it was an ancient song from before the time of the Six Kingdoms. Maybe you would have known what the song was about?"

She shrugged, "Maybe? I'd like to hear it sometime."

He sat for a few minutes and then, when no one else said anything, he jumped out of the wagon. Cynia jumped out behind him and they walked together beside the wagon for quite a while. It had become a common practice in the journey.

She said, "You've got no interest in Meneli."

"Sure I do, why would you say that?"

"You just want in her breeches." She said confidently, like a simple statement of fact.

He wasn't sure if he could deny it without sounding like an idiot, "Well, I-"

"I can see it. Everyone can see it." She paused for a moment. "Sarasa can see it. Sadly for you she is focused on her training, she's not looking for love. Or lovers."

"Is that why Dalen doesn't like me?"

"Oh sure, that's part of it. That and because you're Gentry. Plus you're the Evoker and he never did wanna admit that anyone was tougher than him. It also probably don't help that you're much better looking than him."

"Thanks, but he wanted to be a Champion. He could have picked Evoker."

"Champion is the Order that most suits him. I know that deep down it bugs him that it wasn't the most powerful Order that fit him best."

Dalen called back to them, "Look there, in the trees. Is that a person sitting over there?"

The book slammed shut and Sarasa said, "If that's more of those bandits, don't kill them all before I have a chance to try out this new spell!"

Rissyl and Cynia looked at each other and laughed. Then Cynia whispered, "She's gonna enjoy being a Magi a little too much." They laughed even more, but Rissyl kept a wary eye on the figure in the trees.

The figure was sitting on a stump, and he didn't move as they approached. In a strong voice he said, "Hail travelers. You are those that the Rolimi spoke of, I presume." The old man wore a green and black cloak with elaborate runes on the seams and in several other locations all around the cloak. The cloak flowed like smoke in the light breeze. The man's staff was adorned with a very large green gem, held in place by a very fancy and impressive looking metal attachment.

Sarasa ran up to the man, stopping near him and bowing reverently, "Greetings! You must be Randol. It is an honor to meet you! We are anxious for your guidance and wisdom."

The old man stood up and leaned against his staff for a moment. Then he walked slowly past Sarasa and glanced at her cloak, "Grey? So you are a

Shadow?"

She bowed again. "Yes, I am in the Order of Shadows, I'm Sarasa. We are members of the Sovereign Magi Society." She stated it with extreme pride.

The man held out a hand and said, "It's been a very long time since I have heard anyone speak of such things, and longer still since they did it above a whisper while looking over their shoulder. All of you please come over here. Let me look upon you."

The old man had an aura of authority about him, and Rissyl couldn't help but feel like a child playing make-believe in the presence of such an old and powerful Magi. He was old, but Rissyl had no doubt that the man could destroy all four of them and not break a sweat.

They each made their way closer to the man. As he walked past them he glanced into each Magi's eyes. Then he turned away and beckoned for them to follow him. He walked a short distance and jammed his staff down on the ground in front of him. A large section of the meadow and trees in front of them began to shimmer, and slowly a small wooden home began to appear where there had previously just been meadow and trees. The old man walked slowly forward, and then turned to see if the others were behind him. "Move within the circle so I can raise the veil once again." As soon as they got the wagon moved into the area the old man jammed his staff onto the ground again and there was a brief shimmering all around the area. Presumably the veil was back in place, although from the inside things looked no different.

He led them to the small home, and walked inside. There was a cozy looking bed to one side, a small kitchen and eating area off to the other. The walls were covered with paintings and portraits, all of which looked ancient. On the far side of the room was a stairway going down. The old man led them to the stairs, and walked down them extremely slowly. The stairway was long, descending probably as far as twenty or thirty feet below the ground. The light from his home only lit the top half of the stairway. The old man reached out one hand and several dozen light orbs shot from his hand and formed a glowing line down the stairway.

At the bottom of the stairs was a long hallway leading into darkness. The old man shot a stream of light orbs down the hallway. Rissyl was shocked to see how large the underground area was. The central hallway went on for two hundred feet or more. There were a number of doors on both sides. He followed the old man to the third door on the left, where he held it open and bid them to go in.

The room held several comfortable looking chairs and couches. Bookshelves lined two of the walls, and the other two walls were completely covered with portraits and paintings. Some of them were close up portraits of Magi wearing all different colors of cloaks. Some of the paintings were nature scenes, others depicted epic battles.

The old man bid the four Magi to sit wherever they wanted and Rissyl picked a large comfortable-looking chair made out of some sort of animal hide. He sat down and the chair felt like it was stuffed with feathers.

"Well, first I should introduce myself. I am Randol. At one time I was the Exalted Grand Diviner of the Grand Coterie of Sovereign Magi of Menelia, which is a fancy title for the one chosen to lead the Order of Diviners. Back then, there were dozens of independent groups, called Coteries, all over the Six Kingdoms. The Grand Coterie was the authority over them all."

He paused as everyone introduced themselves.

"I was quite surprised when the Rolimi came to me and told me of your existence, and your desire to rebuild the Magi Society. What are your intensions?"

They all looked at each other, and Rissyl didn't care who spoke as long as it wasn't him.

After a moment Sarasa said, "Randol, it is wonderful to meet you. Thank you for inviting us to your home. Nalria came to us, and offered us her gift. She has directed us to rebuild the Magi Society. My great grandfather was Chardron Dodisen, a powerful Diviner, or so the family stories say. He was also their grandfather as well." She pointed at Cynia and Dalen. "Our intension is to rebuild the Society, as best as we can. Nalria wanted to honor our great grandfather by choosing his descendants to receive her gift."

The old Magi said, "I knew Chardy Dodisen; he was indeed a powerful Diviner and a great man, you are very right to be proud."

Sarasa asked, "The Rolimi said that you may be the last human alive who was a Magi before the Betrayal. How is it that you knew our great grandfather? How can it be that you were a part of a Grand Coterie that was destroyed a hundred years ago? That would make you well over 120 years old at least. You don't look nearly that old."

"Actually I'm just shy of my 150th birthday. I'm still alive thanks to Nalria and powerful magic. I must say that I have prayed to the goddess, asking for a day such as this, where worthy young Magi would take up the banner of the Society and begin to rebuild what was ripped from us. I dare say, the goddess responded more generously than I had expected. She has sent us some truly wonderful Magi to forge a new future."

Dalen stood up and started pacing around, "Alrighty, I'm sorry. I just can't buy all of this. You look as old as my grandpap, but you say you knew my grandpap's grandpap? That's crazy. And how could you possibly know how worthy we are? You know nothing of us, we just met!"

The old man sighed, but did not raise his voice. "Dalen Haris Dodisen. Your mother was Evercia Safortin and your father was Dontol Dodisen. You were born in 3,493 MC or the year 91 on the Ryallic calendar. You were proclaimed a slave in 3,503 MC for the period of five years for getting into a fight with a Gentry teenager. You are a perfectionist and have unrealistically high expectations of yourself. You put forth a tough-guy façade to hide your excessive insecurities and feelings of inadequacy. You harbor extreme resentment toward the emperor and his government for enslaving you. You are fiercely proud of your family's history within the Society, and your loyalty to the Society and your chosen friends is without reproach. You feel a deep obligation to learn as much about the Society, and to gain as much power, as possible. You are unusually selfless and care little for wealth or worldly possessions, but you would give everything you have, including life itself, to see the Society brought back to the power and prominence of former times. You are deeply resentful of Rissyl Sokigo because you feel like he doesn't take the Society as seriously as you feel that he should, and you hold an alarming amount of malice towards him in what can only be interpreted to be an unhealthy and problematic redirection of your anger towards the emperor for your term of enslavement. You are also jealous and mildly resentful of your sister Sarasa Dodisen because she is significantly more intelligent than you, in your opinion, and because she learns things so much faster than you."

Dalen had been making 'okay you can stop now' motions towards the old man for half of his monolog, but when Sarasa was mentioned he finally said, "Okay, you've made your point."

Without pausing, Randol said, "You look down on your cousin Cynia Dodisen because she does not feel the same level of malice towards Rissyl as you do. You feel that she is weak for feeling affection for the son of the slave owner who purchased her."

Dalen sat with both hands outstretched before him, physically pleading with the old man to stop, he said loudly, "Alrighty, that would be enough. Thanks."

115

Rissyl looked at Cynia with a raised eyebrow, but she didn't look at him.

Randol paused and looked directly at Dalen, "Have I judged you fairly and thoroughly enough, Dalen Haris Dodisen? Or would you prefer that I do a more exhaustive peering into your soul?"

"Oh no, that's perfect." Dalen paused for a moment, and then added, "You learned all that from glancing at my eyes for a moment?"

"The eyes are the window to your soul, and your window is wide open. You must learn to close that window. Just imagine what an enemy could do with that much knowledge. I will teach you, later." He looked around the room, "Anyone else feel that they need proof that I judged them thoroughly enough?"

The room suddenly had three people talking over each other, "Oh, no sir!"

"Nope, I'm good!"

"Absolutely not!"

All three of them were sitting with their arms crossed, desperately trying to look at anything except the old man, so as not to get him started on them.

After a while, Sarasa said, "I have to ask. Why is the bottom half of your cloak black? All of the other Magi cloaks that I've seen are white on the bottom half."

"Ah, an excellent question young lady! The Magi who served in the Grand Coterie all wore the black as a sign of distinction. It was a very high honor, but such authority is usually a burden as well."

Rissyl could see how it would be a massive burden to carry so much power and responsibility. That got him thinking about his place within the rekindled society. He asked, "Are there any other Magi alive? Or are we it?"

"I wonder the same thing, my boy. There could be other Magi out there, but it seems unlikely. The Betrayal brought unimaginable death and bloodshed. Any Magi who survived surely hid as I did, and it's unlikely that they would teach others the secrets of magic use for fear of making them targets as well. Eventually they would have passed on."

After a long silence, the old man said, "What do you all know of the Society Stronghold?"

Rissyl knew only rumors and vague legends of the place and he turned to Sarasa who looked lost in thought.

She said, "Only conflicting stories about what it was and what happened to it. Some stories say it was the marvelous headquarters of the Society with libraries, schools, martial training halls for hand-to-hand and weapons combat, and more. Other stories say it was a fortress designed to keep out the Society's enemies and it had dungeons filled with victims of the Society's wrath. I've read that it was impossible to travel there without magic. The stories say that the emperor himself led a legion of his elite Wyverns to capture and destroy the Stronghold. There are countless accounts of the Stronghold being dismantled stone by stone, and the emperor even tearing down several walls of the place with his own hands. It is said that all Ryallic imperial roads contain stones from the place."

Randol let her finish and then he replied, "I would say that the first three statements are fairly accurate. And the final three statements are complete falsehood. The Stronghold stood for many centuries, and as far as I know, it still stands today. It was built in a place that is virtually impossible to travel to without magic, and the emperor was never able to destroy it because we abandoned the place to the Rolimi and caused the portal stone to become inert, making it nearly impossible to reach. We cut ourselves off from our own headquarters, leaving behind a wealth of knowledge on the ways of magic, and an arsenal of magical artifacts, to keep it from falling into the hands of the emperor."

Dalen asked, "You said nearly impossible, but it could be possible to go there?"

"Yes! But that is as much of a problem as it is a solution. If you could travel there it would mean phenomenal magical knowledge and power for you, but most likely none of you would survive to reach the place. It would be a very perilous journey, even for experienced Magi. It's north of the Rukthor Mountains, and there is no known overland route through the mountains. You would have to travel through mountain caves and endless caverns, as well as ancient abandoned dwarven mines. The Stronghold was intentionally built so remotely so it would be forever out of the reach of all nations of the region, so that the Society could truly remain sovereign."

He paused as the four young Magi discussed possibilities excitedly among themselves. After a bit he added, "But that is not the most dangerous part. The necromancers and the Ryallic emperors have sought the Stronghold for generations. If either of them found out that you are looking for it, they will pursue you. If either of them were to reclaim the Stronghold from the Rolimi before you do, it would be catastrophic."

Rissyl asked, "Do necromancers use magic the same as we do?"

Randol shook his head, "No, necromancer magic is completely different. But some necromancers have a magewel, and could learn to use our magic in addition to their own necromancer magic."

"That'd be awful." Cynia shivered at the thought.

Sarasa asked, "What are the Rolimi? They have been teaching us, but we don't know much about them."

"They are magical creatures native to the lands far north of the mountains. They live in our world but they also travel through the plane of magic. They allied with the Society hundreds of years ago and have been the teachers and the curators and protectors of the Stronghold ever since." As he talked he stood up and beckoned them to follow him. He started walking down the hallway slowly, "Follow me, I have one more thing to show you."

As they walked down the hallway, Rissyl noticed a large banner or vertical flag on the wall inside one room. The banner was golden-yellow with elaborate black edges. In the center of the banner was the image of a large shield. The shield was divided into quarters, and each quarter was the color of one of the four Magi Orders. In the red quarter was a symbol that looked like a streaking ball of fire. In the green quarter was a symbol that looked like a hexagon with an eye inside. The grey quarter had a symbol of crossed fists holding daggers, and the symbol in the blue quarter was a horizontal sword crossed with a vertical battleax.

Rissyl said, "Randol, what is this golden banner in here?"

The old Magi didn't stop walking. He said, "The one with the four-colored shield on it? That is the banner of our Society. I took it from the headquarters of the Grand Coterie as we retreated during a brutal attack from Ryal's army."

The four Magi stopped and looked at the banner for a few moments. Then they hurried to catch up with Randol.

He led them upstairs and outside, and then they walked several feet east of his home.

When they stopped, Sarasa said, "There is something that I've always wondered. I don't mean to sound disrespectful, but I don't understand how non-magical armies could defeat a bunch of powerful Magi. I've seen a bit of what we can do, and I can't even fathom how much more powerful the Magi would have been before the Betrayal."

Rissyl nodded his agreement with Sarasa's question. He had wondered the same thing many times of the past month, but he didn't want to be the one to bring it up.

Randol summoned a chair made from the earth around him, and he sat down slowly. He said, "That is an excellent question, and one that I have spent decades pondering. It's something that we'll spend many hours discussing, in the hopes that your new Society can avoid our downfall. But here is a quick answer.

"First, our own arrogance and apathy was our biggest enemy. We were so caught up in our own affairs, and were so convinced of our own invulnerability, that we let our defenses down to the point where we were very vulnerable. There were no walls around our buildings, locks on our doors, or guards at the thresholds because who would dare attack us? By the time we realized that we needed guards, many of those suited for that duty had already been killed.

"Second, the time of the Betrayal was not the 'height of the Society'. If I'm being honest, I have to admit that the Society had probably been in decline for at least two centuries. In my day we were primarily a society of old men who were mostly concerned with tradition, etiquette, and ceremonies. Most of the leadership felt that the youth of the time did not have the moral character needed for membership. Before my time, they implemented severe limits on the number of new Magi accepted each year. By the time I was old enough to join most Coteries would accept only two or three new Magi per year. The selection process was extremely competitive and family members of existing Magi always received first priority. The number of Magi within the Society was not nearly as high as you might guess, and it was significantly lower than Ryal assumed.

"Third, it had been over a century since the Society had fought many magical battles. The necromancers were decimated and virtually eliminated long before I became a Magi, and there simply weren't many battles to be fought. The citizens feared and respected the Magi, so when members of the Society went on patrol it was usually the mere sight of us in our Magi cloaks that was enough to preclude any battle. Most of us focused on spells that made life easier, made money, or could help people in need. Few Magi bothered learning many combat spells because they simply weren't used very often. In the early days of the war many Magi found themselves hiding with a spell book desperately trying to learn how to cast the simplest combat spells.

"Lastly, we were terribly out numbered. Ryal would send an army of hundreds of soldiers to take on a farmhouse where three or four Magi were staying. Even a powerful Magi with an arsenal of combat spells at his disposal can only fight for so long before he drains his magewel and needs

119

to rest."

The four young Magi sat in silence letting the information soak in. It was Sarasa who spoke first, "That's not exactly the same type of story that my grandpa told. He always talks about the Society as a force that stood up for the common people. He never described it as people who mostly cared about their own social events."

Randol stood up and patted Sarasa on the shoulder, "Don't get me wrong, young lady. Even during my day our primary focus was always on helping the common people. We regularly went on patrols helping to keep the cities safe, and make sure that they were a place where even the poorest people could live a pretty good life. The Society provided food and shelter to more common folks than I can count. We helped the farmers ensure that crops received good moisture, even in years of drought. The good deeds and redeeming qualities of our Society are beyond anything that I could adequately convey."

Rissyl felt very proud to hear these things about the Society, and when he looked to Sarasa she was smiling proudly.

The old Magi continued, "What I was saying was that the Society was more concerned with tradition and ceremonies than it was with evaluating its own vulnerabilities or adapting to changing times." He paused for a moment and looked at the four young Magi. Then he added, "So, let's turn our attention to the next lesson." He pointed towards the ground near his feet.

There was a non-descript stone about the size of his fist on the ground, and it looked like many other similar stones nearby. When the old man waved his hand over the stone it started rising up out of the ground. When it stopped rising it was a three feet tall stone obelisk with elaborate runes all around it.

"This is a portal stone. From this stone you can teleport to any other active portal stone. Back in my day we had many of these stones that allowed Magi to travel quickly anywhere we needed to go. It was how we traveled to the Stronghold, and many other places around the Six Kingdoms. Unfortunately, the stones have become inert after decades of neglect. I will teach you how to locate the stones, how to reactivate them, and how to use them."

As Rissyl looked at the portal stone he noticed that some of the markings were the strange characters of the script that Sarasa had been studying during their trip. He said, "Sarasa, can you read this?"

She nodded, "Yes, some of the markings are runes and some are Meneli script." She knelt down next to the portal stone, "These big ones at the top are the number forty-two. Then down the side it says *Salven'Tik: Foriva ay vol strivik ty presiven teh menelican laefe sanctivus*."

Randol translated, "Morality: I will always strive to preserve the sanctity of human life."

Dalen nodded, "From the Covenants."

"Yes, every portal stone has a statement from the Covenants written on it."

Rissyl was excited to see such a wonderful magical artifact. He said, "Wouldn't it be great to have all of the old portal stones reactivated? We could travel all around the empire!"

"Yes, that'd be great! There are so many places I wanna see!" Cynia nodded excitedly.

Dalen said, "It'd be a great advantage for the Society, if it comes to combat."

Sarasa added, "For all of those reasons and more, getting all of the portal stones activated should be one of our early priorities."

They all nodded or voiced their agreement with Sarasa's statement.

Rissyl asked, "What about teleporting? Evokers can teleport great distances. Is that the same as traveling through these portal stones?"

"Yes, my boy! Very good. The portal stones were originally created many hundreds of years ago by powerful Evokers. They were made as a way for the other Orders of magic to be able to travel quickly."

"So, theoretically, couldn't I just teleport to the Stronghold?"

"If you had been there before, and if you were vastly more powerful, then maybe. It takes a great deal of power to travel that far. And you can only teleport to places where you have already been. Otherwise, you have no point of reference to where you're going. Teleporting without a very clear mental picture of where you are going is extremely treacherous, even to the most powerful and experienced Evokers."

Rissyl thought for a moment and then asked, "Then how do we get there?"

"I have a couple of old books that will provide some clues. That's the best information that we have. But first, everyone come closer and I will show you how these portal stones work."

Chapter 14

Vendino

It was an hour into the meeting, and he saw no end in sight. The Council of Ministers had spent more time shouting and slamming their fists on the table than they had spent actually attempting to discuss anything productively. Vendino understood everyone's frustrations. It had been a challenging month as everyone worked long hours trying to make the populating of Misi go smoothly. It was anything but smooth. The biggest problems had been with supplies. Each city was expected to send food, Dregs, and other essentials to Misi to help the new residents get settled in, but several cities had been hesitant to send the expected quantities. The next biggest problem had been with personnel. A number of people selected to move to Misi had been hesitant to comply, and that had created backlogs and problems at all levels.

"That is quite enough." The emperor looked to Thorli, "Minister, I want Wyvern Regiment ready to travel in twelve hours. They will escort every chancellor from each city to personally appear before me to explain their incompetence!" Then he looked to Vendino, "Send word ahead to each city. Tell them that the Wyvern are on their way, and if the cities have not already donated the generous contributions that I asked for by the time that the Wyvern arrive I will be highly disappointed and I will hold the chancellor personally responsible. Also make it known that every person who was honored with a personal invitation to relocate to Misi must comply by the end of Mid-Spring or they will be charged with violating an imperial decree and sentenced to a minimum of twenty years as a Dreg."

A general murmur of agreement whispered through the meeting room, and the tension level dropped quite a bit. Vendino made some notes on his parchment. He was quite pleased that the emperor was taking a firm hold on the situation; it was the kind of leadership that was needed to make things happen smoothly.

"What else do we have to discuss?"

He had been dreading this for days. The emperor wasn't in a very good mood today, and discussions like the next one were never pleasant even on his good days. Vendino took a deep breath and held it for a minute before answering, "Majesty, there are a couple of items that you should be aware of, which are of a magical nature."

The emperor leaned back in his chair, crossed his arms, and gave him a look of warning. Vendino, and all of the ministers, were well aware of the emperor's pride in his grandfather's accomplishment of ridding the empire of the taint of magic and of his fanatical desire to make sure that it didn't make a reemergence under his watch. The few times when items of a magical nature needed to be brought to his attention, it wasn't a pleasant sight. Emperor Ryal I was rumored to have ordered the slaughter of an entire village because of the report of a single Magi living there. Vendino was quite confident that their current emperor would do the same thing if he felt he needed to.

"First, Majesty, there have been several unconfirmed unusual reports from farms and homesteads north of Rahken, near the central gate in our border wall." He hoped the emperor wouldn't be that worried about unconfirmed reports, and would dismiss them off-hand.

"Unconfirmed unusual reports of what nature, Minister Vendino?"

"Reports of a…" He struggled for a soft, non-threatening word, "…a dead things walking and attacking people, sort of nature." He looked around the room, hoping that the usually overly-talkative ministers might jump in and help him out, but everyone was deathly silent. The emperor's steely gaze was aimed directly at Vendino, and they were all fine with that.

"Walking and attacking is uncharacteristic behavior for dead things, don't you think? Could these be some sort of hallucinations brought on by bad food or something?"

He breathed a sigh of relief that the emperor had given him a way out of that mess. "Yes, Majesty. I was thinking the same thing. It's probably a combination of some kind of hallucinations mixed with other people wanting the notoriety of claiming to have gone through similar situations."

"Indeed. And the second item of a magical nature?"

This time he did not need to decide how to word his explanation. Instead, he looked through his parchments and found the one he needed. He pulled it out and sat it before the emperor. He waited for the emperor to read it. It said:

Attention One and All!

Have you ever wanted magical powers?

Now you can have them!

The Sovereign Magi Society is alive!
And it's once again recruiting!
If you want to be a part, meet us by the
Fireplace at the Ugly Buggar Tavern!
Mid-Spring 12th at sundown.
Secret word is Shazbo!

As the emperor stared at the parchment his face grew redder and redder. Finally, he picked it up and read it aloud to the ministers in the room. There were several audible gasps of surprise.

After a long pause, Vendino continued, "This parchment was found by one of the sentinels in Sorgo, on the thirteenth. He turned it over to his captain who gave it to fast-riders to deliver to us at once. It was delivered this morning along with a letter from the captain saying that he talked to the owner of the Ugly Buggar who said that he didn't notice any unusual situations on the evening of the twelfth, so it's entirely possible that the whole thing is a kid's prank."

The emperor shook his head, "That is unlikely." He turned to Thorli, "Minister, let's send in some troops. Isn't Raptor Regiment in that general area now?"

"Not too far from there, Your Majesty." Thorli looked through his notes. "Not far at all. Do you want them to send a platoon and make a statement? Or should we deal with this quietly?"

The emperor thought for a moment. "Let's deal with this quietly, for now. If there is nothing else, I am famished. Let's adjourn for lunch."

Everyone murmured their agreement, and several people had gathered their things and stood up when the door to the meeting room was flung open. Two children ran into the room. Vendino was relieved to see that the interruption was not caused by his staff it was caused by the emperor's children.

The older child was Prince Edal, the emperor's nine year old son, and the younger was his six year old daughter, Princess Anoria. Both children burst into the room and began racing around the large table, with the little girl chasing her brother.

"Edal and Anoria, come here immediately!" The emperor's voice held a tone of slight amusement.

The two children stopped their game, and walked quickly over to their father.

He looked to the open door, and then back to his children. "Where is your nursemaid? Did you escape her keen eye once again?"

"It's my fault, I apologize for the interruption."

Vendino looked over to see Empress Loranol standing in the doorway.

She said, "I was hoping to see you before you head down to hold audience. The kids haven't ridden their horses in ages, and I'm longing for a few days at our seaside villa. Couldn't we all sneak away, just for a fortnight?"

The children jumped on the emperor's lap, begging and pleading with him, in their irresistible way. The emperor squeezed his children tight and then looked at his wife with a small smile. "We will get away to the villa soon, I promise! But with this Misi business, and a host of other problems, I just can't get away right now."

He stood up and picked up both of his children in the process. He walked out the door, talking to his wife along the way.

Vendino waited until the emperor and his family had moved down the hall. Then he said, "Well, meeting adjourned."

Chapter 15

Sarge

Grum'Glin was Sarge's least favorite city to visit. Each city had its own personality, and Grum'Glin's personality was awful. It was primarily a trading city. The river flowed through it, and all over-land trade routes passed through it. On any given day there were almost as many traders, rivermen, merchants, and other outsiders in the city as there were locals. It was a breeding ground for crime and violence. The traders brought guards with them to protect themselves from local thieves. The locals had guards patrolling to protect the city from traveling thieves. Resourceful thieves paid off guards from both groups to ignore their illicit activities. More often than not it was the guards themselves that brought most of the violence.

Some of the Free Cities excelled in culture or the arts. Others produced some of the finest woodworking or metalworking products to be found anywhere. Still others provided vital food and leather goods. Grum'Glin simply aided in the movement of other cities' goods from one place to another, and taxed each of them something terrible.

As he walked down one of the muddy streets along the river he was lost in thought about the various Free Cities, and how they interacted with each other. Their lack of a central government was cause for many of the problems that the cities faced. Each one cared only about their own needs and that seemed to turn the simplest trade questions into problems. If he was in charge, he would unite all of the cities and encourage them to work together. However, since the creation of the empire the Free Cities valued one thing over everything else, and that was their freedom. All of the Free Cities had been a part of the Six Kingdoms before the empire gobbled up most everything. As the new emperor conquered vast swaths of land, the cities of the north were the only territories to successfully resist, and eventually the empire built a massive wall to keep the lands of the empire separate from the Free Cities to the north.

Over the last century, the Free Cities had seen the Imperial Wall move further north as the empire captured one city after another. It had been about a decade since the empire's last attacks, and lately the tensions had been high in all of the cities, as they worried that the voracious southern neighbor was once again looking to claim another city.

He couldn't help but think that if the Free Cities had a single government, perhaps that government could organize a force that could keep the empire from continuing to capture more cities. Maybe they could even liberate cities that had been captured in the past. It was a radical idea, and one that went completely against the fiercely independent mindset of the cities, but eventually there would be no more Free Cities if something wasn't done.

As he turned a corner he noticed something that brought his thoughts back to the city before him. Up ahead, was a large cage with a man inside. The man was wearing rags, he was covered in mud and filth, and he looked about half dead.

He walked over to the man, and the pathetic prisoner must have expected him to throw or kick something at him because he closed his eyes and winced, but he made no effort to move or raise his hands to protect his face. Sarge knelt down in the mud and muck beside the cage. "Hail stranger, why are you here?"

The prisoner could barely talk. It sounded like his throat was too dry to form words, so Sarge took out his waterskin and put it next to the cage. The man inside looked hesitant to accept it at first, but then drank desperately. He let the prisoner drink until the waterskin was empty.

Finally the prisoner replied, "I've angered the gods. They're smiting me."

Given the prisoner's sorry state, Sarge didn't doubt that this was the case. "That I can see. What's your name?"

"Gordo."

"Greetings, I'm Sarge. So, tell me Gordo, what'd you do to get put in this cage?"

Over the next several minutes Gordo told him a remarkable tale of misfortune. He had to stop the prisoner a couple of times to explain terms like Dregs and the Dross, because Sarge had never heard of such things. He wasn't sure what to make of this prisoner. Years ago Sarge had fought against imperial soldiers in the battle to save the Free City of Misil'Kayl. However, other than shouting curses at them he had never actually talked to someone from the empire.

From behind him, someone shouted, "Get away from the prisoner!"

Sarge stood up and faced the large man who approached. "Why is this man in a cage?"

"He is an imperial spy! He was pulled from a mine to the west of here, trying to sneak into Free Cities lands! He's a scout for an imperial invasion!"

"What'll happen to him?"

Gordo pulled himself to a standing position and leaned against the cage. Sarge looked into Gordo's eyes. He opened his magesight to see what it would tell him. He was shocked to see that the prisoner had a sizable magewel. He didn't know how to dig deeper into the prisoner's soul, but he trusted the poor man anyway. He was certain that this pathetic man was not a scout for an imperial invasion. Then he looked back to the angry man behind him.

"I mean to let him starve to death, and then we're gonna put his head on a pike outside the gate of the imperial wall!"

Sarge turned to Gordo and said, "Is this true? Are you a scout, as the man says?"

The prisoner lowered his head as he shook it from side to side. He allowed himself to slowly fall to the ground, and he sat there with his face pressed against the bars of his case.

"Do you want to harm this man, or the folks in Grum'Glin?"

Gordo looked up at his captor, and then shook his head slightly, "No. I just want food. And a soft bed."

Turning back to the captor, Sarge asked, "Why would the empire need spies in Grum'Glin? Have they ever been sneaky? No they haven't. I know, I've fought them. They don't sneak, they overwhelm. They don't sarding care if we know our fate! When they captured Misil'Kayl they camped their massive army at our city gate for a fortnight."

"That means nothing! I still say he is a spy!" The captor planted his feet and crossed his arms across his chest.

"This man is no more a spy than you are. By what authority do you hold him?"

"By the order of Guard Commander Tamlon."

"Bring him here, immediately."

The big man considered the demand and then shook his head, "No, he's a busy man. I'm not going to bother him."

Sarge widened his stance and put both of his fists on his hips. His brown and white cloak opened to reveal several weapons. "Will you dare defy a direct request from the Sovereign Magi Society?"

The man bowed hesitantly, and then said, "No, sir. I will bring him."

The man hurried off and Sarge turned back to the prisoner. "I plan to take you from this place. You'll travel with me as my companion, until we decide what'll be best for you. Is that agreeable to you?"

"Yes, anything is better than this cage." Gordo nodded slowly. "Will I be your slave?"

Sarge's expression turned disgusted, "The Society does not tolerate slavery. You'll be a free man. You can travel with me for a short time, or longer, until you're stronger and ready to move on to wherever you'll go next. But I may need to conscript you into my Society to get them to free you. To join, you'd be required to take an oath of loyalty to my Society. It is an oath to fight for the preservation of life and freedoms of all people. Is that acceptable to you? Once you give your word, I cannot allow you to ever recant."

The prisoner nodded, "Yes, I give my word. With all of my heart!"

Sarge noticed two young women walking past. Both women wore low cut dresses and had their hair tied up in a high pony tail the way he liked it. They noticed him watching them walk past and they stopped and turned towards him. One of the women said, "Hey sweet thing, what brings you to Grum'Glin? Looking for some ale and a good time?"

"I'm always looking for some ale and a great time. What do you got in mind?"

Both girls smiled at him, and he was pretty sure that the quiet one was looking at his coin purse. At least she would be, if his coin purse was hanging in front of his breeches. The talkative girl said, "Well you should stop by Miss Arissa's. The nights are never dull at Arissa's!" Both girls started giggling, and the quiet one winked at him as they walked off.

When they were out of sight Sarge turned back to Gordo. He said, "What were we saying?"

Gordo asked, "Are Magi allowed to do those things, with that kind of girl?"

Sarge nodded at the prisoner but before he could answer, he saw the jailer returning with seven other men. All of the other men wore armor. One of them also had a number of medals hanging from fancy ribbons around his neck. The others looked to be his guards. The man with the ribbons approached Sarge, "What is the meaning of this? I don't have time to be summoned onto the street like a common servant!"

"Greetings Commander, I represent the Sovereign Magi Society. This man is no longer your prisoner. You will release him to me."

The Commander laughed, "Magi, you must be confused. Your Society lost its influence long ago. Grum'Glin no longer even acknowledges your authority. The prisoner stays where he is. I mean to mount his head on a pike!"

Sarge crossed his arms before him, "The ant may not acknowledge the boot, but that will not stop it from being squashed." He paused, not entirely sure that he was doing the right thing, but there was something unique about this prisoner. He couldn't simply allow him to be killed. He took a deep breath, and let it out slowly. Then he said, "I invoke the Right of Conscription. This man shall become a member of the Sovereign Magi Society, and according to Society Law I am entitled to use any and all means at my disposal to free him from confinement. To defy me in this would be most unwise."

"But this man is a spy! He's scouting for an invasion!"

"Nonsense. The only thing he is scouting for is the path to live as a free man. He will become a member of the Society, and I cannot permit him to be caged. Who is your superior, Commander?"

"I report directly to the baron!"

"Excellent. Arrange an audience. I will not unleash my magic fury, as long as I am given audience with the baron before nightfall." Sarge knew that this was a risky maneuver. As far as he knew no Magi had invoked the Right of Conscription in many decades, most likely not since the days of the Six Kingdoms, and most certainly not with a threat of magical violence. Society Law was absolute, at least to Sarge. He would bow to no other laws. Even though the Magi numbers continue to erode, the leader of this city would be hesitant to defy the Society. He hoped.

At first it looked like the commander would defy him further, but finally the man spun quickly and he stormed off, followed by all of his guards and the jailor.

Sarge knelt down next to the prisoner. He pulled some dry bread and deer jerky from his pack and handed them to Gordo. "So, tell me about your home. Where are you from? What did you do before this whole 'slave' portion of your life began?"

The two men spent the next several hours talking. Gordo told Sarge about Sorgo and his life as a street performer, and many of his favorite stories from his childhood. They talked at length about the Society and Sarge's ongoing efforts to stop the necromancers.

Eventually one of the guards returned. He said, "Magi, the baron will see you. Please follow me."

They walked through town to the palace. Sarge was impressed, it was a magnificent structure. He'd never taken the time to venture to this part of the city. It was a stark contrast to the filth of the docks and warehouse districts.

When they entered the building the guard led him through a maze of hallways and passages. He noticed with passing interest some of the beautiful paintings and sculptures around the palace. The city must be doing very well financially for the baron to be able to afford such a lavish home.

The guard stopped at a desk in a small anti-chamber. "Place your weapons on the desk. They'll be returned after your audience with the baron."

Sarge sighed. It wasn't as though he would need the blades if he really wanted to harm the baron, but they had been passed down from Magi to Magi for centuries and he would be highly displeased if he had a hassle getting them back. He pulled out his long sword and long dagger from their belt sheaths and placed them on the table. Then he grabbed two small daggers from his boots, and a variety of little spikes and other random weapons from pockets in his cloak and breeches, and placed them all on the table. He gave the guard a look of annoyance, and then a second long look of warning to care for those expensive weapons.

The guard motioned towards his shoulders, "Cloak too, I'm afraid. Baron's orders."

He removed the cloak slowly and placed it on the table, but he didn't remove his hand from it as he stood, staring the guard in the eyes. "If I don't get this cloak back, exactly as it is now, I will personally turn every last person in this palace into swamp slugs and I will then dismantle this place stone by stone and board by board. So, unless you would like to see this place rebuilt as the fanciest shithouse in the Free Cities as you spend your remaining days foraging for frog eggs for a snack, I would advise taking real good care of that cloak. Clear?"

The guard looked uncomfortable and said, "They'll be safe, Magi. Through those doors, please. The baron will see you now."

As he left his most important earthly possessions on the table, he thought that it would be nice if he could just disregard that kind of order. Being sovereign and all, one might think that Society Magi could do anything they wanted, but that wasn't how it worked. He didn't remember the exact wording, but Society Law basically said that a Magi should be respectful of local laws and customs unless they threaten the Magi's life or mission. Since the custom of going unarmed before the baron threatened neither of those things, and he assumed that custom was probably fairly common around the Free Cities, he left his most important things behind.

The large room that he entered pulled his mind from those thoughts. The room was probably designed to make those who enter feel small and unimportant, and it did a good job of that. He walked past benches of onlookers and approached a large chair at the end of the long room.

When he stopped walking, the baron said, "Magi, I hear that you are making threats towards, and demands of, the Commander of our Guard, and that you are demanding my time. What is all of this trouble about?"

"Baron, your people have imprisoned a slave from the empire, who fled here to find freedom. Instead of helping and welcoming him, you've locked him in a cage."

"I'm told this man is an imperial spy."

Sarge laughed, "We both know that's a stupid assumption. If the empire wanted this water-logged dung-hole, it would march a swarm of soldiers to the gates and camp them there until you all starve, and then they'd sweep in to kill the unlucky fools who clung to life. That prisoner is no spy and we both know it."

"Why do you care?"

The Magi stood a little taller with pride, "I care because that's what the Society does. We care for those who haven't been given a fair chance at life. I care because this wretch can't go home or they'll make him a slave. He knows no one in the Free Cities, and he has nowhere to go. I care because no one else does, but mostly, I care because he means to take the oaths and take on the burdens of becoming a Magi. Therefore, I am honor bound to free him and assist him."

"And what would you do with him?"

"He'll travel with me as he learns the ways of the Magi, until he is ready to strike out on his own."

The baron looked bored, and took a sip of wine before replying, "And what if I told you that the poor wretch is being taken to the gallows as we speak to be hanged for being a spy?"

"I would ask you to give my condolences to the family of the poor guard who tried to open his cage. You see, I've placed a magical trap on that door. If anyone other than me opens it before I disarm the trap, they'll meet a most unfortunate demise." He hoped his bluff was believable. If he had the magical skills to lay that kind of trap he would have, but they don't know that he can't do that sort of thing. Although he was not the most powerful Magi that ever lived, he did pride himself on his ability to lay down some serious bullshit when the need arose.

"Fear not. My guards are all safe and sound, as is the prisoner, for now. Let us make a deal. I'm assuming that you've heard the rumors of Awakened terrorizing the farmland around Grum'Glin. Bring me proof that they're gone, then I'll release the prisoner to you."

Sarge was starting to get annoyed. He widened his stance and put his fists on his hips. He assumed that it was not as intimidating without all of his weapons in their place, but it was a natural reaction to random annoyances. "Sorry, sir, that ain't how it works. The Society does not take commissions and we do not bow to the demands of nations." He paused for effect, and then added, "Or cities. I'm not bargaining for the prisoner's life. I am stating that it is time for him to be released."

The baron took another drink of wine, "And if I refuse to release him to you? The Sovereign Magi Society is effectively dead. It was murdered by insane Emperor Ryal. The demands of the Magi have not carried any weight in our lifetime! But, if you bring me proof of the death of these Awakened then I'll consider releasing the prisoner to you."

This was going about as bad as Sarge assumed it would go. Now that the baron felt like he was in control he was altering the deal, and not even promising that he would release the prisoner at all. He wondered what kept the cities and kingdoms in check for the Society back in the glory days. His initial guess was fear, the kingdoms would be afraid of angering a society of Magi. Then he had a revelation. Perhaps it was protection? If a city or realm refused to follow the Society's Laws, there would be little reason for the Society to protect that place from necromancers and other magical foes.

He decided he would just lay down his cards and wait to see how the game played out. "As I have said, I invoke the Right of Conscription. The prisoner will be coming with me. If you acknowledge the Society's sovereignty, and adhere to Society Law in this matter, then I will continue my regular patrols of this location. When I encounter a necromancer, or other magical threats to the city, I will deal with them as I choose without asking for payment or reward. But if the city of Grum'Glin refuses to acknowledge the sovereignty of the Society, then I will immediately put out word for all Magi to shun Grum'Glin and leave it to the mercy of whatever evils it might face. The choice is yours." He turned and started to leave.

"Magi, wait."

Sarge stopped and turned around.

"Can you really kill the Awakened?"

He nodded, "I killed several of them and the necromancer who controlled them, less than a fortnight ago outside of Ront'El."

The baron sat in his chair and stared at Sarge for several long moments before saying, "Guards, release the prisoner to the Magi. You're dismissed."

Sarge let out a silent breath slowly as he walked out of the large room. He started to feel better as he put on his cloak and slid all of his weapons into their proper place. That had worked out better than he had hoped. Now he just needed to free the prisoner and then they could celebrate a successful day by enjoying whatever wonders might be found at Miss Arissa's.

Chapter 16

Rissyl

A person doesn't realize how much they love their own bed until they're away from it for an extended period of time. As Rissyl enjoyed the comfort of his bed, he thought about how great it felt to be home. The four Magi had arrived back in Sorgo shortly after dark last night and they left the wagon in the warehouse. He was exhausted when he finally got into bed, so he didn't have time to really appreciate how good it felt to be home. Now that he was awake and the morning sun was shining in his window, he was content to stay in bed for a few minutes and just enjoy the moment.

The door to his bedroom opened and Cynia let herself in without knocking. He looked up in annoyance, and then realized that she was carrying a large tray of food. He sat up as she placed the tray over his lap in the bed. He was shocked, "Cynia, you shouldn't have. You're not a Dreg when it's just us, remember?"

She pushed his feet to the side of the bed as she climbed onto the bottom part of the bed, facing him. She said, "I know, but we agreed you'd pay me to keep house and stuff. That's what I'm doing. I thought you'd like to have some breakfast in bed on your first morning back. Besides, I wanted to have breakfast in bed with you."

The journey to Randol's had changed the relationship between Rissyl and Cynia, and he was happy with the changes. He didn't stop to think too much about what type of relationship they had, other than to think of it as familiar and pleasing. He liked her company, and she seemed happy to be around him.

She grabbed a fork and pulled a plate closer to herself.

He smiled, "Well thank you, this is very nice."

They both enjoyed a few bites of the skillet breakfast that she had prepared.

She said, "That was pretty intense, wasn't it? I thought my head would explode with all of the spells and stuff we've been learning."

It had seemed like a whirlwind since they arrived at Randol's place. They spent a few days there, and two of those days were spent in lessons with

Mr. Pyllis. Each of them focused on spells from their own Order. Rissyl was glad to hear that he wasn't the only one to be a little overwhelmed by everything that they'd learned over the last fortnight.

He nodded, and swallowed a bit. "Yes it was. I'm going to need so much practice just to remember all of the trigger words, and the shapes that we form as we manipulate the magic from our magewels."

She smiled as she thought about something. She said, "I thought Dalen was gonna start punching things when he started fizzling his spells the other day."

He laughed out loud. "I thought he was going to start punching you on the way back, when you kept making fizzling sounds in the back of the wagon!"

"Well, he did throw a dagger at me eventually!"

They both laughed, "Yes, but it was still in its sheath."

"Well it still hurt my arm. Look, I got a bruise."

"Aww, you delicate flower, did you get a boo-boo?"

She flipped him an obscene gesture, "Here's my boo-boo, right here." She paused and held a finger up to her lips to hush him. "Did you hear that?"

They got quiet and he heard the sounds of someone climbing the stairs at the end of the hall. They both began summoning magic.

Then Burga called out, "Hey Riz, you home yet?" He came around the corner and looked into Rissyl's bedroom.

"By all the gods, Urg! How'd you get in here? I almost cooked you!" Rissyl was annoyed. He redirected the summoned magic into a light orb and tossed it at the wall. Cynia did the same.

"I've gotta key, moron! How do you think I got in here?"

Cynia said, "But what were you thinking barging into his bedroom? What if we weren't decent?"

He paused for a moment and looked from Rissyl to Cynia and back, "Wait. Why would you be not decent together? Are you...?"

She picked up a pair of Rissyl's socks that were balled up at the foot of his bed, and threw them at Burga. "No, you oaf! I'm just saying, maybe you should knock? On the outside door."

Rissyl laughed, "True, Urg. She is not a big fan of clothing in the morning. We're lucky that she slipped on a nightgown this morning. You might want to knock."

"Who ain't a fan of clothes in the morning?" Burga's little sister walked around the corner. She waved at Rissyl, "Hey Riz. Why's your Dreg in your bed?"

Cynia looked at Rissyl but he shook his head 'no' to indicate that she didn't need to get up. He said, "Hi Jessa. Now that I'm the man of the house, things are going to be different. I'm not going to treat Cynia like most people treat Dregs, but that's no one's business, so let's keep it between us. Okay?"

She shrugged, "Whatever Riz. Get freaky with your Dreg, it ain't my business."

He was sure that his cheeks were getting red. He glanced at Burga, who was making thumbs-up gestures and grinning at him, and that just made it worse. He resumed eating his breakfast. Between bites he said, "So, what brings you two over here bright and early in the morning?"

"So you can teach me to be a Magi!" Jessa was slightly younger than Burga. She had light blond hair that she had bound into four pig-tails on her head. She wore a simple brown and white dress in the current style, which was a little shorter and a little frillier than Rissyl preferred.

Rissyl gave Burga a stern look, "Urg, why did you tell Jessa? She's too young. This is serious stuff. It's dangerous!" Jessa was like a little sister to him, and he didn't like the idea of his best friend dragging her into the middle of it.

"What are you talking about, Riz?" Burga looked offended. "She's barely younger than you."

Jessa looked very offended, "I am a legal adult!"

"Well, you can get married and own land." Rissyl wasn't ready to concede his point, "But you can't own livestock or Dregs for another four years."

Cynia nodded, "She's got a point. She is an adult, and, she's just a year younger than me."

He looked from Cynia to Jessa. When he looked at Cynia he saw a full grown woman. However, when he looked at Jessa he didn't see her that way. Maybe he would always view her as a girl. He had heard his parents say something to that affect several times, about always viewing him and his sister as children.

He carefully climbed out of bed, trying not to spill the drinks. He walked up to Jessa and looked down at her. "Jessa, I'm going to use what is called magesight to look into your eyes. It will allow me to see if you have the gift to become a Magi."

"Will it hurt?"

"Not a bit." He held her by the chin and gazed into her eyes. He opened his magesight for the briefest moment and looked upon her soul. He saw her magewel clearly. It was smaller than Burga's, but she did have some potential. He wasn't sure whether or not he was happy about that. He considered lying and claiming that she didn't have the gift, to keep her safe from the dangers that she would certainly face as a Magi, but that didn't feel right.

"Okay, you have the gift as well. It's up to you guys. Cynia and I will talk to Dalen this morning. Maybe tomorrow we can get you two started in your lessons?"

"What about the others?" Jessa looked from Burga to Rissyl and back.

"What others?"

Jessa looked surprised that he didn't know. "All of the others who wanna be Magi!"

He looked to Cynia to see if he was missing something, she just shrugged. Then he looked to Burga and held out his hands. He made a facial expression to say that he was waiting for more information.

Burga said, "There are lots of people in Sorgo who wanna be a Magi."

"And…" Rissyl continued to hold out his hands, "How do we know this?"

"Because we put up signs!" Jessa looked proud and excited.

From the bed Cynia said, "You did what?"

Burga held up his hands as if he might have to keep her at bay, "They were really subtle signs!"

Rissyl started to pace back and forth across the room as the full weight of what his friend was saying started to sink in. He looked at Cynia and said, "If they put up signs, then surely the sentinels have seen them?"

"And if the sentinels saw them, the emperor knows. Big trouble is coming, soon!"

He was close to a panic, and he was having trouble putting all of his thoughts in an organized and logical order. There was so much that needed done before it was too late. He had so much more to learn, and needed so much practice in the things he had already learned. He assumed he would have months, if not years, to learn and grow before the threat become real. Dammit Burga!

"Dammit Burga!" He said out loud this time. "We've got to warn Rasa! And Dalen."

Cynia stood up. "We've gotta get outta Sorgo before it's too late. We gotta get to…" She stopped and looked at Burga. Rissyl realized that she was hesitant to reveal their goal to him. As much as he hated to admit it, that caution was probably wise.

He rushed to cut her off, saying, "Yes we do. It must be today. Pray to the gods that it's not already too late."

"Why are you so upset? We're trying to help you rebuild the Society!" Jessa looked very hurt and annoyed.

He took a deep breath to try to calm himself down, "Jessa, magic is illegal. The emperor's grandfather murdered tons of people to get rid of magic permanently. Our emperor is not going to be happy to hear that magic is back."

"But Urg said the people have a right to learn magic if they wanna!"

"The emperor doesn't see it that way."

Burga said, "Forty-eight people responded to our flyer."

"By the gods, Urg. Forty-eight people want to join us?"

"Rissyl, listen!" Burga put his hand on his friend's shoulder to get his full attention. "The flyers didn't say no one's name. We met in secret at a tavern far away from here. The emperor may know the Society is recruiting, but he don't know who is in the group."

He listened, and considered the dangers. Burga was right, if they only knew that the Society was recruiting, all they could do was look for more clues about who was in the group. Perhaps they weren't in as much immediate danger as he had first thought. "Who are these candidates? How do we find them?"

"They're supposed to meet us at an empty inn on the southwest side of the Commons, tomorrow afternoon."

Cynia put her hand on his shoulder, "We've gotta warn the others."

Chapter 17

Kimly

Kimly sat on the balcony of an abandoned building in the Commons, eating an apple. The early morning sun was just starting to warm the day, and she stretched out in the comfortable chair. She was surprised that the previous owners hadn't taken the chair with them. She liked how it let her lean back and put her feet up while still mostly maintaining an upright posture.

This spot had been her frequent hang out over the last several days. She picked it because it provided a great view of the apothecary shop where she had followed the Magi named Dalen. It had been almost a fortnight since she'd last seen him, and she was beginning to wonder if he had left town or something. When she wasn't watching the shop she sometimes watched the warehouse where the Magi had met. The warehouse had been empty for that whole time as well.

Her life had certainly changed since she crossed paths with the Magi. She felt well-fed for the first time in ages, possibly for the first time in her life. Instead of sleeping in abandoned buildings, or at the cemetery, she had been sleeping at different inns around the Commons. She also owned some nice clothes, which was something she had never experienced before.

However, the biggest change was the new found desire for power. Since she had been given a tiny taste of power, she craved even more of it. In the past she just wanted to survive, and find a way to avoid the people who wanted to hurt or swindle her. Now she wanted the power to defeat those people, actually she wanted the power to smite those people mercilessly.

The road to that power was right below her, in that little apothecary shop. At least it would be if the Magi would ever return. She was certain that she could manipulate that Magi into sharing his secrets with her, if he would just come back to the shop.

She felt something touch her arm. Looking that way she saw the big brown and white stray dog that seemed to live in this abandoned building. She said, "Hey Slobbers!" She reached down and started petting the dog's head aggressively.

The dog pushed against her, and its tail started wagging rapidly.

"I'm bored outta my mind! Be a good dog and fetch a Magi named Dalen for me!"

Slobbers sat down, looking hungrily at the apple in her hand.

"Oh, you're hungry? I've been hungry loads of times, it sucks." She tossed the apple on the floor at his feet.

The dog ate it in a few quick chomps, and then sniffed around on the floor for scraps. After a bit the big dog padded over to Kimly and put a large paw on her leg.

"You're way too big to jump up on my-" The big dog jumped up onto her lap. She let out an "Oooph!" as the large dog plopped onto her stomach and chest. Its large head nuzzled up against her chest and neck.

She noticed two people walking up to the door of the apothecary shop, and her heart leaped with joy when she realized that one of them was the Magi named Dalen. She hugged the dog tightly! "Good boy! You made Dalen come back, that's such a good boy!"

For a few minutes she forced herself to stay in the chair. It would look odd if she walking in the shop just seconds after he arrived. So, she sat in the chair and petted Slobbers's head for a few minutes.

She was about to get up and head over to the shop when she noticed four people hurrying across the street and up to the door of the apothecary shop. She recognized two of them as the other Magi from the warehouse, but she didn't know the other two.

The four people went into the shop and soon after she could hear heated discussion all of the way across the street at her balcony. She wasn't able to hear what was being said, but clearly someone wasn't happy about something.

She wondered if the flyers that she had seen around town several days ago had anything to do with the shouting. Those seemed like a dreadful idea, and she suspected that they were a certain death sentence to the poster and anyone stupid enough to answer them. She wanted power, but not that bad. Hers had been mostly a crappy life thus far, but it was the only one she would get. She fully intended to make the most of it.

The visitors didn't stay long, and a few minutes later she watched the four people leave the shop and walk back up the street. She waited several more minutes to let tempers calm.

Finally she said, "Okay, you're as heavy as a buffalo, get down."

The dog ignored her command, and it tried to bury its nose under her

141

arm.

"Get up!" She pushed the dog slightly.

She cried out in pain as the large dog stood up, shoving one elbow into her right ribcage and shoving another elbow into her upper abdomen. Then it jumped from her lap, shoving one foot into her lower abdomen just above her leg as it did so.

She said, "Ouch, damya! Be careful, that sucked!" Then she hurried off to the stairs.

Before crossing the street she tried to wipe most of the dog hair from her clothes. She straightened them as much as she could, and then she made her way over to the shop.

The smell of countless herbs and plants battled for her nose's attention as she walked into the shop. Dalen was behind the table and the smaller redheaded Magi girl was arranging some containers on one of the shelves as she walked in. Neither one of them said anything to her, so she stood next to the counter and pretended to look at a container of crushed plant leaves.

After a few moments, Dalen said, "Good morning, miss. Is there something you're..." He paused in mid-sentence when she looked over at him. Then he said, "Oh, it's you. Looking for something special?"

She smiled on the inside, happy that he remembered her, "Well, yes there is! Oh and the herbs you sold me the other day worked wonders. I was hoping you could come to the rescue again." She saw him blush slightly, and she felt a great deal of pleasure being able to affect him so quickly.

He said, "Alrighty, I'm glad they worked. What can I get you today?"

She glanced over at the redhead, but the girl didn't seem to be paying much attention to the conversation. Kimly said, "Sadly, my mother is suffering from a dreadful case of the runny poo. It's been so vile around her house, I don't even wanna visit. Perhaps you've got something to help?" She giggled on the inside. As far as she knew, her mother's digestive system was fine but she knew that the old hag would drop dead if she knew that her daughter was talking about her unmentionable times to a perfect stranger.

If Dalen was embarrassed by her casual discussion of the delicate problem he did a good job of hiding it. She supposed that it might not be as unusual of a topic within an apothecary shop as it might be elsewhere.

He said, "Alrighty, I'm sure we got something for that." He looked to the redhead and said, "Rasa, would you hand me the jar of raspberry leaves?"

The girl walked to a different shelf and brought him a large jar of dried leaves. He measured some of the leaves out, and scooped them into a small pouch. Then he said, "Here you go miss. Just have her make a strong tea from these leaves, twice a day for two days. That should help her." He pushed the bag towards the edge of the counter near her. "That'll be one falcon."

Kimly stepped over to the counter and pulled out her coin purse. "It's gonna be a lovely day out today, ain't it?"

Dalen nodded, "I hope so. I saw some storm clouds off in the distance, so we'll see. How have you been since I last saw you?"

She pulled out a copper falcon coin and set it on the counter near him, "Oh Deary, I've been simply wonderful!" She paused and looked around, and then said quietly, "Have you seen the flyers around the city talking about the Magi Society recruiting people?"

She knew she was taking a chance, bringing up the flyers. However, it seemed like her best way to turn the conversation to magic without sounding too suspicious.

He said, "I've heard about the flyers. You interested in the Society?"

"Maybe. But I was worried that maybe they were a trap from the chancellor's men."

He looked at the redhead and then walked around the counter so he was closer to Kimly. He looked deep into her eyes for a moment. She was half tempted to step back, because his stare continued long enough to feel a little uncomfortable. Then he said, "I trust that you're not working for the chancellor, so I'm gonna let you in on a little secret. Rasa and I are Magi."

She faked a surprised gasp as she brought her hand up to her mouth, "You are?"

The redhead said, "Dalen? You sure about this?"

Dalen nodded, "Yes, miss. We are. I'm sorry, hang on a moment." He stepped over and whispered something to the redhead.

When he came back to Kimly, he leaned against the counter. He said, "By the way, I'm Dalen. That's my sister Sarasa."

She held out her hand to Dalen, "Well met, I'm Kimly."

Sarasa said, "Well met."

"So, tell me Kimly, why do you wanna be a Magi?"

She hadn't expected that question. She kicked herself for not preparing better, if she would have thought about it that was probably one of the questions that she would have been prepared to lie about. She asked herself what answer Dalen wanted to hear. She decided that he probably wanted to hear some nonsense about standing up for the weak or helping the poor.

She finally said, "I'm tired of being a victim. I wanna be powerful enough to stop the bullies. And punish them."

Her heart started racing, and she kicked herself mentally for telling the truth. It just slipped out, and she was about to correct herself and add something about helping the poor when Dalen smiled.

Sarasa stepped over and put her hand on Kimly shoulder. The redhead smiled at her and said, "We can help with that."

Dalen laughed and said, "Kimly, the first time I saw you I knew I liked you."

She smiled back and said, "Maybe we could go for a walk, and you could tell me more about it?"

"Rasa, would you mind watching the shop for a while?"

Chapter 18

Rissyl

Cynia and Rissyl walked up to the old dilapidated inn cautiously. They were in the worst part of the city, very close to the Dross, and Rissyl didn't feel comfortable at all. At least it was the middle of the day, but somehow that still didn't ease his tension that they were about to be mugged at any moment. He wasn't sure if he would be less comfortable out here in the street waiting to be mugged, or in the rickety old building waiting for it to come crashing down on his head. The thought of packing a few dozen people in that old place seemed like a really bad idea.

Again he silently cursed Burga for his stupid choices. It was probably the fiftieth time that he had cursed Burga in the past day.

After standing outside the inn for a few moments, he looked towards Cynia to see if she was brave enough to enter. She shrugged and they pushed their way through some overgrown bushes to get to the door. The inn had been closed for months, so they could be reasonably assured some privacy.

Dalen looked up and smiled when they entered. He was not alone. There was a good looking young Gentry lady standing next to him. Dalen's smile immediately had Rissyl on edge, because Dalen didn't smile all that often. He pointed at Rissyl and Cynia as they walked in the inn and said, "Kimly, this is Rissyl and Cynia. They're also Magi in the Society. Rissyl and Cynia, this is Kimly. I have asked her to join us!" He looked like a proud kid showing off his recently finished painting, he was grinning from ear to ear. Cynia walked over to a nearby bench and sat down.

Rissyl held out his hand to greet her, "It is a pleasure to meet you, Miss."

She smiled sweetly, and he was pretty sure that she winked at him. "Well met, Rissyl." She took his offered hand and held it an abnormally long time after the handshake concluded. Then she looked down at Cynia. She added, "And well met to you, Cynia." She held out her hand for Cynia to shake.

Cynia said, "Well met." Without taking Kimly's offered hand, Cynia turned to Dalen and said, "We should probably summon our cloaks."

"Yes, good thinking." Sarasa walked into the common room from one of the back rooms. As she did, her grey and white cloak reappeared.

The others followed her lead and quickly, all four of them looked imposing in their Society Magi cloaks. Rissyl was surprised at Cynia's reaction to the new girl. She was not normally rude to people she had just met. He wondered if she knew the girl, or if she just didn't like her for some reason.

The front door to the inn opened up. They all turned to see Burga and his little sister enter the inn. After a quick round of introductions, Sarasa pulled Kimly, Burga, and Jessa aside. "Okay, you three will be the hosts. The four of us Magi will each take one of the bedrooms upstairs, and we will use that as our interview room. As people arrive, queue them here in the common room. The four of us can each interview one person at a time. As we finish with one, go ahead and send us the next one. I brought some colored marbles."

Sarasa held up a bag of little balls, some of them were white and some were dark colors. "If we give the candidate a white marble, they have the potential for magic and we are recommending them to join. If we give them a dark marble, we have rejected them."

Sarasa stopped and looked at everyone for a moment, to make sure that everyone was following along. "Take all of the white marble people downstairs to the basement. There is an old gambling room down there. Keep them there until we're done. Try to make sure they're comfortable, this could take a while."

"I brought some drinks and food." Dalen pointed towards a couple of bags piled on a nearby table.

"Take all of the dark marble people down this hall to the storeroom at the far end of the hallway. They can wait there until we're done talking to everyone. Any questions?"

There being no further questions, Rissyl and the other Magi headed upstairs to the bedroom area. He chose a room and stepped inside. There was an old desk in there and he positioned that so it was between him and the door. He sat behind it on a small stool.

It was almost an hour before anyone else arrived, and he was starting to think that all of the planning was for nothing. Then he heard some movement on the stairs and someone entered the room next to his. After a while, there was more movement on the stairs and the door to his room opened.

A woman in her late-twenties walked into the room. She was wearing a long dress that had been mended several times. She was clearly a Denizen woman, and he got the impression that she had lived a tough life. She looked scared and he encouraged her to sit on the stool before him.

"First, I am just going to look into your eyes for a few moments."

She nodded once, quickly. She gathered her dress in her lap a bit, and both hands held tightly to it.

"You have nothing to be afraid of, this won't hurt a bit."

He leaned closer and looked into her eyes. He opened his magesight as the Rolimi had taught him to do, and he gazed into her eyes with his magesight and his regular vision. The sensation reminded him of holding his hand close to one eye. If he closed one eye he saw only his hand in front of his face. If he closed the other eye, he didn't see the hand at all. However, if he looked with both eyes and let his vision become less-focused, he could see the hand and what was behind the hand, and the hand almost looked ghostly as though it wasn't fully there.

That was very similar to what he experienced using his magesight and his regular vision to look into this woman's eyes. He could see her face and eyes before him, but they were almost a ghostly image, and he could see behind them. The vision behind those eyes was something that still felt foreign to him, and he still had trouble fully grasping what he saw.

The magesight vision showed him a large three-dimensional complex geometric shape that floated in the space behind the person's eyes. The shape seemed larger than her head and it slowly rotated and gradually changed its shape slightly as he watched it. The Rolimi explained that this geometric shape was his magesight's interpretation of what the person's soul looked like. Each person's soul appeared different, and this woman's was made up of gently sweeping peaks and valleys.

The geometric shape was mostly opaque and appeared to be a bluish color, and there were dozens of little objects buzzing around in the space surrounding the shape. The Rolimi explained that each of these quick little shapes were conscious thoughts that the person was thinking about as the Magi gazed into her eyes. Mr. Pyllis claimed that the Magi could focus in on any of those thoughts and understand what the person was thinking about at that time, but Rissyl had not been successful at that yet.

If he looked carefully he could sort of see through the mostly opaque geometric shape of her soul. Inside were all of the woman's hopes, dreams, and desires. Each one had a shape and form of its own, and took up space within her soul. He was told that some Magi could focus deeper into the person's soul to see their personality, memories, fears, and so much more. The thought of doing that to someone, especially someone who didn't expect it, made him feel uncomfortable and he backed away slightly.

Remembering why he was gazing at her, he focused his search for a magewel. It should be easy enough to see, if it existed. The woman had many thoughts racing around her head, and they were becoming increasingly distracting to him. Then he caught a glimpse of what he was looking for. It looked surprisingly similar to a Rolimi being, in that it seemed to be made completely from light. As the opaque geometric shape, his visualization of her soul, slowly turned he saw the quickly shifting magewel come into view. It wasn't large, but it was there.

This woman had indeed been blessed by the gods. He slowly closed his magesight and blinked his eyes a few times. It was slightly disorienting to go back to relying solely on his normal vision.

He smiled at her, but she didn't react to his smile at all.

He now knew that she had the potential to be a Magi. Next, he needed to decide if she was the type of person that he wanted to be a part of their Society.

He asked, "Why do you want to be a Magi?"

She didn't answer for quite a while, when he thought that maybe she wouldn't answer at all she said, "I wanna walk down the street and not worry about who is gonna to step outta the alleyway. I wanna be strong enough to help strangers in need, and not have to hide in fear that I might be hurt if I try to help."

She paused, and when he was about to speak she said, "My granddad told me stories when I was a girl. About a group of Magi heroes who helped folks. They cared about the folks that no one else cared about. It seemed childish to dream a group like that existed, and even less likely that it would exist these days."

Again she paused, and she wiped a tear from her eye. "But I wanna believe, and I wanna be a part of it."

He waited a moment to make sure that she was done. "You realize that the Society is still very much against imperial law, and that by joining and becoming a Magi that you will most likely become a target of the empire? You say you don't want to be afraid, but I can assure you that if you become a Magi, and if you're being hunted by the emperor, you will be afraid."

She looked down at the table, "Are you trying to talk me out of this?"

He shook his head, "No, I need to make sure that you understand what you are about to get yourself into. This is not a game, and there is a very real chance that your actions as a Magi could get you seriously injured or killed."

"I know. I knew that before I first showed up at the tavern to answer the flyer. I really figured it'd be a trap, and thought I'd be dragged to the Dross by sentinels that very night. I have nothing left. My husband and my son were both punished for crimes they didn't commit, and both died as Dregs. I am doing this for them."

"Have you been told that all Magi will be expected to make patrols of the city, and possibly the surrounding lands? The goal is to slowly begin to regain our place as defenders of the common folk and that will take vigilance and action from all members. Is this something that you are willing to do?"

She sat up straighter on her stool. "I did not know that, but it makes me even more determined to wanna be a part of this."

He thought for a moment. The woman looked small and meek, but she seemed to have the desire and the right mind set. He reached into his pocket and pulled out a handful of marbles. He handed her a white one. "Please take this to the hosts, and wait patiently until we're ready for the next step."

She thanked him and left the room. As she walked out, he desperately hoped that joining his Society didn't get her killed. That would be hard for him to live with.

Within a few moments the door opened again, and a young man in his early twenties walked in. He sat down on the stool without being invited. The man studied Rissyl's face, and it put him on edge.

There really was no telling if any of these people were actually sentinels trying to catch them breaking the laws. He started to feel uncomfortable with this man as they sat and looked at each other silently.

"First, I am just going to look into your eyes for a few moments." He leaned a little closer to the man.

The man leaned in closer and stared into Rissyl's eyes as he stared at the man and opened his magesight.

Rissyl hadn't used his magesight on very many people. There had been the two strangers today, Cynia and Dalen during practice, and Burga and Jessa the previous day. The geometric shape that Rissyl saw when he interpreted this man's soul with his magesight was different from the others. The shape was chaotic and random. He saw almost no geometric symmetry anywhere. It was just a hodgepodge of different shapes mashed together in a slowly rotating blob.

The other thing that was striking to Rissyl was that the man's soul looked almost completely transparent. Rissyl could easily see all of the thoughts, memories, and so much more scattered all around within the shape. Even the objects within the man's soul seemed to be in a chaotic disarray.

It didn't take him long to see that this man had no magewel, and that was all well and good because he couldn't imagine that the man would make a very good addition to their Society.

He closed off his magesight and sat back. He pulled a handful of marbles from his pocket and handed the man a dark blue one. "Please take this to the hosts."

As the man walked down the hall, Rissyl could hear him saying something loudly. It was some disparaging remarks referring to them as "...a bunch of freaks..."

He sighed as he waited for the next person to walk into the room. Over the next hour or so, Rissyl met with a dozen more people. None of them had a magewel, at least none that he could detect, so he gave them all dark marbles.

When the door opened again it was Jessa who peeked in, "This is the last one for you."

He thanked her and a large man walked in the room. The man had the body of a fighter, but was dressed like a farmer. Rissyl motioned for the man to set down in front of him, and the man did so wordlessly.

"First, I am just going to look into your eyes for a few moments." He leaned a little closer to the man.

The man did not move, and did not flinch. He just stared back at Rissyl as the Magi's magesight kicked in. Once again he was greeted by a sight he hadn't seen before. The geometric shape of this man's soul was an almost perfect circle. It was non-descript in every way, with no noticeable valleys or peeks. The other interesting thing was that the shape was entirely opaque. He could not see into it at all.

As he looked for the presence of a magewel he realized another unusual thing about this man. There were no random thoughts zipping about the space outside of the man's soul. There were no thoughts and no movement of any kind outside of his soul.

Rissyl realized that the man must be consciously clearing his mind and sitting without thought or ponderings. Sarasa had referred to something like that, which they do in her fighting guild. She called it meditating, or something along those lines. He wondered if this man was in a fighting guild.

Was he emptying his thoughts to keep Rissyl from reading them? Perhaps it was something else?

He closed off his magesight and sat back. "Are you meditating?"

The man raised an eyebrow, "Why do you ask?"

"You've cleared your mind of all conscious thoughts. That is uncommon."

The man smiled slightly, "So, you truly are a Magi? You can read my thoughts?"

"Not exactly." Rissyl shook his head no. "At least, not easily, but I can see thoughts, as if they were tangible things, buzzing around behind your eyes. You've suppressed all conscious thought. Why?"

"It seemed like a prudent thing to do, when dealing with a Magi." The man shrugged as he answered.

He reached in his pocket and pulled out some marbles. He handed the man a dark green marble. "Quite possibly. Please take this to the hosts."

The man looked at the marble for a moment. Then he said, "Green? Is that significant?" He held his hand out to Rissyl and said, "My name's Konrad, I look forward to our journey."

Rissyl shook the man's hand and gestured towards the door. With a slight hesitation Konrad made his way downstairs.

Rissyl sat for a few moments, pondering his final candidate. Then he heard the door to the room next to him open and someone walked down the hall. He made his way over to Cynia's room.

"Is that all of them?"

She looked tired. She nodded, "Yes. I'm glad that's over. It sucked."

He hadn't noticed it being all that tiring, but she looked beat. He heard movement on the stairs and he looked down to see Jessa coming up. He said, "Please tell Burga and Kimly to meet us up here."

Jessa hurried back down the stairs and then returned with the other two. The four Magi and the three hosts gathered in one of the rooms. Rissyl said, "Okay, I don't trust some of these people."

That statement was met with a chorus of affirmative replies indicating that the other Magi felt the same way.

He continued, "Okay, let's do this. We'll-"

Cynia stopped him with a hand on his shoulder. He looked at her, and she made a motion towards Kimly. He looked to Sarasa and Dalen, and neither one of them were any help. He said, "Burga, please take Kimly and Jessa down to the room where you put the white marble people. All three of you please wait for us down there."

After some grumbling, all three of them headed down the hallway, and then down the stairs.

"Do you want to tell me what that was all about?" Rissyl continued to be surprised by Cynia's actions towards Kimly.

She shrugged, "I dunno, I just have a feeling about her. Something ain't right and I don't trust her."

Dalen made an annoyed sound, "I trust her. That should be enough."

She laughed, "You hardly know her. How can you trust her? You just want into her dress." Her Rolimi pup clawed its way up her clothes to perch itself on her shoulder.

Rissyl looked around for his, but he didn't see it. It had been wandering around the room earlier, but he hadn't seen it in a while.

Dalen said, "Whatever, I'm just saying that you expected me to trust Rissyl because you trust him. I'm asking the same thing."

She held up her hand, "Fine, Dalen. I'm just being careful. Couldn't you just sard her and not bring her into the Society?"

He slowly gave her a rude gesture and she smiled back. Then he said, "Should we go down stairs?"

"Wait a minute." Rissyl motioned him back into the room. "I have an idea. Dalen, you and Sarasa could deal with the dark marble people. Take them one at a time and tell them that there is one more step to their consideration for admission. Tell them that they have to meet us back here one more time, one fortnight from tonight. Hopefully that'll at least buy us some time."

Everyone nodded their heads in agreement, and Dalen said, "I like that idea a lot, good thinking. Then you and Cynia deal with the white marble candidates. Have them meet us at the warehouse tomorrow night to start their training?"

"What do you propose to do if we find out that one of these dark marble people does betray us?" Sarasa asked, looking at Dalen.

He replied, "We'll deal with them if it comes to that."

She nodded, "We also have to worry about any of the white marble people betraying us."

"There is always that possibility." Rissyl followed them out of the room.

"Excellent! Come on up and get your new cloak." Mr. Pyllis began handing out the brown and white Magi cloaks to each of the newest Magi to

152

join the Society.

Jessa looked over at Rissyl and gave him a huge grin as she put on her new cloak. Kimly and Burga put on theirs and admired each other approvingly. One by one, each new Magi donned their cloak, and soon there were eleven new Magi standing around in the warehouse chatting excitedly and admiring each other's brown and white cloaks.

Rissyl and Cynia were sitting on a large crate off to the side watching things progress. He found it exciting to see the Society grow to fifteen people but he was nervous to leave all of these new Magi unsupervised right after they took the Covenant. He asked, "Are you sure we should leave in the morning? I'm nervous about leaving them while they're so early in their training."

She turned to look at him with a raised eyebrow, "Who guided us? Just the Rolimi. The new Magi will have Rolimi to guide them."

"Yes, you're right. I'm just nervous."

He noticed one of the new Magi walk up to Sarasa, and she bowed to him. The man was middle-aged, but looked to be in good shape. Earlier he was introduced as the guild master of Sarasa's fighter's guild. Rissyl thought that it must be awkward for her to have someone in the Society who she looked up to so much.

Sarasa and the guild master walked over to Rissyl and Cynia. Sarasa said, "You two remember Guild Master Thon? It is so great to have him in the Society with us. He has been my instructor since I was little, so I feel comforted by his presence with us. He has offered to teach hand to hand combat skills to all of our Magi."

He looked at Cynia and they nodded to each other, "Yes, I think that would be great! All Magi are going to need to know how to stay safe."

Dalen walked up, "I wanted to get my guild master involved, but he ain't got a magewel. Oh well, Thon is a good teacher."

The whole group began talking about fighter's guild things, and Rissyl quickly lost interest. He stepped away from the group and moved closer to the other new Magi. After a moment, Cynia followed him.

The one recipient of a white marble from Rissyl walked up to him and Cynia. She smiled and showed off her new cloak. He held out his hand, "Congratulations! I'm glad to have you in the Society!"

She shook his hand, "It's good to see you. Most of you are so young. Or I'm just old."

He replied, "You can't be that old, maybe about my mother's age? What is your name?"

"Thanks for that!" She laughed, "I'm twenty-eight. I'm guessing your mother is at least a little older than that. My name is Eleyne."

Cynia said, "Eleyne, it's great to meet you. You're welcome to punch him. You don't look as old as his mother."

"I'm glad that you're here. Now just keep yourself safe."

Before she could reply, Mr. Pyllis called everyone over. In his rapid and monotone voice, he said, "That concludes the lessons for tonight. Practice the things you've learned! We should have the next lesson in four days."

Rissyl walked over to Mr. Pyllis and said, "The four of us will be going on a journey, and we'll be taking your box with us to continue our studies. How do we go about getting a new box for these students?"

The Rolimi replied, "Just point me towards the new box."

"Does it have to be special or fancy like this one?"

"Any box will do. It just becomes a gateway to tie your location to us."

Rissyl pointed to one of the smaller crates off to the side of the room. "What about that small crate over there?"

With that, the Rolimi began collecting all of the tables, the chalkboard, and other items they had brought for the classroom. One Rolimi walked over to the crate that Rissyl had indicated. He summoned magic and enchanted the crate with several runes that gradually disappeared. The Rolimi then opened the lid and hopped inside. The lid closed behind him.

Before too long all of the Rolimi were gone, leaving Rissyl and his three companions alone with the eleven new Magi.

Dalen gathered the new Magi around them. "Alrighty, the four of us are leaving in the morning. We're going on an important trip for the Society. For your safety, and ours, we're not gonna share the details now. However, we'll tell you everything when we get back. While we're gone, you've gotta learn and practice your spells. Work hard, and practice as much as you can."

"And don't forget to go out on patrol." Sarasa looked from one face to the next as she talked to them.

"Remember that your safety is more important than the patrol." Rissyl stressed this, hoping that the point would be well received with each of them. "Make sure you patrol in pairs. You're just looking for unfortunates who need a helping hand, or those who are being abused or unfairly treated. Give assistance how you can. Obviously we can't help every single person right now, but let's get started."

Cynia added, "Just remember what we talked about earlier. If you plan to use magic or reveal yourselves as Magi, summon your cloak before you draw attention to yourself. The magic in your cloak will offer some protections. When it is time to vanish, remember your trusty *Smoke Cloud* spells. In the confusion, send your cloak back to the plane of magic and blend into the crowd. You could also use your *Shadow Shroud* spell and fade away if you're in a fairly dark location."

Kimly held up her hand, and then began speaking, "I would like to come with you."

Dalen nodded his head, while Cynia and Sarasa both shook their heads no and gave Dalen a stern look.

Several of the other new Magi, including Eleyne and Thon, expressed an interest in coming along.

"No, we need all of you here." Rissyl leaned against a crate, "You must work together to make yourselves stronger Magi, and keep each other safe."

Chapter 19

Vendino

Vendino was in his regular seat in the imperial audience chamber. The room was massive, with a huge dais on the east side of the room, and an elaborate blue and black carpet running the length of the room from west to east. The north and south walls were dominated by huge stained-glass windows, and large tapestries hung above and between the windows. Also along the north and south walls were several rows of benches where the Council of Ministers and other spectators sat.

In the center of the dais was a large throne for the emperor, several feet behind the throne and off to either side were two smaller chairs. These chairs were pushed up against the wall. They were hardly noticeable to those standing in front of the dais because of all of the plants, tapestries, and other decorations along the back wall. That's the way Vendino liked it. He was nearby, in case the emperor needed him for anything, but he was not the center of attention. He looked over to his left, to the other chair at the back of the dais, and saw that Thorli was sitting completely still. The old warrior looked like he was trying to wish himself invisible. The large and imposing minister did not like sitting in front of everyone, but the emperor insisted.

In front of the emperor stood four of his elite Wyvern guards, surrounding a man who looked very out of his element. The man was probably in his mid-twenties, he was dressed in dirty and tattered clothing. His hair was unkempt and dirty. Vendino assumed that the man probably smelled bad too. It was amazing that this scum was ever even granted an audience with the emperor. Had he reported any other crime he would have talked to a sentinel or a sentinel captain and they would have handled it from there. If he had reported a particularly heinous crime, he might have received an audience with a minor clerk, but a report of a magical attack was different. Few sentinels or clerks wanted to bring that to their superior. For that matter, few magistrates or ministers wanted to deal with it either, because that kind of report could be the kiss of death. Not reporting it would be even worse than reporting it, so instead, Vendino assumed that a long line of bureaucrats shuffled this poor scum up the ladder to let him tell his tale himself.

The emperor said, "So, I'm told that you were attacked by four Magi, south east of Sorgo. Tell us what happened."

The man said, "Your most excellent royal highness, me and some friends were hanging out in a grove of trees not bothering no one when a wagon full of Magi came up to us. There was a succubus in the wagon who ensorcelled me with her temptress magic and lured me into her trap. Then the others started to attack us. One of them called a tornado of fire from the sky! It swallowed up seven or eight of my friends and burned them to dust! The Magi were evil and vengeful, and I barely escaped with my life!"

Without betraying any emotions, the emperor said, "And did these evil Magi happen to tell you their names, or where I might find them?"

The man looked at the ground, "No, Your Worshipfulness."

"Did you follow these evil Magi? Can you tell me where they were going, or where they came from?"

"Well, no sir, Mr. Emperor, sir. I wanted to report it right away because I know how evil and illegal magic is. And I heard that there was a reward for turning in folks like that."

"So, if I am understanding you correctly, this nameless band of wandering Magi attacked you with fire tornadoes and vile orgy magic, yet somehow they let you escape to come and tell me of their wicked ways?"

Vendino massaged his temples. He was starting to get a headache, and watching this fool dig his own grave was aggravating it.

The man nodded emphatically, "Yes, Your Excellent Grace, that's exactly it!"

"You and your pals were just hanging out in a grove of trees, out in the open countryside, just minding your own business, and here you are now to collect some imperial coin. This will help with the grief of losing your friends?"

"That sums it up very well, your royal highness-ness." The man smiled and rubbed his hands together.

The emperor sat back in his throne, "Here is what I think happened. You and your gang of hooligans were lying in wait for unsuspecting victims. Somehow, your victims got the better of you, and you thought that you'd make up a wild tale about magic and fire tornadoes to get some revenge, and maybe even score some of my hard earned coin. Does that sound closer to the truth?"

Vendino couldn't help but smile as the realization spread across the fool's face. Only now, when it was far too late, did the low-life realize that he would not be leaving the palace. The man made excuses and begged, but it was useless.

The emperor said, "Guards! Get this filth out of my sight. I order him to be executed for highway robbery, providing false witness, and perjury before the Crown."

The guards dragged the man, kicking and screaming, from the audience chamber.

A few minutes later the doors opened again and a skinny man with a light complexion walked slowly towards the emperor. Lord Jalinox carried a walking stick, but did not seem to need it. He wore a black cape with red and black tunic and breeches. He was so skinny, and his skin so pale, that he almost looked like a walking corpse. Vendino turned to look at anything else. The man gave him the creeps.

The emperor said, "Everyone, clear the room. My two advisors and the door guards should be the only ones to remain." Everyone else quickly left the room.

Lord Jalinox continued his slow walk towards the emperor. Vendino had seen him walk much faster on other occasions. He knew the disrespectful alchemist was walking slowly on purpose to keep the emperor waiting. The senior minister looked over at Thorli to see his reaction to the slow moving alchemist, but the large minister gave no visible reaction. Vendino was fairly certain that this would be the new Minister of War's first experience with Lord Jalinox.

Eventually, the man stopped before the throne and gave the briefest of bows. "You called for me, Your Majesty?" The man's words were formal but his tone sounded annoyed and disrespectful.

The emperor said, "How is the Motlite project coming along, Lord Jalinox?"

"Better than expected, Majesty. I am, if I might say so, truly a miracle worker. Obviously, we have no way to completely test them, but I am confident that the survivors of the first batch will perform marvelously! There is, however, that trifle matter of my compensation."

"That matter was settled long ago. You demanded, I denied, and we moved on."

The alchemist smiled a devious smile, "Demanded is such an ugly word, Majesty. I simply stated the compensation that would be required to retain my services. It was not a demand." His smile faded, "Nor was it a negotiation."

The headache that been brewing in Vendino's temples grew by several degrees. He braced himself for the royal explosion that he knew was pending.

The emperor raised his voice, "Jalinox, I'll not give you a falcon more than you're already making! This project has already cost a fortune!"

The alchemist bowed slightly, "Very well, then. I will turn my genius talents to more enjoyable projects. Good day, Ryal." He turned to go.

The emperor raised his voice even further, yelling, "Jalinox, if you take one step outside of this chamber I will have you hanged immediately!"

He stopped and turned around slowly, "Very well, then. Let's get to it. I've always wondered what it would feel like to be asphyxiated. It's rumored to be quite pleasant, really. Euphoric, some say. I've even heard it said that it was quite the arousing experience, if you know what I mean." The creepy alchemist winked at the emperor.

"Guards! Seize this man!"

The alchemist held out his hands for the guards and said, "Sadly, that means that you'll only have six of the Motlites that you so desperately want. With me dead, you'll have no chance to make more. Guards, come along before my excitement wanes!"

"Belay that order! Did you say six?" The emperor had slid forward in his throne, and was leaning forward to get even closer.

"Yes indeed, six."

"But you promised me fifty!"

"No, Majesty, we started with the prospect of fifty. I made it quite clear that the process was complicated and risky... and expensive. At one point, it looked like twenty-six Motlites would survive. Sadly, because of budget cuts and financial restraints, twenty of them didn't make it, leaving only six."

At this point the emperor rose, which of course meant that the ministers needed to stand as well. He shouted, "You despicable bastard!"

"I am, I really am." Jalinox laughed heartily, "Sometimes it's even difficult to live with myself, but I muddle through. However, there is a silver lining, Majesty."

The emperor paced up and down the front of the dais. Vendino had only seen him do that a couple of times, and it was never a good sign.

He held out his hand, waiting for the alchemist to elaborate.

"The second batch will be ready before too awful long, batch number three will be ready in ten to twelve years, and we have enough of the garroliron to begin a fourth batch of a few hundred Motlites very soon."

He didn't stop his pacing, "How many of the second batch are still alive?"

"Currently?" Jalinox looked thoughtful, "About thirty-five, when I last checked. However, we're getting close to one of the more complicated, and dangerous steps."

The emperor stopped directly in front of the alchemist, "And how much, exactly, is it going to cost me to ensure that all thirty-five survive?"

"Oh, there are never any certainties in this sort of thing. Regardless of how much money we throw at it, we're likely to lose some of them. If I were to be made a member of the Council, that would help. I would, of course, need the regular financial compensation of the other members of the Council of Ministers, and a large villa out away from the city. I am going to need at least two magistrates to work directly beneath me, and they must both be attractive mothers, naturally. For a fourth batch of Motlites, I will need at least two hundred Dreg females of childbearing age, and at least fifty Dreg males. They could be sent in batches of ten or so, but I'll need all of them by the end of the year. Obviously we also need as much garroliron as you can provide."

Sitting back down in his throne, the emperor said, "And if I refuse your demands?"

"There we go with that word again. If my reasonable salary expectations are not within your power to provide, it's unlikely that any from the second batch will pull through, sadly." He wiped an imaginary tear from his cheek.

"So be it, Minister Jalinox." The emperor said the title with venom. "I will grant your requests. You'll be made a member of the Council, but your title will be Minister of Dwarven Relations, and if you breathe one word about the Motlites then I'll kill you with my own hands. Do I make myself perfectly clear?"

Jalinox smiled, "Perfectly."

"I want those six Motlites ready to report to Minister Thorli first thing in the morning. Am I understood?"

The alchemist said, "Yes, Your Majesty." Without waiting to be dismissed, he turned and walked quickly out of the chamber.

Once he was gone, the emperor said, "Gentlemen, join me up here." He waited for the two ministers to walk to the front of the throne. "Thorli, you will form a new unit called Chimera Company. It will be comprised of six squads, three men to a squad. You will assign one of Jalinox's Motlites to each squad. They will report directly to you. Each squad will be autonomous. Get them prepared for deployment within a few days. Then I want one assigned to Sorgo, and one each assigned to each of the other major cities in the northwest."

Thorli bowed deeply, "Yes, Majesty!"

"Vendino, get the word out to every city to prepare the donation of Dregs that Jalinox requires. Oh, and pick a couple of magistrates who are good-looking mothers, and reassign them to Jalinox. Let us pray we never have to hear the details of that assignment." The emperor shook his head in disgust.

"Yes, Majesty. I'll find a couple of suitable clerks who don't have very influential families. Preferably ones who have problematic pasts or possibly those where they were about to be fired anyway. We'll get them promoted to magistrate and reassigned to Jalinox."

"Yes, yes, that's perfect. That'll be all."

The two ministers left the audience chamber. Once they were alone, Thorli stopped Vendino and asked him, "What are these Motlites, anyway?"

Vendino shrugged, "I'm not even sure. Supposed to be immune to magic, or something like that. The emperor and Jalinox have kept the whole thing very hush-hush. The whole project is being done at a secret camp several miles south of the city, well-guarded by Wyvern, and hidden in the forest apparently."

The warrior turned minister shook his head, "I don't like it at all. It gives me the creeps."

"That makes two of us."

Chapter 20

Rissyl

The next morning, bright and early, the four Magi loaded up the wagon and headed north out of Sorgo to find the Stronghold. However, their first destination was the portal stone near Sorgo. After a few hours of searching they found the stone. The spell Randol taught was vital in their discovery of the stone, because otherwise it just appeared to be a random rock on the ground. The spell Randol taught them to reactivate the stone would have been difficult to accomplish with only one Magi, but the four of them working together didn't have any trouble.

The portal stone rose out of the ground and the intricate runes carved up and down the sides glowed to life.

Rissyl asked, "What does the writing say?" Really he didn't care what it said, but it interested Sarasa and he wanted to show more interest in the things that she liked.

She knelt down next to the stone. "This one has the number fifteen at the top. Then it has *Justivik: Teh harimen graevitus shilt isk aven'tiva* written down the side."

The others waited for her to translate. After a moment she said, "Justice: Those grievously wronged must be avenged."

Dalen smiled, "One of my favorite lines from the Covenants!"

Stepping up to the portal stone, Cynia said, "Okay, let's do this!"

The others stepped up to the stone as well. They all placed their right hand on the top of the stone. Rissyl said, "Randol's portal stone was number forty-two, right?"

Sarasa said, "Yes."

Rissyl asked, "Not to sound too stupid, but forty-two is Foer Tov in Meneli, right?"

Sighing, Sarasa said, "Yes. We really need to spend more time on your Meneli lessons."

He said, "Yes. So, what happens if we try to port to a stone that is not active?"

"Let's not find out." Cynia asked, "Are we ready?"

Dalen said, "Ready!"

They all began to summon the magic in the manner Randol taught them, and then Dalen said, "Ty."

All together the four of them said, "Foer Tov Ac'Tovik."

Everything blurred for an instant, and suddenly Rissyl found himself in the woods near Randol's home. He felt like he might throw up, and he held tightly to the portal stone to keep from falling down. After a moment the vertigo seemed to pass a bit.

Sarasa said, "Wow! What a rush!"

With an impatient tone, Dalen said, "Hands on the stone, get ready to return."

She said, "Riz, we're going to portal fifteen. That's Uni Fevin." She looked at Rissyl and grinned.

He wasn't sure if she was smiling in a positive way, or in a mocking way. He decided to take it as a positive thing. He said, "Thanks Rasa." He smiled back at her.

"Come on, Rissyl, focus! Are we ready?"

Rissyl said, "Yep."

They began summoning the magic and Dalen said, "Ty."

Together all four of them said, "Uni Fevin Ac'Tovik."

Once again everything went into a blur for a moment. The vertigo from the port to Randol's had barely faded, and it was back with a vengeance after porting a second time so quickly. Rissyl kept a hold of the portal stone for quite a while.

Sarasa sat down on the ground and said, "I feel like I've had way too much ale."

One by one all four Rolimi Pups appeared and pounced onto Sarasa's lap. They climbed on top of each other trying to crawl up her tunic to get to her face. She giggled and pushed them down but they climbed back up.

Dalen pushed himself away from the portal stone and said, "Daylight is wasting away, let's get moving." He walked over to the wagon quickly, arranged his things, and urged the horse to start walking.

Rissyl and Cynia looked at each other and he rolled his eyes. Rissyl reached out and touched the stone. He summoned the magic to cause the portal stone to sink back into the ground. It was still active, but it was much less noticeable.

Cynia reached her hand down to help Sarasa up. Without taking the offered hand, Sarasa rolled backwards. Rissyl assumed it was some sort of rolling move that she learned in her fighting guild, because at the end of her backwards roll Sarasa was standing on her feet.

With two running steps, Sarasa jumped into the back of the wagon.

Once again, Rissyl found himself walking with Cynia next to the wagon as they traveled through the open meadows. All four of the Rolimi pups bounded through the tall grass before them, weaving in and out as they spent as much time harassing each other as they spent running through the grass.

"That was fun!" Cynia ran forward, causing all of the Rolimi pups to scatter. Then they circled around and started trying to nip at her heels.

From up on the wagon Sarasa said, "I agree! I was a little nervous to teleport, but it was a rush!"

"It gave me a headache."

Cynia laughed, "Dalen, everything gives you a headache. I thought it was fun."

"I won't lie, I was really nervous when we gathered around the portal stone, waiting to use it." Rissyl placed his hands before him, as if he were once again standing in front of it. "Once we all joined hands and reached out to grab the stone, and the magic kicked in... wow. Rasa is right, it was a rush! One moment we were in the open meadow outside Sorgo, and the next moment we were standing next to the portal stone at Randol's place!"

Dalen added, "I wish we could've stayed for a while. I bet the forest near his house has some great herbs and tons of different types of moss growing there. But we really need to focus on getting to the Stronghold."

Cynia was looking at Dalen and not looking where she was walking. She accidently stepped on one of the Rolimi pups! Her foot passed right through it. The pup jumped to the side and started barking at her. "DARP! Darp!" As she walked, the pup chased her foot trying to chew on her ankle.

"Teleporting to Randol's wasn't bad, but going back to the Sorgo stone is what gave me my headache."

Rissyl shrugged, "Yeah, they were both fun though."

Things calmed down after that and everyone fell into their own travel routines. Rissyl spent most of his time thinking about the day, and trying to memorize the Meneli numbers from zero to nine. Before he knew it, the sun was starting to sink in the western sky.

"How much further do you wanna go before we stop for the night?" Dalen pointed up ahead. "There's an escarpment up ahead, do you see that? It's starting to look like rain, that escarpment will make building a shelter a little easier."

"You're the driver, wherever you prefer. If you and Rasa want to hunt for some dinner, Cynia and I can get camp setup."

"Sounds like a plan."

Two hours later, the four of them sat around a large fire, eating rabbits that Dalen had caught. They also munched on dried bread, and some fresh berries that Sarasa had found. The sun was starting to set, and the rain clouds were almost on top of them.

"So, we still haven't settled how we are gonna deal with the problem of slavery." Dalen threw more bones in the fire.

Rissyl groaned. The four of them had gone through this several times, and it always ended with everyone mad at him and no one talking.

Sarasa sighed, "Dammit Dalen, this again? Can't we just enjoy a peaceful night?"

"Yes! This again! We gotta get it settled. It ain't just us no more. We are growing, and we gotta have this issue settled so that we can deal with it as one in front of the new Magi."

"I don't see what there is to discuss." Cynia wiped her hands on the grass. "Society Law is clear. Slavery is not to be tolerated."

Rissyl rubbed his temples. After this conversation, he would surely be stuck with a headache. Then at least he and Dalen would be alike in one way. "Cynia, do you have any idea how long ago those laws were written? The Magi from hundreds of years ago had no clue what modern life would be like. We don't have slavery like it used to be done in the days of the Six Kingdoms. We have a very efficient system of crime and punishment. Those people who are guilty of heinous crimes repay their debt to the rest of us through their servitude as Dregs. What else should we do with them? Lock them in a cage and have them sit around unproductive all day? That would be a horrible waste of manpower. I don't see what is wrong with making criminals do some work!"

As soon as he said it he knew that he stepped way over the line, and the looks on the faces of the others confirmed that assumption. Every other time that this came up, he tried to sugar-coat his opinions and didn't say too much. This time, he said too much.

Cynia was angrier than he had ever seen her. Her face was red, she had tears streaming down her cheeks, and she looked like she just might explode at any moment. Dalen and Sarasa were competing to see which of them could scream at him the loudest. He was sure that they were both trying to make some point, but he could barely comprehend either of them, and together it was just really loud gibberish.

After nearly a half an hour of shouting and tears, things finally started to quiet down. For a bit he thought that they were about to settle into ignoring each other for the rest of the night.

Then the silence was broken by Sarasa, "Do you even know why Cynia is a Dreg?"

"Rasa, no. It don't matter." Cynia was sitting with her legs pulled up to her and her arms wrapped around them. Her chin was resting on her knees.

He shook his head. He had never really thought to ask what had caused her term as a Dreg. He assumed it had to be something bad, to earn ten years of servitude. "No, I don't know why she is a Dreg."

Everyone was quiet for a long time. As it started to rain, Cynia began her story. "My mom was a slave to a powerful soldier. He got her pregnant and she tried to hide her pregnancy from him. I'm told that he was away often, and she spent a lot of her time living in the Dross. So he might not even known he had a daughter with his Dreg servant. Since I was born to a Dreg that meant that I was a Dreg until my age of majority, but that really wasn't awful. I was raised by my grandparents. Dreg children don't live in the Dross; they are raised by Denizen family members or put into an orphanage. I had some schooling with other Denizen children. But when other kids went home to play with their friends, I spent my evenings working in the textile mill spinning wool into cloth. I almost never saw my mom, but other than that I really didn't feel much different from other kids. Sure, the Denizen kids were mean to the Dregs. But I knew lots of Dregs, and we all just sorta stuck together."

She paused for a moment to wipe some of the rain from her face. It was no use, since the rain was picking up. All four of them were getting soaked, but no one moved away from the fire. Even the large fire was starting to lose-out to the increasing rain.

"When I turned the age of majority my time as a Dreg came to an end. By then my older brother had died from our vision with Nalria and my mom had gone mad from grief. She took her own life. After my time as a Dreg was over, I didn't know what to do with my life since I didn't have to work in the textile mill every night. I decided that I was gonna try to find my dad. He couldn't love me as a Dreg, but maybe he would love me as a Denizen? I started asking around, trying to find out who he was. My grandparents begged me to drop it and leave him alone. Over the next several months I slowly started to piece together information about him. His name was Thorli, and he was commander of the Wolf Pack Regiment when he owned my mom. Shortly before my age of majority he was promoted to minister and appointed to the Council of Ministers."

Rissyl's jaw dropped and he sat in stunned silence for a long time, with rain running down his face. "You are the daughter of one of the emperor's Council of Ministers?"

"I'm the illegitimate and unwanted Dreg daughter of a powerful Aristocrat who serves on the emperor's Council. Yes, but you should let me finish." She paused, wiped her face again, and continued. "When I found out where he was I saved coins for months to afford travel to Clornoss. When I finally got there I tried to see him, but I could never get past his army of clerks. For four days they gave me excuses and asked me to wait patiently because he was a very busy man. Finally, on the fifth day I got angry and I tried to barge into his office."

At this point, Rissyl couldn't tell which water streaks on her face were rain and which were tears. He wasn't entirely certain that he wasn't crying too.

"I was dragged away in chains. I was charged with a whole list of things ranging from ignoring a lawful command from a clerk of the empire up to attempting to badger a Member of the Council of Ministers. There were a number of other creative charges thrown in there for good measure. They took me away, sentenced me to ten years as a Dreg, and told me if I ever pestered the minister again, or made my 'false accusations' against him again, then it would be a life sentence as a Dreg."

Somehow, every raindrop felt like it might be a small hammer beating against his head. He felt numb inside and he had no idea what to say. "You are a Dreg because you wanted to talk to your father?"

Dalen threw a dirt clod at him, and it hit him in the side of the head. "Yes you sarding no-good Gentry! She is a Dreg because she wanted to talk to her dad. Is that the sort of heinous crime you were picturing when you were ranting that all of those rotten Dregs deserve what they get? You and your sarding pompous Gentry ideals make me sick!"

Sarasa wouldn't look at him. The two of them stood up and went to their tent.

He looked to Cynia to say something to her, and she looked away. She stood up and walked to their tent. He didn't feel like getting into the tent.

He just felt like sitting in the pouring rain. Somehow, that fit his mood at the moment. It was as if his tidy understanding of how the world worked had just been rudely shocked. He had accepted that Dregs deserved how they were treated because they were being punished for being awful people. His father had explained many times how the system was setup, and it seemed completely fair to him that people who couldn't live like civilized folks would be forced to live differently.

However, this was something else entirely. If what they said was true, and he believed that it was, then people at the highest levels of the imperial government used the punishment of forced servitude as a way to deal with minor annoyances. It was as though they had no concern for an individual whatsoever. If that was the feeling at the top, where the moral character should be at its finest, what was the situation like at the lower levels?

He shivered at the potential magnitude of the unfairness of it all. Perhaps it was because the breeze was picking up, he was soaked, the fire was almost out, and he was getting extremely cold. Maybe it was a mixture of both? Feeling awful, he climbed into his tent.

- = - = -

The next morning, Rissyl woke to the sounds of birds chirping loudly. It had rained all night, and he figured that the worms had come to the surface to avoid their flooded homes. The birds sounded like they were having a grand time.

He heard Cynia moving around. "Hey, Cynia. Still mad at me?"

"Oh, Riz, I wasn't mad at you last night. Not really. I try not to dwell on the unfairness of life, or it will consume me and make me loony. When I get talking about that stuff it's tough not to get angry at the world. Since you were sticking up for those who made me a Dreg, you got to be the main target last night."

"I get it. You really got an unfair deal."

They lay there in the tent, wrapped up to their noses in their thick blankets, looking at each other. He sat up and motioned her closer to him, "Come here, please?"

She pulled her covers a little tighter, "I'm better, but I'm not in the mood for sex games. Sorry." He couldn't see it, but he heard the smile in her voice and that raised his spirits.

He gave her a pretend-annoyed look, "That's not what I meant." He held

168

out his hand to her. "Please?"

She sat up and scooted closer to him. When she did her blanket fell down to her waist and he realized that she was wearing one of his tunics. She saw him looking at it and said, "I was cold."

He held her right hand close to him, with his right hand over her wrist. "I want to try something. Please hold still." He slowly summoned some magic; he molded it and shaped it, and then directed it towards the skin on her wrist. He wasn't sure if the spell was working, but he kept trickling a little more magic as he rubbed her wrist. Before long, black liquid streamed slowly down her arm and dripped off her elbow.

Her eyes were wide, and she gently pulled her right hand back towards herself, but he held it firm. He shook his head side to side, and continued to focus on his spell. They sat like that in silence for quite a while, as the thick black liquid dripped off her elbow onto her blanket.

When he pulled his hand away, his palm and her wrist were covered with the thick black goo. With wide eyes, she pulled her hand back and wiped some of the black goo from it. When they looked at her wrist he realized that his spell succeeded. The tattoos were gone!

She sat there staring at her wrist, with her jaw hanging open. After a few moments she whispered, "Riz, what'd you do?"

He shrugged, "I removed those damned tattoos. As far as anyone knows you are not, and you never have been, a Dreg."

She just sat and stared at her wrist. "By the gods, could it be true?" She rubbed at her wrist as if the tattoos would re-appear. Then she leapt over and gave him a huge hug. She held the hug for quite a while and then suddenly stood up. "RASA! Rasa!" She yelled for her cousin, as she fumbled with the tent door fasteners.

Alarmed, Sarasa was already out of her tent, with Dalen right behind her when he and Cynia climbed out of their tent. The siblings both had their weapons out. Dalen was also wearing his cloak and the hood was up. He was ready for combat. Rissyl couldn't help but wonder if he slept like that.

"What is it?" Sarasa was in a fighting posture, and she had her daggers pointed at Rissyl.

Cynia held up her wrist towards them.

They both lowered their weapons slowly and looked closer at her wrist.

"What happened to it?"

"Rissyl worked some kind of spell, and pulled the tattoo ink right outta my skin. It's gone forever!"

Dalen hugged her and Sarasa walked over to Rissyl. "How did you do it?"

"It was a variation of a spell that I have been reading about in my Conjuration book that the Rolimi gave me to study. The more I read it, the more I was convinced that I could change it a bit to pull tattoo ink out of someone's skin. After our discussion last night, I realized it was time for me to try it."

She gave him a stern look, "Altering spells like that can trigger unexpected results. It can be dangerous. You could have ripped the insides right out of her arm."

He nodded. She wasn't saying anything he hadn't already considered, at length.

"Thank you!" She reached up and gave him a hug. He held her tight, not wanting the embrace to end.

They stood around and talked about Cynia's new freedom for a while and then Rissyl stepped away to find firewood. Before long they were all looking for any relatively dry wood that they could find. Then they worked together to get the fire going once again. Eventually they had a nice fire going and they gathered around it to warm up.

"You could use that spell to free all the Dregs." Dalen made the simple statement sound more like a challenge.

Rissyl had hoped that the goodwill he had earned by finding a way to free Cynia from her term as a Dreg would last a little longer, but it seemed that Dalen was already prepared to bring the tension back. He desperately wanted to ignore the question so he could go on being the good guy for a while longer. "But which ones do we free? They can't all be wrongly enslaved. What about the murderers? What are we going to do with them? If we set them free then we're doing more harm than good."

"I hate to admit it," Dalen said after a long pause. "But that's a valid point. If only there was a way to see who was really guilty and who was unfairly enslaved!"

Very quietly Cynia said, "There is."

Everyone looked to her, waiting for her to elaborate.

After a very long pause, she continued, "The Order of Diviners specializes in *Divination* magic. When we gaze into someone's eyes with magesight we see more than what other Magi see. Remember how Randol told us so much detail about Dalen with just a glance in his eyes? He's much better at it than I am, but when we were judging all of those Society candidates the other day, I could see almost every detail of their lives. Their passing thoughts were as clear to me as my own. Events from their past were as easy to see as thinking of my own memories. In a few seconds I knew their deepest secrets and their most hidden desires. I tried not to see all that. I just wanted to take a glance to see if they had a magewel, but all of these other things came clearly into view."

She paused for a moment and Rissyl thought back to that night. Now he realized why she looked like the experience had taken so much out of her. He thought it would be unpleasant to know so much intimate information about strangers.

"The problem is, when I see those memories they will stick with me. If I gaze into the eyes of a hardened killer, I'll have first-hand visions of what it's like to do those things to people. Not just the images, but the sounds and feelings, and the enjoyment. It is everything that they remember and how they remember it. I know that's part of my burden as a Diviner, but I don't look forward to doing it to a bunch of killers and rapists."

Rissyl watched as Dalen and Sarasa sat in quiet thought. He was sure they were going to try to encourage Cynia to use that skill on as many Dregs as possible. He said, "No, that would be awful. We can't ask her to do that. It will change her in a terrible way."

Everyone was quiet for a long time. Eventually, Sarasa said, "Under Society Law, what is the penalty for heinous crimes?"

They all knew the answer to that question, but it was Dalen who answered, "Death."

"So, what about this? If we encounter a Dreg that we want to set free, we give him a choice. Inform him that within the Society the penalty for heinous crimes is death. We give him the option of having Cynia gaze at his soul. If he is a murderer he won't want to die, so he will turn down the offer. So then, she usually only has to gaze at those who really are innocent." Sarasa looked pleased with her suggestion.

Dalen nodded his approval.

Rissyl looked at Cynia, and she gave him an encouraging nod. He asked, "What are we agreeing on here? Will this be regular practice? The Society is going to battle the empire over Dregs? It will mean a war; the emperor will not tolerate it. The basic fabric of the empire is built on the backs of the Dregs. If word gets out that we're freeing some of them, it will not be pretty."

Cynia replied, "That is exactly what it means. Will this make the emperor want us any more dead than he already does simply because we're Magi?"

"It takes an official vote." Sarasa raised her hand first.

Dalen and Cynia quickly raised their hands as well. Reluctantly, Rissyl raised his hand.

There was clapping, and a couple of them patted Rissyl on the shoulder. He was not sure that he was happy about what he started. He had not agreed to be a part of this Society to free Dregs, but how could he not help those who were wrongly made a Dreg?

"So, how do we get started?" Sarasa looked anxious to start.

He saw no need to rush this. He said, "We go on a case by case basis as we stumble upon Dregs during our travels to the Stronghold?"

"What about all of those Dregs that we saw yesterday who were turning the old dirt road into a stone road?" Dalen looked right at Rissyl, daring him to speak against the idea.

"But that's in the wrong direction."

"It wasn't far from here." Both of the girls gave him a pleading look.

He wanted to say no just because Dalen demanded that they do it, but clearly it meant a lot to Sarasa, and he desperately wanted to win her approval, so he nodded. "Fine. If you all want to backtrack and free some of those Dregs, I'm not opposed to it."

It had only taken them a couple of hours of backtracking to find the group of Dregs who were once again working on the road, along with their guards. The four Magi left the wagon, summoned their cloaks and weapons, and started walking towards the group. Sarasa made herself invisible shortly after they left the wagon, and Rissyl had no idea how far she had gone.

He assumed they must look intimidating in their cloaks with their weapons out. He hoped that the imperial guards thought so. As they approached, the loud sounds of the Dregs laying the stone road masked their approach. Therefore, they were able to get close before the guards noticed them.

"Halt! Don't come any closer, who are you?" The guard wore armor beneath his lion emblazoned tabard. The Dregs saw that something was happening and they stopped working so they could watch the spectacle unfold.

The three Magi did not stop approaching and the guards drew their weapons. There were four guards, spread out around the work area. The one who spoke wore a slightly more elaborate tabard, which set him apart as the leader.

As Dalen continued to walk, he said loudly, "We're part of the Sovereign Magi Society. Slavery is a violation of our laws. For now we will not interfere with your poor treatment of the guilty, but we demand that all of those Dregs who are truly innocent be freed!"

There was a murmur through the Dregs. Some issued taunts towards the Magi. Some made mocking comments. Others professed their innocence. All of the Dregs had a large chain attached to metal bands on both of their ankles, and their feet were chained so they couldn't take very long steps. The other end of the chain was attached to a very large iron ball placed to the side of the work area. Each of these iron balls had about four Dregs chained to it.

The lead guard laughed a taunting laugh. "The scourge of the Magi was smeared across the blood-soaked grass ages ago! You're no more Magi than I am!"

"Once again, I demand that you offer the Dregs to our judgment. Those found to be innocent must be set free." Dalen maintained an unusual level of calm as he talked to the guard leader.

Drawing his sword, the guard leader said, "Lions seize these fools! We'll see how they enjoy working the roads as Dregs themselves!"

Sarasa suddenly appeared behind the guard leader. She grabbed his shoulders with both hands and pulled him back towards her. As she did that she slammed the heel of her right foot into the back of his right calf, which knocked his right leg out from under him as she pulled him to her chest. He was facing away from her as she dragged him to the ground. One of her arms quickly snaked around his neck, putting him in a choke hold, while the other hand drew one of her daggers and pressed the tip of it against his temple.

She said loudly, "Drop your weapons, all of you! Or Captain Nobody here earns a nice breeze on his brain. Now!"

Not waiting to see if they choose to comply, Rissyl summoned a big orb of fire and launched it a few yards in front of one of the other guards. Well, his intent was to have it land a few yards in front of the guard, but instead, it actually landed right at the guard's feet!

The guard jumped back to get out of the fire that splattered all over the grass before him. There was an audible gasp of shock from many of the Dregs and guards alike.

Dalen walked right up to the guard that Sarasa had under control. He placed his long sword against the man's chest. "As I was saying, we are Magi,

173

and we've come to free the Dregs that you've wrongly enslaved. Tell your men to come over here slowly and drop their weapons right over there."

The guard leader said, "Men, do what they say."

One by one, the other three guards walked over and dropped their weapons.

Sarasa ordered the guards to move away from the discarded weapons. Then she took up position behind the guards, ready to deal with them if they tried anything funny.

"Ok Dregs, I need you to separate yourselves into two groups!" Dalen spoke loudly so all of the Dregs could hear him. There must have been close to one hundred of them. "Those who are murderers or vicious criminals, go stand over on the south side of the road. You'll stay here with the guards. Those who are innocent go and stand on the north side of the road. A Magi will read your soul. If you are truly innocent then you will be set free. But if you claim to be innocent, and are in fact guilty, then you will be executed. Do I make myself clear?"

The lead guard said, "This is an outrage! Of course they'll all say they're innocent! You must be mad!"

The guard was right. Every Dreg moved over to north side of the road.

Rissyl groaned. He was afraid this would happen.

"You!" Cynia pointed at one of the Dregs. "You are first, go and stand next to the iron ball that you're chained to."

The man walked to his iron ball. He had to weave through people, and lift one person's chain over his head. Rissyl thought that it must be chaos trying to work while attached to a heavy chain, in a group of a bunch of people who are also chained. He guessed that the Dregs must get tangled together often, but the Dreg didn't seem to have much difficulty moving through the other people and chains so he could stand next to the iron ball.

Dalen and Cynia went over and met the Dreg. Rissyl stood back where he could see everyone. He wanted to be prepared in case several Dregs tried to rush over towards Dalen and Cynia. He also wanted to keep an eye on the Guards in case they gave Sarasa any trouble.

The Dreg stood with surprising arrogance as Cynia approached him, and Dalen took up a position behind him. The Dreg dropped a large section of his chain on the ground at Cynia's feet, and it barely missed smashing her toes. The Dreg had a large "999 RY" tattooed on his wrist. He looked mean, and he stared defiantly at Cynia.

"Do you understand that I'm gonna gaze into your eyes, and I'll be able to see every detail of your life? Your memories, your hopes and dreams. All of it."

He smiled a wicked smile at her and nodded. "Do your best, Magi." The word Magi was practically spit from his mouth with obvious contempt.

From behind him, Dalen said, "And you understand that the penalty for rape and murder is death, yes? If she finds that you are a rapist or a murder, you will be executed."

The man shrugged, "Just look at me, I'm a gentle fawn. As innocent as a newborn babe. Work your magic, so we can get to the freedom part, eh?" The man's voice was rough and gravely.

She stepped closer and Rissyl knew that she was opening her magesight. He saw her quick intake of breath, but she stood fast. For several long moments she stared into his eyes and neither of them moved. Finally, she stepped back and spoke loudly for all to hear.

"You are Hesard Kimorah, born in Tharrin in the year 72 RY to Jary and Marna Kimorah. Your thirst for riches drove you to crime at an early age. You killed your first person at the age of seventeen, he was a Tharrin sentinel who was chasing you down after your robbed an elderly woman in the marketplace. Afterwards, you fled to Khazror where you managed to live for a few months before the desire to kill again became too hard to resist. The next several years were the best days of your life. You traveled from city to city, whoring, robbing, and killing more frequently. Getting' caught was just a matter of time, and in 95 RY you were captured and made a Dreg for life in Sorgo. Since then, you've made friends with several of the Dross Guards by telling rumors and lies about your fellow Dregs."

As soon as she said that, a low rumble of questions and challenges came from the group of Dregs. Hesard put up a hand and whispered, "Okay that is quite enough! Shut up, you've made your point!"

She stepped away from the man slightly and talked louder to make sure everyone could hear her, "Together with a Dreg named Alddon, you've told rumors or outright lies to the guards causing at least forty other Dregs to be killed or tortured. And you have-"

Complete chaos broke loose within the group of Dregs, cutting off whatever else she was about to say. Several of the Dregs seized a man, assumedly Alddon, and began screaming and shouting at him and shoving him around. The Dreg fell to the ground and a swarm of other Dregs began kicking and punching the man savagely. One Dreg grabbed his heavy chain and started beating the man with it.

The guards didn't move a muscle, and Rissyl looked from Dalen to Sarasa and then to Cynia and none of them seemed to know what to do. Did they let the Dregs handle their betrayal their own way? He wasn't going to wait any longer for a decision from the group. He held up his staff in front of him, and then slammed the end in the ground and pointed the gemstone slightly towards the group of Dregs. He summoned a large amount of his magical essence and shaped it quickly. Then he focused it through the staff, gathering magic from the surrounding area with the staff. When he released it, a large streak of blue lightning shot from the gemstone of his staff and struck on the ground near the swarming mass of Dregs. When the lightning hit the ground, the entire area was shaken by a massive wave of thunder! Everyone stopped moving, and the Dregs on the ground stood up slowly. They all placed their hands on their head, facing Rissyl.

His ears rang, so he knew that everyone near the large scorch mark on the ground was probably mostly deaf for the moment. He shouted as loudly as he could, "Stop your attack on that man! Stand in peace and compliance!" As they moved away, his initial instinct was to run over and check on that man. However, even from this far away, he had no doubt that it was too late for Alddon. Vigilante justice had been carried out.

Hesard looked like he wanted to flee, or possibly attack, but he stared at Rissyl's staff and folded his arms across his chest. Without warning, Dalen used his long sword and executed the Dreg. The man slumped to the ground, probably never even knowing what happened.

Dalen turned back to the Dregs by the rock. "This man was judged by the Sovereign Magi Society and he was guilty of murder. According to Society Law, he has been executed! Do you all still claim innocence? Know you now that we will know the truth!"

One by one the Dregs moved over to the south side of the road, indicating that they were guilty and wished to stay with the guards rather than be judged by the Magi. The process took some time, as each man navigated the others and tried to keep their chains from getting tangled. When the movement was done, only eight Dregs remained on the north side of the road proclaiming their innocence. There also was the unmoving body of Alddon.

The guard leader shouted, "This is an outrage! You have no authority to execute Imperial Property! This direct assault upon the empire shall not go unpunished! I will see you all in chains as Dregs!"

Cynia walked over to the guard leader, and Dalen followed her. Sarasa got closer to him, but maintained her watch on all of the guards. Rissyl stayed further back, trying to keep an eye on the entire group.

"So, I should judge you instead?" Cynia got right up to the guard leader's face, and the man quickly closed his eyes and looked away. She said, "Oh, don't be shy. What's your name?"

"I am Lieutenant Rahan of the Sorgo Lion Battalion, Commander of the Cheetah Crew."

"Well, Lieutenant Rahan, open up those eyes and give me a peek at your soul. I'm sure that you're a man of great moral character, and there's nothing in your past that you wouldn't be comfortable sharing with the men under your command. Right?" Cynia spoke sweetly, but there were daggers in her words, and Rissyl knew that she would be more than happy to spill all of Lieutenant Rahan's dirty secrets to the rest of his men.

After a long moment Lieutenant Rahan said, "Fine! Do what you want with the Dregs! Just leave me alone!" The man kept his eyes tightly closed and looked away from Cynia the whole time.

She waited a moment and then walked away from him. She pointed at a Dreg on the north side of the road and motioned for him to come over to her.

The man looked extremely scared, and his hands shook visibly, but he stood still and looked at Cynia as she stood before him. For several long seconds nothing happened. Then she wiped a tear from her eye and placed her hand on the man's shoulder. She said, "I am sorry for what you've gone through."

Then she stepped back from the man and in a loud voice said, "This man does not deserve to be enslaved, and according to Society Law I declare that he will be set free!"

Dalen moved quickly to retrieve the key to the man's shackles from Lieutenant Rahan. He hurried back and released the man from his chains.

Cynia said, "Now, go over to the red Magi and he will set you free." She called the next Dreg over to her.

The newly freed Dreg walked over to Rissyl. "Hold out your right hand." When the man did, Rissyl grasped it with his right hand. "This will not hurt. I am going to remove this Dreg tattoo, so you can live as a free man." Before he even finished talking, the black goo started dripping from the man's wrist to the grass.

After a minute or so, the man held up his wrist to inspect it. Then he wiped it on the rags that he wore for clothes. He stared with disbelief at his wrist, astonished that the tattoo was gone. The man turned to the other Dregs and held up his hand to show them all. The men on the north side of the road broke out into cheers! The men on the south side of the road grumbled and gave obscene gestures.

Rissyl reached into his pocket and pulled out two silver dove coins, and handed them to the newly freed man. "Take these, and go wherever you like. We wish you well. Spread the word that the Sovereign Magi Society is reborn, and we will no longer tolerate the oppression and subjugation of innocent peoples!"

The man shook Rissyl's hand enthusiastically. He looked at the two coins like they were a fortune, and then he turned and started walking quickly up the road to the west.

By that point, Cynia had declared that the next Dreg was also subjugated unfairly, and this process continued for the next few people. Rissyl felt remarkable as he looked at the expressions of unbelievable joy and gratitude from the newly freed Dregs.

With only two Dregs left to judge, Cynia stood before one of them. She had been gazing at the man's eyes for quite some time. When she finally took a step back she said, "My friend, you've the gift of the Magi in you! If you choose, we would offer you a place in the Society. We will teach you to be a Magi, if you agreed to take the Covenant and live as a Magi. Or you can simply have freedom and walk away to wherever you want to go."

The man stood in stunned silence before saying, "Are you serious? A few hours ago I believed the rest of my life would be spent as a Dreg, and now you're telling me that I could be a Magi. I could help free others from their captivity?"

She nodded.

"Then yes! I would love nothing more than to be a part of this amazing thing you're doing!"

"You must know that this is a very serious commitment. You will be hunted by the emperor and all of his men. It could very well be a danger to your life."

"I understand!"

Cynia stepped back a step. She announced, "Not only has this man been enslaved unfairly, he has the gift of the gods within him! He has the talent to become a Magi!" She watched as Dalen unlocked his shackles and then motioned for him to move over to Rissyl.

When the man got to him, Rissyl quickly worked the magic to remove the tattoo from the man's wrist. He was starting to feel more comfortable with the spell, and it didn't take nearly as long as when he did it for Cynia. As the man wiped his wrist clean, Rissyl asked him, "What is your name?"

"I am Hanry. Thank you so much for what you've done! You can't begin to know what this means for the lives of us folks that you've freed."

Chapter 21

Lyro

It was a beautiful morning in the northwestern part of the Ryallic Empire. Lyro and his younger brother Lindin were sitting in the grass tying tips and feathers to arrow shafts. It wasn't his favorite thing to do, but an archer headed to battle needed plenty of arrows, and it was certainly better than many of the other tasks that a young man could be ordered to do around an army camp. A few hundred yards to the northwest he could see the border wall and the western gate. At any minute they would be ordered to march through that gate and his military adventures would finally begin.

Since they were little boys, they had dreamed of the glory and excitement of being imperial soldiers. When he was ten or eleven years old a regiment of imperial soldiers marched down the road near his family's farm, and the brothers both knew at that moment that they were going to grow up and be soldiers. They spent many hours playing war and trying to imagine where those soldiers were marching and what it would be like when they got there.

Even as they got older, both of the brothers remained short and skinny and their father warned them that they'd never make it as a foot soldiers. He encouraged them to improve their archery skills. They took that advice to heart and both boys found that they had a knack for archery. Several years later, shortly after Lindin reached the age of majority, both brothers walked down to the nearest garrison and asked to join.

Before they knew it they were both assigned to Okapi Company in the Wolverine Regiment, stationed in Misi. At first it was odd being stationed in a city that had no population. The city had been captured by Wolverine Regiment almost a decade before, and then workers came in to tear down many of the buildings, build some new ones, and fix the buildings that didn't need replaced. Wolverine Regiment lived in the area that would eventually become Misi's Dross.

During the four years that the brothers had been with Wolverine Regiment, they did nothing but practice. Some days the archers would practice archery all day. Some days they worked on movement and formations, and drills to make sure that the archery shieldmen knew how to do their jobs properly. Occasionally, they would practice defending Misi from invasion from the northern barbarians, but most often they did practice exercises where the whole regiment worked together and invaded as if they were capturing Misi all over again.

A few times the regiment had marched out to the new sections of wall that were built to separate Misi from the barbarian Free Cities to the North. He remembered the large celebration that was held a couple of years ago when the new parts of the wall were finally complete and Misi was safe from attacks from the northern barbarians. A short time later the old sections of the wall to the south and east of Misi was dismantled and the new city finally became a part of the empire.

Although the training was hard and the living conditions were sparse, it had been a great four years. The brothers had earned a reputation of being great archers, they had made some wonderful friends, and overall the training had been fun and exciting. After a while the same old routine began to get a bit dull.

All that changed a fortnight ago, when Wolverine Regiment received orders to leave Misi and travel to the western gate in preparation for an invasion into the barbarian lands. Everyone in Okapi Company was excited to finally get a chance at glory and honor.

"Hey dummy, I'm talking to you!" Lindin smacked Lyro in the back of the head.

The hard, but playful, blow from his brother brought Lyro's thoughts back to the present. "What? Sorry, I was just thinking about the last few years."

"It's been a blast, hasn't it?"

"Yes! But at least we're finally on the move!" He rubbed the back of his head, acting as though he was looking for blood. "What do you think it'll be like to finally liberate another city from those barbarians?"

"Oh, brother it's gonna be glorious! I just know it! The other day I overheard one of the guys from Angel Company say that the regiment brought two wagons filled with casks of ale for the victory celebration!"

He pantomimed drinking from a massive mug, and both of them laughed loudly. Lyro leaned closer to his brother and said, "I heard that we're gonna get so many new Dreg women from the barbarians that every soldier in the regiment can buy one for just a fortnight's wages! You'll never have to wash your own socks again!"

"Who cares about socks? I'll be happy not to have to queue for hours just for a dance with one of the camp amity Dregs."

Lyro shivered and gave his brother a shocked look. "You are so much braver than me! Those Dregs are almost feral! I don't see how you can dance with them?"

Commotion started on the far side of camp, and the ruckus gradually spread towards the brothers. As he looked out across the vast encampment, Lyro saw soldiers moving into organized lines. The encampment was huge. There were forty companies, roughly eight hundred soldiers, and that didn't count squires, stable boys, camp aides, Dregs, and all of the other non-fighting folks needed to support such a large army. The tents and people stretched on for a hundred yards in each direction.

A messenger boy sprinted past and stopped at the sergeant's tent. The boy was admitted and only stayed in the tent for a short time before running off to the next tent. Lyro finished putting away his fletching supplies and closed up his pack before the sergeant emerged from his tent.

"Okapi Company, fall in!" The sergeant shouted, as he stepped out of his tent and positioned himself in front of the formation that quickly materialized near his tent.

The archers of Okapi Company had fallen into a formation like this so many times in the past that it was routine. It took only moments for several perfectly straight lines of archers to form. They stood at attention and waited quietly for their leader to give them directions.

Lyro was so nervous and so excited that he could almost hear his own heart pounding in his chest. That excitement only got worse as he noticed that the west gates in the border wall were being opened and several of the mounted companies were already on the march! He knew that the pikemen and foot soldiers would follow the mounted troops, and then the archers would form the columns in the rear as they marched to war. The columns were surrounded, of course, by a company of mounted scouts who could fan out and watch the perimeter for sneak attacks.

The sergeant continued, "The time has come Okapi! Pack up the tents!"

Within two minutes their portion of the encampment was packed and stored in the back of the wagon. The company formed up once again before their sergeant.

"Prepare to fall in behind Angel Company on the left flank as we march on to liberate Grulin from the barbarians!" There was a shout from the archers of Okapi Company. "For Victory!" He shouted. Okapi repeated him.

"For Glory!" Okapi repeated him even louder. "For the emperor!" The company repeated him and then there was a general roar of shouting as all of the men of the company cheered and stomped their feet. "Right. Face! Forward. March!"

Two hours later, Okapi Company had finally made it through the gate, and the formation spread back out to its regular size as it exited the empire and entered the land of the barbarians. The drummers sounded even more ominous than normal as they thumped their steady drum beat.

Thrump... thrump... thrump... bum bum... thrump... thrump... thrump...

Everyone easily fell into step along with the beat. Eventually one company began singing a marching song and before long the entire regiment sang along. Eight hundred soldiers, plus a few hundred tag-alongs, spread out over a one hundred yard rectangle marching and singing an army song.

One song turned into two songs. Before long, Lyro had completely lost track of time. He might have been marching for ten minutes, or perhaps it had been several hours.

Thrump... thrump... thrump... bum bum... thrump... thrump... thrump...

The drum beat flowed through his body. All thoughts were gone except the thought of putting one foot in front of the other, in time with the steady beat. He sang the songs, but he didn't think about the songs. It was just him, the drum beat, and several hundred of his closest companions walking together to the beat.

Thrump... thrump... thrump... bum bum... thrump... thrump... thrump...

The singing from the front of the formation died down, and slowly the companies at the back of the formation stopped singing as well. This change in what had been the routine for several minutes, or perhaps a few hours, brought Lyro back into the moment. He looked around and noticed a couple of farms in the fields up ahead. Looking back he realized that they were fairly far west of the wall now.

Several companies of foot soldiers broke off from the rest of the formation. Three of the companies ran towards the farm to the north of the road and three other companies ran towards the farm to the south of the road. Even from this far back, he could hear the war cries of the companies as they ran towards their targets.

Thrump... thrump... thrump... bum bum... thrump... thrump... thrump...

The drum beat carried on steadily, and the rest of the division marched at their normal pace down the road while the other six companies sprinted towards the farms.

Lyro watched the large farmhouse to the north as the three companies reached the low white picket fence around the large home. Within two or three seconds the entire fence was destroyed and the mass of people swarmed to the house. They ran in the doors, they crashed through the windows, and in one spot the soldiers used their massive weapons to smash right through a wall!

One by one, soldiers started to emerge from the home. Some carried war trophies of whatever types of valuables they happened to find. Others carried food and provisions. One came out pushing a woman before him. She had her arms tied behind her back. Within a couple of minutes all of the soldiers emerged from the house and set it ablaze.

Turning his attention, as they marched along, to the farm house off to the south he noticed that a family had fled the house and they were being chased by many of the foot soldiers. Lyro thought the family might get away, until one of them fell. The rest stopped to help her, and the foot soldiers caught up. He looked away as the soldiers dispatched the barbarians where they lay and stood, pleading for mercy and cowering from the inevitable doom.

That home was sacked and burned as well. After only a few minutes all six companies had returned to the formation. They placed their loot in their packs, or on company wagons, and then resumed their previous positions within the large regimental formation.

Thrump... thrump... thrump... bum bum... thrump... thrump... thrump...

Lyro was impressed that the whole operation of clearing the homes had happened without the rest of the formation even breaking stride.

As he marched, he noticed the woman who had been taken from the farmhouse was led back to the wagon that carried the amity Dregs.

Lindin smiled as he saw Lyro looking at the woman as she was brought past. He said, "Did you see the diddies on her? I hope that's one of the Dregs they sell to the troops after we liberate that city! She's foxy!"

Lyro started to laugh and agree, but something about the woman caught his attention. She didn't look like a Dreg. She didn't even look like a barbarian. She just looked like a farm wife, just like so many women in his own family.

He said quietly to Lindin, "She looked a lot like our Aunt Chelli."

Lindin looked back at her, and then looked at Lyro with wide eyes, "Creepy. Yes she does."

184

He looked back to the front and let his mind wander as he walked. He started thinking about his family. He thought about all of the happy days he had spent with them as a kid. Sure, there was hard work a lot of time, but there were many good times too. He wondered if today had been one of those happy days for those two farm families. Clearly it was no longer a happy day for them.

Thrump... thrump... thrump... bum bum... thrump... thrump... thrump...

He marched and he thought about his family, back on their farm. He couldn't help but picture an army of barbarians approaching his family's farm. Would the barbarians kill them all? Would they capture some of them and make them Dregs? The thoughts turned his stomach and he pushed them far away.

Soon the drumming and marching took over his consciousness once again. The minutes passed and eventually the formation came across another farm house. He couldn't even look as the footmen ran off to gather trophies and spoils. The bile rose up from his stomach and he had to focus to keep his last meal down. He wondered what it would be like to be one of the foot soldiers. Do they really enjoy the killing and looting as much as they seemed? Were they secretly sickened like he was starting to become? He wasn't anywhere close to what was happening, hadn't seen the horrors that those men saw, and he was already starting to dislike it.

Killing defenseless farm families wasn't the type of glory he had dreamed about as a boy. He looked over at Lindin, and the look on his brother's face betrayed that he was feeling much the same.

Thrump... thrump... thrump... bum bum... thrump... thrump... thrump...

As the minutes dragged on there was more marching, more farmhouses, and more disappointment in the heart of Lyro. It started to seem like it would carry on indefinitely.

When he saw a large building with several smaller buildings in the distance, he was afraid that another farm family was about to lose everything before the army even reached the city. He was relieved when he realized that it wasn't a farm, it was a large temple and several outbuildings. His relief turned to shocked realization when he saw ten companies of foot soldiers rush towards the temple.

As he marched on, he watched in disbelief as the temple and outbuildings were looted, the clergy and monks led out into the yard and executed, and the buildings set on fire. At least two dozen gentle unarmed men of the gods were cut down without putting up a fight. He watched countless centuries of history and toil burn, and he knew that the whole place would be destroyed before anyone who cared even knew it was at risk.

For the first time he wondered if he was truly one of the good guys, or one of the bad guys. At the moment, he didn't feel like one of the good guys.

Thrump... thrump... thrump... bum bum... thrump... thrump... thrump...

As things calmed at the temple, the companies rejoined the formation as it continued to march on slowly.

The army rumbled slowly towards its goal.

When the sun finally began its slow descent in the western sky, the company commanders began ordering their troops to halt, and directed them to large swaths of land where they were instructed to setup camp.

Several hours later Lyro sat in the dark playing with the campfire, lost in thought. The small fire near him, and the dozens of other campfires around the area, cast long flickering shadows onto the tents and other items scattered around the area. It was a calm night, and the lack of a breeze meant that the smoke from all of the campfires lingered in the area leaving the open meadow smelling like wood smoke and providing an ominous haze in the flicking campfire light around the area. His entire company was asleep, and it was his turn to keep watch. Fifteen to twenty feet in each direction was another campfire. Each one had another Fire Guard keeping watch over his company as the others were sleeping.

The hardest part of being Fire Guard was staying awake for an hour after being asleep for part of the night. According to his training, his duty as Fire Guard required him to walk around the camp near his company and watch for threats. He wasn't supposed to be sitting, and he surely wasn't supposed to be looking at the fire because that messes up a soldier's night vision, but in all actuality everyone just sat and played with the fire and tried to stay awake until the bell rang to indicate it was time to change the guard.

Memories of monks and farmers cut down for no reason flickered in the firelight as he poked the hottest embers with his stick. He felt sick to his stomach, and his zeal for the campaign was completely gone.

The sounds of horses whinnying nervously sounded from several places around him and brought his attention back to what he was supposed to be doing. He stood up and looked around, but the night looked much darker after staring into the fire for a long time. He could not see much as he stared through the haze looking for what might have set the horses on edge.

He drew an arrow and readied his bow when a scream pierced the darkness behind him, only to be cut short right after it started. He turned slowly in a circle, scanning for threats, but he couldn't see any.

Then, in an ever growing wave, the whole encampment descended into chaos. At first it was shouts of concern, commanders awoken from their sleep issuing hurried orders, and frightful screams coming from all sides. He started shouting for his company to wake up. He kicked his brother hard in the leg. "Get up! Get up! Everyone get up now!" He ran from person to person kicking or shaking everyone as he went by them.

Within moments the shouts of commands were overshadowed by screams of pain, and the sounds of battle. They seemed to be coming from every direction, and Lyro still had no idea who they were fighting! Had the barbarians attacked in the middle of the night? His sergeant stepped out of his tent with his armor half on, and his sword in hand.

Then several soldiers came running past Lyro's campfire at a full sprint, screaming at the top of their lungs! He knew that these were foot soldiers. To see them running from a foe in the dark sent a chill down Lyro's spine. He raised his bow and drew the arrow, looking for the men who were chasing the soldiers, but the shapes that appeared from the haze were not men at all, they were wolves!

The first wolf stopped its chase when it saw the sergeant standing near the tent. The wolf leapt at the sergeant, knocking the man down. The wolf ripped and tore viciously at the sergeant's face and neck with its deadly teeth. The other wolf redirected its motion from chasing the fleeing soldiers. It instead lunged at an archer who was still trying to put on his boots. The wolf knocked him to the ground and tore at him relentlessly. The archer didn't stand a chance.

Lyro fired his arrow at the beast, hitting it in the side of the head. He felt cold satisfaction hearing the arrow smack into the creature, but the beast did not fall dead, it simply stopped and looked at him. That was when Lyro realized that the creature's eyes glowed a dull eerie red in the hazy night. He also noticed that the creature looked like it had been dead for weeks and that decomposition had already claimed much of the animal's fur and muscle. Bones of the wolf's legs and pelvis showed through the gaps in fur. He fought down the bile that threatened to come up from his stomach. The stench of death followed the creatures into the camp.

He brought another arrow to his bowstring and drew it quickly as the hideous beast began to stalk towards him. He barely noticed the screams from all around him, as he gave this creature his full attention. Arrows flew from the right and the left at the wolf as it stalked him. Several of the arrows struck the wolf in the legs, side, head and stomach but none of them slowed it down! Lyro took a deep breath and then let most of it out to calm his hand a little. He held the breath and loosed the arrow; it drove deep into the wolf's chest. He was afraid that the creature was indestructible. It had many arrows sticking out of it. As soon as Lyro's arrow slid home in the wolf's chest it fell to the ground and the red glow left its eyes.

The desire to cheer faded quickly as the other wolf pounced at another archer. Lyro quickly looked around to find his brother. After a moment of panic, he found Lindin behind him trying to nock another arrow. Lyro did the same, aiming for the other wolf in their section of camp. Before he could fire, another soldier came running through the camp. The wolf noticed the man running and it took off after the new prey. Lyro followed the wolf with his arrow aimed, but never got a clear shot because of all of the people running around in a panic.

Soldiers and archers ran and stumbled around the encampment in complete disarray. Most of them were wearing no armor, or just bits of armor.

He breathed a sigh of relief that the immediate threat was gone. However, new screams from nearby drew his attention to his left. Several yards away he saw four men walking towards him awkwardly. At first they seemed like wounded soldiers, but as they got a little closer Lyro could see the red glow of their eyes and the rotting of their dead flesh!

He had heard fire-side stories of undead monsters, the Awakened, but he never thought the stories were real. The scary stories had just invaded their camp!

As he drew his bow level with the new threat, he watched a panicked soldier run past the monsters. One of them took off quickly after the man, catching him in no time and pouncing on top of the fallen man. The Awakened reared back its head and let out a horrible howling scream before leaning forward to bite at its victim.

Lindin grabbed Lyro's shoulder and pulled him close, "There are more coming from that way too! We've gotta get outta here!" Both men started running. They didn't know where they were going, but they became one of the many men just running in a mad panic to get away from the creatures.

As they ran, they realized that the entire encampment was in shambles. He had no idea how many of the monsters there were, but as widespread as the panic seemed to be, there must be a lot of them. Everywhere they passed had soldiers locked in deadly combat with more Awakened.

After a short time of running deeper into the encampment, they came to the clearing where the amity Dregs wagons were setup. This area was as chaotic and trampled as the other parts of the camp, with people running around in a disorganized and panicked mob. As they entered the area a woman started screaming at them, pleading for them to release her. She pointed wildly at some of the other cages, where two of the monsters had ripped open the cage and were viciously mutilating the unfortunate Dregs who had been locked inside.

He was half tempted to ignore the woman and continue to run. However, he realized that the woman was the new Dreg that they had just captured, who reminded him so much of his aunt. He stopped abruptly and Lindin ran into the back of him.

"Why the sard are you stopping?"

He pointed at the woman, "We can't just leave her locked in there!"

"Yes we can, let's go!"

Lyro elbowed his brother in the chest, hard. "No we can't, they'll eat her! Look for the keys! They have to be here someplace!"

He started looking on the bodies of the soldiers that were laying around the area. After a few quick checks he found a ring of keys on one of the bodies. He ran over to the woman's cage and struggled frantically for the right key. One of the Awakened looked up from its current meal to take an interest in all of the clanking noise.

With a loud CLICK the lock came open. He reached in, grabbed the woman's hand, and pulled her along with him as he started running. As he did so he called out, "Let's get outta here, Lindin!" The three of them sprinted through the camp and he didn't waste time looking behind to see if the monster had followed them. If it was like the others, he assumed it would get distracted by slower easier prey if they didn't dally around.

They weaved in and out of wagons, horses, people, trampled tents, and a myriad of other obstacles as they sprinted through camp. They slowed and turned left to avoid a wagon when they came to a startling new sight that brought them to a halt. Several feet from them, facing away, was a man in black robes with a large staff. The staff had a glowing purple gem on top. As the man pointed it at soldiers, glowing orbs of purple light shot from the staff and slammed into soldiers, dropping them on the spot.

The woman said, "Is that the leader of these monsters?"

"Let's go!" Lindin and Lyro asked simultaneously.

She replied, "If it's leading these things we should kill it!"

As she said that a soldier ran up to the necromancer from behind, screaming a battle cry along the way! The necromancer turned to face the new threat. He reached to his empty belt and grasped ahold of air, and drew forth a magical sword that seemed to be made entirely of purple light! The robed man continued the motion of his turn, spinning the magical sword and slicing the attacking soldier completely in half!

The necromancer then pointed his staff at the dead soldier and poked the top half of the corpse with the purple glowing gem. The soldier opened his dead eyes, and they glowed a dull red. It used its arms to pull the lower portion of its body back to its torso, and with a movement that looked like a man trying to slide on breeches that were too tight, the creature mashed its two halves back together!

The newly created Awakened began to stand as the necromancer launched a volley of purple glowing orbs at Lindin. He evaded the first several and took off in a flat out sprint. As he ran, he yelled, "Sard that! Let's get outta here, now!" Lyro didn't need any more convincing! The woman followed them and they sprinted away. The necromancer must have turned his attention to other victims, because Lyro didn't see any more purple orbs coming at them.

A piercing trumpet song rang out loudly. It was answered by several other trumpets playing the same tune together with the first. He didn't recognize the tune at first, and then he realized that it was the signal to retreat. He was shocked to hear the imperial army sounding the retreat. However, what else could they do?

Things were in chaos before the signal to retreat, and it descended even further into full-on rout as the entire army, or at least what was left of it, gave up trying to fight the creatures off and instead turned to run towards the safety of the border wall.

The woman shouted at Lyro as they ran, "These Awakened will follow the army, killing them all. We've gotta get away! I know someplace safe!"

She turned and began running to the left. Lyro debated quickly whether to follow, and then shouted for his brother to follow them. He pushed against the tide of soldiers who were running east up the road. Eventually, he got out of the thickest mass of people and saw where the woman was heading. She was running away from the army, heading north. He turned and saw that Lindin was following, as were a handful of other soldiers who were desperate to get away from the Awakened.

They didn't stop running, even as they moved far away from the rest of the army. Eventually, the woman couldn't run any longer and she slowed to a fast walk, holding her side. Lyro and the others caught up to her and they followed her silently at a fast walk.

The remaining men of the proud imperial army ran for their lives along the old road leading to the west gate and the safety of the empire. He knew that many of them probably wouldn't make it. It would be hours of travel, and no one could run that long.

Chapter 22

Kimly

Somehow she had been paired up with Eleyne, the world's most boring person, for these patrol missions. Overall, Kimly didn't mind doing patrol. It gave her a chance to practice some of her newfound skills in a practical setting. It also gave her an excuse to spend a few hours people-watching, and that was one of her favorite activities anyway.

Of course it had also presented a couple of good opportunities to separate a few unsuspecting Gentry from their coin purse. She had stopped counting all of the money that she had collected, because knowing how much she had just made her want to spend it. Instead of counting it she just hoarded it all in her secret hidey-hole in the mausoleum. Eventually she was going to reinvent herself and buy a big house somewhere, but right now she was having too much fun playing Magi and gathering more and more coin.

The unexpected benefit of going out on patrol had been the satisfaction of helping the unfortunate souls who were being treated unfairly by others. Okay, it would be more accurate to say that going out on patrol provided the satisfaction of getting a bit of revenge on the maggots who treated unfortunate souls unfairly. She had been treated poorly by people all of her life, so every opportunity she had to keep that from happening to someone else was one more point for the good-guys.

Before any of that could happen, she needed to ditch the dead-weight. She was standing in a plaza near the bazaar, where she had just met up with Eleyne. This was their normal meeting spot to go out patrolling each night. When Burga was assigning partners she would have preferred absolutely anybody in the room other than Eleyne. She had almost said as much, but she didn't want to make waves so she kept quiet.

"We should patrol separately tonight." Kimly tried to keep her tone matter-of-fact. This was the pair's third time patrolling together. It was also the third time that she had suggested patrolling separately.

Eleyne looked upset, "We're supposed to patrol in pairs! I don't really feel comfortable patrolling on my own."

"Great, see you at the lessons tomorrow. You'll do awesome. Bye!" She giggled to herself as she turned.

"Wait, Kimly, don't leave…"

As she walked away, she summoned a little bit of magic and wrapped herself in it. Invisibility! Okay, it wasn't the fancy *Invisibility* spell that Shadow Magi use; it was the easier *Shadow Shroud* version. It worked about the same, except it could only be used in darkness or in places with fairly low light. It was one of the first spells that she challenged herself to learn as the Rolimi began letting them experiment with slightly more complex spells. She was practically invisible in the evening twilight in the middle of the plaza. The experience still filled her with elation every time she did it.

Behind her, Eleyne said, "Dammit, Kimly."

She stopped and looked back at Eleyne. Part of her felt guilty. The woman was nice enough, but Kimly knew that she would have no fun at all on patrol if she let that woman roam with her. She waved goodbye, and knew that the woman couldn't see her.

Luckily, the moment of feeling bad passed quickly. She turned and made her way to the bazaar. She was tempted to hum a happy tune as she walked quickly to the merchant area of the Commons, but that would mess up her *Shadow Shroud* spell. She had found, through trial and error, that if she bumped into someone she would become visible to that person at least until she moved and faded out of their view. She wasn't certain how that worked, and she had meant to ask the Rolimi about it. It was her guess that since her *Shadow Shroud* was an illusion, when someone came in contact with her it would dispel that illusion in their mind, at least briefly. She wasn't too caught up in the details of these kinds of things. It was slightly interesting, but mainly from the standpoint of making sure that she didn't get herself caught in any of her little schemes.

After a couple of blocks, she was in the bazaar. It wasn't very busy, considering that it was the end of the day and the sun was setting. She figured she didn't have much longer before the shops closed down for the night. She found an out-of-the-way spot where no one was likely to trip over her, and sat down on a large rock to watch the events of the evening.

As she sat there watching people going about their normal routines, she thought about the whirlwind that had been the last few days. Once Dalen and the other Magi left town on some important mission, Burga had assumed leadership of the Magi who remained in Sorgo. That was fine with her, someone had to do it and she surely wasn't going to volunteer.

He and his little sister organized the patrols and the training schedule.

Burga decided that the pairs could patrol as often as they wanted, but they should try to go out at least every two or three days. That would ensure that at least one Magi pair was patrolling the streets of Sorgo pretty much every day. She wasn't convinced that a handful of patrols would make a great deal of difference, but Burga and the fighting guild master Thon both explained a few times that the group had to start somewhere and that rumors of their deeds would spread quickly. Thon described their actions as the spark that would ignite a blaze.

So far, she hadn't seen any sign of that blaze, and she figured she wasn't likely to be the spark lighter. She had revealed her brown Magi cloak a couple of times and intervened on behalf of the Society, but both times had been relatively minor offenses, and no one seemed overly impressed with her Magi announcement.

The first time was on the day of her first patrol. She noticed a group of thugs who were trying to get some poor chap to give up his coin purse. She summoned her cloak and pulled the hood up. The thugs looked shocked that a small-statured woman with a soft, high-pitched, voice was standing there in an odd cloak and commanding them to leave the guy alone. For a moment Kimly thought the men might attack her, but they backed away into the shadows instead.

The second time also happened the day of her first patrol. She had been walking through a section of the Commons with small homes on either side of the road. As she walked, she heard yelling and crashing coming from one of the homes. She found the front door unlocked and she let herself inside. Standing in the dark home using the *Shadow Shroud* spell, she watched as one large man held a smaller man by the shirt as he had him pushed up against a wall. The smaller man had red marks on his face and looked as though he had been hit. A woman was standing nearby begging the larger man to leave the little guy alone. At first, Kimly wasn't going to get involved with a family squabble. Then the big man started punching the little guy relentlessly. Kimly moved quickly behind the big man. She summoned her cloak, pulled a dagger from a sheath at her belt, and dropped the *Shadow Shroud* spell. The woman had gasped as Kimly grabbed the hair of the big man, pulled his head back and placed the cold steel of her dagger at his throat. He didn't need too much coaxing to leave, and he seemed to take her stern warning to heart as he ran from the place.

That one had felt good. The woman was relieved, and it was a little good will towards this new Society. The Society had given her magic and riches beyond her dreams, the least she could do was spread a little good will towards it.

She saw four imperial soldiers walking down the street, and they brought her thoughts back to the present. At first she assumed that they were sentinels, but their tabards were different. These men wore a black tabard with a silver animal of some kind, something she had never seen before. Whoever these men were, they certainly were not sentinels. As they got closer she noticed that three of the men looked like mean experienced soldiers and one looked young and misshapen. The misshapen one was shorter and thinner than the others were, and it walked with an unusual gait like one leg was longer than the other. The freaky creature-of-a-man's face was malformed and its teeth were an odd greenish color and so over-grown and twisted that it couldn't seem to close its lips all of the way. When the freak turned its face to her she almost gasped. Not only was it hideous to behold, there was something fundamentally wrong with it more than just the physical appearance. What was wrong she couldn't guess, but most disconcerting was that it saw her! She didn't know how it saw through her *Shadow Shroud* illusion, but it very clearly looked directly at her.

As the guards passed her, she heard them stop someone on the street. One of the guards said, "Pardon, sir. Have you seen anyone claiming to be a Magi in this city?"

Kimly didn't hear the man's answer, but he shook his head no. Then she heard the guard say, "Well, have you heard stories from others about people in the city claiming to be Magi?" The man shook his head no, and the soldiers moved on.

She sat there in stunned silence. How had the misshapen man seen her? Did the illusion not work on some people, or was there something unusual about that freak of a human? Her gut told her it was something about that creature. She would need to be more careful.

They moved down the street, frequently stopping to talk to people as they walked past. The freaky man never looked back at her, but she kept an eye on them until they moved out of sight.

She was about to move on to a different location when she noticed a young man approach a nearby merchant. Kimly knew the merchant; he was a farmer who brought produce, jams and jellies, fresh baked breads, and other food items into the bazaar every few days. As merchants went, this man was one of the few that she actually liked. For the most part the merchants knew the folks who didn't have much coin. They knew many of the folks who tried to swipe a loaf of bread because they were too poor to buy it. They watched for these people and ran them away from their stand, but this merchant was one of the few who actually tossed a piece of fruit or a small section of bread to the needy who wandered past. The old farmer was nice to everyone, even the folks too poor to pay. He had given her many fruits and things over the past few years. When she had coins she always went to his table first to give him back a little to say thanks.

She watched the young man as he looked at the merchant's wares. She could tell right away what the man was doing. He was pretending to look at the food, but he spent most of his time looking at the merchant and trying to find an opening to steal something. The merchant didn't seem to notice anything wrong with the man because he was too busy dealing with a loud and fussy woman who showed up right before the shady man arrived. Kimly realized the two might even be working together.

She never thought that she would be defending merchants, but this farmer was different and she wasn't about to let some loser get away with more than a fruit or two. She slipped down from her perch on the large rock and summoned her cloak, and then stepped over near the merchant's tables.

As she suspected, the shady man was planning to steal but his target surprised her. As the rude woman made a stink over imagined bruises on some of the fruit, the man stepped around the other side of the merchant's table and reached for the merchant's money box. He grabbed it and stepped away in one quick motion.

Kimly was ready. She ran forward and grabbed the man's shoulder as he moved away from the merchant's table. She allowed the *Shadow Shroud* illusion to slip away as she pulled the man around. As the man turned to confront her she held her dagger between them, her white and brown cloak clearly marking her as a Magi.

She said, "Return the money box. Now!"

The man looked around like he was going to try to run. She released his shoulder, held up her hand, and said, "Krol'Tu!"

A small ball of fire appeared in her palm. She tossed the flaming orb at his feet, and the sticky fire splashed near his legs and continued to burn for a short time before burning out. There were gasps from a few people nearby as she looked him in the eyes and said, "The next one is larger, and it cooks you like a roasted pig! Now return the money box!"

The man stared at her with wide eyes. He reached out with shaky hands and held out the money box to her.

"I don't want the damned thing!" She glared at him and pointed to the merchant. "Give it back to the man you stole it from!" By this time, a few people had stopped to watch what was going on. The merchant looked shocked, and a few people around her were speaking in hushed whispers.

The young man placed the box on the table before the merchant.

Kimly looked to the merchant, "How do you want the man punished? Shall I cut off a hand? Should we just call the sentinels and have him made a Dreg?"

The old merchant shook his head no, and still looked bewildered by the whole thing before him. "He doesn't need punished, I have what is mine."

"I'm sorry, sir. The man does need punished." She looked from the merchant to the thief, and back. "If you'll not have him turned in, or his hand struck off, then what can this man do to help you? How can he repay his debt to you?"

After a few moments the merchant said, "I'm an old man. I could use help loading and unloading my product on and off my wagon on the days when I'm here. It is almost dark, and I have a lot to load up tonight."

She was satisfied with that. It seemed like a good solution. "Very well." She looked at the young man, "Do you agree to come and help this merchant for an entire fortnight? Load and unload his wagon, and help out however you can, without stealing from him?"

The man nodded his head quickly.

"I'm a Magi, I will know if you're lying!" She tightened her grip on the man's shoulder, and brought the dagger back up near his chin.

The young man said, "I'll do it, I swear! I just took his coin box because my family has nothing."

She nodded, "I get it. It's hard to have nothing, but you can't take from others who have very little! You'll help this man for a fortnight. You'll keep an eye on him, and help him keep safe from other thieves. If you're good to him, he might even slip you a little loaf of bread or a fruit sometime."

The merchant and the young man both nodded, and she released him. She felt around her pouch for the smallest coin purse that she had in there. She had no idea how many coins were in it, but she figured anything was better than nothing. She handed the coin purse to the merchant, "If you're satisfied with this man's help, and you'd like to give him these coins at the end of the fortnight that would be kind of you."

She looked around at the growing crowd of onlookers and said, "Tell your friends that the Sovereign Magi Society is active once again! We are watching out for the common folk! We may not be everywhere, but we are watching. Evil creeps be warned!"

She turned and walked away. As she did, she summoned a little magic and draped it around her in a *Shadow Shroud* spell. She heard the gasps as people watched her fade from view. It was a great feeling, and her heart was racing at the excitement of it all! She felt an odd sense of satisfaction to take a coin pouch that she nicked from a Gentry and give it to someone who has nothing. Circling around, she went back to the rock that she had been sitting on earlier.

From that vantage point she watched the crowd erupt into loud discussions. Several people went up to the merchant and asked him if he knew that the Society was protecting him. Kimly watched the people gathering. As new people came over to find out what all of the ruckus was about, the story spread. Just as Burga and Thon predicted, people were anxious to gossip about things, and she realized that this could very well be the spark they mentioned.

The other times she had revealed herself as a Magi, it had been fairly secluded and there weren't many witnesses, but this time her actions were seen by several people in the middle of the bazaar. She smiled to herself as she watched the people discussing what they saw.

Even the young man and the merchant got in on the story telling. She felt great, and she hoped that the merchant was happy with the outcome. She was happy that the young man didn't get away with the merchant's coin box. Clearly, Kimly didn't have a problem with one person's coins being taken by someone else, but she could not stand the idea of someone stealing from someone who was already struggling. Stealing from Gentry was one thing, but stealing from a poor old farmer was very different.

She sat there and watched the would-be thief help the old merchant load his cart. As nighttime fell, the bazaar gradually grew quiet as all of the shops closed for the day. She hopped down from her rock and removed her *Shadow Shroud* spell. She wanted to grab something for dinner before the last of the shops closed. She dismissed her cloak back to the plane of magic and headed deeper into the bazaar to find some food.

Someone had been cooking up some lamb or something similar earlier, and the smell had been calling her name, so she headed towards the source of the aroma. After a while she found the vendor with the side of lamb over a fire. He had his shop mostly closed, but he still had a small amount to sell and he was eager to sell it instead of letting it go to waste. Before she could buy a large chunk of the delicious smelling meat, she noticed the four odd soldiers once again. They were walking up the road towards her.

She bought a slab of meat quickly and sat down to the side of the road to watch the soldiers walk past. This time they were walking with a purpose, and they weren't alone. The four soldiers were followed by eight large men in everyday clothes. The eight men may not have been dressed in armor or wearing tabards, but she was certain that they were all soldiers. If they had been separate and walking around the city casually, she probably wouldn't even have noticed them. However all of them walking in step with each other in that usual soldier way, with their chests out and chins held high, it was impossible to miss the signs that these were soldiers.

Her first instinct was to let them walk past and just ignore them. Wherever they were headed at this time of night, it probably didn't concern her, and she was perfectly happy with that. Earlier, the four had been asking about the Society, so some internal alarm yelled at her that these soldiers meant danger. If not to her specifically, then for the Society in general, so she decided to follow them.

She had been following people since she was barely old enough to walk. Even without magic she could track almost anyone through the city streets without them having any clue that she was there. This was a large group of men who were not trying to hide. She was confident that she could follow them with no problems.

The group of soldiers moved quickly through the streets of the Commons, turning at a couple of corners, and they seemed to know exactly where they were headed. Without warning, all of them started running. For the time-being she chose not to pull the *Shadow Shroud* spell over her, in case that creature saw her. There was no sense drawing that type of unneeded attention from those soldiers. Therefore, she couldn't rush without blowing her cover, but the soldiers didn't run far. They ran up to one of the homes on the left side of the street.

The men didn't slow their running as they arrived at the home, and they didn't bother to knock. The first soldier to the door just lowered his shoulder and smashed right through the door! All of the soldiers rushed into the home, and Kimly moved closer so she could hear what was going on.

There was only silence for the first several seconds and she started to think that perhaps no one was home. Then she heard a scream from within the house. That was followed by crashing and more yelling. She saw a flash of light from one of the windows upstairs, which was followed immediately by more crashing and yelling.

A tiny little voice in the back of her head suggested the idea of rushing into the home to help whoever was in there. That triggered a cynical chuckle from her as she continued to watch the home, waiting for people to emerge. It was more likely for the house to grow wings and fly around the city than it was for her to rush into a home and protect a stranger from imperial soldiers. A small crowd of people had stopped to look at the home and they began murmuring, asking each other what was going on within the house. She moved over to blend into the spectators.

Within a couple of minutes, all of the soldiers had returned from within the house, and they carried one person out with them. She recognized the young man as one of the new Magi. She didn't remember his name, but he was bound with manacles and chains upon his wrists and ankles. One of the soldiers carried him out of the house and out onto the street. The Magi was weak and badly injured.

By the time all of the soldiers were out of the home and reassembled in the street, the soldier had placed the Magi on the ground. A different soldier knelt down next to the Magi, and then looked over to the freakish soldier and said, "Dammit, you weren't supposed to kill him!" He reached down and took off the manacles and chains. He said, "Rollins throw this body back in the house. It does us no good now."

One of the other soldiers carried the Magi's body back to the house and threw it inside. He then returned to his place in line. The soldiers reformed their organized lines and continued marching down the street.

She followed the soldiers through the Commons and to the north internal gate that led to the Gardens district. This was shocking to her; she never expected imperial troops to move against one of the Gentry. There was a nagging feeling in the pit of her stomach that she might know where they were headed next.

A few days before, she had followed Burga and his sister when they walked home after a lesson with the Rolimi. She didn't really have a goal in mind at the time, she was just curious where they lived and how wonderful their house was. It turned out that they lived in a very nice home in the Gardens, and she wouldn't soon forget how splendid it was.

As she followed the soldiers through the Garden District, she was certain that they were headed to Burga's lovely home. The little voice in the back of her head kept pestering her to do something to warn Burga. She didn't owe him anything, but he was the self-appointed leader of the Society in Sorgo in the absence of Dalen and the others. After a few more moments of indecision and internal debate, she suddenly turned to her right and darted down an alleyway. Abandoning all attempts at being sneaky, Kimly sprinted through the streets of the Gardens District. She was pretty sure that she could get to Burga's home far enough ahead of the soldiers to get everyone out safely. She hoped.

A few blocks later, she turned up the road to Burga's house. She sprinted down the block and glanced to her left as she crossed the road and ran up his family's front walkway. "Dammit!" She cursed to herself. The soldiers were barely two blocks away and they were running!

She flung open the door and ran into the home. "Everyone get the sard outta here, now! Soldiers are coming!" She was out of breath and she took a moment to put her hands on her hips and try to slow down her breathing.

"Who are you? Get out of my home!" An older man, she assumed he was Burga and Jessa's father, rushed out of his study.

An older woman walked out of the kitchen area with Jessa and an elderly woman who was dressed like a Dreg servant. Loud stomps from above announced Burga's sprint down the upstairs hallway. As he ran down the stairs he said loudly, "Kimly, what's going on?"

"Dammit Burga, let's go! Imperial soldiers will be here any moment. We've gotta go now!" She tried to run down the hallway towards the kitchen, but the father caught her arm and stopped her.

"You're not going anywhere until you tell me what's going on! Why have you-"

He was cut short by the unmistakable sound of breaking glass! Soldiers poured into the home through the door and windows!

Kimly broke away from the father's grasp and ran forward towards the kitchen. She grabbed Jessa as she ran past and tried to push her away from the soldiers. "We've gotta get outta here!"

With a jerk of her arm, Jessa pulled away, "I can't abandon my family!"

Summoning a small amount of magic quickly, Kimly wrapped herself in a *Shadow Shroud* illusion. The house had some candles spread around for light, but it was dim enough to provide plenty of cover for her spell.

It was too late to save Burga, but she might still escape out the back unharmed. When she took a step towards the kitchen exit several soldiers ran in from that door, including the freakish creature of a man in the weird animal tabard.

201

One of the soldiers said, "You two guard this door! We'll follow the Motlite into the house." The soldier patted the large creature on the shoulder.

Kimly turned and ran back down the hallway towards the living room.

When she entered the room it was complete chaos. The father was on the floor covered in blood and clearly dead. Burga was still at the bottom of the stairway. Several soldiers were trying to get at him, but he kept lobbing orbs of pure lightning at them. On the floor before him were the bodies of three soldiers.

Two soldiers stood at the far side of the room, and they were all that stood between her and freedom. From their actions, she was sure that they weren't able to see through her illusion. The entire house was filled with screams, and the crashing of treasured family possessions being trampled and destroyed.

As she was about to make her rush towards freedom she heard the unmistakable death screech from a woman behind her. She turned to see Burga's mother fall to the floor beside the old servant who was already lying there. She saw the freakish creature-man, the Motlite, grab ahold of Jessa by both wrists. The Motlite pulled her close and stared into her eyes. At first, the girl thrashed against the Motlite's grip, desperately trying to pull away from it, but within moments Kimly could see the strength drain from the girl. Jessa quickly looked so weak that she could barely stand on her own. The Motlite yanked one of Jessa's arms, throwing her into the arms of one of the other tabard-clad soldiers.

Kimly felt glued in place. Part of her felt like retching. Part of her wanted to flee, but that stupid nagging voice in the back of her mind pleaded with her to do something for Jessa. She watched as the Motlite walked calmly down the hallway towards her. It sent chills down her spine as it looked directly at her as it walked past.

On the stairs, Burga continued to launch orbs of lightning. With four soldiers dead at his feet, the others had backed off some, but the Motlite walked directly towards Burga. The Magi launched a lightning orb at the Motlite, hitting it right in the head, but the orb simply dissipated when it touched the creature's skin! Shaken and surprised, Burga sent a steady barrage of orb attacks at the Motlite! One after the other he lobbed fire, ice, acid, lightning, and water orbs! Each one hit the creature, but every one of them just petered away to nothing as they touched him.

The attacks didn't even slow the Motlite's pace as it walked directly up to Burga and grabbed him by the arms. The Magi realized too late that he should flee, and once the creature had him in his grip, the outcome was assured. Kimly watched as the Motlite somehow sucked the strength completely from Burga, and the other soldiers rushed forward. They didn't even attempt to capture him. Instead, the soldiers unleashed their fury on the weakened Magi in vengeance for their fallen comrades.

The sight of Burga's violent death at the hands of the merciless soldiers broke Kimly out of her shocked inaction. She rushed back to the kitchen and drew one of her daggers. The guard who was holding Jessa had no clue that she was even there, and she slit his throat before he knew his life was in danger! She caught Jessa as the girl started to fall. Attacking the soldier tore her concentration away from the illusion. So, as she carried the girl towards the back exit she was completely visible and vulnerable. After a step towards the door, they encountered another soldier who had been guarding the rear exit.

She paused long enough to try to figure out her next plan when she felt cold hands clamp down on her wrists from behind her! Her body was filled with the shock of cold, as if she had jumped naked into freezing cold water! She felt herself being turned around, and she looked into the eyes of the hideously deformed creature of a man. It smiled at her with its twisted and gnarled green-tingled teeth.

Then everything went dark.

Chapter 23

Rissyl

"Isn't it a little early to make camp?" Sarasa sounded annoyed as Dalen stopped and dropped his packs. "The Free City is nowhere in sight, and we're probably still several days away from the mountains. We're never going to get there if we spend all of our time sitting around!"

"Yes, but we also need time for Hanry to get some training. Besides, we've been pushing hard for the last few days since we crossed the border wall into Barbarian Lands. Plus, we're carrying a lot of crap after leaving the wagon and horse on the other side of the border wall." For the first time in days Dalen didn't seem all that stressed. He rubbed his shoulders after dropping the heavy gear. "Also, it's practically dark out. Let's get camp setup."

Turning to gather some firewood, Rissyl set about doing his routine chores for camp setup. Cynia and Sarasa began setting up tents, and Dalen went out hunting with Hanry as had become their routine. At least it had been dry in these parts recently and that made it much easier for him to find good wood for the fire.

Half an hour later Rissyl and the girls were sitting around the fire. Both tents were set up, and Cynia cleared off an area for Hanry to set out an extra bedroll. They had offered to change up the sleeping arrangements somehow so he could sleep in a tent as well, but Hanry flatly refused. He insisted on sleeping under the starlight. After years in the barracks in the Dross, he seemed to like sleeping in the outdoors.

Rissyl said, "It sure would have been easier getting here if we could have gone through a gate. Then we could have brought the wagon with us."

Sarasa nodded, "Yeah, but the empire restricts travel into the barbarian lands without special merchant tokens. You didn't want to kill the guards or fight our way through them."

"Personally, I thought it'd be harder to get over the border wall than it was." Cynia smirked at Rissyl as she teased him, and both of the girls broke out into laughter.

"Yeah, thanks for the reminder. My butt still hurts, thank you very much!" He knew he was blushing heavily. Even after all these days of traveling together, he still felt nervous and awkward in front of Sarasa. He wanted desperately to impress her at… well, anything, really. Instead, he just routinely found new and creative ways to look stupid in front of her.

"The look on your face as you fell from that rope!" Cynia made a mocking face of surprise and horror, as she flailed her arms around wildly, pretending to fall. The girls continued to laugh raucously. He couldn't help but laugh along.

He shoved Cynia playfully, "You would have felt bad if I would have broken my butt! That was a long fall!"

Sarasa took a deep breath between giggles, "Luckily the sticker bushes at the bottom broke your fall. But don't fear, Cynia would have kissed it better for you."

Cynia threw a handful of sticks and dirt at her cousin, "Real classy, Rasa. Sure I would, if I could find a clean spot. At least I offered to pluck the stickers from his cheeks!"

He dropped his arms to his lap heavily and turned to give her an incredulous look, "By all the gods, Cynia! Must you try to humiliate me at every opportunity?" He stood up, "Okay, I'm going to study my books. Goodnight ladies."

"You know, Riz, you should thank Cynia." Sarasa said to him as he walked past her, "I don't think I would have pulled stickers from your butt." Both girls resumed laughing as he walked to the tent.

As he pulled back the flap he heard someone running from the northwest. He looked up and saw Hanry rushing towards them.

"Everyone come quick, Dalen wants you to see something. It looks like some sort of magical fight is happening not far from here!" He turned and ran back to the northwest, and the others ran behind following him.

After a mile or two he slowed down as they approached the spot where Dalen knelt down, watching something to the northwest. Off in the distance, they could see streaks of purple light shooting from a dark robed person. Many other creatures moved around the tall grass, and they all seemed to be focused on reaching one person. That person had a bow and fired arrows rapidly. The arrow tips glowed with a faint orange glow as they streaked towards their targets.

The sun was fully set, but it was a cloudless night. The moon shone bright, spreading its light across the meadow and keeping the night from growing too dark.

Dalen asked, "Do you think it's two necromancers fighting?"

Without even waiting to see if the others were following her, Sarasa summoned her cloak and weapons and started walking quickly towards the battle. "No, it is a necromancer attacking some poor guy!" She started running as she caused herself to turn invisible.

The others took off after her. Dalen called out, "Wait, Rasa! Dammit!"

As they got closer, they could see the situation clearer. Everyone was out in the middle of a meadow with no buildings or landmarks anywhere nearby. The robed person was obviously a necromancer, and it was commanding a large swarm of Awakened.

Cynia gasped as they got closer, "That man is a Magi! He's wearing a Magi cloak!"

"Yes, and he's firing an enchanted bow! Let's get to him before the Awakened do!" Dalen increased his speed and changed his heading slightly to get to the Magi.

Slowing to a walk, Cynia focused on a summoning. She pointed the gem on her staff at a large group of Awakened to her left and waves of green light swirled around her from the gem. Up ahead, the plant life all around a group of Awakened began moving, growing, and grasping at the unnatural creatures. It clung to their arms and legs, and stopped them in their tracks.

Rissyl slowed to a fast walk also. He lowered his staff to point the red gem towards a group of Awakened slightly to his right. Red light swirled from the gem as orbs of fire shot from the gem and streaked towards the closest undead monsters! The fire orbs slammed into their targets and the creatures screeched in rage and pain as they shriveled to the ground in agony and a second death.

With war cries, Dalen and Hanry raised their swords and rushed the closest Awakened!

The stranger in the Magi cloak continued to fire his enchanted bow, but when he noticed the other Magi he shouted, "We must kill the necromancer!"

Almost as if on cue, an orb of purple magic slammed into Rissyl from his right! A wave of intense pain spread from his shoulder where the orb hit him. He turned towards the necromancer and started walking that way. Another purple orb slammed into him, sending more waves of pain through his chest and slowing him slightly. He wanted to yell out in pain, but he fought it back. The purple magic spread across his cloak, which shielded him from the worst effects of the necromancer's attack. He knew he would be on the ground, seriously injured or worse, had it not been for his cloak's protection runes. He lowered his staff at the unholy caster and sent forth a series of fire orbs, but the robed person fired a series of purple orbs which impacted Rissyl's orbs in mid-flight causing them all to explode in a brilliant explosion of purple and red light, illuminating the meadow!

He held up his right hand and summoned a globe of pure lightning. The orbs summoned using the staff did not drain his magewel nearly as quickly, but they were not as powerful as the ones that he could conjure using purely his internal magical reserves. He sent the powerful ball of lightning flying at the necromancer, but the evil caster was able to counter the magic sphere with a summoned orb of its own purple magic! Again the meadow glowed brightly for a brief moment, as the two magics collided in a wondrous display!

Rissyl was beginning to get frustrated, and slightly nervous that perhaps he couldn't beat this necromancer. Then he noticed Sarasa appear directly behind the dark robed servant of evil. He could see the necromancer's eyes grow wide as her blade thrust through its chest! The evil caster looked down at the blade sticking out of its chest in shock and horror as it slumped to the ground, dead!

As the necromancer fell, all of the Awakened fell to the ground as well. Suddenly, the only ones left standing in the field were the Magi. The bow wielding Magi approached the others quickly, and they all met at a center point between them. The man was older, probably in his mid to late fifties. He walked with a limp and he slung his enchanted bow across his back as he walked.

He stopped before the group of Ryallic Magi and whispered, "By the gods!" He slowly knelt to the ground and bowed low before them. Rissyl and the other Ryallic Magi looked at each other in surprise. Sarasa was the first to speak, "There is no need to bow like that. Please stand. Who are you?"

The man slowly stood up. It was clear that his knees hurt and that it pained him greatly to get up from the ground like that. Once he was back on his feet he said, "Are you truly Order Magi? I thought all of the Magi of the four Orders were long dead?"

Dalen replied, "They were, but we are the chosen of Nalria, she appeared to us and bid us to take on this burden. It is her will that the Society be brought back to its former glory! We have been chosen to bring that to reality!"

The man fell to his knees once again and bowed so low that his face touched the ground, as his arms stretched out before him, "Praise be to Nalria! May the Society of the Magi grow strong once again! Praise be to Nalria!" The brown cloaked Magi continued to bow deeply, as the Magi from the empire looked at each other.

Rissyl hit Dalen gently with the back of his hand, and whispered, "Now look what you did."

Dalen shrugged and made an obscene gesture towards Rissyl.

It was Sarasa who knelt down and held out her hand to the man, "Please stand, sir. You wear the cloak of a Magi. Where did you get it?"

The man took her hand, and with her assistance he stood up once again. "I am Uli Lau, and the cloak was my grandfather's. I have been a Society Magi for almost forty years."

Each of the Ryallic Magi shook his hand and introduced themselves. Rissyl said, "I didn't realize that Society Magi still lived in the barba…" He caught himself about to say Barbarian Lands, and realized that this man might take offense to that, "The, ah, lands of the Free Cities? How many of you are there?"

Uli shook his head, "There are not many any longer. For decades, the Ryallic Emperors sent soldiers into these lands to hunt down and kill Magi. Over the past twenty or thirty years, that has stopped, since the border wall was completed. However, the threat of the imperial soldiers has been replaced by an increasingly active group of necromancers. They must be recruiting somehow, because their numbers have been growing quickly over the last decade or two. Now we're down to thirty or so practicing Society Magi, but only about a third of us are young enough to do much patrolling. The others focus on studying and teaching whatever new members we happen to draw. It seems that low pay, constant travel, and an almost constant threat of getting killed has not been helpful in bringing on new Magi." He paused, and then asked, "How are the numbers in the empire?"

Rissyl started to answer, and Dalen cut him off, "Not as high as they need to be, but we're working on it. Do you have any way to gather your Magi together so we can all meet? It is dangerous, but we should really get some things organized."

"Of course we all have nexus gems." Uli pulled a yellow translucent gemstone, about three fingers in diameter, from his pocket. It was irregularly shaped, and inside was a multitude of crystalline patterns and shapes. Seeing the expression on the faces of the Ryallic Magi, he said,

"Don't you have them?"

The others looked at it with curiosity. Dalen answered, "No, many of our artifacts have been lost or destroyed over the years. I've never heard of nexus gems, what are they?"

His face lit up when he realized that he had something that the Order Magi didn't possess. "These are wonderful. I can send a short message to one or many other nexus gems. The message can only be a couple of seconds long, but I can send it to anyone who has one of these gems, no matter how far away they are. Their gem won't allow another message until someone summons the existing message and empties the gem."

All of the other Magi stood with their mouths agape at the amazing magical gem.

He held the gem close to his mouth and they could see the magical summoning as the brief flash of light filled the Magi's hand. The gem glowed softly red as Uli said, "Urgent meeting at the ranch, all Magi." The gem glowed red briefly and then faded to its previous non-glowing state.

After a few moments, Cynia said, "I can see how that'd be very handy."

Uli nodded, "If you're ready, we can head to my ranch, I may have enough gems for all of you. I have a couple at least. The ranch isn't far from here."

Everyone looked to Dalen, "Time is short, but lead the way. We can talk further as we walk."

"First, we have to deal with this dead necromancer." Uli stepped away from the group, over towards the fallen caster.

Cynia pointed to the southeast, "And then we have to head back to camp and get our supplies and packs."

"This necromancer is a woman, too."

Rissyl moved closer to the fallen necromancer, "Is that uncommon?"

"It's been a lot more common recently. I've been tracking this one for a fortnight. It was near the imperial wall south of Ront'El and it's been moving west until I caught up with it here." Uli began checking through the necromancer's possessions.

Shortly before dark on the following evening, Rissyl sat at a campfire with several other Magi. The ranch that Uli had referred to turned out to be a nice piece of land several miles south of the Free City of Sothral. The fire was built in a large pit quite a distance from the house, near an old barn, on the top of a hill with a good view in all directions. All around the fire pit, there were several large logs, split down the center to form nice seats near the fire. After a few hours of hunting earlier in the day, the group had cooked several pheasants over the fire, and Uli had brought out other fixings for a good meal.

Rissyl and the four other Magi from the empire were seated at the fire along with Uli, three elderly Magi, and two middle-aged Magi.

Uli had introduced Rissyl and his companions to the three elderly Magi as they sat down at the fire. They were Makah, Gimroe, and Thain. They sat close together and hadn't said much since everyone had gathered near the fire. The three elderly Magi were already at the ranch when the group had arrived; Rissyl assumed that perhaps they lived there.

Aruk and Baeldin, middle-aged Magi, had arrived and sat down at the fire shortly after the pheasants finished cooking. Uli introduced everyone, and offered Aruk and Baeldin some pheasant when they sat down.

Aruk was a clean-shaven middle aged man of small stature, with bushy brown hair, who wore a white and brown cloak over his traveling clothes.

Between bits of pheasant, Uli said, "Aruk, would you like to tell the Order Magi about yourself?"

He mostly looked at the fire as he quietly said, "Greetings fellow Magi, I'm Aruk and I'm a Society Magi from the Free City of Oodas. My father was a Society Magi in Oodas and his father was a Diviner. Lately, I've been traveling with Baeldin. We were actually on our way to the ranch for supplies when we got Uli's message on our nexus gem." He looked at Baeldin, and motioned for him to speak.

Beside Aruk was Baeldin, who was the opposite of Aruk in most every way. Baeldin was a large man, both in height and girth. He had already given the group the impression that he was loud and boisterous. His large head was almost completely bald, and he sported a big bushy brown beard. He was dressed similar to Aruk. "Imperials, you'll forgive me if I don't curtsy. I was born in the Free City called Misil'Kayl, you may know of it since your empire slaughtered most of its people when they captured it. They built a large wall to separate it from the Free Cities and absorbed it into the empire along with the other Free Cities it has stolen over the years. My entire family, and everyone I grew up with, died in that invasion. So I'm not really feeling warm and welcoming towards imperials even after all this time."

Baeldin continued talking loudly, but Rissyl's mind was reeling. He knew that the empire captured one of the Free Cities several years ago, but he had never really stopped to think what that meant for the existing people who lived there. He just assumed that they became residents of the empire, but as he put the pieces together he realized that Misil'Kayl must have been the name of the city before the empire captured it and renamed it to Misi. It was the new city that the empire was in the process of populating, the city where his parents and sister just moved.

He felt sick to his stomach thinking that many citizens of Misil'Kayl had been killed so that his family and others could have a nice newly rebuilt city to populate. He wondered why the emperor would go through the trouble of capturing an existing city, killing everyone, tearing down their stuff, and then rebuilding it all. Why not just build something new in a large open meadow somewhere? However, he didn't understand all that went into running an empire, and maybe there were some circumstances that he didn't see.

He put his hand on his head. He wondered what circumstances justified killing all those people. Were they a threat to the empire somehow? It was something he would have to look into further before he could fully wrap his head around it.

Cynia patted him on the leg to get his attention, and when he looked at her she motioned with her head and eyes that Baeldin had asked him a question. He looked over at the large Magi, and Baeldin was clearly waiting for a response.

Rissyl said, "Ah, I'm sorry, I didn't catch your question. Would you repeat it?"

Pointing at Dalen, Cynia said, "I believe you missed Dalen throwing you under the stampeding horses."

Dalen gave her a dirty look, "Baeldin asked if we were a secret imperial weapon sent to help capture more cities. I told him that your father was a major figure in the imperial government, and he'd have to ask you."

"And it was a sarding awful thing to say." Cynia made a rude gesture at Dalen and he returned it.

As they were talking, four additional people walked through the field towards the campfire. There were two men and a woman wearing the brown and white cloaks of the Magi, and a large man without a cloak. They walked up quietly and stood near the elderly Magi.

Rissyl was incredulous. He barely noticed the new arrivals. He leaned forward and placed his hands on his knees, "How do we expect to rebuild this Society if we can't even get along with ourselves! This is stupid." He pointed at Dalen, "Stop being a creep." Then he looked at Cynia, "Please don't antagonize him further." Finally he looked at Baeldin, "And you can't possibly be serious? The Ryallic Emperors have hunted and killed our Magi ancestors just as mercilessly as they killed the people in Misil'Kayl and other Free Cities!"

Baeldin sat up straighter, puffing up his chest, "They killed our Magi ancestors, except your father apparently! If you're from a Magi family then how is it that your father just happens to be one of the imperial rulers?"

As Cynia started to reply, Rissyl noticed that Sarasa was no longer sitting next to Dalen. He looked around for her, but didn't see her.

Before the words could come from Cynia's mouth, the fire suddenly exploded into a massive inferno! A bright fireball erupted from the fire pit, expanding violently, flashing so large as to engulf the ring of log chairs and all of the Magi sitting upon them. The explosive expansion of fire was accompanied by a loud boom that rattled the air and pierced the night. All of the Magi threw themselves backwards off the log seats, desperately trying to escape the explosive flames!

When Rissyl opened his eyes he realized that the fire looked exactly like it had a moment ago. The fire was peacefully and harmlessly flickering in the pit. The explosion must have been an illusion, but the sound was real. His ears were ringing and he could barely hear anything. He stood and helped Cynia up as Uli slowly stood up on his own. The four new arrivals hurried over to the three elderly Magi who had also fallen backwards off their log chairs.

Rissyl noticed that Dalen had somehow sprung a few yards away from the fire, and Hanry moved back towards him. Aruk and Baeldin were standing behind their log chair, looking around warily. Sarasa stood directly beside the fire. With the wind blowing in her hair, an angry expression on her face, and her fists on her hips. She looked ferocious.

One of the three elderly Magi, Gimroe, brushed the dirt from his clothes and asked in a shaky voice, "By the gods, what was that?"

Sarasa gave a quick look at Gimroe and asked, "Do I have everyone's attention now?" She walked over towards Dalen and said loudly, "Dalen, try not to be a sarding troll for a while, will you?" Then she walked over to Baeldin, "And you need to put away your whiny crap and be a man! I'm sorry that the empire did awful things to people you care about. We had nothing to do with that. Rissyl had nothing to do with that, and his father had nothing to do with that. The sooner you accept that, the sooner we can start getting this Society onto the path of being rebuilt!"

Taking a step forward, Baeldin got into Sarasa's face. He stood more than a foot taller than she did, and he was easily twice as wide. Clearly not ready to back down, he said, "And maybe I don't have any interest in being a part of an imperial Society?"

Rissyl took a step forward as one of the four newcomers walked up to the fire next to Sarasa. The Magi walked with the grace of a panther. Rissyl wasn't sure what to expect, and readied a spell to keep Sarasa safe in case things went sideways. He realized that Dalen had moved next to Sarasa as well. This could get ugly quickly.

Baeldin looked to the newcomer Magi who had stepped up next to Sarasa and said, "This ain't your argument, Sarge. Step back, I'll handle this."

Sarge crossed his arms, raised his chin, and looked down his nose at Baeldin. The two men were about the same height, but Sarge was much more physically fit, although he looked noticeably older. "Bullying young ladies these days, Baeldin?"

After a short pause, Baeldin backed up and then pointed at Sarasa, "She started it."

A little chuckle escaped Aruk's mouth, and that got Sarge and Baeldin laughing softly. With that, the tense mood seemed to lift slightly.

The three elderly Magi sat back down slowly on the log bench. One of them whispered loudly to the other two, "Back in my day a girl would get the belt to her naked backside if she dared talk to a man like that." The three men laughed to themselves, and Sarasa gave them a sour look but said nothing.

Uli cleared his throat, "Magi, please sit down and let us continue this meeting with a little bit of tact. Please remember, these Order Magi have been blessed by Nalria the Goddess of Magic herself! If we reject these Order Magi, we are truly rejecting Nalria as well!"

Everyone who was standing took a seat.

"That's better." Uli pointed to Sarge, "Would you continue introductions, please?"

Standing, Sarge said, "It would be my honor. Fellow Magi, I'm Sarge. I've been a Society Magi for many years, and my old adventures and tales aren't really of any interest right now. Lately I have spent a great deal of time tracking down necromancers. They seem to be looking for something, and they've been raiding farms and ranches. For some reason they haven't bothered any of the cities, but it's probably just a matter of time." He nodded his head in greetings. Then he continued, "This here is Gordo." He

213

motioned for his companion to rise. "Gordo was an imperial slave. He escaped the imperials and was quickly captured by paranoid miners from Grum'Glin. I freed him from a cage in that city. He has taken the Oath and wishes to join the Society. I've begun his training and we were headed back to the ranch to get him a cloak and a decent weapon. Along the way we met up with those two a few days ago."

Rissyl looked to Cynia in surprise. He was surprised to hear of an escaped Dreg in the Barbarian Lands. She shrugged, and he assumed that she was as surprised as he was.

Taking his nod from Sarge, the other brown and white cloaked male newcomer stood up. He said, "Greetings everyone, I'm Ranik." He was about Rissyl's height and had long dark hair and a dark mustache. "And this is my sister Firana." She stood up and waved. Like her brother, she was in her mid to early twenties. She had long dark hair and fair skin. "We're from the Free City of Kha'Mu, a coastal city in the far west. We didn't even know that we were Magi descendants until a few years ago. So until Gordo came along, we were the new people in the group. We're still learning, and we'd love to pick up any knowledge that you want to share with us."

Everyone sat back down and Sarge added, "Order Magi, Ranik's desire for magical learning is shared by us all. One of the biggest problems that we have suffered over the years is stagnant interest, because no one was really learning anything new. Those with advanced knowledge too often kept that knowledge for themselves. If you are truly Order Magi, then I expect there is a lot you can teach us."

"Obviously, they have things they can teach us! Did you see that illusionary explosion that the girl summoned? That was impressive!" Firana looked impressed, and she gave a nod and a smile towards Sarasa.

"Impressive?" Makah, the elderly Magi, scoffed, "That dammed girl almost killed me with a heart attack, and I think Thain crapped himself!" Gimroe scooted away from Thain a little.

With a laugh, Sarge said, "Makah, you're too grouchy to let a little thing like that kill you. And it takes much less than an illusionary explosion to make Thain crap himself."

Everyone laughed at that, and the mood around the fire improved a bit more.

Once the laughter and whispered side-comments died down, Sarge stood up, "There is one piece of important news that you all may not have heard yet. The empire sent an army to capture Grum'Glin, almost a fortnight ago."

That led to an uproar of gasps and outrage. Everyone tried to talk at once as some urged Sarge to provide more details, and some expressed anger and concern. Rissyl watched in growing dread, certain that the mood was going to turn against him and his companions once again.

"No, the imperial army never reached the city!" Finally, Sarge waved his arms and spoke over everyone. There was a stunned silence, and everyone waited for more details. "In their first night camped on our side of the wall, they were attacked by a 'mancer and a horde of Awakened! Many imperial soldiers were killed, and the entire army was routed back to their side of the wall! Gordo and I saw much of the battle, from afar."

There was a cheer from the Free Cities Magi, and an uncomfortable silence from the imperial Magi. Sarge continued, "Me and Gordo had been tracking that 'mancer. We ended up following as it chased the routed army. I am sure that it crossed into imperial lands, and we did not follow it there. These 'mancers have been searching for something, and they've increased their searching lately. Now it looks like they're taking their search into the empire."

Again chaos broke-out around the fire as everyone started talking on top of everyone else.

Rissyl grabbed Cynia by the hand and led her over to Sarasa, Hanry, and Dalen. He said to them, "The closest city to that gateway is Sorgo. If that necromancer is loose inside the empire that is very bad news for Sorgo. It might be focused on farms and ranches now, but for how long? Surely our new Magi recruits are not experienced enough to battle one of those?"

Dalen shook his head no, "Not with a horde of Awakened, it would be a slaughter. Other than a couple of them, they don't even know how to fight. We've gotta do something."

"Perhaps the army was able to kill the necromancer once inside the wall. We don't know. We need to stay focused on our goal." Sarasa put her hand on Dalen's shoulder to get his attention. "Once we get to the Stronghold we can find the spells and magical artifacts and weapons that we need to properly fight the necromancers! Then we should have access to a portal stone and we can port directly back to a stone a few hours from Sorgo. We might actually get there sooner if we press on. We surprised that necromancer last night, and we were lucky. Next time we need to be better prepared."

"What if it doesn't have to be one or the other?" The others turned to

215

Rissyl, but they were all already shaking their heads no. He realized that they probably thought he meant that they should split up. "That one Magi said that the necromancers seem to be raiding farms and ranches. It sounds like Sorgo is not in immediate danger. But the farmers and ranchers are. What if some of the Magi from this area travelled to Sorgo to warn the new Magi about the necromancers, and help them learn to fight them, while we continue on to find the Stronghold?"

They nodded their approval of his plan, and turned their attention to the other Magi who were loudly expressing their desire to travel to defend Grum'Glin. Rissyl sighed as he realized this would not be an easy plan to sell. He moved back to stand near the fire, in the middle of the gathering of Magi. He cleared his throat and raised his hand.

Then he started talking loudly, "Magi, if I might have your attention. Cynia, Dalen, Sarasa, Hanry and I are on a mission to travel to the north side of the mountains to find the Society Stronghold. It houses a vast library of magical spells and research, as well as an arsenal of magical relics, artifacts, and weapons. You have talked about the growing threat of the necromancers, and we're all aware of the threat of the emperor. Finding the Stronghold is the key to re-establishing the Sovereign Magi Society as a true force for justice and peace throughout the known world!"

The group was quiet for a moment as Rissyl's words sunk in. Finally Sarge said, "I've heard rumors of the Stronghold, of course, but I never gave them much credence. As far as I know there is no way to travel to the north side of the mountains. But when you describe the Stronghold that way, maybe that is what has made the necromancers so active lately. Maybe they're searching for clues on how to find the Stronghold? It would explain a lot."

Makah stepped forward slowly and put his hands to his sides. His long grey beard was tangled, and his posture was slouched, but his eyes were bright and burned a passion that Rissyl had not yet seen from him. The old man turned slightly, looking to everyone to make sure that he had everyone's attention. He said, "I first started fighting necromancers seventy-two years ago, barely three decades after the Betrayal of the Magi. These days, I fight them by teaching others to confront them, but I can say I've never seen them as active or as ruthless as they've been in the last several years." He paused to cough and clear his throat. "However, I've heard many stories of the Society Stronghold! Mark my words, if the necromancers gain control of the Stronghold, there will be no one that can stop them. The massacre of the Magi will look trivial next to the catastrophe that we can expect if that happens. You cannot let that happen! The imperial Magi are right; securing the Stronghold is of utmost importance!"

Everyone nodded their agreement to the elderly Magi's statement. Rissyl said, "There are three things that we must do, and they all need to happen simultaneously. Some of us absolutely must secure the Stronghold. Some of us must assist in the defense of that Free City. And some must travel to Sorgo inside the empire to hunt down that necromancer, and teach our new Magi there how to battle the necromancers."

Once again, chaos ensued as all of the Magi from the Free Cities began talking at once. The vast majority of them insisted that they would defend Grum'Glin. Rissyl looked at Cynia and then Sarasa for advice or suggestions.

It was the elderly Magi, Gimroe, who finally waved his arm and asked for calm. Eventually, everyone quieted down and turned their attention to the old man. He quietly said, "Like Makah said, some of us have been Magi for a very long time. Many of you have countless battles that you speak of around a pint to impress the ladies, and no doubt most of us feel that we own the honor of being Magi. I became a Magi almost eighty years ago. I was taught by men who lived decades in a Magi Society that we only dream about. The stories I could tell you of things they told me could fill fortnights of campfire tales, but I dare say that the rag-tag band of Magi individuals that we've become is nothing like the organized group of Magi who were so powerful before the Betrayal. As I watch you lunatics argue and bicker like idiots, I realize that we have no hope of regaining any semblance of our former glory without organization and leadership!"

The old man paused and looked around the group. Many of the Magi from the Free Cities cast down their eyes and looked contrite, but others looked more defiant.

The old Magi continued, "In the days of old, all Magi belonged to groups, called Coterie. Back in the days of the Society's power and influence, there was a separate Coterie in almost every city. These groups included Magi from the four Orders, and those Order Magi were the most powerful and influential. The Coterie also had many of the Society Magi who wore the brown and white cloaks did not belong to one of the Orders, were not as powerful, and held almost no influence. Each Coterie had a leader from each Order, and those four Order leaders made decisions for the entire Coterie."

Again, he paused and looked around. Everyone waited quietly for him to continue. "For decades we have plodded along fighting necromancers, and wishing for knowledge. We longed for a way to rebuild the Society to be something of pride like it used to be. Ladies and gentlemen, I urge you to look right over there." He pointed to Rissyl and the other imperial Magi, in their blue, grey, red, and green cloaks. "Nalria has answered our prayers! But most of us, on this evening, have been so blinded by our own prejudices and so worried about our own interests and desires that we can't see what is standing among us! I was resentful and blind at first too. All three of us were." He pointed to the other two elderly Magi.

He walked over, very slowly, to stand right before Rissyl and Dalen. "Order Magi, blessed of Nalria, I greet you anew and ask for your forgiveness of our lack of manners and decorum." The old man folded his hands and bowed respectfully. "On behalf of myself and these other idiot Magi, I ask that you agree to take on the burden of leadership in a new Coterie of Magi. I ask that you accept me as a member of this new Coterie. I also ask that you judge all Magi who are present for acceptance in one of the four Orders. Lastly, and most importantly, I ask that you begin to teach us. Guide us to knowledge and increased power so that we can stand against those that threaten us all."

One by one the other brown cloaked Magi lined up behind Gimroe. They all bowed, and Rissyl felt a shiver run down his spine. Was it excitement or the realization of a destiny that he never fully realized that he wanted? He felt someone grab his hand and squeeze it, and he looked over to see Cynia smile at him slightly.

He looked to Dalen, who held out his hands to encourage Rissyl to speak. Rissyl said, "First let's talk about the four Orders, and what types of things they focus on. Then I think the four of us will show you some examples of the types of magics used by each Order. We will then use magesight to see who possesses a magewel with the potential to excel in one of the four Orders. Finally, in a few days, after you've had a chance to practice some new spells and think about your choices, we'll give some of you a chance to choose an Order." He looked around at everyone. "Does that sound like a good plan? We can spare a day or two to teach and grow, before deciding who will go to Sorgo, who will go to defend that Free City, and who will come with us to secure the Stronghold."

Dalen nodded, "Yes, this sounds like a good plan."

From the back of the group Uli added, "That would be good. There are other Magi who have yet to arrive."

Rissyl motioned for Cynia to follow him, and they walked over to Gordo. He said, "But first, let's see if we can't get rid of that Dreg tattoo for good."

Chapter 24

Rissyl

"This is really crazy, ain't it?" As she whispered to him, Cynia sat down on a bench next to Rissyl. They were in the large barn on the Magi Ranch outside of Sothral.

"Yes." He nodded, "It's surreal."

Not counting Rissyl, Cynia, Dalen, Sarasa, and Hanry there were nineteen other Magi in the barn. The ten Magi who were around the campfire two nights ago were there, and there was an additional nine Magi who had arrived since then. Eight of the new arrivals were elderly Magi and one was another young necromancer-hunting Magi named Zahr. They were all seated on benches at one end of the large barn, facing the five imperial Magi.

Dalen stood up and said, "Uli is everyone here?"

"There are fourteen Magi from the Free Cities who are not here yet. Five of them are very elderly Magi who are not healthy enough to travel this far. Seven of them are elderly Magi who will not be personally traveling to battle necromancers, the empire, or to try to reclaim the Stronghold. That leaves two young Magi who will eventually be joining us here, but they still have almost a week of travel before they arrive." Uli sat back down when he was finished speaking.

"Ok, everyone who is gonna be here, is here. So let us get started." He took their special box and placed it on the floor. He said, "Sovereign Magi Society. Class is in session."

The box opened and the Rolimi instructor, Mr. Pyllis, climbed out of the box. The gathered crowd of Free Cities Magi began murmuring and whispering, apparently they had never seen a Rolimi before. Then a large arched doorway popped up from the center of the box. Several other Rolimi started coming through the doorway.

"I am Mr. Pyllistacaillian. You may call me Mr. Pyllis." Other Rolimi pulled a chalkboard out of the box and placed it beside Mr. Pyllis, and he arranged it so the Free Cities Magi could see it. He wrote his name in the top left corner of the board. "Under no circumstances may you call me Mr. P." He looked at each student to make sure that they were paying attention.

"In case you don't know, I am a Rolimi. We are a race of gods-blessed beings from far from here." Mr. Pyllis continued with the same speech that he gave Rissyl and the others when he first began teaching them. When he was done with that, he said, "The goddess Nalria has blessed these four Magi, and the Rolimi acknowledge them as the legitimate leaders of the four Orders of the Sovereign Magi Society. As the leaders of the four Orders, they have examined each of you, and they have found that nine of you meet their criteria for admission into one of the four orders. When I call your name, please go and stand over there." He pointed at a spot just to the left of the benches. One at a time, pausing between names to let the individual start making their way to the appointed spot, the Rolimi said, "Uli. Sarge. Gordo. Aruk. Ranik. Firana. Zahr. Makah. Widdel."

Once all of those who had been called made their way to the side of the benches, Mr. Pyllis said, "Everyone else, please move to the back of the barn to continue your lessons as a Society Magi."

Dalen patted Hanry on the shoulder, and encouraged him to follow the others to the far side of the barn to practice lessons as one of the brown and white cloaked Society Magi.

The Rolimi teacher motioned towards the box with the arched doorway over it. Quickly, several Rolimi started coming through the doorway carrying a tall irregularly shaped table with four sides. It was placed near the wall.

Pyllis walked over to the nine Magi who had been chosen by name. "You have all been chosen for membership in one of the four Orders." He pointed to the tall table. The top of the table was divided into four quadrants, and each quadrant was a different color. In the center of each quadrant was a small cup filled with some sort of liquid.

He gave a quick refresher about the types of magic used by each of the four Orders. Then he said, "It is time to choose your order, and take the Covenant of the orders. Have you all considered your choices carefully?"

The nine Magi nodded or gave an affirmative answers so Mr. Pyllis pointed at Uli, "Okay sir, you're first. Walk over to the table, grab the cup of the color of your choice, and state that you choose whichever order you are picking. Then drink the entire contents of the cup."

Uli walked around the table looking at each color, considering his options. Then he stopped next to the grey cup. He drank the contents of the cup, and Pyllis motioned for him to go and stand next to Sarasa. Then one of the Rolimi hurried over and refilled the contents of the grey cup.

Over the next several minutes, one at a time, the other eight Magi walked over to the table and drank from one of the four colored cups. Then they went and stood next to the leader of their Order.

Once everyone had made their selections, Rissyl looked at each group. Aruk and Firana stood in his group. He didn't know too much about Firana, except that she was young and inexperienced. Aruk seemed quiet and not overly confident. He was satisfied with the people in his Order and he was anxious to see them learn their first Evocation spells.

He looked over to Cynia and saw that she had three Magi standing next to her. Both of the elderly Magi that had been selected, Makah and Widdel, had chosen the Order of Diviners. Zahr, the younger Magi who arrived yesterday, also chose green.

Next he looked to Sarasa. She was standing with Uli and Gordo. Uli had proven his skills with the bow when they fought the Awakened together a few days prior. Rissyl thought about how deadly Sarasa could be with her sneaking and invisibility, he shuddered to think how affective that would be from afar with a bow. Gordo, on the other hand, had been very quiet since Rissyl had met him, so he didn't know what to think of the former Dreg.

Finally, he looked over to Dalen. The new Champions were Sarge and Ranik. Rissyl wasn't too surprised to see that Sarge had chosen blue, because the man carried himself like a warrior.

Mr. Pyllis motioned for the new Order Magi to get closer to him, "Okay, time for the Covenant." One by one they each took the Covenant.

Rissyl knew it would take a long time for each new Order Magi to go through the whole Covenant. So he let his thoughts wander. He had been worrying a lot over the last couple of days about what might be going on in Sorgo. Part of him felt guilty for initiating a group of new Magi and then basically abandoning them. He kept telling himself that he, Cynia, Dalen, and Sarasa didn't have anyone to protect them when they were just getting started, but they had the benefit of no one really knowing that the Magi Society was being reborn. These new Magi were new, under-trained, and likely to draw unwanted attention. He tried to tell himself that he was just being too much of a worrier. His parents had counseled him about that so many times as he was growing up. He was always stressed out about something. This was probably no different.

After a while his thoughts turned to the elaborate box to which the Rolimi were tied. He thought about the first time they used it. Cynia often talked about how the box couldn't be opened except with the touch of all four of them. That was why they needed him, because they couldn't open the box and start their training without him, but now they open the box all of the time with just one of them touching it. He guessed it must have been some kind of one-time locking spell that prevented it from being opened without the touch of a Magi from each Order. He made a mental note to ask Mr. Pyllis about it sometime.

Then he realized that they were about done with the Covenants, and he brought his attention back to what was going on around him.

When they were finished, Mr. Pyllis had each of the new Magi stand in a line facing him. Other Rolimi brought a pile of items and set them next to the teacher. He said, "Please remove your white and brown cloaks."

Mr. Pyllis called each of the new Order Magi one at a time to receive their new cloaks and weapons. They looked proud and excited to be a part of one of the Orders.

The next few hours went by quickly for Rissyl. The Rolimi split all of the new Order Magi into their individual Orders, so he was with Aruk and Firana working on basic evocation spells. A Rolimi had brought over a couple copies of the basic evocation spell books, and the group worked on the simple spells for quite some time. Even though he had already been through all of this, Rissyl still learned some new things. When he first went through this training everything was so new that it was like drinking from a waterfall. Now that he felt comfortable with many of the basics, he picked up many new things that he missed the first time through.

Aruk and Firana both learned their new spells extremely quickly. He was a little jealous because they already had quite a bit of experience as a Society Magi, so they had a good foundation upon which to build, and the new lessons from evocation came quickly to them.

Before he realized how much time had passed the Rolimi announced that lesson time was over. Mr. Pyllis and the other Rolimi quickly picked up the chalk board and other items they had brought, and returned through the magic doorway in the box to wherever they had come from.

Uli addressed the gathered Magi, "Ladies and gentlemen, if I could get your assistance we can get an evening meal prepared."

Rissyl was impressed with how quickly everyone fell into a role. He paired up with Cynia to gather some firewood and get the fire going. By the time they had gathered a good amount of firewood for several hours of a large fire, a team of hunters had already returned with a large deer. Being a Magi did have its advantages when it came to hunting for food.

Before long, most of the Magi were sitting around the fire with several large chunks of deer meat cooking over the open flame. Uli and Aruk brought out a couple of large baskets of breads and vegetables, and Sarge rolled out an entire barrel of ale.

From the other side of the fire, Rissyl heard the boisterous Society Magi, Baeldin shout, "I ain't your servant! Get your own sarding mugs!" The large man shoved Zahr and Sarge aside and walked off alone.

Ranik asked, "What's his problem?"

"I asked him if he'd mind running back to the house and grabbing several mugs. Everyone's been helping out and none of us are servants. I don't know why he's so angry." Sarge pushed the barrel up onto its end and then watched Baeldin walk off.

Aruk said, "He is angry that the rest of us were accepted as Order Magi and he was not. He is the only younger Magi that remained a brown cloak."

"Alrighty. Well, he's gonna have to grow up and deal with it. He's not the only one. Hanry wasn't ready either. Baeldin's poor attitude is part of the reason he is still a Society Magi. I'll get the mugs." Dalen walked off quickly.

Conversation quickly turned to happier topics. Once Dalen returned with mugs and the ale started flowing no one really seemed to notice or care that Baeldin had stormed off. Sarge got out his recorder and started playing. Soon the meadow was filled with music, singing, dancing and merriment.

Rissyl didn't normally like dancing, but as he saw the rest of the Magi stand up and start dancing around the fire, he couldn't resist getting in on the fun.

The catchy tune that Sarge played drew everyone into one of the elaborate dances that had been around for ages. It was one of those dances that everyone seemed to know, whether they were Gentry or Commoners. Even folks from the barbarian lands knew the dance. He was caught in the flow of the dance. Step, step, step, turn, step, and change partners. Step, step, step, turn, step, and change partners. Around and round he went, some people flowed in the same direction he was going, and the other half of the dancers flowed in the other direction.

Then, Gordo turned in the wrong direction and Cynia smacked right into his chest. That brought a chain reaction of crashing and chaos to everyone nearby, and the entire group burst into laughter.

More ale, less dancing, and a lot more laughing followed that. Eventually, the songs and dancing gave way to sitting around the fire telling stories of adventure and glory.

Ranik told a story about a time when he and Firana were hunting for herbs in the foothills and stumbled upon a group of goblins that had come down from the mountains. According to his story, the two of them fought off at least thirty mean goblins with just their limited magic and crafty ingenuity. He told, in great detail, how the two of them lured the goblins into a valley and then climbed trees and attacked them from the trees. Rissyl couldn't help but wonder how much of the story was accurate and how much was being embellished.

Then Dalen started telling the story of when several rogues ambushed them on their way to meet Randol. Rissyl didn't really want to hear the story of the first time that he had used magic to kill, so he stood up. He needed to get away and just have some quiet time.

It was fun, and everyone seemed to be bonding, but he didn't normally enjoy large gatherings. He was about ready for this one to end. He didn't want to ruin everyone's fun, so he thought he'd take a little walk. The ale didn't help, he wasn't normally a drinker and this ale was much stronger than he was used to. A nice walk would help, hopefully.

As he walked away from the campfire, he realized someone was following him. He assumed it was Cynia, but as he looked over at the person walking up to him, Firana said, "Do you mind if I walk with you?"

"Oh, no. Not at all. I'm just going for a walk. The smoke is burning my eyes." Really he wanted to tell her that he'd rather be alone, but he didn't want to hurt her feelings.

"I think it's probably the ale that's burning your eyes! That stuff is strong!"

They both laughed as they walked. He nodded, "Yes, that stuff is way too strong for my liking. I'm a light-weight when it comes to ale."

"Yeah, me too. I don't normally drink the stuff, but I didn't want to look like the fuddy-duddy, so I drank a little. I think it burned the hair off of my toes." She giggled at her own joke, and he joined in the laughing.

They walked for a long time after that, talking about funny and light-hearted stories from their childhood. He lost track of time as they walked towards a grove of trees off in the distance. He had heard that there was a pond in the middle of the wooded area, so he decided to head that way.

Once they reached the woods, he sat down on a large rock near the water. He skipped a couple of rocks and she sat there quietly watching him.

After a while she cleared her throat. She said, "Are there any rules about Magi having a relationship with other Magi?"

He was shocked by her question, and he stopped his throwing motion to turn and look at her. He hadn't expected something like this. She was very pretty, and he was flattered that she would want a relationship with him, but he wasn't sure how to tell her that he was only interested in Sarasa. The last thing he needed was a broken-hearted Magi in his Order. That kind of drama would really complicate things.

When he didn't answer right away, she added, "Is Dalen seeing anyone? Do you think he has even noticed me?"

Rissyl suddenly felt stupid, and a bit embarrassed, at having assumed that she was talking about him. He should have known better. "Ah, no, I don't think that he is dating anyone at the moment." He didn't want to mention that Dalen wasn't exactly his favorite person in the world.

"He seems like a caring man, not the kind of man who would hit a woman. He seems protective of his sister, that's a good sign, right?"

"Oh yes, he is extremely protective of his sister. And his cousin." He thought about the day in the apothecary shop when Dalen had slammed him up against the wall.

"I have a hard time trusting men. My parents died when Ranik and I were little, and we went to live with my aunt and uncle. They fought terribly. My uncle was very mean and violent to us and to my aunt. I grew up knowing that I could never live a life like that. When I choose a husband, he will be a gentle and loving man."

He was shocked to have her share so much private information, since he barely knew her. As much as Dalen annoyed him sometimes, he felt like he should give her some kind of assurances about him. "Dalen is passionate about the Society, and he is very focused on our goals, but he is a good man, and I am sure that whenever he settles down he will be a good husband."

"Do you think he's noticed me? What kind of girl does he like?"

"I don't know. Just sit down and talk to him. If you ask about our mission, or his ideas on how to make the Society great again, you'll get him talking to you for ages."

"Thanks, I'll try that! How about you? How long have you and Cynia been a couple?"

He almost laughed, "Wait, what? You think that me and Cynia...?" He rubbed his temples and then looked at her, "Why would you say something like that? Cynia and I are not a couple."

She looked surprised, "You're not? But you tent together, and you both act like such a close couple, we just assumed that you were."

"Everyone thinks that we're a couple? No, she's just my friend. Okay, more than a friend. But no. We're not dating. I..." He stopped short. He wasn't sure that he wanted to admit his feelings for Sarasa to someone that he just met, but she had already shared personal things with him. They were in the same Order, maybe sharing personal things and building a bond would be a good thing? "The girl that I dream about is Sarasa. She barely knows that I exist, but I have been infatuated with that girl since the first time I saw her."

There was an uncomfortable silence for a bit, and then she replied, "Maybe she does notice you, but she assumes that you're seeing Cynia? Or maybe she is jealous of the relationship that you have with Cynia?"

"There is nothing to be jealous of with me and Cynia. She's more like family to me!"

She looked away and said, "You don't act like family. You act like a couple."

He said, "We're just really comfortable around each other. We..." He was starting to get flabbergasted and he couldn't put his thoughts into rational sentences. It was all very simple, but he couldn't explain it. "Cynia and I have been through a lot together over the last couple of months. It's not a relationship or anything like that."

She looked over at him and smiled slightly, "I think you might be fooling yourself. It's not my place to judge, but if you're wondering why Sarasa doesn't seem interested in you, that might have something to do with it."

They sat in silence again for quite a while and then she stood up. She placed her hand on his shoulder, "I should get back. I'd like to try to talk to Dalen before bed. Thank you for the talk, I really appreciate it."

She walked off and he sat by the pond and thought about what she said. He didn't want to admit that she was right, but he thought she might have a point. He was about to get up and head back to the others when he heard a noise behind him. He turned and looked and he saw the silhouette of someone standing not too far away.

Cynia pushed herself away from a tree and walked over. Well, walked might be a bit of an exaggeration. She had enjoyed a bit too much ale and her walking was aided by leaning against trees a few times as she made her way to him.

He wondered how much she had heard, and how long she had been there. He didn't say anything to Firana that he wouldn't have said to Cynia's face. Nevertheless, he wondered if somehow he had hurt Cynia's feelings

226

by saying those things to the girl.

She plopped to the ground next to the rock that he was sitting on, and she rested her head against his leg. He considered saying something to explain his conversation with Firana, but he couldn't think of the right thing to say.

"Well look at us, all alone next to a pond. Under the stars on a gorgeous night." She spun around awkwardly. She leaned the other side of her head against his leg, and she wrapped her right arm around his leg so that his inner calf was against her elbow and her hand rested on his inner thigh. She looked up at him as her fingers caressed his leg.

He almost fell off the rock when he felt her hand moving on his thigh. He looked down at her and wanted to say something memorable or meaningful, but all he could squeak out was, "Yes, it is a great night."

She giggled and he could tell that she really had enjoyed way too much ale. Her fingers continued to caress his upper leg. It wasn't unusual for her to play with his hair, but she had never touched him in such a provocative way. She asked, "Have I ever told you how turned on I get when I've had a lot to drink?"

His heart was about to pound right out of his chest. She grabbed onto his tunic and pulled herself up, ungracefully, and straddled his legs facing him. She pressed her breasts against his chest and wrapped her arms around him while she buried her face in his neck. The feeling of her against him, and on him, was almost more than he could take. It was like a dream, and he didn't want it to end.

She had a great body, and he certainly enjoyed seeing her at her most immodest when she insisted on changing her clothes in front of him. He had occasionally wondered what it would be like to be with her. However, he didn't want her this way, when she was drunk. He didn't want her to regret it. As much as it pained him to do it, he gently pushed her away with his hands on her shoulders. He looked into her eyes and said, "Cynia, not like this. I don't want you to give yourself to me when you've been drinking."

She kissed him quickly, "Shut up. Yes you do." She pushed him backwards and he fell backwards off the rock, and she fell on top of him. She leaned forward and kissed him again.

He started to roll over but someone was laying on his arm. Rissyl opened his eyes and looked around, and then he closed them quickly. He hoped that last night had been a dream, but looking over he saw Cynia laying on her back using his arm as a pillow. Her shirt was off and she was partially covered with her cloak as a blanket. He stayed there a while admiring her naked breasts, and tried not to breathe too much so that he didn't wake her and spoil the moment.

His head felt terrible, and there were several sticks and rocks in his back. The smell of old vomit was coming from somewhere nearby and he groaned internally as he remembered that unfortunate detail from the night before. She was going to be so embarrassed, or angry, or something when she woke up. He really wasn't looking forward to that. As uncomfortable as he was, he did appreciate having a nice view to look at while she slept.

Too soon, she started to stir, and then she groaned loudly. She opened her eyes and looked at him, and then she rolled away from him and sat up. She looked around for her clothes and started dressing without saying anything to him.

He was afraid that she was so mad that she would never talk to him again. He didn't know what to say, so he said "I'm sorry, Cynia."

She finished pulling down her shirt and looked at him. "Sorry for what?"

"That I let things go too far. You were drunk, and I didn't stop it. I hope you're not angry at me."

She threw a rock at him, hitting him in the stomach. "Stop being such a wuss. I knew what I was doing, stop apologizing for it. If you want to apologize about something, apologize for scraping my bare back and butt across the rocks. Or for making my hips hurt so much." She paused and gave him a wink, "Or for running out of steam when I wasn't done yet."

His jaw dropped, "It... wasn't good for you?"

She threw another rock at him, "Dammit Riz, I was joking! It was great, you didn't leave me hanging. I was just teasing!" She smirked at him. "But you did scrape up my back and butt."

He smiled back at her, "You almost killed me, shoving me backwards off of that rock."

"You liked it. But I'm sorry I puked in the middle of things. We were shaking up all of that ale, and it wouldn't stay down no longer!"

He laughed, "That's okay. At least I was behind you at that point." They laughed together and they both stood up and finished dressing.

As they walked back to camp Rissyl considered whether Firana had a point about them acting like a couple. He wondered if their night of sexual adventures had changed their relationship in Cynia's eyes. He didn't want to ruin the morning after such an enjoyable night, but he needed to make sure that she understood that his desires for a relationship with Sarasa hadn't changed.

He struggled to find a gentle way to say it, and he finally gave up and just said, "You know, Cynia, last night was great. But I want… Well, what I mean is I…"

"You want me to know that Sarasa makes your heart go thumpity-thump and she's the girl you want to be with?" she said.

"Yes, that's basically it. I probably sound like a troll, after last night?"

She was quiet for a while, and then said, "Riz, I didn't come to you last night to try to win your heart. I know that you want her. I was drunk and turned on, and I wanted to be with you. I was pretty sure that you wanted me too. We're both adults. It was a fun time, and I don't regret it at all."

He was relieved that she felt the same way he did. "So, you won't be jealous if Sarasa finally comes around and throws herself at me?"

She laughed, "No, of course not. You're my best friend and I want you to be happy. But I would have to warn her about that weird grunting sound you make during sex." She gave him a playful smirk.

His face turned bright red, "You wench! That's terrible; I don't make a grunting sound!"

They walked for a while in silence and then she started making a loud mocking grunt sound. They both started laughing and he pushed her gently as they walked.

He said, "You're a wench!"

She winked at him and said, "I know."

When they arrived back at camp everyone else was awake and finishing breakfast. As they got close to the fire he whispered to her, "Well, this is going to be awkward."

She didn't respond. As they walked up to the fire, several people were staring at them. She grabbed a kettle of tea from over the fire and poured herself a cup. Then she turned and said, "What's wrong, haven't you ever seen two people return from a night of dirty sex by a pond?"

Rissyl started coughing as he choked on his own saliva, and she smiled at him and patted him on the chest as she walked past. All of the gathered Magi suddenly looked very busy attending to whatever menial task they happened to be doing. Firana and Dalen were sitting together eating breakfast. Sarasa was sitting with them.

He walked over to grab some breakfast. He sat down at a bench by himself. As he chewed on a dry muffin, Sarasa walked up to him. She said,

"Hey Riz, can we talk?"

"Of course Rasa, what's up?"

She motioned for him to follow her and she led him away from the campfire. They walked around the big barn and she climbed up onto a large bale of hay and sat down. He climbed up onto it with her, and he sat down facing her with his legs crossed.

The breeze picked up a little and he could smell the subtle sweet smell that he sometimes noticed when he was near her. He didn't know what it was, but he really loved that smell. After a few moments he said, "What is that smell? I like it a lot."

She smiled slightly. "It is Jasmine. I love how it smells too."

He sat in silence for a bit, waiting for her to reveal why she wanted to chat privately.

She pulled some hay from the bale and started playing with it. She said, "Firana came back to camp last night and talked to me. She said that you told her how much you like me and that you want us to be a couple."

His heart was pounding wildly, and he wasn't sure if he should be angry at Firana or if he should thank her for saying something to Sarasa about his feelings. He nodded, "I've had feelings for you since the first time I saw you. I didn't think you felt the same and I've been afraid to really say anything about it."

She wasn't looking at him; she just looked at the long piece of hay in her fingers. "Of course I have feelings for you. You're a strong Magi, you're handsome, you come from a respected family, and you're a gentleman most of the time. Any girl would be lucky to have a guy like you. But you're my cousin's man, I couldn't try to take you from her. That would be wrong."

He shook his head, "No, Rasa! I'm single, I'm no one's man! If you'll have me, I would love to be your man!"

"Dammit, Riz! How can you say that? You were sarding her just a while ago! You told Firana how much you wanted me and then you spent the rest of the night doing gods-know-what with Cynia! Can't you see how twisted that is?"

He didn't know what to say. Every response seemed wrong. "I'm sorry, Rasa. I didn't know you had any interest in me. If it matters for anything, Cynia was extremely intent on getting her way last night." She dropped the piece of hay and looked at him with an annoyed look on her face. He stammered, "But that don't really matter."

After a few moments of awkward silence she said, "While you and Cynia were gone last night, Dalen announced who would be assigned to which mission."

He looked at her with his mouth agape. "He did what? How could he do that without working out the details with the rest of us? This is bullshit!"

She held up her hands to calm him, "Don't get worked up, he talked it over with me and the other Magi."

That made him even angrier, "So everyone knew his plans but me? Nice. So, what are the assignments?"

"Dalen wants to make sure that there is an equal distribution of the four Orders in each group, as much as possible. So the group going to help defend the Free City is Firana, Ranik, Uli, and Baeldin."

He hated to see Firana assigned to the group going to defend that barbarian city from the emperor's armies. He was afraid that it would be a suicide mission. All three of them might be suicide missions, though, and she knew what she was getting into, so he didn't complain about the first group.

She continued, "Heading straight to Sorgo will be Aruk, Zahr, Hanry, Dalen, and I."

He slammed his fist against the side of the barn, "He can't split us up! We're in this together! We all need to go to the Stronghold together!"

She put her hand on his knee, "Dalen is worried about the necromancer attacking Sorgo, our family is there. He needs to head up that group, and I need to go with them. Sarge and Gordo can help you and Cynia secure the Stronghold."

He leaned against the barn and felt his heart start to ache. He knew that Dalen was trying to keep him and Sarasa apart. Rissyl wanted to keep her close so he could keep her safe. He hated the thought of her heading in the opposite direction, especially after just finding out that she has feelings for him.

"He wants to keep you and I apart, doesn't he?"

She shrugged, "I don't know, Riz. That might be part of it. But right now that is up to you."

He was still angry, and his emotions were a jumbled mess, so he had no clue what she meant. He said, "What is up to me?"

"You have a choice to make, Riz. Do you want to be with her, or do you want to be with me?"

He took a deep breath and looked at her for a moment. He thought she was the most gorgeous woman he had ever seen. "I've already told you that

I have feelings for you. Do you want us to be together?"

She smiled at him slightly, "That choice is yours. If you want me, then you can't sleep with her any more, it must be just us. If you bed her again, you've made your choice. However, right now we must focus on our missions. The Society is more important than individual relationships. When we meet again you can tell me the choice you've made."

He just looked at her and gave a little nod. He didn't know what to say.

She jumped down from the large hay bale gracefully. Then she held out her hand to help him down. They walked back to the campfire together.

When they got close to the campfire, Dalen said, "Let's get things packed up, Rasa. We should be leaving soon."

He watched her head to her tent and once she closed the flap behind her, he turned to his own tent. Inside he saw Cynia was putting things away.

She said, "You two were gone for a while. Making out a little bit behind the barn before we split up?"

"Dalen told you about his plan? I think it's stupid."

She shrugged, "It has its merits."

"Sarasa and I weren't making out behind the barn. But Firana told her about my feelings for her. Sarasa has feelings for me too. We talked about becoming a couple. She told me that I have to choose between you and her."

Cynia didn't answer right away. Without looking at him, she asked, "What did you tell her?"

He was starting to feel uncomfortable for some reason that he didn't understand, "Well, I haven't answered her yet, but if I choose her, I can't bed you again. She said if you and I are lovers again, that it means that I'm choosing you."

Cynia made an annoyed face, "Well that's crap! I wouldn't make those kinds of unreasonable demands on you." She gave him a playful wink. "Okay, let's get stuff packed up so we can go."

He watched as she stood up and began packing away her things. After a few minutes he stood and started getting his things arranged as well.

When he had finished packing he stepped out of the tent. He saw Sarasa sitting on a bench by the fire by herself and he walked over to her. They didn't have much time to say their goodbyes before it would be time to break camp.

Chapter 25

Kimly

She had never felt so weak in her entire life. Even the time when she was deathly sick with dysentery as a child, and everyone said that she had one foot in the grave, was not nearly as bad as this. She worked up enough energy to open an eye, and she wished that she hadn't. Looking around, she realized that she was lying on the hard floor of a small stone cell. One might even call it a dungeon, but she thought that might be a little cliché so she decided just to think of it as a cell.

Kimly tried to sit up, but she just didn't have the strength. Instead, she thought she might curl her arm under her head to prop her head up off the hard floor. When she tried to move an arm, she realized that her wrists were cuffed together with some kind of greenish metal manacles.

She turned her thoughts inside, and tried to call some magic to summon a light orb. However, as she tried to use the tiniest amount of magic she realized that her magewel was almost entirely empty.

How could that be? She had been taught that it refills naturally over time, and it had been days since she had used it.

She felt light-headed, and thinking seemed to make it worse. She didn't even know how long she had been in this place. The last thing she remembered was that strange magic-dead creature touching her.

That was it! She remembered a feeling like the Motlite had sucked the life from her, but it must have sucked the magic out of her. The Rolimi had warned them about using so much magic as to leave the magewel completely empty because a person couldn't live without magic inside them. Somehow, that Motlite had drained almost all of the magic from her.

That still didn't explain why the magic wasn't coming back. She looked back down at the manacles around her wrist. Could they be somehow blocking or draining the magic from her?

Then she heard a horrible screech that echoed through her cell. Whoever was making the sound was quite far away, as the scream was faint. It was a haunting screech of despair, hopelessness, and pain. As soon as she heard it, she realized she had heard it many times over the… however long she had been there. The sound sent shivers down her spine. Someone was being tortured, and there was no reason to think that she wouldn't be next.

Every few hours, or possibly every few minutes, the hideous screech of agony and despair happened again. Sometimes it sounded closer than others, and sometimes the sound came from a woman, and other times it sounded like it came from a man.

She tried to drown out the sound, but it was no use. She tried to sleep, but she couldn't drift off. So instead she just stayed there on the floor.

When the clanking at the door started, her heart sank. This was it, she was certain that it was now her turn to scream. The door opened and two large mean looking soldiers walked in. They reached down, grabbed her under the arms, and dragged her down the hallway. Her knees and feet dragged along the hard stone floor, smacking into irregular spots in the stone, and rubbing off little chunks of flesh as she went. She tried to lift them off the ground, but she simply didn't have the strength so she hung there limp in the soldiers' arms.

When they finally dropped her back to the ground she looked around and found that she was in a large room with a table in the middle. There were other people in the room, she could hear them talking. She heard footsteps approaching her.

A man said, "Jarla, dear, clean her up. She smells like the middens. Then get her dressed for dinner."

Jarla replied, "Yes, Lord Jalinox."

Kimly realized that someone had placed a key in her manacles and with a CLANK the manacles released her wrists. Then she felt someone tugging her pants off her lower body. If she had more energy she might be angry at the violation, but at this point she was mainly annoyed at being jostled around so much. After Jarla pulled off her trousers and undergarments the woman started tugging off her tunic.

As she lay naked on the hard stone, she desperately wished for some sort of blanket between her and the floor. It was cold, and seemed to suck the warmth from her further.

She hadn't noticed the woman, Jarla, walk away from her, but she noticed her footsteps return and suddenly the contents of an entire bucket of freezing cold water dropped onto her! She sucked in breath quickly and curled up into a ball trying to warm herself. A few seconds later more freezing cold water splashed onto her!

"Lay on your stomach and stop moving! I'm trying to clean you up for dinner! Spread your legs."

Kimly did as she was told, and freezing cold water slammed into her nether-regions, sending her crawling away quickly. She sat up and curled her legs up to her with her back against the wall. It was only at this point that she realized that she felt slightly better than she had earlier.

The manacles were off, and she was slowly regaining some strength. Maybe if she played along and let this draw out long enough she would regain enough magic to escape from this freakish nightmare.

Jarla walked up to her with another bucket of water. She said, "Spread your legs."

She bit her tongue to keep from yelling, but she refused to spread her legs. That sucked, and she wasn't falling for that again. Jarla kicked her legs apart, and poured the cold water on her. When the water hit her sensitive parts between her legs she shouted, "Dammit! Enough of that!"

The woman stepped away and returned with a large brush, like the kind a person would use to wash a horse. She said, "Lie on your stomach." When Kimly complied the woman began scrubbing her all over with the large brush. It actually felt somewhat good, until the woman got over-aggressive in the sensitive areas. After a while she said, "Roll onto your back."

She complied, and as the woman began scrubbing the rough brush aggressively across her breasts, the door opened again and she watched the soldiers drag Jessa into the room. They dumped her in the corner on the other side of the room.

The rough brush on her feet and legs felt pretty good, but when the woman started going to town with the brush between her legs Kimly bit down on her arm to keep from screaming. Then the woman worked her way back up Kimly's body to her face. The filthy brush scraped across her cheeks and nose, and pushed her lips open as the woman vigorously scrubbed her face with it. Kimly tasted dirt, feces, and untold other nasty things as the woman continued to scrub her face with it.

As soon as Jarla pulled the brush from her face, Kimly turned and spat onto the ground. She exclaimed, "Sard! You couldn't do my face first? Dammit, yuck!"

She closed her eyes and lay there without moving as the woman grabbed another bucket of water and dumped it across her.

"Can you stand?"

She doubted it, but she tried. It was difficult, and she had to use the wall to hold herself up, but she got herself upright.

The woman refilled the bucket, returned, and dumped it over Kimly's head. This repeated a few more times, and then the woman brought over a cloth to wipe the water from her body. Finally, she brought a plain white dress and pulled it over Kimly's head.

The woman pointed at a chair over at the table. She said, "Go sit over there."

Kimly walked carefully over to the chair and sat down gratefully. She shivered and tried to hug herself to warm up. Being fairly dry helped, and the dress helped as well.

Then she heard Jessa scream as a bucket of water was dumped onto her. Kimly looked over and saw that a different woman had pulled the clothes from Jessa and was dumping water on her body. Jessa was naked, filthy, and shaking from the cold, and she was cursing loudly.

Kimly turned her chair slightly and watched the show as the woman set about scrubbing the filth from Jessa. Kimly tried to suppress a smirk as the girl cursed and yelled at the woman who vigorously scrubbed her naked body with the large horse brush. She felt a little bad for laughing at the girl, remembering how much it sucked, but watching it done to someone else was actually fairly amusing.

"Do you find her suffering enjoyable?"

Kimly looked to see who spoke to her. She hadn't noticed that the man, referred to as Lord Jalinox, had sat down at the table with her. He stared at her quizzically. She shrugged, "It sucked when it happened to me, but, yes, it is mildly entertaining to watch."

He laughed heartedly, "Does it excite you?"

She looked back at Jessa, and saw the woman shoving the brush back and forth under and between the girl's breasts. She looked back at Jalinox and shrugged, "If you're into that kinda thing, I guess. She's naked and pretty, so I'm sure that some might get their jollies by seeing that."

He laughed again, "Oh, I like you a lot. We're going to have great fun together."

Somehow, she didn't expect his idea of fun to be something that she was going to enjoy all that much. She turned her thoughts inward, and she reached for the magic deep inside herself. She could feel a little magic essence beginning to fill her magewel. She was quite sure that it wasn't enough to summon her cloak, at least not without completely draining the magic from her and possibly killing her. She just needed to be patient; eventually she'd be strong enough to use magic.

He pulled something out of his pocket and sat it on the table. "Jarla, dear, kindly put these on our guest. I think she has plenty of strength to feed herself now."

The woman picked up the pair of bracelets that he had placed on the table. She walked over and placed them each on Kimly's wrists. Each one was hinged and locked with a loud CLICK as she pressed it closed.

Kimly brought her wrist close to her face to examine the bracelet. These were not nearly as thick as the manacles that she had been wearing, and they were not connected together, but they were made of the same greenish metal from which the manacles had been forged.

Jalinox said, "These should keep your magic from returning, but shouldn't drain you as quickly as the manacles did. If you behave properly you can continue to wear those. If you cause me the slightest annoyance, we'll go back to the manacles and Jarla here can scrub your filth from your arse each day before dinner because you're too weak to even care for your most basic needs."

She gave him a sarcastic smirk, "No, these'll be fine, thanks."

The chair next to her moved, and she looked to see Jessa sitting down carefully in the chair. She looked cold, weak, and miserable.

"Jarla, please have a seat." Jalinox pushed a chair out for her with his foot. Then he turned to the other girl, "Lovely Narinda, kindly run along and fetch dinner."

She wasn't gone long before returning with a tray of meat, and two soldiers who carried other trays of food. It was all placed in the middle of the table.

"Very nice, doll. Now put these bracelets on our guest over there and then have a seat. Everyone dig in and enjoy!"

The woman placed the bracelets on Jessa, who looked at them and then looked at Kimly. With a sympathetic smile Kimly shrugged at her, and held up her own wrists.

After dinner, Jalinox stood up. "Ladies, please accompany me." He walked to the door and opened it.

Outside, four guards walked behind the women as they followed Jalinox down the hallway. They followed him through a maze of twists and turns, until Kimly was thoroughly lost.

Eventually, they came to a door with a soldier stationed outside of it. The soldier opened the door and the women followed Jalinox into the room. He said, "Lady Magi, I'm going to have to ask you to take a seat over there and strap in until we're done."

Kimly and Jessa walked over to a bench and sat down. One of the soldiers attached their hands and feet to manacles that were chained to the wall. Kimly didn't know what was about to happen, but she was pretty sure that she wasn't going to like it.

Then another soldier walked to the other side of the room and opened double doors. Inside that room were two small children perhaps around 7 years old, both were strapped to some sort of wooden platform. The platform was almost perpendicular to the floor so both children almost looked like they were standing. The children started yelling and crying "Mommy!" when they saw Jarla and Narinda. Both women rushed forward to embrace their children.

In a loud voice, Jalinox yelled, "Stop!"

The two women stopped and looked back at him.

He said, "Ladies, please calm down. This is the moment you've been waiting for since you arrived for your new assignment with me. Here is your chance for one of you to take your place at my side as my assistant."

The women looked confused and looked at each other, and then at their child, and finally back to Jalinox. Narinda said, "How the sard did you get my child? What is he doing here? I left him with relatives back home!"

He smiled and put his hand on her shoulder supportively, "Yes, yes, dear. It was actually quite the pain to find the little rascal, but my men eventually found him. That endeavor is what set us back several days. I digress. Notice the large lever on the side of each child's platform."

He pointed at the young boy, "Jarla, dear, please go and stand next to Narinda's son and take hold of that lever. Don't pull it yet." He laughed merrily, "Oh heavens don't pull it yet. That would spoil the fun!"

Then he pointed at the young girl, "Narinda, my sweet, kindly go and stand near Jarla's daughter and take hold of that lever."

He waited for the two women to get into position and then he said, "Okay ladies, here is how this is going to work. One of you is going to kill the child of the other, and whoever does will become my assistant."

Both women let go of the lever and stepped away from the platforms. Jarla said, "That's insane! By all the gods, I will not! How horrible!"

Narinda looked like she might throw up. She said, "You're a madman! I won't do it either!"

Jalinox laughed, "I am, I really am! That's what makes my job such a good fit! Only a madman could do it!" He laughed maniacally. Then his face grew steely cold. "However, I recommend that you put your hands on those levers and let me finish explaining the rules."

Both women slowly approached the platforms, reached out, and touched the levers gently. They almost seemed afraid that the levers would bite them.

"Let me draw your attention to the contraptions above." Jalinox pointed at the ceiling. Before each platform was a large wooden device with two iron poles sticking from it. "When you pull one of those levers, the crusher thing up there will swing down and impale those two nasty looking poles completely through the chest of the sweet little innocent kiddie on the platform before you."

Both women looked like they were about to step away from the lever again. Jalinox said, "But wait, there is more. I have my own lever over here." He pointed at the wall near the double doors. "If I pull this one, then both of those crushers come down at the same time, and both of the precious little angles get the life impaled out of them."

The women both gasped at the same time and Narinda exclaimed, "Oh, no, no, NO!"

He laughed triumphantly. "Oh yes, yes, YES! So, let me go over this again. I will count to five. As soon as I start counting one of you will intentionally murder that sweet little baby before you, and that brave woman will win two things. First, you get to become my personal assistant. Second, your kiddo gets to continue to breathe. The cowardly woman who failed to pull her lever is the loser, has a squished kid, and instead of being my personal assistant she will take a job that is significantly less pleasant. If I happen get to five before one of those brats gets squashed then I get to pull this nifty lever over here and you both lose."

He held out his hands and smiled. After a moment he said, "Are we ready?" He took hold of his lever. A soldier moved behind each of the women.

Jalinox looked over at Kimly and Jessa and winked at them with a big grin.

Jessa looked as far from Jalinox and the children as she could. Kimly was shocked. She had met many genuinely evil and twisted people in her life, but none were anywhere near as crazy and twisted as this Jalinox seemed. At the same time, she couldn't help but wonder which woman would be willing to kill someone else's child to save her own.

Jalinox looked back at Narinda and Jarla. He started counting loudly and quickly, "One! Two-"

As he started to say "Three" Jarla screamed and slammed down her lever! The large wooden bar swung down and the two iron poles slammed hard into the chest of the small boy with a loud squishing crunching sound!

Narinda screeched, "NO!" The soldier behind her grabbed her by the waist and pulled her away from both platforms.

Kimly shut her eyes tight and looked away from the scene in the other room. She had a strong stomach, but that was too much even for her. She could hear someone, probably Jessa, getting sick nearby. There was shouting and screaming and crying coming from the other room, and Kimly kept her eyes closed tightly. Then she put a hand over her eyes, just in case they popped open on their own.

She heard Jalinox say, "Get Narinda out of here and clean up this mess." There was a pause and the sounds of movement and more hysterics. Then he said, "Get the little girl down and take her and my new assistant to their new quarters."

After a few moments Kimly opened her eyes in time to see Jalinox approaching them. He said, "Guards, get these ladies unshackled from the wall so we can continue our tour."

He waited for the guards to get them unchained and then he led them from the room. Now there were two soldiers following them. They passed through a number of doors and corridors before coming to a large door that was barred on this side with two guards watching it.

Jalinox looked at one of the guards and held his hand towards the door, and the guard hurried over and unbarred the door. He opened it and Jalinox walked in, motioning for everyone to follow him.

Before she even walked in Kimly felt her heart sink as the haunting echo of countless soft cries and sobs emanated from the room. The smell of excrement and filth was heavy and she covered her nose as they walked into the room.

When Kimly got in the room she was shocked at what she saw. The room was narrow and extremely long, with bright lanterns every few feet to keep the room brightly lit. The room was lined on both sides with a long row of cells created by iron rods going from floor to ceiling.

He walked the group over to the closest cell on the right. Kimly looked into the cell and saw that it was about ten feet square with no decorations or furnishings. The walls and floors were stone, and there was no bed or mats on the floor. Huddled together in one corner were five women. They were mostly naked having only a crude piece of cloth wrapped around their bodies. They were filthy and each of them had very short, roughly cut, hair.

"This is the Wellsprings room." Jalinox spread his hands wide as he slowly motioned to the entire room. He continued proudly, "All of the Wellspring Dregs live and work in this room. As you can see, each Wellspring Dreg is given a comfortable environment for work and leisure time. Follow me please."

As they walked through the long room, she couldn't help but look into every cell. Most of them housed several young women, but some of them housed several young men. The Dregs were all mostly naked, and the majority of them were huddled into groups on the floor in the back of their cells. Some of them were standing against the cell door, holding the bars and staring at Kimly with pleading eyes. Every once in a while a sudden scream or loud sob echoed through the large room sending shivers down her spine.

She noticed six large devices spread through the middle of the long center room. Each device looked like a table or workbench. Nevertheless, each one was slightly different. Some had flat surfaces like a desk, others were angled so one end was closer to the ground. One of them was almost upright. All of them had manacles scattered around the edges. Many of the tables also had ropes, clamps, leather straps, and a vast array of implements that Kimly could only guess were used for some sort of torture.

Jalinox exited the room into a long hallway. Kimly wasn't sure if he was taking the Magi through the place to brag about what he had built, or to warn them where they would be taken if they didn't do as he wanted. Whichever was the case, she was going to do everything in her power to keep herself out of those cells.

They passed a few doors and then he turned left and he led them into a small dark room. There wasn't much room for more people in there. The room was maybe fifteen feet per side, and large tables sat along each wall. Tubes, beakers, vials, jars, and glass containers of every size and shape were spread out across all of the tables. Some of the beakers and containers had colorful liquids in them. Some sat on top of fires where an unknown liquid slowly cooked over the flame. On one corner of one desk was a large green metal bar of raw ore.

"This is where the magic happens." Jalinox pointed at the bar of ore, "Where we take that ore, shave it down into small bits, and melt it into a wonderful little syrup with some of that goop over there. That is injected into the Wellspring Dregs. One treated Wellspring Dreg can go a full six

241

months without needing another treatment! That's good because even though we use an incredibly small amount of the garroliron ore, the stuff is terribly difficult to acquire. It's also quite deadly after a few treatments."

She wasn't sure that she wanted to know the answer to her question, but Kimly asked it anyway, "And what is the purpose of the treatment?"

He looked at her for a moment and then answered, "The creation of Magi-killing Motlites, of course. Okay, off to the next room!" Ushering them out of the room, Jalinox led them down the hallway again.

They passed several doors before entering one on the right. The large room that they entered had about a dozen chairs spread out around the room. Several nearly naked women with breasts heavy with milk sat in the chairs. The women sat with a bucket on their laps in front of them and they were each expressing milk into the bucket.

"Once a Wellspring Dreg successfully accomplishes her duties, she becomes a Salubrious Dreg and gets to move to the nicer facilities in this section of the camp. This is the Salubrity Room where the Salubrious Dregs package food for the new little Motlites. The Dregs are brought to the Salubrity Room a few times a day to work, and then they get to retire to rest and relaxation in their quarters until milking time comes around again."

Kimly didn't know what these 'nicer facilities' looked like, but she was pretty sure that they were anything but nice. She decided that she would be quite happy not knowing.

She looked closer as one of the women expressed her milk, and she realized that the milk was a sickly green color. As she looked around, all of the milk being expressed was the same shade of green. Without thinking she let the question come out, "Why is their breast milk green?"

He looked impressed, "I'm glad you asked! That is a bi-product of the garroliron in their system. It turns their milk green. And that garroliron milk fed to the little Motlite babies is what helps give them their Magi-killing powers." He paused, and then added, "Well, we think. We're not exactly sure how much they are born with and how much is acquired from the milk. We're still testing that."

He led them out of the room and back to the hallway. "Now, let's head out into the fields and I will show you the pasture where all of the little Motlites are free-ranging as they grow big and strong!"

- = - = -

Fallen leaves were scattered across the altar, and all around the dais. Kimly reached down and picked up a dead leaf. She turned it around in her hand and felt its surface. The leaf had been coated in some substance to keep it from crumbling, and it was stiff and sturdy. She nodded to herself. That explained how they had fallen leaves in the springtime.

Standing at the back of the dais was a chaplain in the black and purple robes of Viator, the god of death. Over his robes the overweight chaplain wore a long purple stole, which hung down the front of his robes on either side of his chest. At both ends of the stole was a black fallen leaf, the symbol of Viator.

The room was elaborately decorated with symbols of Viator and murals of death and violence. Candles were everywhere, and most of them were burned down to the last few inches, with dried candle wax pooled at their bases.

The chaplain stepped up to the altar to give the exhortation. He looked around the sanctuary, and then, with a booming voice, he pointed down at Jessa and said, "Whom-so-ever cowers in the night fearful of mighty Viator shall surely be consumed by him!" He made a broad sweeping motion with his hands and then brought them to his bosom as if gathering something to his chest. "But he who invites death will be called upon by death to aide in the gruesome work, endless and ever-lasting, unsavory but indispensable!" He raised his right fist out before him. "All people must die!" Then he slammed his fist into his chest, as if he held a dagger. "But those who worship death, who toil in the fields doing the deeds of Viator during this brief time among the land of the living, shall surely enjoy riches beyond measure for all eternity when they finally pass through the Gate of Death!"

In the two days since she had been awake enough to know what was going on, this was the sixth exhortation that she had attended. Three times a day, every day, the followers of Viator were expected to attend to ritual exhortation. She had seen it done many times as a child. Her mother worshipped Viator. Not fervently, of course. Few people did, but occasionally she would see her mother attending to the exhortations, especially if there was something bad going on or if her mother needed a prayer answered.

However, she had certainly never seen the exhortation done with such zeal! This chaplain believed in the message, and he wanted to make sure that everyone else believed it too. She looked around the sanctuary. She and Jessa were seated up front. Nearby, sat Jarla and her daughter. On the other side of the sanctuary was Narinda, who spent the whole time crying quietly into a rag. Scattered around the back seats of the sanctuary were a number of nearly naked Dreg women, Wellsprings and Salubrious Dregs most likely. Along the back wall of the sanctuary were several soldiers who quietly ensured that peace and order was strictly maintained.

When the chaplain left the altar, the soldiers escorted the Dregs and Narinda from the sanctuary. Kimly and Jessa sat patiently, waiting for Lord Jalinox to return for them, or to be escorted somewhere else. She was surprised at the amount of freedom that she had been given over the last couple of days. Clearly, she was a prisoner, but she was allowed to attend exhortation or walk around most areas of the underground lab. Yesterday, she had spent several hours in the Wellsprings room because she was bored and she was curious what actually went on in there. She always had a soldier escorting her, but at least she spent very little time in her cell. Jalinox had said that her stay could be as pleasant or as unpleasant as she wanted, and she fully intended to make it suck as little as possible. If that meant listening to three exhortations a day, so be it.

She was a little worried about Jessa. The girl had become sullen and withdrawn over the past couple of days. Kimly thought that wasn't entirely bad, because the girl was always chatty and a bit annoying in the past. So the new, quiet, Jessa was a welcomed change, but Kimly worried that the girl might be plotting something stupid, and Kimly fully intended to ensure that she didn't suffer because of stupid choices made by Jessa.

Behind her, she heard the little girl ask her mother, "Mama, why don't Dreg girls wear nice clothes?"

Jarla laughed, "That's silly, child! Why would Dregs wear nice clothes? We don't put nice clothes on our horses, do we?" The girl giggled and shook her head no. "We don't put nice clothes on our chairs do we?" The little girl laughed loudly and shook her head no. "We don't put nice clothes on our doggies, do we?"

The girl giggled loudly and said, "No!"

"Then why would we put nice clothes on Dregs? They're just things we can buy, like watermelons and dishes. You wouldn't put pretty little dresses on your watermelons, would you?"

The girl pushed her mom playfully as she laughed. "No! That's dumb." The girl sat and thought for a moment and then said, "Yesterday, you said the Wellspring Dreg's job is to make Motlites to keep us safe from the evil Magi."

"That's right, sweetie."

"Only the Motlites can keep us safe from Magi? And only the Wellspring Dregs can make the Motlites?" The girl's expression had turned serious and quizzical.

"Yes, baby, and these are dangerous times."

The girl looked extremely confused. "Then why do the Wellspring Dregs act like they don't want to get Motlite babies? Don't they want to keep us safe?"

Jarla looked at her daughter with a sad expression, "That's the sad part. Dregs only care about themselves. That's why Lord Jalinox has to keep them in cages, or they would just run away and we wouldn't have any Motlites to keep us safe!"

The little girl's expression changed to anger and she clinched her little fists in her lap. "I hate Dregs!" Her mom patted her on the knee, and the girl was quiet for a while. Kimly watched her sitting there, deep in thought. Before long she looked at her mother and said, "Yesterday, one of the Salubrious Dregs said that Lord Jalinox was evil. Is he a bad man?"

The woman turned to her daughter and took both of her little hands in her hands. "Tali, listen to me very carefully, because nothing is more important than this. Good and bad don't exist; they are just concepts that change from person to person. What one person thinks is good, someone else thinks is bad." She paused and the girl looked confused. She asked her daughter, "Do you like turnips?" The little girl shook her head no and made a disgusted face. Jarla continued, "I love turnips! To me they are good. To you they are bad. Who is right?"

Tali shrugged, "Me?"

"Yes! To you, you are right, but to me, I am right. Does that make sense?"

She nodded slowly, "Yes, I think so."

Jarla continued, "Lord Jalinox is a very powerful man. If he wants good things to happen to you, they will. If he wants bad things to happen to you, they will. We can choose to view him as good, or we can choose to view him as evil. Both would be right, but one would be stupid."

The girl thought for a moment, "So, be happy and don't worry about good and bad?"

"Exactly, baby! If you want to get ahead in life, you can't get all caught up in good and bad. You must always worry about what is good for you! If you are happy, what else could matter?"

"Yeah!" The little girl seemed excited again, and she smiled brightly at Jarla.

"Think about how things were before we came to live with Lord Jalinox." The girl nodded. "Remember how mama was always away working, and you spent all of your time at your cousin's house?"

"Her boys were mean to me!"

"Yes they were, and we never had any money or nice things, or much food to eat. Remember that?" The girl nodded yes again. "But now look at us. We're like queens! We have wonderful rooms and clothes, and great food!"

Tali added excitedly, "And the smelly Dregs have to do anything we tell them!"

"Yes baby, the Dregs have to do whatever we tell them. All we have to do to hold onto this wonderful life is keep Lord Jalinox happy with us. Do you think you can do that?"

The little girl gave her mom a thumbs-up sign and said, "Yep!"

Kimly's attention was dragged away from the exchange between Jarla and her daughter when she heard the door at the back of the sanctuary open.

Lord Jalinox walked quickly into the room and said, "Ladies, I have great news! A new Motlite is being born right now! Come quickly and you can witness the birth!"

"Yay!" Little Tali cheered as she stood up.

Kimly followed the mother and daughter out of the room, and Jessa followed quietly behind her. Several soldiers fell in line behind them.

They followed Jalinox through the twisting hallways to a fairly large room that Kimly hadn't seen yet. In the center of the well-lit room was a bed with a pregnant Dreg laying on it. The naked woman's abdomen was heinously large, and it looked like her skin would pop open at any moment. The movement of the baby inside could clearly be seen as the woman lay there. Two midwives attended the woman. In one corner of the room were soldiers and in the other corner were two Salubrious Dregs. The woman on the table moaned in pain.

Jalinox walked over to the pregnant Dreg and then looked at his guests, "Behold! The Motlite is already trying to escape his confinement!" Then he walked over to the two Salubrious Dregs who were standing in the corner. He motioned for Tali to come closer and then he said, "Tali, dear. We have two Salubrious Dregs here. One of them gets to be the first to feed our new

Motlite, and the other one has to go back to the Salubrity Room. You get to pick which one!"

The girl's face lit up. She asked, "I do?"

"Yes you do! The one you pick will have all of the powerful green milk sucked right out of her breasts. Sadly, the little Motlite will also pull all of the magic from her blood in the process and it will surely cause her death."

Both Dregs gasped and moved away from Jalinox, and Tali looked less certain. "He will kill her?"

Lord Jalinox smiled and placed his hand on Tali's shoulder, "Of course, dear! The god of death requires payment for his gifts. Get a life, give a life. Besides, both of these Dregs will soon be dry of milk and they can't make more babies. Whatever else would we do with them? Do we need more servants and dishwashers? We can't just throw them out, can we?"

She shook her head no. Then she looked at the two women and asked, "How do I know which one to choose?"

He turned to look at the Dregs, and put his hand behind Tali's back and urged her forward. "That, dear girl, is entirely up to you."

Tali stepped over to the first Dreg woman and looked her up and down. Her nearly naked body was dirty and scarred. The woman looked terrified and she held her hands up near her mouth, both hands were shaking. The woman pleaded with her eyes. She whispered, "No, no."

"What is your favorite color?" The little girl's question was asked loud and clear.

The woman stammered, "What?"

Tali said, very slowly, "What. Is. Your. Favorite. Color?" She sounded like she was talking to someone extremely dense.

In a shaky voice the Dreg woman said, "Red, I guess. Red."

Then Tali stepped over to the other Dreg. This one was crying and had her arms folded tightly in front of her. The girl asked her the same question. She said it slowly, apparently assuming that this Dreg was slow in the head also.

The woman quietly said, "Blue."

Tali's eyes lit up and she jumped up and down. "My favorite color is blue too! You get to live, yay!" Then she pointed to the other Dreg woman and said, "You get to feed him." She ran over to her mother.

The chosen woman howled in despair, and at the same time the pregnant Dreg screamed out in pain as contractions hit her.

Jarla hugged her daughter tightly and whispered, "I am so proud of you!"

"Get that one back to the Salubrity Room!" Jalinox instructed one of the guards. Then he looked at the two Magi women. "Do you want to help with the birth?"

Kimly shook her head, and said, "This Salubrious Dreg ain't a Magi, is she?"

He shook his head, "She is not."

"The Motlite will kill her? Just from nursing on her?" She looked perplexed.

"The Motlites can't control their magic consuming abilities. Prolonged contact with someone will drain the magic from them, eventually killing them even if they're not a Magi. It's an occupational hazard, and something we're hoping to control in the next batch."

"They don't kill the mothers before they're born, why is that?"

Jalinox laughed and patted Kimly on the shoulder, "That's a perplexing puzzle that we've struggled to understand since the earliest days of our research. From what we've seen, the Motlite doesn't gain the magic consuming talents until it starts nursing from one of the Salubrious Dregs for the first time."

Jessa said, "Then why bother with Dreg mothers who are tainted with the garrol stuff? Why not just take normal babies and feed them the green milk?"

"Ladies I'm beaming with pride at your astute observation skills! We have tried feeding the Salubrious milk to many normal babies, and sadly it kills regular babies every single time. The Motlite babies survive the initial feeding almost half of the time."

The Dreg on the table screamed again and one of the midwives said, "Here it comes!"

Chapter 26

Vendino

"General Kraesthorn, commander of Wolverine Regiment?" The emperor stood before his throne in the audience chamber with his arms crossed in front of his chest, his head held high, and his eyes planted firmly on one of the elaborate windows near the ceiling of the chamber.

Vendino was fairly certain that the emperor had not looked at the general since he had entered the large room. He knew that wasn't a good sign. The emperor had been infuriated since word had arrived that Wolverine Regiment had been routed without even reaching the barbarian city. For days the emperor demanded that every last member of Wolverine Regiment be executed immediately, but Thorli had argued fiercely against that. At times, the emperor seemed to redirect his rage towards the minister, but eventually he calmed down slightly.

The general answered stiffly, "Yes, Your Majesty! General Kraesthorn, reporting as ordered!"

"Tell me, general, how did you manage to fail your troops so badly that an entire regiment was routed and fled the field of battle without even engaging the enemy?"

He paused briefly, and then cleared his throat. Then the general replied, "We were ambushed by zombies, in the middle of the night, Your Majesty."

"Zombies?"

"Yes, Your Majesty."

"Was your regiment not properly trained to battle zombies, general?"

"That answer seems self-evident, Your Majesty."

"You were in charge of the regiment, were you not, general? Why did you not prepare your men for the obstacles that they might encounter on the way to their objective? Isn't that the primary duty of a commander?"

He looked like he wanted to defend his actions, but instead bit his tongue. "No excuses, Your Majesty. I've failed you and my men."

"Indeed you have, general! Indeed you have, and what do you think is the fitting punishment for a general who fails his emperor and his men in such a way?"

The general raised his chin slightly and answered, "That he be relieved of his command and forced to retire on some quiet out-of-the-way farm somewhere?"

The emperor laughed a loud and boisterous laugh that was devoid of all humor. "You're partially right, Mr. Kraesthorn. You are hereby stripped of command, and stripped of all rank! You and every officer of Wolverine Regiment shall be hanged for cowardice by the end of the day. The Wolverine Regiment will be immediately and forever disbanded and scarred by shame for all time! Every last member of that regiment who is not hanged will be ordered to serve 999 years as a Dreg! And most importantly, every last member of your family will join your men as Dregs for the remainder of their life! Every one of them, from your oldest grandparents to your second cousins! Your children! Your children's children! Until the end of their lives every Kraesthorn alive today will live the remainder of their lives as Dregs!"

The beleaguered former-general fell to his knees, "You wouldn't!"

A murmur rolled throughout the chamber as all of the spectators whispered and muttered to each other.

The emperor turned to one of the guards, "Get this man out of my sight! He is not worthy to walk upon the rugs of my chamber! Have my orders carried out immediately!" He turned back to Vendino, seated near the wall at the back of the dais, "Minister Vendino, have the paperwork drawn up to carry out my orders!" Then he turned to Minister Thorli on the other side, "Minister Thorli, have every person that I have mentioned rounded up and taken to the Dross or the gallows immediately! If needed, dispatch whatever troops are necessary to travel wherever is needed to have this order carried out! I want the order executed before word spreads to these people and they try to flee!"

Together the two ministers responded, "Yes, Majesty!"

Several hours later, Minister Vendino sat at his regular spot at the table of the Council of Ministers. The room was abuzz by the disruption caused by adding a thirteenth minister to the meeting. He looked over to the empty chair provided for Minister Jalinox. However, Vendino had more on his mind than whether the creepy old minister deserved a chair at this table. The events with the former general clearly indicated that the emperor was becoming more volatile, and sitting to his immediate right could be extremely hazardous if he wasn't careful. The emperor was becoming more unpredictable by the day, and that had everyone in his inner circle on edge.

250

Across from him sat Minister Thorli, as usual. The tough-looking old minister seemed to have aged several years in just the past few months. Thorli looked at him and said, "Jalinox is late."

Vendino just nodded.

"The new minister is lucky the emperor is not yet here. He doesn't seem to be in a patient mood today"

The minister to Thorli's left said, "How old is Jalinox?"

Vendino replied, "Forty or fifty, maybe? I'm not sure."

The minister next to Vendino said, "My father sat on this council for almost fifty years, and he died twenty years ago. He once mentioned that Jalinox was a special agent for the emperor before my father became a minister! That would mean that Jalinox served our emperor's grandfather, Ryal I!"

"That's impossible." Thorli shook his head, "That would mean that Jalinox has been an agent of the empire for over seventy years? He certainly doesn't look over ninety years old."

Before Vendino could reply to the Minister of War, one of the guards at the door to the emperor's office announced "The emperor approaches!" All of the ministers stood and assumed the Royal Reverence Bow.

The emperor walked quickly into the room and sat down without observing any of the typical formalities. As the ministers sat down he said, "What is the status of our efforts to snuff out the weeds of magic which have popped up?"

Thorli answered, "Majesty, we have killed two of them, and captured two."

"Is that all of them? What about the others?" The emperor looked like he was about to explode, as he looked from one minister to the next.

Then the main door to the Royal Hall opened, and Jalinox walked in with his new assistant, Jarla, close behind him. He wore his traditional black and red tunic with a black cape flowing behind him, and Jarla was dressed similar to him but her black cape had red trim around it.

"Thank you for joining us, Lord Jalinox. We've started without you. Who have you brought with you?" The emperor spoke quietly and with obvious strain on his ability to remain calm.

The new minister grabbed his new chair, pulled it around the table, and then pushed it up to the far end so that he would be seated directly across from the emperor. In the process of doing so, he pushed Minister Aribeth's chair several feet to her left with her still sitting in it. She gave him a dirty look, but didn't say anything.

With a pleasant smile Minister Jalinox replied, "Good evening, Majesty. I would really prefer that you not start without me. I do have such a long distance to travel to attend these things; you could at least give me the courtesy of awaiting my arrival. Please let me introduce Jarla, my acolyte."

The emperor's face reddened slightly, and Vendino fully expected him to explode, but, with clinched fists, the emperor said softly, "Only ministers are allowed to attend meetings of the Council of Ministers. She'll have to wait outside."

The new minister laughed with genuine humor, "Your Majesty is such a jokester. Seriously, I'm much too busy to attend these things very often. Jarla here will be attending in my place most of the time, so, of course, she should be here with me this time to start to get acclimated with the nuances of dealing with all of these esteemed ministers."

Thorli scooted his chair back and away from the emperor slightly, and Vendino mentally braced himself for the onslaught that he fully expected from the emperor. The other ministers, who normally fought to talk over each other at every opportunity, sat in complete silence. He assumed that they were all hoping to keep from making themselves the next target of the emperor's rage.

However, the emperor just interlaced his fingers and smiled. After a brief pause, the emperor replied, "But, of course, the Lady Jarla would be welcomed in your place, Minister Jalinox." He took a deep breath and then continued, "So, where were we? Oh, yes. I'll repeat my questions. The two we killed, and the two we captured, is that all of them? What about the others?"

Vendino flipped through some papers before him and then answered, "From the reports I've received, Your Majesty, those are the only ones that we have captured or killed. Our people in Sorgo reported that the other suspected Magi have either fled the city or given up using magic."

"Fled the city? Fled to where? Do we even know where they've gone?"

"Not to the best of my knowledge, Your Majesty." Vendino paused, because he was extremely hesitant to say what he needed to report. "There have been a couple of reports of Magi Society activity in Kazror."

He slammed a fist down on the table, "A couple of reports? Have we taken action? Have we killed those who were reported? We must take every single report of this seriously! We must take action!"

"Your Majesty, it would be problematic to kill everyone just because of a single accusation. It would be chaos. People would turn in their neighbors as revenge for completely unrelated reasons. Do we really want to jump onto the slippery slope of mass killing of those simply accused of using magic? It would be a return to the final years of the Purge."

The emperor slammed the table with both fists together. "Yes! That is exactly what we want, if it's the only way to kill off these wretched Magi! My grandfather was a tactical genius, and he freed us from the taint of magic!"

Jalinox said, "Your grandfather was a fool!"

Standing up quickly, the emperor shoved his chair away with a kick of his foot. It crashed backwards behind him. "My grandfather was the greatest ruler the known lands have ever seen! He built this empire! He defeated the Magi!"

The new minister stood up slowly, and Jarla pulled his chair out of his way as he did. "Your grandfather murdered almost one hundred thousand innocent loyal citizens of his own lands in a maniacal bloodlust. He sent another thirty thousand soldiers to their death battling Magi and conquering neighbors who had been peaceful allies for centuries. He sent the entire economies of six kingdoms into a complete failure, to the point where almost a quarter of the surviving population needed to be enslaved and forced to work endless hours just to provide enough food and basic supplies to get by. All of this, just to kill a few hundred Magi?"

The emperor clenched his fists and closed his eyes as he shouted. "That is enough, Jalinox! You've crossed the line!"

Jalinox held up his hands, palms forward and bowed his head slightly. As he sat down, Jarla was there to push in his chair. He looked over at Vendino and flashed him a quick wink and a smile.

The emperor didn't see Jalinox's wink, however, because Thorli had stood up at the same time and the emperor looked to him. The Minister of War said, "Your Majesty, I beg you to ignore the insolence of our newest member. We all know and acknowledge the brilliance of your grandfather, and on a daily basis we enjoy the sacrifices that our forefathers made for our happiness today."

Thorli sat down and the emperor turned to look for his chair. One of the guards hurried forward and righted it, and the emperor sat down as well. He still looked on the edge.

The Minister of War continued, "But these are different times. After growing up on stories of the Purge, the citizens of today are going to be more volatile if they feel that another Purge is eminent. If we repeat the actions of the past, we could quickly be faced with widespread unrest throughout the empire. I recommend that we table this issue for the moment. We could task every minister in this council to consult with his or her top advisors and come up with a recommended course of action to deal with this problem. This will also give us time to further evaluate the threat and assess the validity of these reports."

"Fine. One fortnight, and then I want recommendations from each of you. Unless there is a plan I like much better, I am still leaning towards another Purge. Where are these captured Magi, I would like to speak to them myself."

Jalinox made an exaggerated expression of sadness, "I'm sorry, Majesty, they're all dead. They killed themselves to avoid captivity during transport to Clornoss. It was really quite tragic, but admirable that they would give their lives for their beliefs like that."

The emperor looked to Thorli, "I thought they lived?"

"Your Majesty, at your bidding we had them taken to Lord Jalinox. According to my men they were delivered to him alive."

With a smile and a shrug, Jalinox said, "And according to my people they were all dead when the soldiers brought them. Maybe Thorli's soldiers killed them for some reason. I just know they didn't survive the trip to Clornoss. Pity."

"Minister Thorli, the next time we capture Magi I want them immediately brought here." He paused and prepared to stand, "Are we finished?"

Thorli shook his head no, "One more matter to address, Your Majesty. Shall we assign another regiment to finish the job of capturing that barbarian city?"

Emperor Ryal shook his head no, "We've tipped our hand there, minister. I'm sure you'd agree that we'll meet unnecessary resistance there now. Is there a more suitable target for our next acquisition?"

Minister Aribeth, the Minister of the Treasury, said, "Your Majesty, I would recommend the city of Ront'El. Our reports talk of vast silver and gold mines just north of that city. It could mean a huge boost to our precious metals reserves."

"I agree, Your Majesty." Thorli nodded, and then continued, "If we extend our border wall directly north, all of the way to the mountains, we would also effectively cut the Barbarian Lands in half. It would significantly hurt their trade, and limit the level of resistance they could muster against us during further expansion efforts."

For the first time all meeting the emperor smiled. "Yes, I like that very much! We do need direct access to the mountains and all of the resources that they hold. Ministers, let's make it happen. Without failures this time."

Vendino asked, "What shall we call the new city?"

"Let's call it Ronel. One more thing, Minister Thorli, you will personally lead this army as their general."

The table got quiet as all eyes turned to the Minister of War. After witnessing the results of a general's failed campaign, there was no question about the implied threat upon a member of their own council.

Thorli nodded to his emperor, "It would be my honor, Your Majesty."

Chapter 27

Rissyl

Rissyl looked around the room. He was surprised at how many people were at an inn out in the middle of nowhere near the mountains northwest of Sothral. He and the other Magi on his quest had been exploring the base of the mountains for days, looking for an entrance into tunnels or an underground lair that eventually led through the mountains to the Stronghold. After several unproductive and frustrating days, Sarge suggested that they rest and relax at this nearby wayside inn.

The *Moose Tail Inn* was a fairly new building. It was large and sturdy with a spacious stable off to the side. It was positioned on the only road through these parts. It was built as a gathering place for local farmers and ranchers and as a stopping point for dwarven trade caravans as they leave their kingdom and head into the human lands to trade. Over the last decade it had become the single busiest place north of Sothral, according to Sarge.

When they entered, the first thing that Rissyl noticed was the smell. The large common room still smelled of fresh cut wood and varnish. The serving wench had joked that the place still had that 'new inn smell'. After the smell, he noticed all of the dead animals mounted on the walls. There were elk heads, wolf heads, and countless other heads and entire bodies of a wide variety of woodland creatures. In one corner was an impressive bear, standing on its back legs and looking ferocious. Interspersed with the multitude of dead critters on the walls were miscellaneous farming and ranching tools and implements from days gone by. Also scattered around the walls were a few paintings of old farmers and farmland.

The people in the common room were mostly local farmers. It was late in the day, and many of them had come to the inn for drink, food, and fellowship. After picking a table and ordering drinks, the Magi quickly became the center of attention for the whole place. Everyone slowly gravitated to tables near them, to ask them news from the nearby cities.

At first, Rissyl had felt uncomfortable sitting around a group of strangers with his Magi Cloak visible, but Sarge and Gordo insisted on keeping theirs visible, so there had been no point for Rissyl and Cynia to hide theirs.

After the Magi had enjoyed their meal, one of the farmers brought out a wooden box and asked for a challenger to play him at Goblin Squares. He sat down at a table near the Magi and opened the box. He sat a square playing surface on the table. It had sixty-four squares on it, arranged eight by eight which alternated in color between white and black. Then the man took out sixteen white playing pieces and arranged them in the first two rows of squares next to himself.

Sarge looked at Rissyl and Cynia and asked, "Do either of you wanna play him?"

They both shook their heads no, and Rissyl said, "I don't even know what it is, or how to play."

"What? That's awful." The old warrior Magi shook his head sadly, and sat down at the farmer's table. He began arranging his black pieces on the two rows closest to him.

Gordo stepped over to Rissyl and Cynia. He said, "Sarge loves this game, and he's really good at it. The front row of pieces are the grunts. There are eight of them, each with a different color head. The colors don't mean anything, it's just to tell them apart."

Rissyl looked at the pieces that Sarge had arranged in his front row. From left to right the colors were brown, purple, red, orange, yellow, green, blue, and grey.

"The pieces in the back row are the important and powerful pieces. Those two in the middle are the goblin king and the shaman."

He leaned closer to get a better look at the pieces. The goblin king was shaped like a big fat goblin with a crown and scepter, and it was taking a big bite of a leg of some large animal. The shaman piece was shaped like a goblin in robes with a large gnarled staff, and several magical talismans hanging off his robes.

Gordo explained, "The two pieces on either side of the goblin king and shaman are the two goblin scouts. On either side of those pieces are the goblin archers. And the two outside pieces in the back row are the wolf riders. The heads of the back row pieces were painted the same color as the head of the grunt in front of it."

Rissyl was impressed with the detail of each figurine. Whoever carved them was quite skilled. He guessed that the game set was probably expensive, since it was so well crafted, but these pieces looked very old and worn, so perhaps it had been passed down from the farmer's father.

Once Sarge had his pieces setup, the old farmer said, "What's the wager?"

Digging into his coin purse, Sarge pulled out a single silver coin and placed it beside the game board on his side. He said, "One dove?"

The other farmers in the room had gathered around the game table, and they all started muttering and mumbling to each other as Sarge placed his bet. The farmer across the table from Sarge shook his head no. "We're not all rich, Magi. I've got two falcons to wager, and that's it." The farmer sat two copper coins on the table next to the game board.

"Fine, two falcons it is." Sarge put the silver coin back in his purse and pulled out two copper coins. Then he said, "Red Grunt to C-6." He moved the goblin-shaped figurine, with a red head, to a square bordering the one where it had been sitting.

The man on the other side of the table said "Orange Grunt to D-3." He moved a white goblin-shaped figurine, with an orange head, one square closer to Sarge's pieces.

Gordo leaned over and said quietly, "The grunts can move one square in any direction, but moving diagonally counts as two moves, so Grunts can never do that."

The farmer and Sarge took turns moving grunts, and they both seemed to be trying to form some sort of defensive pattern with them. Then Sarge said, "Red scout, B-5."

Rissyl was surprised to see a piece move so far, and it moved forward diagonally. He looked to Gordo who said, "The scout can move four squares in any direction. He can move through other pieces, but he can't land on them, so this turn Sarge moved the scout up one, diagonal one which counts as two, and then up another one. They are great pieces to get anywhere on the board pretty quick, and sneak past defenses, but they're not very strong."

"This is a pretty complicated game." Rissyl didn't think he would be very good at this game.

"It is sort of complicated until you understand it. There are a lot of options and a huge amount of strategy involved. Kings and generals have played this game for hundreds of years to improve their minds for military planning. Sarge said that it was designed by a great general to teach battlefield strategies and planning to his officers."

Rissyl laughed, "And now it's a bar room wager game."

The farmer said, "Purple archer, B-2."

Gordo explained, "The archers, and the goblin king, move just like grunts, but the archers can attack any piece up to two squares away. Every other piece on the board has to move into a square with another piece to attack that piece. The other nice thing about archers is that they don't die if they lose a battle. All other pieces either die or kill their opponent when battle happens."

"Brown wolf rider, B-7." Sarge moved his wolf piece diagonal one square.

Pointing at the piece, Gordo said, "Wolf riders move like the scout, but they can only move two squares. And they're more powerful than scouts. They're the most powerful pieces, after the shaman. The shaman can move as far as it wants, in a straight line, in any direction, but it can't move through other pieces."

Rissyl asked, "How does someone win?"

"They kill the goblin king, of course."

"You know a lot about this game. Have you played it a lot?"

Gordo shook his head no, "No, I've never played it. I've just watched him play it a lot of times."

The farmer moved his archer piece one square towards Sarge's pieces and said, "Purple archer, B-3. It attacks your purple scout!"

Both men took dice from the box and rolled them. All of the dice were cubes with between one and six dots on each side.

The farmer rolled one die, and it showed four dots.

Sarge smiled and rolled two dice. One was a one and one was a four. He laughed and said, "My scout lives!"

Gordo explained, "Archers battle with one die, and scouts battle with two dice. Whoever rolls the highest number wins the battle. If there is a tie, then it comes to the next number. They both had fours as their highest number, so they went to the next die. A one beats nothing, so the archer lost, but since it's an archer it doesn't die. If he would have rolled a five instead of a four, then the farmer's archer would have won."

He thought about it for a moment and said, "Intriguing! So a weak piece always has a chance to beat a powerful piece, if the weak piece's player rolls that one die really good, and the other player rolls bad. Okay, that makes sense. How many dice do the other pieces roll for battles?"

"The goblin king, grunts, and archer all roll one die. The scout rolls two. The wolf riders roll three. And the shaman rolls four."

Rissyl looked at Cynia, "That makes the shaman, or one might say the Magi, the most powerful and important piece on the battle field. Interesting.

It makes me wonder about what real battles were like hundreds of years ago. Did Magi battle side by side with non-magical soldiers? I can see how that would really turn the tide of a battle."

Sarge gave him an annoyed look, "And it makes me wonder if you're going to yammer on through the whole game. Surely there is someplace else where you can chit chat? I'm trying to focus."

He got the hint. Cynia elbowed him gently in the ribs. When he looked at her she made a goofy face, mocking Sarge, and they both laughed quietly. He pulled a chair over so he could watch while sitting, and she pulled a chair next to his.

Over the next couple of hours he watched Sarge and the farmer play the game. As far as he could tell, it was a pretty even game, but he didn't know any of the strategies or hidden plays, so one of them could be poised to win at any moment and he would have no clue. Both of them had lost several pieces and now, other than grunts, Sarge was down to both wolf riders, one scout, the shaman, and his goblin king. The farmer had one wolf rider, both archers, the shaman, and his goblin king.

At some point during the game, Cynia had rested her head against his shoulder, and he put his arm around her without really thinking about it. Eventually, she put her feet up onto the side of her chair and curled up against him. That got him thinking about Sarasa again. Would she be upset that Cynia was leaning against him? She had forbid him from bedding Cynia again if he wanted to have a relationship with her, but she didn't specifically say that Cynia couldn't curl up against him. It was confusing. As far as he was concerned what he and Cynia had was different from what he wanted with Sarasa. He liked having Cynia at his side, it had become second nature and comfortable. What he wanted from Sarasa was more emotional and loving, the relationship stuff. Well, he wanted that and the physical things, of course. Okay, so maybe it wasn't that much different from what he had with Cynia. The more he thought about it, the more confused he got. He did know that he didn't like having to choose between the two. It would be much simpler if he didn't have to make the choice. It was complicated being a man; his father must have forgotten to warn him about that.

He thought about using his nexus gem to send Sarasa a message to see if things were going well. It had been a couple of days since she had sent him a message, and that was when they had first arrived in Sorgo. If he could get to the nexus gem without disturbing Cynia then he would, but instead he decided to wait until they stood up.

Several people cheered, and Sarge groaned, and that brought his attention back to the game. Sarge reached out and plucked one of his wolf riders off the board. Then he slid his shaman most of the way across the board, to share the square with the farmer's shaman.

He said, "Shaman to F-2!" There was confidence, and a hint of a challenge, in his voice.

Both players grabbed their dice. Sarge, as the attacker, rolled first. He rolled two sixes, a three, and a one. The Magi leaned forward with a grin.

When the farmer rolled his dice, many of the people gathered around the table leaned closer so they could see the roll better. The first die stopped on four. Then one stopped on six. The last two stopped on a one and a two. The gathered spectators roared in excitement or dismay.

Sarge reached out and said, "Let me help you with that." He picked up the farmer's shaman and moved it off the board. He smiled slyly at the farmer, "Can your grunt save you?"

Without replying, the farmer moved a grunt into the square with Sarge's Shaman, "Blue grunt to F-2." He didn't sound very hopeful. He picked up one die and rolled it. It landed on a one. He growled a curse in frustration, and several spectators groaned.

With a big smirk Sarge picked up four dice and blew on them. Then he shook them in his hand for quite a while, while looking at the farmer. After the dramatic pause, he dropped them to the table. The dice stopped on two fives, a four, and a one.

The farmer grabbed his dead grunt and set it beside the game board, with a little more force than was necessary.

"Ladies and gentlemen, boys and girls, this is the moment we've all been waiting for! The death of the evil white goblin king!" Sarge stood and encouraged the spectators to get noisy in anticipation of what might be his final roll.

Some of the gathered locals had moved over to Sarge's side during the course of the game, and they started chanting, "Sarge! Sarge! Sarge!"

"Just make your move, this ain't over yet." The farmer smiled at the theatrics, as he encouraged Sarge to move.

"Shaman to F-1! Royal Threat!" He moved the shaman piece into the square with the white goblin king piece. Sarge grabbed his four dice.

Rissyl and Cynia both stood up so they could better see, since everyone else was standing and cheering.

Sarge held the dice out, palm open, towards Cynia. "Blow on them, for luck?"

She rolled her eyes, and then blew on the dice. He rolled them across the table, and the first die landed on a four. Then next die landed on a one and the next on a four. The final die spun on a corner longer than then others, and then dropped to a six.

Part of the crowd erupted in cheers and Sarge started giving high fives to everyone nearby.

Several people patted the old farmer on the back. There was no need for him to roll, because the goblin king only rolls one die, and even if it was a six he would still lose.

Rissyl wasn't sure that he followed all of the details of the game, but it did seem pretty straight forward. Perhaps he would try a game sometime. It certainly looked challenging, and people seemed to enjoy watching it.

The spectators slowly moved away from the table. Sarge reached out and took his two copper coins. Then he said, "Keep your coins, I play for the enjoyment of the game."

The farmer took his coins and said, "Good game, Magi. Just for the record, I'd have kept your coins if I would've won."

Both men laughed and Sarge replied, "I figured as much. Do you have time for another game?"

"Ok, I'm headed to bed." Rissyl said to no one in particular.

The farmer nodded and pushed the copper coins back to the side of the game board. They both started setting up their pieces.

Gordo looked over to Rissyl and said, "I'm gonna stay and watch the game. G'night."

Rissyl and Cynia wished him a good night at the same time and they walked up the stairs together to the sleeping quarters. They stopped by one of the doors and she took ahold of one of his hands. He said, "I should probably sleep in this room with the men tonight. Good night." He turned to go into the room they had rented for the men, but she held onto his hand.

He turned back to her and she said, "You could at least come back and talk with me until I fall asleep."

He glanced back down the stairs and then back to her. He didn't reply.

She looked distant and maybe even sad. After a moment she said, "I hate that she is making you choose. It ain't fair." She led him down the hall to her room.

"Well, one woman and one man is sort of how it works for most people."

She stopped at her door and faced him, "I'm not most people." She turned around, unlocked the door, and led him into her room.

When she sat down on the bed to take off her shoes he remembered the nexus gem in his pocket. He pulled it out and was surprised to see that it was glowing a soft green color. He held the nexus gem up near his face so he could hear it well and summoned the magic to activate it.

Almost instantly, he heard Sarasa's voice. She spoke quickly, and he could hear the urgency in her voice, "Our Magi have scattered. Emperor's soldiers ambushed them."

He felt his heart drop at her words. This was exactly what he was afraid would happen. He looked at Cynia, and she looked as shocked and concerned as he did as she stepped over to him. He lifted the gem to his mouth and summoned the magic to activate it. It glowed red slightly as he said, "Is everyone okay? Are you okay?"

For several long minutes he just stood there looking at the gem waiting for it to light up indicating that she had replied. Eventually he sat down on the edge of the bed. Cynia climbed onto the bed and crawled up behind him. She sat on her feet and put one knee to either side of him, and then she rested her head against the base of his neck. She wrapped both arms around him, stroking his arm softly with one hand.

When the gem took on a green glow his heart jumped. Then he paused another moment, not really wanting to know, but at the same time he needed to know the answer. He activated the gem, and Sarasa's voice said quickly, "Kimly and Jessa captured. Burga was killed. I'm so sorry!"

He jumped up and bolted for the door. His heart was pounding wildly, and everything seemed like a blur. He couldn't believe that his best friend since childhood had been killed. Jessa was like a little sister to him. He had no idea what he was going to do, but his soul screamed out that he must do something. He sprinted down the hallway, and bounced down the stairs two at a time. He was going too fast to make the quick turn at the base of the stairs, and he crashed loudly into the wall. He pushed himself away from the wall and sprinted over to where Sarge and Gordo sat.

"We've got to go, now!" He was out of breath, and not thinking clearly. He wanted to cry, or shout and scream. Burning something down might feel pretty good, but mostly he needed to feel like he was doing something helpful.

Sarge stood up and looked at Rissyl, "What's going on?"

He glanced down at the gem in his hand before he answered, and it was glowing a soft green. He held up his finger to tell Sarge to hang on. He took a deep breath and tried to catch his breath. Then he activated the gem. Sarasa's voice said, "We're headed to Clornoss. You finish your mission! We're counting on you!"

Gordo stood next to Sarge, both of them looking at him with expectant expressions. "The emperor's men have ambushed some of our Magi in Sorgo. My close friend Burga was killed. His sister Jessa and our new Magi Kimly were both captured. Apparently, the rest of our new Magi in Sorgo have scattered. Dalen and the others are headed to the imperial capital of Clornoss right now to try to rescue Kimly and Jessa."

A great deal of banging and thumping echoed down the stairs, and when Rissyl looked that way he saw Cynia carrying her packs and dragging his pack down the stairs. She dragged the load over to the others and dropped Rissyl's bags at his feet. She said, "Pack your gear, gentlemen. It's time to go."

He was relieved that she was thinking the same thing that he was.

"Well, slow down." Sarge held up his hand. "What exactly do you suggest we do, at this time of the night? We're tired, it's already nighttime, and we have rooms paid for. There is no reason to run off hastily. I'm sorry about your friends, but the things we have to do can wait until morning. We still don't even know where we're going."

Rissyl said, "I've been thinking about where we need to go. This inn was built to handle dwarven trade caravans, so this road must take us to the entrance of the dwarven kingdom. We're going to start there."

"The text books do talk about abandoned dwarven mines, maybe the dwarves can at least point us towards those mines?" Cynia nodded enthusiastically. "Good thinking!"

"That settles it, then." Sarge nodded his agreement, "First thing in the morning we'll head that way."

Rissyl was about to respond, but Cynia stepped in front of him and got into Sarge's face. He was almost a foot taller than she was, but she poked him in the chest and said, "We're leaving now. You will go and grab your gear and come with us, or you might well head down to Grum'Glin to help the others, because you'll just slow us down."

With that, Gordo turned and made his way to the stairs. Sarge looked at her in surprise, and then slowly turned. He pushed his copper coins towards the farmer and then followed Gordo up the stairs.

"I'll carry our bags out to the new wagon, if you'll go to the stable and get the horse. I'd like to be traveling as soon as possible." She nodded to him and headed outside.

They traveled through the night, taking turns sleeping in pairs in the back of the wagon as it bounced noisily down the road. By the time the sun peeked over the hills in the east, everyone had enjoyed a few hours of mostly sleepless rest.

Gordo drove the wagon and Sarge walked out in front of it as they made their way up the rough trail towards the entrance to the dwarven kingdom.

Rissyl felt like troll dung. His back hurt, and his head didn't feel much better. He looked over at Cynia and she looked worse than he felt. "You look terrible."

She made a rude gesture at him and said, "Yeah? I feel worse than that. What genius came up with the idea of sleeping in the wagon? That sucked."

From the front of the wagon, Gordo said, "That would be Rissyl. Yes, it did suck. And that's coming from the ex-Dreg who used to sleep on gravel and boulders."

Cynia said, "Next time just tie my feet to the back of the wagon, and pull me along behind it while I sleep. At least then I'll have some soft dirt clods and clumps of grass for my head to bang against, instead of slamming into the side of the wagon repeatedly."

Gordo laughed and added, "I was thinking about grabbing a net and suspending myself under the wagon. I might get run over a few times, or get horse dung splashed on my head, but it'd be much better than trying to sleep in the back of the wagon and sliding slivers into my legs all night."

"Oh, you guys are hilarious. Really, please don't stop." They both laughed at him, as he slid on his boots and jumped off the back of the wagon.

"We're just giving you a hard time, Riz." She put on her shoes and jumped off the back of the wagon, walking over next to him as he walked beside the wagon.

They walked quietly for a few hours. Slowly, the hills to the sides grew taller, and before long the road traveled through a valley with high walls on either side. The valley was dozens of feet wide, and the closer they got to the base of the mountains, the more steep the walls along the valley became.

"Is it just me, or does this place give you the creeps?" Rissyl scanned the ridges of the valley walls on both sides of them as they walked.

Cynia shook her head no, "It ain't just you." She pointed ahead, "Look, Sarge is slowing down to let us catch up. He must feel uncomfortable too."

Before long, the wagon caught up with Sarge and he whispered, "Have you noticed how quiet it is in here? No birds. No creatures of any type making noises? Something is not right. Stay on guard." He picked up the pace, drawing his sword as he walked.

Rissyl and Cynia both summoned their staffs as they walked next to the wagon. Before long, two Rolimi pups appeared, walking between them. Both pups were quite a bit larger than they had been the last time Rissyl had seen them. They were about the size of small watermelons. Both pups walked slightly ahead of them, Rissyl's reddish pup on the left and Cynia's greenish pup on the right, sniffing the ground and looking around as they walked. Neither one made a sound.

For several more minutes, they walked quietly through the valley. They continued to pass various terraces traveling up and down the valley walls where people or animals could climb up and down the valley walls fairly easily. Nothing happened. Rissyl was starting to think that all of the caution and stress was unwarranted.

He looked over at Cynia and asked, "What does your magesight show? From what I've read, we're just starting to scratch the surface of the possible uses for our magesight. Especially for a Diviner."

She nodded, "That's a good point. I hadn't thought of that. Lemme try."

Almost immediately, she gasped and started to fall. He grabbed her quickly, barely able to keep her head from slamming into the ground. He knelt at her side, "Cynia! What's wrong, are you okay?"

She looked all around, blinking quickly. Then she looked at him and said, "We've gotta get the sard outta of here, now!"

He picked her up, carried her to the back of the wagon, and placed her onto it. Then he ran up next to the front of the wagon and said to Gordo, "We've got to get out of this valley now, get that horse going faster!" He started running to catch up with Sarge.

The old warrior heard the rhythm of the horse steps change, and he looked back to see Rissyl running. He started running as Rissyl caught up with him. He asked, "Why are we running?"

As he ran next to Sarge he said, "Cynia used her magesight and had some sort of vision. She insists that we need to get out of this valley quickly."

The two Magi continued to run with the horse pulling the wagon wildly right behind them. Slowly, the wagon overtook them and Rissyl and Sarge both grabbed the end of the wagon and pulled themselves up onto it.

Gordo continued to push the horse to gallop faster, and it pulled the wagon as fast as it could for several long minutes. Eventually, the sides of the valley sloped away from them and the valley opened up. Being near the base of the mountains, there were still sharp slopes nearby, but the road no longer felt enclosed and dangerous.

He slowed the horse considerably, and let it travel at a quick trot for several long minutes before Sarge said, "Okay I think that's good. Let's stop for a minute and rest that horse." Then he looked at Cynia and asked, "What did you see?"

She held her head in her hands as if she was trying to keep it from coming apart. She massaged her fingers on her forehead and temples and then answered, "I saw a caravan of dwarves in that valley, and there was a rain of arrows from both sides of the cliff walls! Right after that, the walls became alive with monsters! They poured down the terraces from the cliff walls and swarmed the dwarves! Within seconds the entire valley floor was crawling with these creatures!"

"What did the creatures look like?" Sarge asked.

Rissyl added, "Were they goblins or something?"

"I dunno! They were bigger than goblins, I think. Meaner! They were green and brown in color and many of them had dark hair on their heads. Lots of them had large hair spikes, with tattoos or markings all over their faces."

Sarge nodded, "Orcs. There are several orc clans in these parts, and they commonly tattoo their faces and bodies, but I haven't heard of them ambushing dwarves. Are you sure that what you saw was a vision and not just some sort of dream or illusion?"

She shook her head, "No, it wasn't a dream. I saw it with my magesight, I'm certain that this either happened recently or will happen soon. We didn't notice any signs of a battle, so I'm guessing it hasn't happened yet."

"Ok, then we'll let the horse rest a bit, and then we'll carry on, but keep your eyes open." Sarge climbed down and started walking ahead of the wagon. After a minute, Rissyl and Cynia hopped down from the wagon and Gordo urged the horse forward.

Up ahead, a wagon came into view, coming from behind a hill off in the distance. As it got closer, Rissyl could see it was pulled by several mules, and there were several armored dwarves walking in formation on either side of it.

Cynia exclaimed, "That's the dwarven caravan from my vision!"

"Let's go warn them!" Rissyl and Cynia both hurried to catch up with

Sarge, who was already waving his arms to get the caravan to stop.

When it stopped, five dwarves walked down to meet the Magi in the middle of the valley.

Sarge said, "Hail, dwarves. Beware of danger ahead."

Four of the approaching dwarves were dressed the same, in full platemail armor with a grey-plumed helm, and a large two-handed battleax strapped over one shoulder. The fifth dwarf was also in plate armor, but he wore a green and grey sash across his armor, and a number of pins and medals adorned the sash. This dwarf wore a green-plumed helm, and he reached up and opened the visor as he stopped before Sarge. "Magi, yer interferin' with the emissary to King Drilzad the Fourth, Chief of the Imlak Clan and the High King of Mazbakhar Halls! Stand aside!"

Cynia stepped forward, "Respected dwarf, I've had a vision of the valley ahead. There will be an ambush of orcs, and your caravan will be slaughtered!"

The green-plumed dwarf slammed his visor closed, "You ain't seen dwarves fight, have you? We're fierce! Ain't no foul orcs could best us!" The dwarf turned around and his guards followed him back to the caravan.

The three Magi stood and watched the dwarves walk back. Rissyl scratched his head. He didn't know if the dwarves planned to ignore their warning. He looked to Sarge, "Will they ignore us?"

The old warrior shrugged, "I doubt it. Dwarves are stubborn and braggarts, but they ain't stupid. We'll see."

The group of dwarves returned to the caravan and several dwarves got together and talked for quite a while. Several times, they looked or pointed down towards the Magi or further down the valley. Eventually, several dwarves began walking back to the Magi.

The dwarf with the green sash led the way, with a dozen grey-plumed dwarven warriors along with him. When they reached the Magi he said, "In yer vision, was the orcs comin' from the east or comin' from the west?"

Cynia thought about it for a moment and then pointed east, "Most were coming from that way."

Without another word, the dwarves started walking towards the east side of the valley.

Rissyl and the others followed the dwarves, several feet behind them. When they got near their wagon Sarge said, "Gordo, park the wagon over there. Tie the horse to something, and then come join us."

The Magi followed the dwarves down the east side of the valley. As soon as the dwarves found a place to get up on higher ground, they moved up there. They continued to make their way across the tops of the hills on the east side of the valley, and slowly the valley walls grew higher and higher. Before too long they were walking across the tops of the east side of the valley wall. They reached the spot where the valley narrowed down to an effective ambush point.

Gordo caused himself to become invisible, and the two Rolimi pups bounded ahead until they were even with the dwarves. Eventually, the group of dwarves stopped and took up positions behind some rocks. They whispered to themselves making some sort of plans as Rissyl and the other Magi got close enough to see what was going on.

When he got closer, Rissyl hid behind a large boulder, and peeked around to see what everyone else was looking at. Far ahead, back away from the edge that looked down onto the valley, was a crude hide tent, with several large orcs seated around a crude table. Standing near them was the unmistakable form of a necromancer in black robes. Ahead and to the right, near the edge of the cliff, he could see several large orcs behind boulders, looking down into the valley.

He pulled Cynia closer and whispered, "Can you control the magesight? Can you make it show you what's going to happen soon? How much control do you have over it?"

She shook her head no and held up her hands in question. She whispered, "From what I've read I can. I ain't never tried it! I dunno if I can?"

He said, "You've got to try! We need every advantage! If these dwarves storm that tent, all of those orcs are going to swarm us."

She nodded and said, "I'll try." She held tight to the boulder, and peeked around to see the orcs with her magesight.

Rissyl looked over to the dwarves and saw that Sarge was talking to them. He didn't think he wanted to know what they were planning.

Cynia leaned back against him, and then turned to him and held him tightly. She whispered urgently into his chest, "We've gotta go, let's just run back to the wagon now!"

He pulled her away and said, "What did you see? Anything that can help us?"

She shook her head no fiercely, "No! You're gonna die! And Sarge, and all of the dwarves!"

He shook her slightly. "Stop it! Focus! How do we die, what happens?"

"I dunno! I just see you lying a few feet from here, with a thousand arrows in your body! The dwarf leader is dead with a large crossbow bolt in his chest. I can't do this, Riz!" She whispered through tears.

He squeezed her shoulder, "Yes you can! Take a deep breath, and calm down. Try the magesight again. Try to see what happens before we all die."

She gripped the boulder again, and looked out towards the orcs with her magesight.

Sarge came up to Rissyl and said, "The dwarves are gonna focus on those archers, and they want us to handle the 'mancer."

Rissyl held up his finger to urge Sarge to be quiet for a moment, and he looked at Cynia.

After several long breaths, she turned back to him and looked over at Sarge. She said, "This is what my magesight shows me… The dwarves are gonna engage the archers, while we try to attack the necromancer. One of the orcs at the table is gonna pull a crossbow and kill the dwarf leader instantly. The archers are gonna turn their attack on us, because we're not armored and our cloaks won't protect us much against arrows. You two will both be killed by arrows not far from here. The necromancer will begin raising our dead to fight against us, as the other orcs swarm over that wall and overwhelm the rest of us."

Rissyl hugged her and whispered, "That's great!"

Cynia and Sarge both looked at him as if he had lost is mind.

"No, listen. Now we know that won't work, and we have an advantage. Gordo, where are you?"

A soft voice near Rissyl said, "Right here."

"Good! Now, get over there and get ready to kill that orc with the crossbow! As soon as you see the dwarves emerge from these rocks, you kill that bastard!" Rissyl waited for an answer.

Gordo whispered, "Got it!"

"I am going to teleport to the far side of the orc camp over there. I'm going to try to kill the necromancer quickly, and then I will turn my fiery attention to orcs." Rissyl looked to Cynia and Sarge for their input.

Sarge thought for a moment and said, "Then maybe I'll take out some of those archer bastards before they make us all holey. I'll see if I can get the dwarves to focus on that table of orcs, and whatever swarm comes after us."

Pulling a textbook from her bag, Cynia said, "Let me see if I can find something really fast!" She started turning pages quickly.

"But first…" Sarge stopped and turned around to face Rissyl. He grabbed

Rissyl's shoulder. He concentrated for a moment and then whispered, "Arg'Tholba!" Then he did the same thing while touching his own shoulder. Finally, he grabbed Cynia's shoulder and cast the spell on her as well. Without another word he hurried over to the dwarves.

"I found it!" Cynia whispered, as she pointed at something in the book. She began reading quickly.

Rissyl thumbed through his textbook quickly. He had only tried teleporting a couple of times before. Both of those times he had only teleported a very short distance, and never under pressure. He just wanted to review the spell really quick to make sure that he had everything down properly. As soon as he got to the right page he heard some sort of commotion coming from the orcs.

Suddenly he saw Sarge and the dwarves rush from behind their boulders with savage battle cries!

He saw Cynia still reading her spell book intently, and he assumed she would be safest behind the boulder anyway, unless the orcs swarmed the place. He stepped to his left to give himself a clear shot between him and his intended destination. He watched as Gordo became visible and grabbed the shoulder of the orc at the table with the crossbow. Rissyl's heart sunk when he realized that Gordo hadn't even attempted to kill the orc! It turned to face Gordo, and then it turned back the way it had been facing. The orc grabbed its crossbow and aimed it right at the necromancer! The evil spellcaster didn't even have time to react. The orc squeezed the trigger and a large crossbow quarrel slammed directly into the heart of the necromancer! Rissyl wanted to shout with joy! Apparently, Gordo had been paying attention during the charm spells lectures after all.

A loud trumpet sounded a single note from his right, near Sarge and the dwarves.

Rissyl snapped himself out of spectator mode and began to summon the magic to teleport himself to the other side of the orc's tent. He molded and formed the magical essence within himself, using just as much as he needed to blink a few hundred feet. He said, "Kur'Gezbar!"

~ Fizzle ~

He cursed to himself. He hated that sound! Nothing announced that someone was a loser Magi like the unmistakable metallic buzzing sound of a spell failure. He started the summoning again and felt something bump up against him. He looked at the ground and there was an arrow laying on the ground next to him! Sarge's protection spell must have worked! He just hoped that it continued to work as another arrow ricocheted from his shoulder. He quickly formed the spell, molding the magic as quickly as he could. He said, "Kur'Gezbar!"

All of a sudden he felt slightly disoriented as he disappeared from where he was, and immediately reappeared on the other side of the orc tent! The necromancer was already dead, and he hoped that Gordo could deal with the remaining orcs at the table. He turned his attention further to the south, which he could now see much better since he was on the south side of the orc tent.

The swarm was already heading towards them! Tons of orcs were running from their hiding places, climbing from the wall terraces, and racing to answer the trumpet call. He wanted to shout to his companions to warn them, but they were busy with their own battles. That left this mass of orcs to him. He waved his right hand in the air in a circle as he summoned the magic for his spell. He shouted, "Krol'Tu Salindi" and a large ball of fire appeared in his hand as it circled around for a final time. The motion of his circling propelled the five foot wide ball of fire through the air at the orcs that were racing forward.

The large ball of fire landed on the ground slightly in front of a large group of the creatures, and then it burst and splattered in the direction that it had been traveling. It spread across the ground and quickly covered several of the screaming creatures with fire! The sticky fire coated the orcs unlucky enough to be in its path, and within moments, those flaming orcs fell to the ground dead!

Rissyl wasted no time. He started circling his hand again to summon another large ball of fire. Even though his last one had taken out nearly a dozen of the ferocious creatures, more and more spilled up onto the ledge every second and he knew that he didn't have enough magic in his magewel to kill them all this way.

He shouted, "Krol'Tu Salindi" and launched another ball of fire at the creatures!

To his right, he heard Cynia's voice as she yelled the vocal component to whatever spell she was casting. He glanced over at her in time to see her slam her staff into the ground. The earth before her began to shake and a large crack formed in the ground before her! The crack raced away from her and travelled south towards the approaching mass of orcs!

The ground below Rissyl's feet began to shake and he looked to his left to see the crack Cynia created begin to expand and swallow up some orcs as it raced forward. The shaking ground intensified, and soon several large boulders began to topple off the edge of the cliff. The screams of orcs falling from the cliff terraces and being crushed by falling rocks continued to grow. However, they were mostly drowned out by the shaking earth and rocks from Cynia's spell.

As quickly as it started, the motion of the ground began to quiet. The crack that had formed became more stable, and eventually everything stopped shaking. The screams of dying orcs echoed through the area. Then a single trumpet called out a three note melody that started low, then went high, and then went to a note between the first two. This melody repeated over and over. Soon more trumpets issues the same three note melody.

Orcs began to retreat! Rissyl watched as the mass of orcs that remained south of him turned and started running at full speed to the southeast. The few orcs that remained alive to climb up from the cliff-wall terraces also ran to the southeast.

He turned and ran to Cynia. He held her protectively with one hand as he looked around to assess the situation in this area. She had moved to the east of the crack that she had formed, which was narrow and not very deep near her.

When he looked to the orc tent he saw several orc bodies lying on the ground. Gordo was injured and bleeding quite a bit.

Cynia said, "I'll go see to Gordo's wounds!"

He let her go without saying anything and turned to see how things had gone with the archers. Near the cliff edge, he saw Sarge helping one of the dwarves to his feet. Rissyl saw several dwarves, including the one who wore the green sash, wiping blood from their battleaxes. He quickly counted ten dwarves plus the leader. That left two dwarves missing. Orc archers and other orc warriors were lying dead everywhere.

The trumpet sounds continued to ring through the area, as they faded into the distance. To the south, Rissyl saw a handful of wounded orcs straggling behind the rest of the group as they struggled to climb to the top of the cliff and chase after their retreating companions.

He walked over to Sarge slowly. He assessed his magewel and found that he hadn't drained it too badly. He felt like he still had about two thirds of his magical essence available to him.

The greying Magi held out his hand to Rissyl. "Great job, kid. I'm glad you didn't get yourself killed, blinking into the thick of things like that."

He laughed, "Well, old man, I'm glad you didn't break a hip killing all these orcs, but I think we all owe our lives to Cynia over there."

Sarge laughed. "We'll see if the hip is broken. I'm sure gonna be sore tomorrow. I'm getting too old for this crap." He paused and looked over at Cynia. "Yes, she did a great job. Let's go see if Gordo's gonna pull through."

The green-plumed dwarf followed them over.

Cynia said, "It ain't too bad. He'll make it, but he's gonna need stitches."

Looking to the dwarf, Sarge said, "Sorry to make you late in your travels for the king."

The dwarf looked at him, and then looked around the battlefield. He said, "Magi, this day you saved our arse! Where you headed?"

Rissyl answered, "We are trying to travel through the mountains, to reach the lands on the north side."

"I dunno if that's possible?" The dwarf put his fists on his hips and looked north. "Let's go ask the king. My mission can hold a few hours. We got a fortnight of travelin' before we get to Clornoss; few more hours ain't gonna change much."

"Wait, you're traveling to the capital of the empire? Are you merchants?" Rissyl was surprised, and his shock was easily apparent on his face.

The dwarf shook his head. "No, the vile emperor double-crossed us. He took as captives several dwarves and he's demandin' a huge delivery of garroliron or he ain't gonna release them."

Sarge and Rissyl looked at each other in question, and then back to the dwarf. Rissyl asked, "Garroliron?"

"Garroliron! Very rare ore that can only be mined in the deepest mines. It's supposed to have anti-magic powers. Ryal's been buyin' small amounts of it for years, but now he demands a crazy amount and he's holding dwarves hostage to get it!"

Rissyl let out a curse, but when the others looked his way he just shook his head. He made a mental note to discuss the situation with the other Magi when they were alone. He realized that the emperor must have found a way to use this garroliron to his advantage, which might explain how the Magi in Sorgo were ambushed.

He said, "Yes, if you would be willing to take us to your king that would be fantastic. Thank you for your offer."

"You saved our skins, it's the least we can do. By the way, I'm Marshal Gruknor, commander of the armies of Imlak Clan, second son of King Drilzad, and second heir to the throne of the Mazbakhar Halls."

The chambers within the Mazbakhar Halls were breathtaking. Rissyl found himself staring around in wonder as they followed Marshal Gruknor through the maze of corridors and chambers. The stone work was exquisite, and he marveled at the detailed artwork in even the most mundane locations. Every stone column was finely carved. Every door frame and baseboard had elaborate details and designs. He realized that it must have taken dwarven artisans several centuries to craft such amazing structures throughout their underground kingdom.

Every hallway was clean. He was astonished at the lack of dust and trash in an underground fortress filled with presumably thousands of dwarves. The further they travelled into the halls, the more crowded the corridors became. It took many dwarves to make twenty foot wide corridors seem crowded.

Rissyl was utterly lost by the time Marshal Gruknor stopped at a large set of double doors. Two fully-armored dwarves with halberds stood guard at the door. The doors were elaborately carved with large dwarven script and a detailed battle scene. The marshal approached one of the guards and said something to him quietly.

The guard pointed towards a long stone bench and said, "Humans, have a seat there. Prince Gruknor, you may enter."

The four Magi sat outside the doors for several hours. Rissyl was pulled from his thoughts by a new sound. It was a low rhythmic bell tolling. He looked to the others and they looked as surprised at the new echoing sound as he was. The guards didn't seem alarmed so Rissyl stayed on his bench.

Shortly after the bell started sounding, Gruknor returned and took a seat with them. He said, "Shouldn't be much longer." He then began giving the Magi instructions for proper etiquette when meeting and speaking to the dwarven king.

Soon, a crowd of dwarves arrived and began filing into the room beyond the doors, and still the Magi waited. A few minutes later, the guard called Gruknor and the Magi forward. He opened the door wide and motioned for them to enter. Marshal Gruknor went in first, followed by Sarge, Gordo, Cynia, and finally Rissyl. The guard walked into the room and announced loudly, "Junior Prince Gruknor, and guests!"

The room was a massive circle, at least two hundred feet in diameter. The ceiling was a huge dome. The room was shaped like a shallow bowl, with benches lining the outer portion of the room in concentric circles, taking up more than half of the diameter of the room. The center part of the room was separated from the benches by a low wall. Long narrow tapestries lined the low walls, depicting large battles between dwarven warriors and fantastic creatures of all varieties.

At the far end of the room was a small platform with a single throne upon it. The dwarven High King Drilzad sat upon it with four guards standing motionlessly behind him. The rows of benches around the room were filled with hundreds of dwarves, most of whom wore colorful outfits made from fine cloth.

Gruknor led the Magi to the far side of the room, and stopped before the king. He said, "Most Illustrious High King Drilzad, these're the brave Magi who fought beside me and me caravan."

The king stood and bowed slightly to the five people before him. When he did so, the entire group of dwarves in the benches stood and bowed low to the five people in the middle of the chamber. The king stood straight again after a moment and said, "Honored guests of Mazbakhar Halls, tell us yer names and yer home cities."

The four Magi looked at each other quickly and Sarge held out his hand for Rissyl to go first. He stepped forward and said, "Most Illustrious High King, I am Rissyl Sokigo, of the Order of Evokers of the Sovereign Magi Society. I was born in Sorgo, within the Ryallic Empire."

The king's jaw dropped open slightly in surprise as he leaned forward in his chair, as a collective gasp of shock and a scattered muttering could be heard around the room. He said, "An imperial?" He looked from one Magi to the next as they stood before him. "What business has an imperial in the lands of the Free Cities, and within me halls?"

Rissyl straightened his back slightly in pride. "Honored King, the Society acknowledges no boundaries or arbitrary borders of men. I was born in the empire, but I am not an imperial. I am a Magi, and we are on an urgent Society mission."

King Drilzad looked like he may ask another question, and then he held out his hand encouraging the next Magi to introduce themselves. Cynia stepped forward next, as Rissyl stepped back.

She said, "Most Illustrious High King, I'm Cynia Dodisen of the Order of Diviners of the Sovereign Magi Society. I was also born in Sorgo, within the Ryallic Empire. I was a Dreg, and Rissyl freed me."

Holding up his hand, the king said, "Tell me of this class, Dreg. I do not know the term."

"Dregs are slaves of the empire."

He made an expression of disgust, "Slaves? Haven't even humans moved beyond slavery?" He paused, and then added, "Even the savage orcs don't enslave their own kind." The king motioned for the next Magi to introduce himself and Cynia stepped back.

Sarge took a step forward, "Most Illustrious High King, I am Theodonis Sinclaritis, of the Order of Champions of the Sovereign Magi Society and formerly the First Sergeant of the Misil'Kaylian Army, but I'm more commonly called simply Sarge. I am originally from the Free City of Misil'Kayl."

The king nodded his head to the Magi, "Then yer truly a hero. Stories of the bravery of the Misil'Kaylians have been told by many bards. Yet one more example of the bravery shown today as you fought beside me kinsmen."

Finally the king motioned to Gordo, who stepped forward. "Most Highest Honored Dwarf, sir." He bowed awkwardly.

Rissyl groaned internally. Gordo had always been a bit awkward in social situations, but Rissyl really thought that going last he would see how the others acted, and that he would remember the instructions that Gruknor had given them. He clinched his teeth together hoping the odd fellow could keep it together for just a brief introduction without saying anything too embarrassing.

Gordo continued without pausing, "I'm Gordo Swann, but you can call me Gordo. All my friends call me Gordo. Not that we're exactly friends yet, but then I did help save your son and all."

The king raised an eyebrow and glanced at Gruknor. Rissyl wanted to cover Gordo's mouth, and then perhaps crawl under a rock.

Still Gordo kept talking, "So, like those two, I'm also an imperial. Well, I used to be an imperial, and then they made me a Dreg which really sucked, but I escaped, and Sarge here rescued me from a cage. And then Rissyl over there freed me from being a Dreg! Oh, and now I'm a Magi and in the Shadows Order." He paused and started to step back. Then he said, "And I have to say, this place is great! You little dwarves really know how to carve stone! This is really very-"

Sarge grabbed Gordo by the collar and pulled him back in line. Rissyl could hear Sarge whisper something, but he couldn't make out what he said.

"Thank you Gordo." The king paused for a moment, and Rissyl had the horrifying thought that the king was trying to suppress a laugh. The last thing he wanted was for the king of the dwarves to not take them seriously. "Me son told me of yer extreme bravery. You could've carried on past the caravan and not even warned them. Instead, you followed them into the face of a powerful enemy. Together you all brought a glorious victory over our hated foes!"

The king motioned for one of the guards to step forward, and he took something from the guard. Then the king walked down from his platform. He walked up to Rissyl first and held out a shiny golden medallion suspended from a green and grey ribbon. Rissyl was shocked, and wasn't exactly sure if he should take it from the dwarven king, but the king held it up as if he meant to put it over Rissyl's head. The top of the king's head only came up to Rissyl ribs, so he knelt down and bowed his head forward. The king placed the ribbon over Rissyl's head and then he stood back up.

Then the king moved and put a similar medallion, on the same kind of ribbon, over the heads of the other three Magi. When he was finished, he stepped back and said, "That's the Mazbakhar Valiant Warrior medal, one of the highest honors given by dwarves, given for yer valiant victory today. In five thousand years, never before has a Mazbakhar Valiant Warrior medal been given to a human. May Renarx, patron deity of all dwarves, sound his titanium hammer in yer honor and rain blessings down upon you!"

As the king walked back to his throne, Rissyl looked down at the medal around his neck. On the front was a beautifully carved image of a dwarf with a war-cry expression, holding a battleax. Also on the front of the medal, around the outside, was an intricate interwoven pattern. Across the bottom was written Mazbakhar Valiant Warrior. On the back was an engraving that said his name on one line and Sovereign Magi Society below that.

Once he got back to his throne, the king sat back down and said, "Magi, for nine centuries me ancestors have been distrusting of the Magi of yer Society. Long before the human civil war brought the death of yer Society, we dwarves denied all requests for friendship and trade with Magi. Dwarves and magic don't mix. In our long history, today is the first that a Magi has stood there before the High King!" He paused long enough to stand. "Let it be known to all, by the power of the Hammer of Renarx, that the Mazbakhar Halls and all of her clans shall treat the Sovereign Magi Society as a friend and ally."

The king sat back down and Rissyl felt himself fill with pride. Never in a million years, did he expect that they would be able to establish a meaningful friendship with a mighty new ally. He was overwhelmed, and felt more than a little unworthy.

"Prince Gruknor says yer lookin' for a way to the lands in the north. Tell me of this quest." The king looked from one Magi to the next.

Gordo started to take a step forward to answer the king, and Rissyl saw Sarge grab him by the scruff of the neck and pull him back as Rissyl took a step forward. His eyes got wide as he noticed two Rolimi pups bound up the stairs to the king's platform and plop onto the ground at the king's feet, one on either side of the dwarven king. He paused just for a moment to see if the king noticed or would react to the small Rolimi dogs, but the king didn't seem to notice them.

"Honored King, many centuries ago, the Magi established a Stronghold on the far side of the mountains, far from the influence of the human kings, to serve as their headquarters and the center of magical learning and study. After the Betrayal, when the Magi were being slaughtered, the remaining Magi took the drastic step of sealing our Stronghold completely to ensure that it didn't fall into the hands of the evil emperor. Now, as we work to rebuild our Society, we desperately need the knowledge that is locked away in the Stronghold. According to ancient textbooks, a route through the mountains exists, but it is said to be deadly and nearly impossible to successfully transverse, but we have no choice. We must make it through the mountains to our Stronghold. Even as we speak, the Ryallic Empire has resumed its attacks upon the Magi. I had a lifelong friend who has already been killed, and another who has been captured. If we have any hope of surviving another attempt by the empire to purge magic from the known lands, we must reach the Stronghold!"

The king leaned back into his throne and interlaced his fingers on top of his round belly. He thought for a long moment and said, "You'll excuse me bluntness, but if all the powerful Magi of old couldn't survive a ruthless emperor, how can the four of you be victorious? You now count the dwarves as yer allies, but surely yer allies won't fight yer battles for you."

He shook his head quickly, "Certainly not!" He struggled for a moment to come up with an answer to the king's challenge. He didn't want to sound arrogant, or fool-hearty.

Cynia took a step forward and gave a brief account of the events of the Betrayal and how the Society had been ill-prepared for the attack. After summarizing many of the points that Randol had explain to them, Cynia paused for a breath and held her head high, "Honored King, today we know full well that we are at war. We don't expect allies to fight for us, we will bring the war to the emperor, but first we must get ready. This time, we have surprise on our side. He may know that the Society is active, but he dunno how much we've grown, and he has no idea what we have planned. He has hit us and drawn blood, but the war is just getting started. Reclaiming our Stronghold is the first major step towards victory."

The king looked thoughtful. He asked, "What's yer goal? How will you know you've been victorious?"

Without pause, Cynia said, "The death of the emperor. The break-up of the empire into a number of smaller kingdoms as originally existed. And the end to slavery throughout the known world." She stood with her head held high and her arms crossed before her.

Rissyl looked at her in shock, and saw Gordo and Sarge looking at her with equal surprise. These sounded like good and valiant goals, but they had never been discussed. He looked back to the king and tried not to look too stunned at Cynia's declared goals.

The king stood up and started clapping, and every dwarf in the chamber stood up and joined in the applause. Soon the clapping was joined with rhythmic stomping and a chant that Rissyl couldn't understand. He assumed they were saying something in the ancient dwarven language.

Then the king held out his hands for silence. He sat down and the assembled crowd sat down as well. There was a buzz of whispered conversation until the king began to speak, and then people grew quiet to listen to him. He said, "Those are good and noble goals. This new empire has shown itself to be untrustworthy, warlike, and despicable. Know that the dwarves of Mazbakhar Halls support yer cause and yer goals. I am not yet willing to provide warriors for yer goals, but that day may eventually come."

The king paused, and then sat forward in his throne. "We dwarves might've been unknowingly makin' it harder for you. For decades we've traded anti-magic ore to the empire. What they're doin' with it, there's no tellin'. But startin' now, we dwarves will not provide another ounce of garroliron to the empire! They've betrayed our trust and detained one of our caravans. They're demandin' a large amount of garroliron as ransom. The caravan you protected was travelin' to bring this bounty to the empire. That was foolish! Dwarves will not be bullied or blackmailed! We will find a different way to rescue our kinsmen."

Rissyl heard murmuring through the crowd and looked over to see a dwarf step down from the benches and walk down to stand with the Magi and Gruknor. The dwarf was slightly shorter than Gruknor, but in the face he bore a strong resemblance to the marshal. He was wearing a brightly colored outfit, with many greens and greys, and he had a wide sash similar to Gruknor across his chest. He turned and faced the king and awaited to be recognized.

The king said, "Magi, lemme present me eldest son, the Sub-Chief of Imlak Clan and the High Prince of Mazbakhar Halls, Khatohar."

The dwarven prince turned and bowed slightly to the Magi. Then he turned back to the king and said, "Honored King, will our kinsmen suffer in an imperial dungeon so we can aide these humans? We owe them some trinkets and maybe coins for protecting my younger brother, but will we sacrifice the lives of our dwarven brethren for them? We must deliver the garroliron as the human emperor demands!" Several people in the crowd vocalized their support for their prince.

Two palms smacked solidly against the arms of the throne as the king pushed himself from the chair. Both Rolimi pups jumped and moved out of his way. He took a step towards his son, "There was a sick feeling in me gut when we decided to send the garroliron as the humans demanded. T'was a rash decision, and it was wrong! Do we really think that the empire who slaughters and enslaves its own race would be honorable to us? They've captured Mazbakhar dwarves for no reason. This is an act of war! We were fools to think of cowering before them like whipped dogs! Maybe seeing the courage of these brave Magi was the kick in the dwarven arse we needed to remember that dwarves do not bow to the demands of humans!"

The crowd erupted into thunderous cheering and applause. Even prince Khatohar clapped loudly.

"Marshal Gruknor, alert yer top StoneWalkers squad to prepare to rescue our brethren from imperial captivity!"

Stepping forward, Gruknor bowed deeply. "Yes, Honored King!"

"Prince Khatohar, you'll get the Halls into a wartime routine! We need to assume our rescue mission will bring war with the humans. We must be prepared. Have the smithies start makin' plenty of armor and weapons for battle. Recruit and train new warriors, our army's size needs to be tripled as quickly as possible. Make all other plans as needed for food, ballista, siege machines, and the like. Assemble the commanders to begin making these and other plans."

The king paused as his eldest son bowed and said, "Yes, Honored King."

Then he continued, "Ladies and fellow dwarves, the Magi bring stories of slavery, warfare, and a nation willin' to murder its own people. Let this remind us, we can't sit back in apathy like the Magi of old. Next, the human emperor may show up at the door of Mazbakhar Halls to slaughter and enslave us! We've been blind, and that ends today. We value peace, but it's time to prepare for war. We'll not cower before any threat!"

The crowd of dwarves was worked into a frenzy, and a roar of yelling and chants echoed throughout the chamber. Rissyl felt proud and inspired, and he wasn't even a dwarf. He hoped that his arrival to these halls did not lead to unnecessary dwarven deaths, but he felt confident that the king had taken their warnings seriously, even if he hadn't originally intended to warn them about anything.

The dwarven king waited for the crowd to calm down. Then he said, "And finally, Magi. There's a way to the north side of the mountains, through the Mazbakhar Halls. The route you spoke of is indeed extremely treacherous, but that is a different route. The route through the Mazbakhar Halls has been closed off for centuries, but you'll have a team of dwarven miners lead you to the other side. It'll take several days, but soon you'll reach yer goal of finding yer Magi Stronghold!"

At once, all of the Magi expressed their appreciation to the king with cheers and happy-dances. With a huge smile Rissyl stepped forward and said, "Honored King, thank you so much for your generous offer of support!"

At the king's feet, Rissyl's reddish Rolimi pup suddenly jumped on top of Cynia's greenish pup and started biting its ear. That resulted in a rolling blur of Rolimi pups wrestling around the platform at the feet of the dwarven king, and no one even noticed except the Magi. Rissyl looked over at Cynia and grinned.

Chapter 28

Kimly

As had become routine, Kimly was sitting in the chapel listening to the chaplain deliver the morning exhortation. Like normal, the chaplain wore the black and purple robes of Viator, with a long purple stole hanging down the front of his robes on either side of his chest. The symbol of Viator, a black fallen leaf, was at both ends of the stole.

She looked around the room. Jessa was sitting next to her, quietly saying the morning exhortation along with the chaplain. They had heard the same speech many times, so it wasn't surprising that Jessa might have it memorized, but Kimly was a little surprised to see her quietly saying it along with the chaplain. The girl seemed to enjoy these times just a little too much.

Sitting further away was Jarla and her daughter Tali. Both of them quietly mouthed the words of the exhortation along with the chaplain as well. Kimly rolled her eyes. She had heard the message of the god of the dark mind since she was a child, but she didn't feel all that compelled to chant his exhortation. It was more of a game to her, something fun to do to get some attention but not something to take too seriously.

In the back of the room, sitting by herself, was Narinda. Kimly watched her for a few moments, and the woman just sat there with an angry expression on her face like normal.

As soon as the exhortation was finished, the chaplain stepped away from the altar as he had done every other morning, but this time, Lord Jalinox walked in the side door and up to the altar. Kimly watched him in surprise, this was the first time she had seen him at the altar. It was also the first time that she had seen him dressed in black and purple robes like the chaplain, but he did not wear a stole.

He said, "Our god Viator demands much of his followers. In return, he offers so many blessings. Now, ladies, it is time for you to learn some of them." Lord Jalinox stepped down from behind the altar and said, "If you would follow me, we shall begin."

Jalinox led all five of them out of the chapel and down several hallways, many of which Kimly had never been in. Eventually, they came to an iron door in a large guard room. Several guards stood as Jalinox and the ladies entered, and one of the guards opened the door at Jalinox's request.

To Kimly's shock and amazement, the door opened up to the outdoors. Jalinox led the five ladies outside, and two guards followed them. He led them deep into a wooded area, to a small clearing near a pond.

The guards stopped at the tree line and simply stood guard. Jalinox encouraged the five ladies to step closer as he stood near the pond. He said, "Behold!" He held out his hand, palm up, and caused a purple orb of fire to appear in his palm! He threw it at a small rabbit nearby. The unsuspecting critter tried to run when the glowing orb flew towards it, but by then it was too late. The orb hit the rabbit, and it fell over dead.

Jalinox walked over to the rabbit carcass and picked it up. He held it by the hind feet, and held it up to Tali first. The girl looked sad but didn't turn away. Then he held it up to Jarla, Narinda, Jessa, and finally to Kimly. He said, "What is unusual about this dead rabbit?"

Jarla said, "There are no signs of damage?"

He cheered and pointed at her, "Exactly! Magical fire thrown by a Magi would cook the rabbit alive, and in looking at it, you would see burn marks, but Khalius Fire does not produce heat, and it does not burn the skin. It simply sucks the life force from the victim, leaving it dead without markings or damage. While fire consumes its fuel source as it burns, Khalius Fire consumes life force as it burns."

Jalinox began teaching all five of them how to call forth the Khalius Fire. He said, "To call Khalius Fire, you must pray to Viator with your whole heart! It doesn't matter if you thank him for blessings, beg him to smite your enemies, or if you simply curse your foes in his name. Be creative! Your new lord enjoys your hate-filled curses and prayers for vengeance and revenge! Dig deep; don't be afraid to show your distain for those beneath you! Remember, each orb of Khalius Fire takes a little part of your life force with it, be careful not to visit Viator in the purple fire pits of Khalius prematurely by calling on his gifts for too long."

He spent the next few hours teaching them the nuances of how to harness the power of the prayer into Khalius Fire.

Soon after, all five ladies stood at the far side of the forest having different levels of success calling the purple fire. As much as she didn't want to admit it, Kimly did enjoy learning the new power. Calling the Khalius Fire felt completely different from summoning magic as a Magi, which currently she couldn't do because of the dreadful metal bracelets. At this point, she welcomed every chance for power that she could get. Calling Khalius Fire took a sincere prayer to Viator, the god of death. That was the hardest part for her, as she had never been very good at sincere prayers.

The ladies practiced for quite a while. Eventually all of them, even little Tali, were able to toss purple fire orbs at will. The extended practice left Kimly feeling weaker and drained, like she was in the middle of an ugly case of fever.

Eventually, Jalinox called them back over to him. He said, "Our lord Viator will restore the life force that you consume to use his powers, but he rewards those who help themselves. If you want to restore your life force without waiting for it to recover naturally, you can always take it from something else. For instance, this dead rabbit. It doesn't need its life force anymore, and every hour that it lays there decomposing is another hour that its life force will slowly drain on its own. The Khalius Fire consumed enough of the rabbit's life force to cause it to die. However, there should still be some life force in the corpse for you to claim for yourself. Better for you to consume that life force than let it seep into the dirt. I'll show you how."

He looked at the guards standing near the tree line and said, "We're going to be a while. One of you run back and fetch us all some food and drinks."

Kimly completely lost track of time as she listened to Jalinox explain how to reach into a corpse and steal its life force. She spent the first few hours being completely confused. She had never even considered such a thing, and certainly had never heard anyone talk about it being done, but eventually she learned how to do it. She was shocked at the amount of life force she could feel within the little dead rabbit once she understood the basics. It was creepy and more than a little repulsive. The life force felt tainted, and she realized that introducing it into her own body was probably unnatural and unholy. She thought that doing it very often just might drive her just a little loony, but it was also oddly intoxicating and exhilarating.

As the sun began to set, the six of them sat down in the dirt to eat a quick meal retrieved by the guard. As they ate, Jessa looked over at Jalinox and said, "My lord, are you teaching us to be necromancers?"

He flashed her a big smile, "Necromancer is such an ugly word, with such a bad reputation. We prefer to use the title Dark Apostle. Or for someone of a lower status we would use the title of Priestess of Death, but both classes have their missions to carry out."

Tali looked up and said, "What mission will we have?"

"I'm glad you asked! Some of you will have the most important mission of all. A mission of exploration and discovery! We are trying to find an ancient ring that unlocks the most important treasure of the Dark Apostles! Whoever finds that ring will receive rewards beyond their wildest dreams, but which of you get to take on that important mission still remains to be seen."

Kimly felt a chill run down her spine. She wasn't sure whether she was afraid she would get that mission, or afraid that she wouldn't.

After they finished eating, Jalinox said, "Narinda, dear, please take our little bunny over there and bury it."

She looked at him with a disgusted and annoyed expression and said, "I don't have a shovel."

"The ground is soft, use your hands."

The woman wasn't gone long, and when she returned Jalinox pulled a large oddly-shaped stone from a pocket. It was about the size of his fist. He said, "Do any of you know what this is?" They all shook their head to indicate a negative response. "This is a Khalius Wicket. It is used to open a portal to the Outer Plane of Khalius."

"Khalius, as in the fiery pits of Khalius? Khalius the place of eternal death and damnation? That very same Khalius?" Kimly was incredulous that one would choose to go to Khalius.

He nodded, "Yes, but the Outer Plane. The section of Khalius that is nearest to us. It is devoid of fire and brimstone." He tossed the Khalius Wicket on the ground and it looked like a hole opened up in the ground beside it. Jalinox looked at the ladies and said, "Well, don't just stand there. Jump in."

Without hesitation Tali jumped in, and Jarla jumped in right behind her. Kimly was pretty confident that both of them had lost their minds. She looked to Jessa to express her surprise that the first two had jumped in so quickly, but as she looked to her, Jessa stepped forward and jumped into the hole.

Kimly took a step back and looked to Narinda. She looked at Jalinox and he motioned for her to jump in. With little hesitation Narinda jumped in. Kimly asked, "How long will that hole stay open?" She looked into the hole and it was just a vast, empty, black nothingness. She couldn't see any of the people who had already jumped in.

"I'm using my power to hold it open. Once I jump in, the hole will close behind me. Then it will just look to those up here, like any random stone sitting on the ground." He motioned for her to jump in, and with just another moment's hesitation she did!

She felt the sensation of falling a few feet, and then she landed in what seemed to be a circular pit about ten feet in diameter. She saw the others who had already jumped in, they were standing motionless all around her. When she looked up, it seemed like she was looking out of any large hole at the dark and starry sky above. She watched Jalinox jump into the hole with them. When he did, the roof closed and the pit became entirely dark.

She heard Jalinox calling to her, but his voice seemed to be in her head! She couldn't see anything and she couldn't hear anything. She tried to pinch herself and she realized that either she couldn't move her arm, or she couldn't feel anything with her arm. As the panic started to set in, she heard his voice in her mind again.

"Move away from your body. Come to me!"

It took a few moments to understand what he meant. She had to stop trying to move her legs, and just let her mind wander over to him. She moved away from her body and right through the wall of the pit. Looking back, she could see her body standing motionless where she left it.

"Come to me!"

His call was more of a command this time. She turned to heed his call, moving through what should be solid dirt, but felt more like walking through water. She was able to see a short distance ahead, and after a while she found the others, but they didn't look anything like she remembered them. Jalinox was no longer his normal small and skinny physique. She now saw him as large and powerful, with bulging muscles. He was at least eight feet tall and impossibly strong. At his feet were two dogs, one was obviously a puppy and the other was an adult dog. They both stayed right at his side trying to push each other out of the way in hopes of winning a pat on the head from their master. To her surprise, the bigger one started talking, and she then realized that the two dogs were Jarla and her daughter Tali.

Off to the side, she saw Jessa and Narinda. Jessa was dressed like the chaplain, but on the bottoms of her stole was the face of Jalinox. She was waving and winking at him like a young girl flirting with her first crush. Narinda, on the other hand, looked more like an animal and she was growling and hissing at Jalinox. She was slobbering profusely as she paced back and forth stalking him.

Kimly was a bit confused. Why did everyone look so different? Is that what their soul truly looked like?

Jalinox's voice flooded her mind again, "What do you see when you look upon me?"

She replied, "A large man, with powerful muscles. Why do you appear like this now?" She realized that she didn't speak out loud, but she didn't have any doubt that he could hear her.

Without responding to her, he started moving away. Everyone followed him. After a few steps, they approached a strange creature that seemed to float just below eye level. It wasn't moving, and it didn't seem solid.

Lord Jalinox said, "Tali, dear. Describe to me this creature lying up here."

She hopped forward like an ungraceful puppy, and looked up at it. She said, "I see a beautiful, fuzzy, white bunny with big floppy ears and hearts and candy floating all around him."

Then he asked, "Kimly, describe to me that creature lying there." He indicated the same creature that Tali had just been asked to describe, but it looked entirely different to her.

"I see a large rat with a long creepy tail and big, fuzzy, white floppy ears."

He made a thoughtful sound, "I wonder why this same creature looks different to everyone here. Does anyone have any idea why that is?"

Everyone was quiet for a moment, and then Jessa said, "Down here our minds show us how we view things, not how the thing really looks? Lord Jalinox, when I look at you I see a wise old man, a scholar who's holding books in one hand and a golden key of knowledge in the other."

"Yes, excellent Jessa! Very good, indeed. Here is that poor little bunny that we killed a while ago. I had Narinda bury it, so now it is accessible from within the Outer Plane of Khalius! All things buried in the ground in our world can be found by entering the Outer Plane of Khalius. We just need to use a Khalius Wicket near where the item is buried and then walk through Khalius until we discover it here. We can even bring it with us when we return to our world!"

Kimly was shocked, and intrigued. What kind of buried treasure could she find if she wandered around the place long enough?

Tali asked, "If I bury my favorite toy, someone in Khalius could come and take it?"

Jalinox nodded, "Oh yes! And not just buried toys. Anything buried in the ground in our world!"

"Treasure?" Kimly couldn't help but smile when she said it, but she wasn't sure if anyone could see that she was smiling. Maybe she just looked like a non-smiling squid or something to them?

He replied, "Most definitely yes! We often find lost treasures."

Jessa said, "Dead corpses?"

"Yes! And when a Priestess of Death is hunting, it is common for her to descend into Khalius and gather up a few corpses to use as her own soldiers. That is another gift of Viator." He waited to see if there were any questions, and when none were asked he said, "Let's take this little bunny with us. Time to head back. Open your senses; you should be able to feel the direction of your body. We'll head back there now."

As she moved through the thick nothingness of Khalius, she occasionally passed little rocks and sticks. She even walked through what she assumed were tree roots, but none of those things were any more solid than the dirt. It was just thick, and felt like walking through deep water. It was almost relaxing. She reached out with her mind and captured some sort of rock. Then she grabbed what she thought was a long straight stick. She continued to grab little odds and ends with her mind as she walked, most of them she couldn't really make out in the haze.

Even the little dead bunny that Jalinox carried seemed as insubstantial as the roots, rocks, and even the other people. It was a difficult concept grasp. Then they were back at the pit, and she could see her body. She moved towards it just as the roof ripped open revealing the starry sky of the clearing that they had left quite a while ago.

There was a sudden rush of sensations as she returned to her body. She hadn't noticed the lack of sensations when she was traveling beyond her body. However, on her return, she was acutely aware of the temperature of the air, the feeling of the fabric of her clothes against her skin, and the smells of dirt and pine trees.

The roof was opened to the night sky, and she realized that all of the things that she had mentally grabbed while leaving Khalius were in her hands. She dropped the things into her pockets without looking at them. Then she grabbed the edge of the pit and climbed out, back into the world of the living. She rubbed her hands around her face and arms, happy to be able to feel her own body once again.

When she looked over, she noticed the rabbit. It had glowing eyes and it looked vicious, but other than that, it walked around and didn't even look dead. She guessed that in a few days it would start looking dead. Tali rushed over and started petting it.

As Jalinox reached out and grabbed the Khalius Wicket, Jessa asked him, "How long can someone stay in that pit? How long can they explore Khalius without returning to their body?"

He said, "The Khalius stone can only open a portal between our world and Khalius when it is dark outside, when Viator's power is strongest. It is unwise to remain within the pit longer than twenty-four hours without returning to the world of the living."

That got Kimly wondering about that stone, "Lord Jalinox, what happens to the stone while we are in the pit? Is it still visible in the land of the living? What if someone steals it while we're in Khalius, would we be stuck there?"

He laugh, "Oh, no! That would be terrible. No, once the stone is in use and one of us enters the pit and seals the entrance behind us, the stone becomes immovable and virtually indestructible until we return from Khalius."

"That's good."

Jalinox caused the Awakened rabbit to hop over to Narinda, "Do you like how I can animate the dead rabbit?"

She stepped away from it and crossed her arms across her chest.

"Would you like it if we animated your son? Let him walk around? Maybe give his mommy a big hug?"

Narinda screamed at him and clinched her fists at her side, "You're a freak!"

He smiled at her and stepped closer. "I know where his body is, we could go to it now."

She turned her back to him, and Kimly could hear her sobbing.

Jalinox said, "What if I told you we could bring him back to life? Not as an animated corpse, but as a living and breathing boy?"

Narinda spun around quickly. She had tears streaming down her cheeks. In a soft voice she asked, "What?"

He stepped even closer to her, "We could return him to life! That is another gift that Viator can grant."

She reached out, grabbed his robes with both hands, and pulled him to her. "How? Is this for real, or one of your games?"

"It's not a game! He could be returned to life, good as new. Well, probably with a couple nasty scars on his chest, but you could live with a little blemish on him, couldn't you?" He gently pulled her wrists to release her grip on his robe, and he stepped away slightly.

"Yes! Of course! Let's go do it now! Make him alive again!"

He shook his head sadly and said, "Unfortunately, the ritual to bring him back was stolen from us centuries ago. It is now locked away. We can't recover that, or countless other spells and rituals, without the ancient ring that I mentioned earlier. Perhaps you would like to help me recover it? Would you be willing to learn the ways of the necromancers? Would you become a Priestess of Death, and join the search to find this ring?"

Narinda planted her hands on her hips and spread her feet. She gave him a determined look, "I would step into the Inner Planes of Khalius if it gave me a chance to save my boy!"

Jalinox smiled at her and patted her on the shoulder, "That probably won't be necessary, but the search is going to be long and difficult. We've been at it for a long time."

She said, "I don't care how hard it is. Make me a Priestess of Death, let's get this started!"

Kimly nodded to herself. So many things were starting to become clear to her. She hadn't understood why the boy had to die, or why Jalinox was keeping Narinda around when she was so clearly combative towards him, but now it all made perfect sense in a horrible, evil, and entirely twisted way. He would use the boy's death, and the promise of a new life, to control her. How could she not be faithful to him? Kimly wondered how many others were being manipulated like that.

To her left she saw Jessa step towards him. She said, "Lord Jalinox, what about my brother? Could we bring Burga back to living?"

With an evil grin Jalinox stepped over to Jessa and said, "Of course we can, dear! Of course we can. If you join me, together we will bring him back. I have special plans for you, but I must be able to trust that you are completely loyal. With your skills as a Magi, and the things I want to teach you as a Dark Apostle, we are going to do great things together!"

Jessa fell to her knees at his feet. Between sobs she said, "I am completely loyal, Lord Jalinox!"

He patted her on the top of the head, "We shall see, Jessa. In time, I am sure that you will prove yourself to me." He looked at Kimly as he said it, and the look sent chills down her spine.

For the last few days, she had been guessing that Jalinox was evaluating the two Magi to see which one he could use in some way. With Jessa's public display of loyalty, and her desire to bring her brother back, Jessa seemed to be the stronger choice to join the evil squad. Kimly realized that she had just about worn out her welcome, and fun-time at crazy-camp was coming to an end. It was time for her to move on.

291

When Kimly finally got back to her room, she was worn out. When she heard the door to her cell lock behind her she started pulling items from her pockets. The first item was the straight stick she had brought back from Khalius. That turned out to be a flat metal rod about a foot long. It was dirty and slightly rusted, but it seemed sturdy. Perhaps she could use it as a weapon? Turning it around a few times she wasn't sure what it had originally been, but the item may have been buried for thousands of years, so there was no telling what it was.

She emptied her pockets and found a number of smallish stones, a couple of tiny animal bones, and an old copper coin. She sat down on her bed and looked through the items. It was a long shot, but she had hoped to find some kind of weapon or key or something to help her escape from the place.

She shrugged and curled up on her bed to sleep. She expected sleep to come quickly, but instead she just lay there lost in thought. Grabbing the metal bar, she started to absently play around with it while she thought about the day. If she had a chance she'd like to grab one of those Khalius Wickets. One of them might come in handy. She started thinking about her sleeping arrangements over the last few years and decided that a cemetery would be an unpleasant place to use one of those wickets.

Looking down at her wrist, she realized that she had shoved the metal bar between her wrist and the bracelet, as she absently fiddled with it. As she turned the bar, it pushed the bracelet against her wrist with a great deal of force. If only her bones were unbreakable, she might be able to pry the bracelet to the point where it would break. Unfortunately, her arm bones would break long before the bracelet did. She tried steadying the bracelet with her feet, but that didn't work at all. Growing frustrated, she sat back against the wall with a huff.

For a while, she just stared at the wall and zoned out. She wasn't one to dwell on negatives, but she was starting to get nervous about her situation. She rolled her head to one side and looked at the door, and then an idea struck her. She rushed over to the door and put the metal bar back through the space between the bracelet and the back of her wrist. Then she tried to shove the bracelet into the space between the door and the wall. It was a very tight fit, but after beating against it with the other hand she finally got it wedged into the space. Now she had a way to hold the bracelet still while she tried to use the metal bar to break the bracelet.

For several minutes, she pried, pushed, shoved and slammed the bar into the bracelet, but it would not break. Her arm was turning black and blue from the bar sliding down the bracelet and smashing into it, and if she wasn't careful she was liable to break her arm. That wouldn't help anything.

After a few more attempts, she jerked her arm from the door, pulling the bracelet out of the space between the door and the wall. She sat down on the floor and pressed her wrist hard against the floor. Then she took the metal bar and started banging the bar down onto the bracelet in growing agitation.

"Dammit!" she cursed in pain as she missed the bracelet entirely, and bashed the back of her hand with the bar! She threw the bar across the room and jumped onto her bed. Burying her face in her pillow, she screamed in anger and frustration!

Chapter 29

Rissyl

For days, they had traveled through the unimaginably long and elaborate passageways of Mazbakhar Halls. The king had assigned three dwarves to guide them through to the north side of the mountains. For the first day, the seven of them traveled through the residential areas of the dwarven subterranean city, making their way through endless passages of shops and homes. That first day, their guides had to stop every few minutes to talk to friends and explain why humans were being escorted through the dwarven underground fortress.

The first night they stopped to sleep at the dwarven equivalent of a wayside inn. The evening was filled with boisterous stories, rousing music, a few impromptu competitions of strength, and a whole lot of strong dwarven ale.

The next morning, the guides led the Magi to a stable filled with large lizards. Rissyl had never seen such large lizards before, but he was sure they were the creatures that his father called the Rukthorian Giant Horn-Crested Lizards. The dwarves just referred to them as Spike Heads.

The next few days were spent on the backs of the Spike Heads. At first, Rissyl was very nervous, and Gordo was openly terrified as the lizards sprinted through the underground maze. As he grew accustomed to the mounts, however, the experience was actually quite fun. During that time they encountered a number of situations that had slowed them down, including getting lost three times and needing to back-track several miles. Twice they came to sections of the cavern that had been completely sealed off, and the dwarves spent several hours tearing down the barricades.

"Not much further now!" Drellis shouted from the back of his lizard. Of the three guides, Drellis had been the friendliest and most talkative.

Rissyl was hopeful, but the dwarf had been saying that for well over a day. "How do you know?"

"I'm a dwarf! I can sense these things in me bones!"

The lizards were running along in a single file line, with two dwarves in the front followed by Sarge, Gordo, Cynia, Rissyl and finally Drellis. They had been making good progress since breaking camp that morning. They were no longer in precisely-crafted dwarven passageways. Since the guides had broken through the last barricade, they had progressed to a series of naturally occurring mountain caverns.

A few minutes later, they came to a wide cavern with a high ceiling. There were so many stalactites and stalagmites throughout the cavern that the lizards had to slow down considerably to keep from crashing into them.

Up ahead Gordo said, "Hey, I smell flowers!"

Drellis exclaimed, "See! I told you that we're almost there!"

"Gordo, I think you're delusional. I don't smell any flowers; just musty stale cave air" Rissyl frowned in disappointment.

The lizards lumbered on at a slow canter, weaving left and right to avoid the naturally formed columns of stone. After a while, the first lizard came to a stop and in turn each of the others stopped too.

Rissyl groaned, "Dammit, are we lost? Again?"

Pointing in front of them, Drellis said, "No, look!"

Before he had a chance to turn to see what the dwarf was pointing at, he heard Sarge growl, "Fires of Khalius!"

Cynia and Gordo had climbed off their lizards and Rissyl stood up in his saddle to get a better look. Then he sat back down slowly. Up ahead was a large chasm, at least sixty to eighty feet across and extending the entire width of the cavern.

He jumped down from his lizard and walked up to the edge of the chasm.

Gordo dropped a rock from the ledge, and they all stood for a long time waiting to hear the rock hit the bottom. After a bit Gordo said, "So, who wants to cross the Chasm of Certain Death first? Someone not named Gordo. Anybody?"

Looking to Drellis, Rissyl asked, "Can the lizards cross that thing?"

The dwarf nodded, "They can walk across walls without riders, but we'll not be crossing that."

Rissyl breathed a sigh of relief, "Oh, good. So this was the wrong way?"

He shook his head, "No, this is the right way. Yer going to cross here. But we dwarves'll be heading back. Our work is done."

"Wait, you're leaving us? We haven't found the other side yet."

The dwarf made an over exaggerated display of taking a deep breath, "Smell that? That's the smell of the outside. Yer almost there and you don't need guides no more."

He sniffed the air again, "Okay, maybe I do smell something that smells remotely like nature. How much further past the chasm do we have to go?" Rissyl felt uncomfortable being abandoned in the middle of the massive caverns.

Drellis shrugged, "How would I know? Maybe a mile, maybe lots of miles. No dwarf's been to these caverns since the passage was sealed over five hundred years ago. But it can't be far now that we can smell the outdoors."

The dwarves helped the Magi unload their bags from the lizards' saddles. One of the dwarves dropped a large bag at Sarge's feet.

Drellis pulled the supplies from the bag. It contained a large rope, a grappling hook, hammer, pitons, and other miscellaneous implements for rock climbing. The dwarves spent several minutes explaining the proper use of the equipment and demonstrated several methods of tying solid knots.

They wrapped one end of the large rope around a stalagmite, tied the end, and secured that end with pitons to keep it from coming loose. Drellis said, "Now someone needs to get to the other side and tie the other end of this rope around one of those pillars. Then the others can shimmy across the rope."

"Okay, I'll teleport across. Give me the hammer and stuff." Rissyl grabbed some pitons and a hammer, and stuffed them in his pocket. He looked at Cynia for a moment and then said, "Be careful!" Then he looked to Sarge and Gordo and added, "All of you."

Without another word, he looked over to the other side of the chasm and began summoning the magic for his spell. He visualized a nice clear spot on the far side of the chasm, a safe distance from the edge, and whispered, "Kur'Gezbar."

His stomach lurched as he experienced the vertigo of jumping between the two places. He blinked a couple of times to clear his head, and then looked around. He saw the others standing on the far side of the chasm where he had left them.

This side was noticeably higher than the ground where the others stood, and he took a moment to look around for the exit. Far to the north end of the cavern, or what he assumed was the north since it was in the opposite direction from where they had come, was a large tunnel out of the cavern, but the more he looked around this side of the cavern, he noticed lots of holes and tunnels that all seemed to be exits. Some of them looked easy to get to, and some were high up towards the ceiling.

He reminded himself to focus on one thing at a time. He needed to get the others over first, and then they could explore exit options. He looked back to his companions and held out his hands, waiting for them to throw the rope to him. Drellis threw the heavy rope, and the bundle didn't come anywhere near reaching him. Rissyl watched as the rope uncurled and dangled down into the chasm, on the far side.

Gordo said, "What kinda throw was that? You throw like a dwarf!"

Drellis made a hurt expression, "What's that supposed to mean? I'm a miner, not a rope thrower! Damned thing's heavy!" The dwarf started to pull the rope back up, to throw it again.

Rissyl said, "Leave it there, I'll grab it." He reached out with a spell and grabbed a hold of the bottom end of the rope. He pulled it to himself using magic and then grabbed it with his hands.

From across the way, the dwarves looked to each other and nodded. Drellis said, "Very nice, Magi. Yer powers are impressive."

He didn't respond to the dwarf's compliment, because he was busy wrapping the end of the rope around a stalagmite. Once he got the rope tied, he hammered a couple of pitons in place to make sure the rope didn't come loose while people were crossing it. He tugged on it a few times to test it, and then he said, "Okay, you should be ready!"

Drellis finished making a hasty safety harness from a small length of rope. He tied it around Sarge's waist, and then Sarge climbed out onto the rope. He was hanging upside down, with his feet still on the ledge where Drellis was standing. The dwarf reached down and used a metal clamp to fasten Sarge's safety harness to the rope.

The dwarf said, "Okay, Magi, just pull yerself across. Keep yer feet crossed over top of the rope, push with yer feet while you pull with yer hands. Easy as snot. The safety harness should keep you from falling to an early death if you slip."

Sarge looked down into the bottomless chasm below him, and then looked back to the dwarf. He was white with fear, "Should? That don't sound too encouraging!" He started pulling himself across the deadly drop.

As he pulled himself across, the dwarf started to tie a make-shift harness around Gordo.

Rissyl watched the older Magi pull his way across the Chasm, and his heart raced in fear and excitement. He was extremely happy that he had the power to teleport, so he didn't have to experience the terror of dangling upside down over the fiery pits of Khalius.

Eventually, Sarge pulled himself to Rissyl's side of the chasm, and he helped the warrior Magi up onto the ledge.

Over on the other side, the dwarf got Gordo's harness clipped to the rope and the Magi started pulling himself across. At first, Rissyl thought Gordo might cross the chasm with no problem, but once the Magi was about halfway across he stopped to look down.

Gordo stopped pulling. He tilted his head backwards to look at Sarge and said, "I dunno if I can do it, Sarge! My hands are getting tired!"

"Don't stop! Just keep going!" Rissyl hoped encouragement alone would be enough to get him across.

Sarge said, "Hanging there is just going to make it worse! Pull, dammit!"

For several breaths Gordo just hung there. When he let go with one hand to reach forward, the other hand slipped off! That sent him dangling upside down, looking straight into the bottomless maw beneath him! The harness was holding him for now, and he still had a hold of the rope with his legs.

Rissyl yelled, "Gordo!"

From the other side of the chasm, Cynia hollered, "Reach up and grab the rope! You can do it!"

Gordo reached up to grab the rope, but missed. That sent him spinning and caused him to let go with his feet! For a few moments he spun in circles, supported only by the harness!

Cynia screamed and Sarge lunged forward a step like he wanted to try to reach out to Gordo, but he stopped and kneeled near the edge of the chasm. He yelled, "Stop screwing around, dammit! Reach up and grab the sarding rope!"

From behind him, Rissyl heard some sort of noise. He couldn't tell what it was, over all of the yelling, but as he started to turn around, something slammed into him from behind and sent a shockwave through his body!

All around him, streaks of light fell to the ground. Sarge screamed in anger and pain as Rissyl jumped to the side and rolled behind a stalagmite to shield himself from the rain of light streaks. He peeked around the stalagmite to find where the streaks were coming from. Standing in several tunnels along the back side of the cavern were small creatures. They looked humanoid and they walked on two legs, but they were really small, maybe half the size of a dwarf, Rissyl guessed. They were mostly lost in shadows, but each of them held short bows that seemed to be made completely of light, much like the Rolimi creatures. The arrows that they were shooting were arrows of light. An arrow landed near him and Rissyl saw that they seemed insubstantial. They were simply traced in light just like the Rolimi.

Sarge called out, "Fires of Khalius! What's that?"

Rissyl saw Sarge shielding himself behind a stalagmite. The barrage of light-arrows continued until a large wind started blowing through the cavern from the south. He glanced back and saw Cynia standing with her arms outstretched and he surmised the wind was some sort of transmutation spell from her. The strong wind blew all of the light-arrows back at the archers, knocking them harmlessly to the ground far away from Rissyl and Sarge. The wind continued to blow, and the creatures stopped firing their arrows.

Rissyl stood up and summoned his staff. He caused a stream of fire orbs to race towards the creatures, sweeping his staff as the orbs shot from it. The orbs impacted the back walls of the cavern in a line, one after the other, from the right to the left and then left to right. Several of the orbs went into the tunnels and came close to hitting the creatures, causing them to squeal and retreat from sight. He paused the barrage of fire orbs to walk closer to the tunnels. When he saw one of the creatures peek out of a tunnel, he sent several orbs streaking into each of the tunnels where he had seen the creatures previously.

He watched for several moments to make sure that they didn't reappear. The creatures seemed pretty skittish, and he hoped that he could keep them busy long enough for the others to cross.

Behind him he heard Sarge shout, "Hurry up, Gordo!"

After a few more warning shots from Rissyl's staff, he heard Gordo and Cynia both behind him. She said, "Come on, Rissyl, let's get outta here!"

He looked back to see the dwarves riding away on the lizards, leading four rider-less lizards along with them.

Together, they moved towards the large tunnel at the far side of the cavern. Rissyl broke into a run towards the tunnel and the others followed him. Once they reached the tunnel, Rissyl felt much better. He wasn't entirely sure that they were headed in the right direction, but at least they were not exposed in the center of the cavern with creatures shooting them with magical arrows! His back still hurt from where one of the arrows had hit him, but there was no blood so he was hoping that his cloak protected him from the worst of the damage.

Once inside the tunnel they slowed to a fast walk. Sarge said, "I'll take up rear guard. Just remember, look before you cook! If those creatures come after us, try not to blast your blue-cloaked pal."

Rissyl motioned for Gordo to take up the scout position in front. Then he replied to Sarge, "I can't make any guarantees, but I'll sure try."

299

Sarge slowed and turned his attention behind them. He said, "That don't fill me with confidence."

"How did you get across the rope so quickly?" Rissyl looked over to Cynia with a raised eyebrow.

"A little spell I learned in one of our first lessons. It gives me cat-like balance for a short time, and I ran across the rope."

"Mother of all the gods, Cynia! Tell me that you didn't! That's nuts!" He looked at her in shock.

She smiled at him and said, "Thanks, I thought so too!"

About an hour later, they were still following the same tunnel. Rissyl noticed that Sarge had started traveling relatively normally, only glancing behind them occasionally, since it became clear that the creatures probably weren't following them.

They had been walking in silence, and Rissyl's thoughts turned to Sarasa. He wondered what she was doing, if they had been able to free Jessa and Kimly, and mostly if she was safe. He checked the nexus gem for the billionth time but it was still dark.

Once again, his thoughts returned to the morning next to the barn with Sarasa. Soon he would have to give her an answer, and the choice didn't seem as easy as he first assumed it would be. He tried to force his thoughts to other things, but they kept returning to a choice he didn't want to make.

He walked faster until he was next to Cynia. "So, what do you think those creatures will do? Do you think they're still tracking us?" He didn't expect her to know, but he hoped that conversation would take his mind off other things.

She shrugged, "I've been thinking about that. They did attack us, but they didn't seem vicious. Maybe we intruded on their lair and they just wanted to drive us away? If that's the case, then they'll probably just follow us long enough to be sure that we're gonna leave them alone."

He hadn't considered that, but she made a really good point. "Yeah, I was kind of thinking the same thing."

"No you weren't."

"Okay, no I wasn't, but it's a good point. If I had thought of it, then I would have been thinking the same thing." He flashed her a goofy grin.

She smacked him playfully in the head, "That's profound."

He pretended to be hurt, "Hey, it's tough being one of the great minds of our time!"

"How do you know, have you met him?"

Rissyl gave her an offended expression and she stuck her tongue out at him.

He whispered, "Mayl'Hok" and a little light orb appeared in his hand. He flicked it at her head, and it stuck on her right cheek.

She ignored it and kept walking. Every time he glanced over at her he saw a glowing orb, bouncing to the rhythm of her gait, stuck to the side of her face. He couldn't help but burst out laughing.

"Take it off." She didn't sound entirely pleased.

He reached over, plucked it from her cheek, and placed it on the top of her forehead. Then he said, "Cynia, I never realized that you were a miner." He barely suppressed a laugh at his own joke.

Suddenly, she leaped on him and shoved him to the ground. Over and over she summoned light orbs and stuck them all over his face and chest. Then she leaned forward and kissed him on the forehead. When she pulled away she had a light orb stuck to her chin. She plucked it off, and placed it on his forehead.

She stood up and kept walking.

Rissyl just lay there for a few moments. When Sarge got to him he reached out and helped Rissyl stand up.

They walked side by side for a few steps as Rissyl plucked light orbs from himself one at a time and tossed them onto the cavern wall.

Sarge said, "You have light balls on your face."

"Yep." He continued to pluck them from his chest and shoulders until eventually they were all off. After walking for a while, he realized that he had never really taken the time to get to know the old warrior Magi. The man probably had a hundred stories and adventures to share. They didn't have anything better to do as they walked through the endless caves.

He looked over and said, "So, Sarge, you must have had some exciting adventures over the years."

The tough old Magi glanced at Rissyl and then looked back to the front. For a few moments Rissyl thought that Sarge wasn't even going to respond, but then he said, "Is this the part of the journey where we grow a bond of friendship by sharing tales of our trials and tribulations?"

Rissyl laughed quickly, "Well, I suppose it is."

"Yeah, let's not do that."

He felt dumb. Without saying anything else Rissyl walked faster to catch up with Cynia.

From behind him, Rissyl heard Sarge say, "If you two are going to screw around some more, you might want to wait until we make camp."

He felt dumb earlier, but he now felt offended and annoyed. The old warrior was usually sarcastic, but this time it bugged him more than normal. He reached down and grabbed Cynia's hand, just to be spiteful.

That got him thinking about spiteful people. He had known some really spiteful people in his life. He realized, as he looked over to Cynia, that she must be the least spiteful person he had ever met. She had been a Dreg, serving him and his family, and yet she didn't seem to harbor any bad feelings towards him at all. He realized that she was a better person than he'd ever be. He was certain that he would harbor resentment if he went through the things she faced.

He thought back to the incident with Tommis. The creep had locked her in a dog cage and treated her like a mutt. He wondered if she secretly wanted to get revenge on the man. He said, "Now that you're a powerful Magi, do you ever think about confronting Tommis?"

She looked at him in confusion. She asked, "Tommis?"

"The neighbor. He locked you in a dog cage."

"Oh, him."

She was quiet for a long time, then she said, "He is a sad pathetic man. Sometimes I feel bad for him, but I really don't give him much thought."

"You don't think about getting revenge?"

She shrugged, "What would that gain? No, I don't see the point of it."

They all walked in silence for a while longer and then Gordo shouted back, "I see light up ahead!"

Gordo started running, and the others followed him. Before long, they found themselves outside!

Everyone stopped and looked around at the scene before them. Rissyl leaned against the side of the mountain at the mouth of the cave, and stared in awe.

The view was breathtaking. The mouth of the cave was in the low foothills, fairly far from the larger peeks of the mountains. Out before him, he saw large trees unlike any he had ever seen, with long narrow trunks and long narrow branches that extended far to the sides of the twisted trunks. The trees were extremely tall, and had what looked like big flat platforms of leaves at the top.

Far off to the front right was a large lake that stretched out as far as he could see. To the front left was a seemingly endless expanse of yellow grasslands, dotted with the unusual trees. To the immediate left and right, the foothills stretched far off into the distance. Back behind him the foothills quickly gave way to the massive mountain range.

The sun was high in the sky, and it was hot. Without much shade he expected the upcoming walk to be hot and uncomfortable. Then he realized that he didn't have any idea which direction the Stronghold might be. It had never occurred to him that it wouldn't be visible when they emerged from beneath the mountain.

He cursed to himself. "So, any guesses on which way to go?"

"Any guess as to which way is north?" Gordo looked up at the sun as he asked.

Sarge walked a short distance away, picked up a long stick and shoved it into the ground. Then he took a short stick and shoved it at the tip of the shadow cast by the long stick.

Rissyl shrugged, "The mountains are back that way, so I'm assuming that's south, but which direction do we need to travel to find the Stronghold?"

"I've been worried about this." Cynia stepped closer to Sarge and looked off, to what Rissyl assumed, was the east and north. "I've been looking through the old texts since before we started this journey, and there is nothing written that describes the location of the Stronghold, other than saying that it is on the north side of the mountain range."

Gordo, Rissyl, and Cynia talked for several minutes. They discussed the landscape, and offered theories about where would be the logical location for a Stronghold. Sarge sat down near his sticks and looked off into the distance quietly.

After a while, Sarge placed another short stick in the ground at the tip of the shadow from the large stick. Then he grabbed another long stick and laid it on the ground touching the two short sticks. He stood up and pointed at the long stick lying flat on the ground. "This long stick is lying in an east-west line. So north is that way." He pointed in the direction that Rissyl assumed would be northwest.

Rissyl walked over to the arrangement of sticks and looked at Sarge, "That's pretty slick, how does it work?" The others moved closer as well. Rissyl was relieved to see that he probably wasn't the only one who didn't know how to make a compass from four sticks and the sun.

"It's pretty simple, really. The sun moves from east to west, right?"

The others nodded, and Rissyl braced himself for a condescending answer.

Sarge continued without pausing, "So the tip of the shadow will move east and west as well. The shadow point starts in the west and travels to the east, as the sun travels to the west."

Rissyl was impressed by the cleverness of the technique, and the fact that Sarge could explain it without being a jerk.

"That's great, but which way do the sticks think we should travel to find the Stronghold?" Cynia sounded more than a little sarcastic. Rissyl turned away so Sarge couldn't see his smile.

Sarge sighed, "You're the brains of this group, kiddo. I'm just here for my rugged good looks, witty commentary, and freakishly deadly sword arm."

Gordo poked Rissyl in the arm, and said, "You're the Conjurer. Too bad you can't just teleport us there."

Shaking her head, Cynia said, "No, it doesn't work like that. He can't teleport somewhere that he's never been. Besides-"

Rissyl cut her off, exclaiming, "Wait, that's it!"

Everyone looked at him in confusion. Gordo asked, "What's it? Teleporting? I was just joking."

"Yes, sort of! The portal stone!"

Cynia smiled and smacked herself in the head, "Yes! Why didn't I think of that?"

"I'm still confused." Gordo held his arms to the side, "I thought it was deactivated, and that's why we had to walk under an entire mountain range to get here. Are you telling me that we could've just magicked our way there?"

"No, but do you remember the spell to help us locate the nearest portal stone?" Rissyl started to summon the magic to cast the spell.

Sarge smiled, "Now who is the clever one? The portal stone is probably, hopefully, near that Stronghold. I'm impressed."

Rissyl smiled and pointed, "The portal stone is to the southeast, a few miles at least."

After several days of traveling underground, the walk to the Stronghold was a refreshing change. Rissyl pulled the hood of his cloak up over his head to shield himself from the sun. It was a hot day, but the breeze felt nice, and for the most part he enjoyed the walk.

A few hours into the trek, Sarge stopped the group and moved to try to sneak up on a huge wild pig. However, the beast sensed his approach and charged him. Sarge quickly killed the beast and carried it to a spot that he picked for a quick meal. They cooked the pig over a large campfire, and it was delicious. After gorging themselves on the first fresh meat that had enjoyed in days, everyone lounged around the campsite for a short while.

Rissyl repeated the portal stone locating spell, to make sure they were still headed in the right direction, and reluctantly everyone continued on their way.

As the sun started to sink low in the western sky, Rissyl led them to the large non-descript rock that was the top of the portal stone.

"Should we activate it?" Cynia asked.

He shrugged, "I guess so. I was hoping it would be at the front door of the Stronghold."

"Is that it, over there?" Gordo pointed to the southeast. Far off in the distance was a sprawling structure surrounded by some sort of light.

Rissyl jumped in the air and pointed, "Yes! I think that's it!"

They activated the portal stone, and then walked quickly towards the Stronghold.

As they got closer, he heard Cynia mutter under her breath, "Mother of the gods!"

He stopped daydreaming and focused on their surroundings. He realized that the Stronghold was getting closer, and it was massive! He expected a large building, or maybe a small castle, but he never even dreamed the Stronghold would be such a sprawling complex of buildings and defenses. The sky was starting to get dark as the sun sank lower, so he couldn't see the details clearly, but if he had to guess, he would say there were many dozens, if not over a hundred individual buildings. There were towers and buildings of all shapes and sizes.   Around it all was a massive, and probably impenetrable, wall. Something glowing red stretched around the base of the entire wall.

The group picked up the pace again as they grew closer to the Stronghold. Eventually, he realized that the red glowing thing extending all around the Stronghold at the base of the wall was some sort of net or mesh fence made from the same magical material as the weapons of the creatures back in the cave. It also seemed like the same magical material that the Rolimi appeared to be made from.

Gordo asked, "What's all over the ground in front of that glowing net?"

"I'm not sure. Is it rough ground, maybe large clumps of dirt?" Cynia guessed.

"It's not dirt." Sarge shook his head, "They're bodies."

As they got closer, Rissyl could see that he was right. Hundreds and hundreds of bodies, most of them just skeletons, were scattered all of the way up and down the perimeter of the Stronghold. He asked, "Do you think they're from the time of the Betrayal?"

Sarge replied, "No, most of them look like they've been dead much less than a hundred years. Some of these have only been dead a few months."

"This one is dressed like a necromancer!" Cynia pointed at a corpse not far from her.

"Yes, so is that one over there." Sarge pointed at a different corpse.

Rissyl carefully stepped between bodies as much as he could, trying to get closer to the Stronghold.

Suddenly a huge Rolimi creature appeared before him, on the other side of the glowing net. This wasn't a cute little Rolimi Pup, or a thin little Rolimi instructor like Mr. Pyllis. This creature was made entirely from light outlining all of its features, like the other Rolimi that he had met, but this one was a deep red color. It was also almost seven feet tall and was shaped like someone with massive muscles. It was hollow like the other Rolimi, but this one had a deep red glow inside of it, like some sort of power or aura was pulsating within its chest. In one hand, it had a large halberd, made from the same magic properties as the Rolimi.

The giant Rolimi creature had the halberd planted in the ground, blade side up. In a deep booming voice, which resonated throughout the area, the creature said, "Magi, present Bisangar's Signet Ring to claim the Magi Stronghold!"

The Magi looked at each other in confusion. Sarge and Cynia both motioned for Rissyl to talk to the creature. He sighed. "Friend Rolimi creature. We are the rightful rulers of the Sovereign Magi Society, and I request that you return the Stronghold to us." He paused, and then added, "Thank you for guarding it."

"Present Bisangar's Signet Ring to claim the Magi Stronghold!"

He put his fists on his hips and tried to look confident, "Rolimi, servant of the goddess of magic, we are the chosen ones of the goddess Nalria! It is her desire that we rebuild the Magi Society! To fulfill our goddess's wishes we must take possession of the Stronghold! Our predecessors asked you to guard this fortress, and today we ask you to hand it back over to us."

The deep voice replied quickly and in a monotone cadence, "Our mistress Nalria demands the strictest obedience to our promises. The Rolimi Guardians promised your Magi predecessors to hold and guard the

Stronghold against all trespassers, both Magi and non-magic, until the day when the rightful owner returns bearing Bisangar's Signet Ring. If you attempt to pass without it, you will certainly join the other carcasses littering the landscape! Present the ring now, or lie down with the dead who came before you."

Rissyl raised his hands slightly, "Okay, I think we will return at a better time." He turned and carefully walked back to the others. He shrugged, "I guess we need to find a ring."

Looking back to the corpses and skeletons scattered around, Sarge said, "I guess we now know what the necromancers are looking for."

They started walking back the way they came. Rissyl's head hurt, and his heart ached. They had travelled so far for nothing. He sighed, "So the necromancers have been trying to claim the Stronghold? We have to make sure they don't claim it before we do!"

They walked in silence for a short while. It was almost full night-time, but the moon was almost bright and the sky was clear, so they were still able to walk without too much trouble.

Rissyl said, "Let's get back to the portal stone. We can teleport back to the others and maybe do something useful?"

"At least this portal stone is active now, so we can teleport back here and we won't need to bother the dwarves again." Cynia smiled at Rissyl and tried to cheer him up.

His face lit up at her statement. He hadn't thought about the portal stone being active and how much easier it would be to get back here. "I guess this trip wasn't a complete waste of time after all!"

Chapter 30

Rissyl

The four Magi ported from the stronghold to the portal stone near Clornoss. Dalen and his group of Magi, along with some Magi who had been left behind in Sorgo, had been traveling to Clornoss to rescue Kimly and Jessa when Rissyl sent a message through his nexus gem asking to meet them to assist with the rescue.

The first person Rissyl saw when they arrived at the portal stone was Sarasa. He knew that he should take a moment to let the vertigo of teleporting pass before he tried to move around, but when he saw her standing there, he was so excited to see her that he ran over to greet her. At least that was the intention, but his legs were like jelly. His head felt like he had been drinking so he instead staggered forward, grabbed Gordo's shoulder for balance, and half-fell into her arms. She was strong and easily kept him from falling. Unfortunately, Gordo had never experienced portal stone travel before, so the dizziness and disorientation hit him harder. When Rissyl grabbed his shoulder it almost pulled him backwards. He lunged for the portal stone for balance, missed it, and fell hard into Sarge, knocking them both to the ground.

Sarge groaned as Gordo rolled across him, trying to stand up. He growled, "Get off of me! Ouch! Dammit, are you a buffalo?"

Rissyl squeezed Sarasa tightly, and she hugged him back. When he pulled away he kept his hands on her shoulders for a moment. She looked up into his eyes, and he thought he saw… something. Was it concern? Perhaps it was affection? As well as he understood women it could very well be a look that said she was desperately trying to not pass gas. He pulled away and looked to the others.

"Does everyone know each other?" Cynia looked around the group and then said, "No, I think some of you haven't met. Before we press on, let's do basic introductions. First our Order of Evokers. This is Aruk."

Aruk waved his hand to the group and then pulled back the hood of his red and white cloak. Rissyl remembered Aruk as the friend of Baeldin, both of whom they met a fortnight ago around the campfire. He was the soft-spoken one, and his friend Baeldin was loud and a bit rude. Looking around the group, Rissyl wasn't disappointed to see that Baeldin wasn't around. Baeldin was sent to defend Grum'Glin.

"The man who needs no introductions, the fearless leader of our Evokers, Rissyl!" Cynia gave him a wink, and he gave a little bow to the others. "Moving on to the Order of Diviners, we have myself, and..." Cynia paused for a moment. Then she said, "I'm sorry, I forgot your name."

The green and white cloaked Magi stepped forward and said, "I'm Zahr." Rissyl remembered almost nothing about Zahr, except that he showed up later than the others, so Rissyl hadn't really had a chance to get to know him very well.

Cynia smiled at Zahr, and then continued, "Our Order of Champions are Dalen and Sarge."

Both of them stepped forward, one at a time, and waved. Rissyl looked to Dalen hoping that there was no new bad blood between them now that he was making some progress with Sarasa, but it was hard to tell with Dalen. He decided to talk with him later and smooth things over.

"Next we have our Order of the Shadows, Sarasa and Gordo."

As Sarasa stepped forward and waved, Rissyl couldn't help but feel excitement and nervousness. Seeing her brought the realization that it was nearly time for him to make his choice.

"And of course we have our Society Magi: Hanry, Eleyne, and Thon."

Hanry stepped forward and pulled down the hood of his brown and white cloak. He waved at everyone briefly. Rissyl waved back to the former Dreg.

When Eleyne stepped forward, Rissyl felt a great sense of relief. He hadn't noticed her standing in the back of the group, and he was happy to see that she was well. When they left Sorgo he was concerned that she might not be ready for the burden of being a Magi. Not that she was weak, but she was inexperienced and she lacked confidence.

Lastly the Guild Master, Thon, stepped forward. He looked right at Rissyl as he waved to the group. Rissyl realized that Thon had been Sarasa's fighting guild's instructor since she was a little girl. There was no telling what Dalen had told the man about him, and her.

For a short while everyone milled around greeting each other, and in some cases introducing themselves to Magi that they hadn't met before.

Then Dalen said, in a loud voice, "Okay, ladies and gentlemen. Pick up your gear, pack up the wagons, and let's get going!"

"Are we going to travel through the empire, just south of the capital, with our cloaks and weapons visible?" Rissyl pulled his hood over his head.

Dalen nodded to him, "Yes we are! Listen up, folks. The emperor started this battle when his men killed and captured our Magi. Today we bring the war to him! We'll travel openly as Magi, and we will slaughter every last imperial soldier we meet along the way! The camp where Jessa and Kimly are being held is several miles. It's well guarded, and there's no telling what we'll face when we get there, but we'll rescue our Magi, and we'll deal a severe blow to whatever else is going on in that place!"

His speech was met with spirited applause and shouts of excitement. Rissyl was impressed. It was a good speech. He hoped that things went as smoothly as Dalen had implied.

Once the supplies were loaded into their two wagons, a few Magi jumped into the back of each. Dalen drove one wagon and Hanry drove the other, and soon Rissyl found himself walking through the meadow next to one of the wagons. He hurried to catch up with Sarasa.

"It's crazy to have so many Magi traveling with us! Eleven of us, travelling together, are heading out to take on the emperor's forces? It's surreal." He hoped to get her talking about anything at all.

She shrugged, "I guess. I'm starting to get used to it. The seven of us have been travelling together for almost a fortnight now, while you four were out searching for the Stronghold. We've gone through a lot together recently. This is a good group of Magi."

He hadn't really given a lot of thought to all of the adventures and difficult times the others might be facing without him. He knew that they had been in Sorgo looking for a way to save Kimly and Jessa, but he had been more focused on his own day-to-day troubles. It seemed odd to think of Magi battling, or going out on some mission without him.

"Yeah, that makes sense. I'm glad to see everyone is still well. I'm glad you didn't attempt the rescue without us, did you have to wait long?"

Sarasa shook her head, "No, we didn't know where they were being held until two days ago. Once we got near Clornoss we started ambushing imperial patrols and doing some magically enhanced interrogation to see if the soldiers would tell us where to find the girls. Every patrol that we hit was a dead-end until the night before last. Zahr has proven himself to be quite talented at using his magesight to discover information he wants. We were actually heading down to attempt the rescue on our own when I got your nexus gem message last night."

She was quiet for a moment and Rissyl almost asked something else, but then she added, "Dalen didn't want to take the time to find the Clornoss portal stone and activate it so you could join us, but the portal stone was pretty close, and several of us persuaded him."

He felt his anger starting to build. "It was stupid of him to suggest that you all try to raid the camp alone. What was he thinking?"

She looked to see if Dalen had heard Rissyl's rant. Then she looked back and said, "Dammit Riz, we're not incompetent! You had a mission to find the Stronghold. We had a mission to assist the Magi back in Sorgo, but that mission turned into a rescue mission to save two of our Magi. We fully intended to complete our mission. The fact that you happened to finish your mission in time to help us complete ours, and the fact that the portal stone was not too far out of our way were the only reasons that I urged Dalen to redirect us so that you four could join us. I am glad you're here, but this isn't all about you. It's much bigger than that, now."

He felt stupid for saying it the way he did, "I know, I'm sorry. I didn't mean it like that. Of course the seven of you can take care of yourselves. I was just trying to say that we have no idea what we're facing, and I'm glad that we're all together now."

From the driver's seat of the wagon Dalen said, "Okay Shadows, let's get our scouts out there so we're not surprised!"

Sarasa turned to look at him for a moment, and then she said, "A Shadow's job is never done." She started to jog and then faded from view as she dropped the invisibility on herself.

Rissyl wanted to be annoyed at Dalen for sending her away. He had hoped to have some time to talk to her, but Dalen was right to get the Shadows out ahead of the group to scout things.

Off to his left, Rissyl noticed Aruk walking a short distance from everyone else. The Evoker had two large wolves padding along next to him.

"Pretty impressive, huh?" Cynia bumped into him as she talked, and it startled him. He hadn't noticed her approaching.

"What's impressive?"

"Aruk and his wolves!" She pointed where he had already been looking.

He nodded, "Oh yes! That is impressive. I've read about summoning creatures, but I've never tried it."

Cynia responded, "I know what you mean, that's what I was thinking when I saw Zahr a minute ago."

Rissyl gave her a confused look, "What about Zahr?"

311

She pointed to the other side of the wagon. They slowed down their walk to let the wagon pass them, and then they walked behind the wagon and crossed over to its right side. Speeding their walk again, she pointed slightly to the right.

His jaw dropped when he saw Zahr. Actually he saw a large gorilla, wearing a green and white cloak, walking casually next to Eleyne. "Zahr is a gorilla? Is that some sort of Transmutation spell?"

She nodded, "It is, and it ain't a beginner spell. I've read about it, but I haven't been brave enough to try it."

"Why a gorilla and not a lion or dragon or something?"

"The more different the new shape is from his original shape, the more difficult the spell would be. Gorillas aren't shaped all that much different from us, so it's probably one of the easier shapes to assume."

Rissyl was intrigued, "Can he talk? Does he understand us? Most importantly, is he likely to pop off any of my arms?"

Cynia giggled, "Not too likely to pop off your arms. I doubt he can talk, but he can understand us. From what I've read, he keeps his sense of 'self' and his own knowledge while in a changed shape, but this ain't an illusion spell where he makes us think he looks like a gorilla. He has actually changed his shape into a gorilla. Since he now has the vocal parts of a gorilla he probably can't speak. He also has the gorilla's strength and speed."

"Does he need to be changed into a gorilla already? Isn't he wasting magic that he might need later?"

She shook her head, "No, actually it's the opposite. Most of the magic used happens when he changes shape, and from what I've read it ain't difficult to keep the shape. As we travel to the camp he'll be recovering some of the magic that he used to change his shape. Plus, the spell is very complicated so casting it in the middle of a battle would likely lead to fizzles."

"Does it hurt?"

"Dunno." She shrugged, "I'll tell you after I try it."

From his left, Dalen said, "Look there, soldiers up ahead!"

Rissyl looked ahead and noticed the road off in the distance. There were four soldiers on the road heading north.

Dalen said, "Aruk, release the wolves! Diviners and Evokers, wait until the Shadows show themselves so you don't hit them by mistake! Ready…"

Both of the wolves raced towards the soldiers. The soldiers stopped and drew their weapons, waiting for the wolves to get closer. Gordo appeared beside one of the solders, with his hand on the soldier's back. Gordo's charm spell overpowered the guard's conscious thoughts and he instead obeyed Gordo's will and attacked one of the other soldiers. A moment later, Sarasa became visible as she drove her sword deep into the back of another! It dropped to the ground as the wolves arrived and quickly knocked the fourth soldier to the ground.

The one that Gordo had charmed succeeded in defeating his fellow soldier, and Sarasa calmly stepped behind him, and cut his throat. The charmed soldier slumped to the ground before he knew he was even in danger.

To his right, Rissyl heard the gorilla known as Zahr start grunting and beating his chest wildly. It was clearly angry, and it was looking at Dalen.

Eleyne said, "Dalen, you didn't even say fire!"

He shrugged, "They were dead before I had a chance."

"You've gotta let them get closer next time or the Shadows are gonna have all of the fun!"

They resumed their march until they reached the road, and then Dalen replied, "Fear not, Eleyne, there will be plenty of soldiers for everyone once we get there."

They turned south and began following the road towards the emperor's secret camp. Over the next few hours they encountered two other patrols of soldiers, but like the first one Rissyl had no part in defeating them. Gordo and Sarasa made quick work of them, with a little help from Aruk's wolves.

He looked over to Cynia and said, "Maybe they didn't need our help after all? They seem to have things well in hand."

"Let's hope that continues to be the case. I have a bad feeling about this secret camp."

Rissyl stepped a little closer to the wagon and said, "Hey Dalen, what do we know about this secret camp? What can we expect?"

"That's a good point; you all need some basic info. We should probably stop and do some planning anyway." He whistled loudly, and then pulled the wagon far off of the road, behind a small clump of trees.

Once everyone was nearby he said, "Okay, let's do some planning. First, Rasa, please give the newcomers an overview of what we know about this camp."

She stepped to the center of the group and said, "The guard that Zahr questioned didn't have any personal knowledge of the camp, but his brother is a guard at the camp. From what we can tell much of the place is underground and it is highly guarded and fortified. The guard didn't know what actually went on at the camp, except that it was very secret and authorized by the emperor himself. He was certain that the Magi were brought there and he believed that they were still being held there. Whatever else is happening there, he didn't know and we can only guess at."

Dalen said, "While we're outside, try to stay spread out some. The Shadows and Champions should be out front, with the Evokers and Diviners hanging back to bring death from afar."

He looked around and Rissyl assumed he was waiting to see if there were any questions. Then Dalen continued, "Once we get inside, we'll probably have much smaller areas to work in. Let's keep one Champion at the rear of the group, and the other Champion and the Shadows up front. Evokers, remember that some of your spells can be just as dangerous to us as they are to the enemy."

Rissyl rolled his eyes, "Really, Dalen? Yes, I'm quite familiar with the destructive power of my spells. I'll be careful not to cook anyone that we like." His voice was filled with contempt and sarcasm.

Dalen responded, unfazed by Rissyl's tone, "That would be great, thanks. Now, if this place is a maze, we're likely to get split up. Aruk, Eleyne and I will be team one. Team two will be Sarasa, Zahr, and Thon. Team three will be Gordo, Cynia, and Hanry. Team four will be Sarge and Rissyl."

He waited and several of the Magi pointed at teammates, or went over to stand with the members of their team. Dalen said, "Remember these teams! This grouping puts an in-close fighter and a ranged Magi in each group. If we gotta split up, teams one and two will stick together, and teams three and four will stick together. If you gotta split up again then go down to your individual teams. Does that make sense? Are there any questions?"

Hanry put up his hand and Dalen turned to him, "So, what specifically is our goal?"

"Our primary goal is to rescue Jessa and Kimly. After that, we wanna kill as many imperial soldiers as we can, destroy as much of their camp as possible, and ruin whatever secret work they have going on there and, most importantly, get back out alive!"

Sarge said, "We may not be far from that camp. Look over there, off in the distance by the edge of that forest. Several campfires."

"I think you're right, old man. Okay everyone grab whatever gear you need for battle. Leave everything else with the wagons. We'll go on foot from here. Weapons out, and be ready for anything! Before we go, step over here so I can drop a little protective magic on you. It ain't perfect, but it'll help some."

After Dalen provided a little magical protection, the group headed out towards the camp.

The walk from the wagons to the forest seemed to take forever. As they got closer to the forest, it became clear that Sarge was right. This was the secret camp. A wood and rope fence stretched out in a huge circle that seemed to include much of the visible forest. A large sign near the fence said, "Keep Out! By order of the emperor!"

Gordo and Sarasa appeared behind the two guards at the gate. Neither guard had time to shout in surprise before they both fell to the ground, lifeless. Before the second guard even hit the ground, Gordo shouted out in pain!

Rissyl heard the buzzing sounds of several arrows cutting through the sky at once. He yelled, "Archers!"

"Over there, in the trees!" Eleyne pointed to the tree line. She tossed a small fire orb towards the archers. As a Society Magi, she had a limited number of spells that she could cast, and most of them would not be as powerful as what one of the Order Magi could cast, but Rissyl was impressed at her determination.

"There are some over there as well!" Thon pointed to another area, as an arrow zinged past, barely missing him.

Dalen shouted, "We have to get into that bunker, over there! My group will deal with the archers! Group two and four, get us into that bunker!" He started running towards a group of archers. He hollered back over his shoulder, "Group three, help Gordo, and then get us into that bunker!" As he ran, he cast a spell causing a semi-transparent disk to form in front of him, which moved with him as he ran. Rissyl saw two arrows hit the magical disk and fall to the ground harmlessly.

"Let's go, group four!" Sarge grabbed Rissyl's shoulder as he ran past, and Rissyl fell into step right behind him. The zipping sounds of arrows continued to tear through the air as they ran. Although he couldn't see most of the arrows, the sounds indicated several came very close to hitting him. He pulled the hood down further as he ran, trying to keep up with Sarge. As he ran past Gordo, he saw Cynia and Hanry helping him up. As much as he wanted to help them, he needed to focus on his assignment.

Up ahead a large hole was dug into the forest floor with a gradual incline leading down into the hole. Inside the hole he could see Sarasa and Thon fighting several soldiers with large swords. Zahr, the gorilla, was bashing on a metal door within the far wall of the hole trying to break it down. Rissyl assumed that door was the fortified entrance to the secret underground camp.

Sarge charged into the hole with a battle cry, his rune covered sword dancing before him. Rissyl was right behind him, but he was at a bit of a loss as to how to attack the soldiers without hurting his allies. Evocation was a high-damage Order, and most of the spells he had mastered did indiscriminate damage to an area. That was no good with several friends locked in combat with his targets.

He followed Sarge down into the hole. Everything was a blur of motion as Thon, Sarasa, and Sarge were locked in a vicious sword battle against four guards. One of the soldiers stepped and then turned quickly, placing himself directly behind Sarge. His blade arced up, and Rissyl knew it would only be a second before the arc turned downward at the back of Sarge's head. He wanted to call out in warning, but Sarge was busy dealing with a different attack from the front.

Rissyl leaped forward and grabbed the back of the neck of the soldier that was about to cleave Sarge in half. He quickly summoned a deadly amount of lightning into his palm. Instead of tossing it, he released it directly into the body of the soldier that he was grasping! A loud clap of thunder echoed through the forest as the lightning discharged! The soldier screamed briefly as he began to gyrate wildly, and then he fell to the ground with smoke rising from his body.

Near the door Zahr stopped beating on the door. He reached out and grabbed the nearest soldier by the arm. The massive gorilla began smashing the soldier up against the door, over and over. At first the gorilla held the soldier by an arm, and then by both legs, as it smashed the door repeatedly.

Sarasa, Thon, and Sarge made quick work of the two soldiers who were left. The gorilla dropped the lifeless body of the soldier that he had been using as a club, and resumed beating on the door with thunderous punches.

Cynia and Hanry ran down into the hole, with Gordo following them. Rissyl yelled, "Is he okay?"

"Arrow to the side, probably not horrible." Cynia pointed towards an arrow still sticking from Gordo's lower back.

There was a loud bang and the sound of something sliding on the other side of the door. The metal door started to open out into the hole, and two swords poked their way out.

Rissyl shouted, "Dammit, Zahr hold that door closed a second! Everyone else get away from this hole!"

The gorilla pushed against the door, holding it closed and trapping the swords between the door and the wall. The other Magi ran out of the hole.

"Now, Zahr! Get out of there!" The gorilla grabbed the ledge above him and pulled himself gracefully up onto the forest floor, and the door burst open!

Rissyl finished forming the powerful spell and swung his right arm like he was throwing a large object. As his arm was almost at the end of its throw, he spoke the verbal component of the spell, "Krol'Tu Salindi!" A large ball of fire appeared in his hand, and as his arm finished its swing, the ball of fire flew in through the door! He jumped to the side, as the fireball exploded inside the room! The explosion threw sticky fire throughout the room, and some of it shot back out the door. A chorus of blood curdling screams cried out, and they were almost as quickly silenced.

Dalen and the rest of team one rushed up behind Rissyl. Aruk and his wolves ran into the underground room first. Dalen put his hand on Rissyl's shoulder and said, "Nice work. Let's go!" He ran into the still smoldering room with his sword drawn. Rissyl and the others followed him in.

The room was completely destroyed, and small fires still burned in several places. A loud bell sounded in a slow repetitive pattern. Dalen rushed down the hallway leading out of the destroyed room and deeper into the underground camp. Within a few feet, the hallway split into two directions. He called back to the others, "Okay, here we go. Teams one and two, with me this way. Everyone else go that way. From the sound of that bell, the whole place knows we're here. May Nalria bless and protect us all!"

Rissyl watched as Dalen led his people down one corridor.

Sarge said, "Alright, Gordo, you dead yet?"

With a quick shake of his head Gordo said, "Not yet." He turned and Rissyl saw the arrow still sticking from his lower side.

The loud bell continued to slowly beat out its low warning.

"Get over here." Sarge grabbed him by the shoulder to pull him close. Then he grabbed the arrow as close to Gordo as possible with one hand, and then snapped the arrow in half with the other.

A howl of pain echoed down the hall as Gordo screamed out.

"Can't take it out yet, kid. We can't have you bleeding out right now, but at least now you won't catch it on something and make it worse." Sarge patted him on the head, and then pushed on his back to send him down the hallway, in the opposite direction of the other two teams. "Now, get up here

317

and run scout. I'll be right behind you. Hanry, you've got rear guard. Rissyl and Cynia, you're in the middle. Let's go!"

Gordo covered himself with his invisibility, and Sarge followed him down the hall. Rissyl and the others followed close behind. The hallway was wide, and it frequently had doors leading off to either side. Sarge stopped to check every door, looking in quickly before continuing down the hallway.

At the first bend in the hallway, Rissyl heard shouts and the sounds of battle ahead. Before he and Cynia even got to the bend and looked down the hallway, Gordo and Sarge had already taken out both of the guards in the room.

The room had only one other exit and it was securely locked. Cynia quickly searched the guard's bodies and found a set of keys.

The bell droned on as Gordo rested himself against a table. Rissyl stepped over to him, "You look like crap, are you okay to continue?"

Gordo nodded and waved Rissyl away.

Sarge smiled as Cynia found the set of keys. He took them from her, "These might come in handy!" He tried several keys on the ring before Rissyl heard the CLICK of success. Sarge followed Gordo out of the door and out into the corridor beyond.

This area looked different from the section they had been in earlier. Before, it had looked like a military compound, but this section was decorated more like a nice home. The walls had portraits and murals, and there were even pedestals with potted plants scattered around the hallways.

Up ahead, Sarge opened the first door to the left and then closed it quickly. "That was a bedroom or something."

As the bell continued its slow tolling, Rissyl grew determined to find it and melt it into a nice silent goo.

"Another intersection." Sarge stopped and looked back. "Team three will go this way, Rissyl and I will go that way."

Rissyl wanted to countermand that order and demand that they stay together. He hated the idea of leaving Cynia with Gordo and Hanry, but he said nothing, and watched as team three hurried off without him. When he turned back, he saw that Sarge was already rushing ahead.

The doors never seemed to stop, and neither did the dreadful slow tolling of the bell. Rissyl followed behind, with his staff in hand. He had already used a good portion of his magewel, and decided it would be best to use his staff as much as possible to save magic.

Sarge opened another door and said, "Hello!" as he rushed into the room. The man inside was dead before Rissyl even got into the room. Sarge turned to leave, but Rissyl didn't step out of his way.

"Remember, there are two women here who are friends. Try not to kill them before we can save them, okay?"

"I'll see what I can do." Sarge pushed his way past Rissyl and continued down the hallway.

As they continued through the complex, systematically searching every room they found, Rissyl could hear sounds of battle echoing down the corridors periodically. They passed several intersections, and Sarge just seemed to choose a direction at random.

After several similar intersections Rissyl asked, "Haven't we been past here already?"

"No, look at this!" Sarge was looking into a room adjacent to their hallway. "I think this one is a cell of some kind. There was a lock mechanism on the door, but it wasn't locked." The room was empty, other than a small bed.

Rissyl looked down the hallway, he said, "Those other doors have locks also?"

They hurried down the hall, checking each door, but all of the rooms were empty.

"Guess we found a prison area. Where are the prisoners?" The hallway was a dead end, so they backtracked to the previous intersection.

The sounds of battle were getting closer. Rissyl said, "Some of the others must be close!"

"And that dammed bell finally stopped! Someone must have found it!" Sarge checked several more doors and then turned a corner.

Sarge opened the door and said, "Think we found them."

He heard a gruff voice say, "Drop your sword, now! Or they die!"

He hurried to the door as Sarge slowly entered the room. When he got to the door, he realized the room was some sort of chapel. There were four guards, two of them near the door, and two of them pointing swords at two women, Jessa and Kimly! There was another woman in the room, off by herself, and an overweight man in priests robes wearing a stole with a black leaf on both ends was up front on a dais.

Rissyl called out, "Jessa!"

Lunging at one of the guards, Sarge thrust his sword forward, but he withdrew the strike before it landed, using it as a distraction. Continuing the lunging motion forward, he quickly circled his sword around, completely avoiding the soldier's defensive strike, and cleaved his sword deep into the shoulder and neck of the first guard!

Rissyl lowered his staff, pointing the red gem forward, and sent a wave of lightning from his staff shooting towards the guard next to Jessa! A low rumble of thunder shook the room as the lightning slammed into the guard, sending him flying back into the pews!

Kimly stepped back and then kicked hard into the back of her guard's knee, sending him stumbling forward. He caught himself on the back of a pew and turned to strike her with his sword!

With another wave of lightning, and the dull rumble of thunder, Rissyl sent another blue glowing streak from his staff. This one caught the guard next to Kimly directly in at the base of the neck. The guard flew into the pew before him.

When he looked over, he saw that Sarge had already finished off both guards by the door. He looked to the priest on the other side of the room, who raised his hands in surrender.

Sarge said, "Don't worry, ladies, you're safe now." He started moving forward, with his sword pointed at the priest.

"Wait, you can't trust-" Kimly's warning was cut short by a sudden stream of purple orbs launched from the woman who had been standing off by herself!

The first couple of orbs struck Sarge, but his cloak seemed to protect him.

Rissyl was entirely shocked. Why had one of the prisoners attacked them? He looked to Jessa in time to see Kimly running towards them, and Jessa started firing purple orbs at Sarge!

He was frozen in confusion. Why was Jessa attacking them? Why was she using necromancer magic? None of it made sense!

"Get out of here, Rissyl! I don't wanna hurt you, but you're not taking me from him!" Jessa's voice sounded desperate, and he was sure that she was crying.

Sarge started to rush towards the woman who was off by herself. The woman continued throwing purple orbs at Sarge as she screamed incoherently. The orbs slowed him, but Sarge kept pressing through.

Rissyl lowered his staff at the woman, preparing to send a lightning bolt at her when he heard a hideous, otherworldly, scream like nothing he had ever heard before. He turned toward the noise in time to see the priest make an upward motion with both hands, like he was trying to pull water from a pond. The priest's screeching echoed on, and suddenly there was a blinding flash of purple to Rissyl's right!

He looked and saw purple necromancer magic ripping up from the ground, completely surrounding Sarge! The magic swirled and whipped around Sarge, catching him in a maelstrom of energy! He flailed out in pain and then fell to the ground. Still, the blinding purple magic swirled and churned around him, battering him and tossing his body around. The runes on his cloak glowed brightly.

When the screeching ended, Rissyl looked back to see the priest and Jessa trying to flee out a back door. Further away, the lone woman retreated towards the back door as well.

Rissyl wanted to cook the priest, but he was afraid of accidently hitting Jessa. As a wave of fury enveloped him, he reached out with his left hand and said "Krol'Tu Salindi!" The large ball of fire appeared before his hand and he shoved it forward with a magical force of rage that sent it hurling across the room. The ball of fire slammed into the lone woman as she ran towards the door, hitting her so hard that she crashed against the back wall of the chapel! The sticky fire exploded outward, incinerating decorations and items across the dais. When the smoke cleared, the back wall of the chapel was scorched black except for a woman-shaped void left where the lone woman had once been.

Kimly ran up to him and hugged him quickly. He didn't know what to do, or who to trust. He pushed her away and said, "We've got to go after them! We have to save her!"

"Dammit Rissyl, she don't want saved! They have warped her mind. If you catch them, they will kill you! That door leads to a secret tunnel and an exit deep in the forest. Leave them be, and they'll be long gone soon."

He stood for a long second, and then ran over to Sarge. The old warrior lay motionless on the floor. Rissyl knelt beside him and put his hand on the old warrior's neck. "He is still alive!"

Rissyl stood up and paced back and forth for a few seconds, pushing both hands against his forehead. Kimly approached him but he put his hand up to keep her from talking. He knew a spell that would make getting Sarge's body out of here much easier, but he was too angry to remember exactly how the spell went.

He paced for a few more moments, calming himself. When the spell came to him, he summoned the magic quickly. A glowing disk of magic appeared on the ground next to Sarge. "Help me move him on to the magic disk."

With her help, he got Sarge rolled onto the disk, and he was able to easily push the old warrior as the disk floated a few inches above the ground.

"Now, tell me what in Fiery Khalius is going on!"

She shrugged, "Jessa is a Dark Apostle now."

He looked incredulous, "A what?"

"Dark Apostle, that's what they call some of the necromancers."

"How did this happen?"

"She's been twisted by them and their obsession with death and Viator. They promised her they could bring her brother back from the dead."

"Dammit, I knew she shouldn't get involved! We have got to get the sard out of here. Let's go!" He shoved Sarge out the door and started to walk behind him, pushing him occasionally as he floated above the floor.

Kimly said, "Wait. There are Dregs here, we gotta take them."

"You're not making any sense, what Dregs?"

"This place is a monster breeding camp! Lots of Dregs are trapped here, forced to breed these anti-magic monsters for the emperor, to fight us. He calls them Motlites"

"Anti-magic monsters? Mother of every one of the sarding gods, could this get any worse?" He looked to her, "Where are these Dregs?"

"Follow me."

He followed her as she raced down the halls. He shoved Sarge before him, occasionally sending him bouncing off a wall as Kimly turned a corner unexpectedly.

Up ahead, the sounds of battle were rapidly approaching.

They turned a corner again, and came face to face with Eleyne. Behind her, Dalen stood in the hallway directing a steady stream of nearly naked women as they ran down the halls.

Rissyl's heart filled with relief when he looked down another hallway and saw Sarasa directing the line of nearly naked Dregs.

In the other direction, he saw gorilla Zahr and Thon in a battle against several guards. Thon moved with unbelievable speed. Rissyl watched the man fighting three opponents at once, and he didn't seem to be outmatched. To his side, and slightly ahead of him, was Zahr. The large gorilla tore through the line of soldiers. He grabbed two of them and smashed them together, then slammed a soldier's head against a stone wall, and then picked up the body and tossed it into two soldiers before him.

Rissyl stepped over to Dalen, "What's going on?"

Dalen motioned with his arms, pointing the direction the Dregs should run. He said, "Hurry up, dammit! Follow the person in front of you, quickly!" Then he looked to Rissyl and said, "These Dregs were prisoners, breeding something. Aruk and his wolves are leading them out. Hopefully, he can get them to the wagons, and we'll meet him over there soon."

Finally the last prisoner passed them, and Rissyl watched briefly as the line of mostly naked Dregs hurried down the hallway away from him.

Rissyl asked, "Should we follow them out, and get out of here?"

Dalen looked to Rissyl and then noticed Kimly. He pulled her to him and engulfed her in a big hug, "Are you alright? I'm sorry it took us so long!"

She nodded, "I'll be fine."

Letting her go, he turned back to Rissyl, "Yes, let's get outta here!"

"No, not yet." Kimly said, "There are more that way." She pointed down the hall towards Thon and Zahr. "Plus, just outside you'll find the creatures that these Dregs are breeding."

"Dammit!" Dalen swore angrily. "Fine, let's go that way. What happened to Sarge? And where is Jessa?"

"Sarge got taken down by a nasty necromancer priest. Jessa attacked us. She refused to come with us, and then she fled with the necromancer that hurt Sarge. That's all I know, let's go."

Up ahead Thon said, "Okay, this way is clear!"

Dalen shouted, "Rasa, we're going this way. Hurry up!"

She moved up front, and Dalen followed her. Kimly ran to Dalen and the others followed them through another maze of corridors. Rissyl let the others move in front of him, as he pushed Sarge down the hall. Eleyne walked behind him, guarding the rear.

Before long, Rissyl heard brief sounds of battle and then he found the guard room where the others had already taken out the guards.

Kimly said, "Down that way are the pregnant Dregs and the other Salubrious Dregs."

Sarasa asked, "Salubrious Dregs?"

"Dregs who give breast milk for the Motlites. The anti-magic creatures that they're breeding here."

As the others discussed the details, Dalen went through the doors and started opening cells. He started lining up the women, and assuring them that they were being rescued. Some of the women cried and some of them cheered as they complied with Dalen's instructions.

He stepped back into the guard room and said, "Eleyne and Sarasa, lead these women back to the wagons. Wait there with Aruk until the rest of us meet you there!"

They hurried back down the hallway, and Dalen encouraged the Dreg women to follow them. Then he turned to Kimly. "Okay, lead us to these Motlites!"

Kimly led the group through a maze of corridors, and then she suddenly stopped. She pointed to a door and said, "Garroliron!"

Dalen said, "What?"

"It's a greenish iron. This is the room where they make the mixture to create Motlites." She opened the door and entered the room. Dalen followed her in, but Rissyl couldn't see what they did inside the room.

A few seconds later they both came out of the room and Kimly continued to lead them through the halls to the exit. They came to an empty room with a large metal door that stood open. It was then that Rissyl heard Cynia scream.

He shouted, "Get out of my way!" and started pushing his way through the others, leaving Sarge on his disk floating in the corridor. Kimly and Dalen beat him outside.

When he got outside, he found himself in a pit with an earthen ramp up to the forest floor, just like at the other entrance. He ran up the ramp and looked to find Cynia. Off to his right he saw her holding a large stick like a spear.

In front of her was an impossibly large and misshapen man. He wore pieces of imperial armor and an imperial tabard, but barely looked human. The features of his twisted face were distorted and freakish, and his over-sized mouth seemed frozen in a hideous half-smile.

The Motlite grunted and swiped its hand at Cynia, and she stepped back to avoid the attack.

Rissyl shouted at the Motlite, to draw its attention away from her. He ran forward and lowered his staff to attack. Dalen ran past him, sword drawn, charging the creature.

Cynia looked over and shouted, "No! Stay away! It sucks in magic! You can't hurt it!" The Motlite lumbered past her, heading towards Dalen.

Rissyl unleashed a short bolt of lightning from his staff, and it streaked towards the Motlite! It was about to strike the creature right in the shoulder, but instead it somehow bounced off it and redirected into the ground nearby. The Motlite didn't even seem to notice the attack.

Further away, he saw Gordo locked in combat against three soldiers in the same type of tabard that the Motlite was wearing. Zahr rushed past

Rissyl heading out to assist Gordo.

When Dalen got close to the Motlite, he attacked it viciously with his sword. The runes down the sword danced with colors as he attacked. He landed blow after blow with the sword, and every attack bounced back, as though the sword hit against solid stone!

The Motlite reached down and grabbed Dalen by both shoulders and its freakish smile grew wider.

Dalen screamed.

As Cynia got close to attacking the creature with her spear, Rissyl saw several purple orbs shoot past his head from behind him!

He ducked to his right and spun around to see Kimly shooting the purple magic of the necromancers! He stared in shock for a moment. He couldn't believe that Jessa and Kimly could both turn against them! He lowered his staff at her, ready to unleash a deadly stream of fire and end the treachery once and for all.

Thon stepped in between Rissyl and Kimly and shouted, "Rissyl, look!"

He glanced to his right to see where Thon was pointing. Then he realized that Kimly was not attacking the Magi, she was attacking the Motlite! Her attacks had dropped the creature to the ground.

Cynia and Dalen stood over it as Kimly continued to launch purple orbs one after the other into the Motlite. It finally stopped moving, and she lobbed one more orb at it.

A scream turned his attention to Gordo. He looked in time to see one of the soldiers pull his sword from Gordo's chest. Zahr got to the battle as Gordo fell to the ground. Cynia and Dalen rushed over to help as well, and Rissyl pointed his staff that way, looking for a clear shot.

One soldier rushed Zahr, and the gorilla reached out and grabbed the soldier by the neck. The soldier tried to stab Zahr, but the gorilla shook the man violently by the neck and then used his body to pummel the next closest soldier. The man tried to get away but Zahr tripped him, and then used the body of the first soldier to pummel the fallen soldier. By the time Cynia and Dalen got close, Zahr had already taken out two of the three remaining soldiers. The last one didn't stand a chance. Rissyl rushed over to Gordo.

He bent down and checked Gordo, but the Magi was dead. He carefully closed the man's lifeless eyelids. He looked around the battlefield and saw what he was hoping he wouldn't see. On the ground nearby was Hanry's obviously lifeless body.

Rissyl moved over to the Motlite and Cynia joined him. He put his arm around her, and drew her close. He whispered, "Are you okay?" but he didn't take his eyes off the Motlite.

She stood up straight, "Hanry and Gordo are both dead."

He kept his arm around her, "Sarge is hurt really bad. I think the others are doing pretty well. We rescued a ton of Dregs. Sarasa and the other Magi took them to the wagons."

Cynia said, "Then we need to get back there. The sooner we're outta here, the happier I'll be."

Kimly stepped up next to Rissyl, "Not yet. There are a lot more of these Motlites, off in that direction."

His heart dropped to his stomach. "What? How many more?"

"A lot, but they're all babies, or very young. They should be easy to kill with rocks or clubs."

Dalen said, "I'll get some large rocks then."

- = - = -

Half an hour later, Rissyl pushed Sarge back to the wagons as the other Magi walked beside him. Dalen carried Gordo's body and Thon carried Hanry. Rissyl found the task of destroying all of the little unnatural creatures to be bloody and more than a little traumatizing. The battle was a partial victory, and he was ready to lay down for a few fortnights.

Nearly naked Dregs were huddled in the backs of both wagons, and into little groups scattered around the area near the wagons. Many of them were standing in small groups talking. Some were crying but most of them seemed extremely happy to be free of the camp.

Sarasa, Aruk, and Eleyne met Rissyl and the others as they approached the wagons. Dalen said, "We can't stay here. Riz, what's the closest city to Clornoss?"

He thought quickly, "I'm pretty sure it's Libur, a coastal city south east of here."

"Alrighty, Aruk, Eleyne, Zahr, and Thon take both wagons and take these people to safety. Try the city of Libur, but in the end it'll be up to you which city or cities would be best for the safety of these people. Maybe some farmers or ranchers along the way can give some kind of clothing? Just keep them away from the imperial army until they can get somewhere safe."

Rissyl said, "Aruk, let me show you how to pull the ink from their skin. Without those tattoos they are free."

"What about the unborn babies?" Eleyne asked, pointing to one of the nearly naked and very pregnant Dregs.

Dalen shook his head, "Clearly, they cannot be allowed to live. They're abominations. Try to find a midwife along the way, maybe she can help. Deal with it however you think is best. One way or another, everyone plan to meet back at the Sorgo portal stone on the last day of Late-Spring at dusk. Then we'll regroup."

Kimly stepped up, "What about me?"

Rissyl said, "You're a necromancer now?"

She sighed, "No. Okay, sorta, but not by choice! I'm not with them, they're crazy!"

Dalen stepped between them, "You're coming with us. There'll be plenty of time to talk later. We're gonna see Randol."

Chapter 31

Rissyl

Randol sat back in his chair, and crossed his arms over his chest, "Bisangar's Signet Ring?"

"Yes, that's what the Rolimi Guardian demanded." Rissyl sat across from Randol in a large room in Randol's basement. Cynia and Sarasa sat on chairs to his right, and Kimly and Dalen sat together on the couch to his left. Sarge was laying on a make-shift bed over in the corner of the room.

Dalen asked, "Have you heard of it?"

"Well of course I've heard of it. Bisangar was one of the founders of the Magi Stronghold. He was an immensely powerful Magi. Items of his creation were some of the most prized artifacts in the Stronghold archives. For hundreds of years his Signet Ring was displayed in the foyer of the Weingart building of the Stronghold. I assumed that it was still locked inside the Stronghold with all of the rest of the items."

"That's disappointing." Rissyl propped his elbow on the arm of the chair, and then rested his chin in his palm.

Sarasa asked, "Do you have any idea how we can find it?"

"That will take research... and time."

Everyone was quiet for a moment until Sarge moaned weakly.

"What was that herb that you gave him?" Rissyl walked over and knelt down next to him.

"Just a strong herb to make sure he stays asleep. Necromancer magic sucks the life right out of a person. The only way to recover is to rest."

"Will he live?"

Randol shrugged, "It's too early to know. He was drained worse than I've ever seen for someone who didn't die outright. The spell cast by that priest you described sounds like nothing I've ever heard of before, so there is no telling what effect that might have on him, long term. Most of the Necromancers had been killed off by the time I was born; their Order was weak back then. It sounds like they're growing now."

Rissyl went back to his chair, "Sarge said that the necromancers were looking for something. Then we found necromancer corpses outside of the

Stronghold, and we came to the conclusion that the necromancers are trying to claim the Stronghold for some reason, but I don't have any clue why they would want it."

"Me either." Randol shook his head, "Necromancer magic is nothing like our magic, and it works entirely differently. Our artifacts and spell books would be no use to them. It makes no sense."

Kimly said, "I know why."

Everyone looked at her in surprise.

Dalen said, "You do?"

"Yes, during one of our chats Lord Jalinox claimed that long ago the Magi stole many valuable artifacts and ritual books from the necromancers, and locked them away in the Stronghold. He thinks that this Stronghold could unlock fantastic powers for himself and his followers."

"Is that true?" Rissyl asked.

Randol shrugged, "I have no idea. That is something else we'll need to research."

Dalen turned back to Kimly, "Who is this Jalinox?"

She replied, "He is a madman, but he is powerful and persistent. I think he's someone important in the emperor's court, but I dunno for sure. I do know that you were lucky he wasn't around when you raided the place, or we might have all died."

The room got quiet again. Finally, Rissyl said, "We were probably lucky for a thousand different things, or maybe it wasn't luck. Perhaps Nalria was guiding our steps? The real question now is... what do we do next?"

Dalen looked at Kimly. He asked, "Are you a necromancer now?"

She shrugged and didn't answer right away. "In a way, I guess. Jalinox taught me how to use Viator's power, if that's what you mean."

Rissyl rubbed his temples. He was still in disbelief that Jessa would choose to stay with the necromancer priest. He had known her all of her life. If she could be corrupted by Jalinox, he found it hard to believe that Kimly didn't succumb to that evil as well. He said, "So we're going to have a necromancer in the Society?" That brought grumbling from Kimly and Dalen both. Rissyl ignored them and turned to Randol, "Was it common for Magi to also practice necromancer magic?"

The old Magi shook his head, "No, I don't know of any Magi who was also a necromancer. Any Magi corrupted by Viator would have likely been killed. Or at the very least they would have been made magic-barren and banished from the Society."

Dalen stood up and said, "You'll do no such thing!"

Kimly reached up and grabbed his hand, and pulled gentle until he sat back down. She asked, "What is magic-barren?"

Randol said, "It's a punishment the Magi used to prevent someone from using magic. The person's magewel is drained and blocked so it can no longer store magic."

"We don't really gotta do something like that to Kimly, do we?" Cynia looked from Kimly to Randol.

"No, we don't!" Dalen crossed his arms in front of his chest.

"That decision is up to you." Randol leaned forward in his chair. "But I will remind you that necromancer magic is different than ours. It can only be used by people who truly worship Viator, the god of death."

Rissyl said, "Is that a chance we're willing to take?"

"I think it is." Dalen gave Rissyl an annoyed look.

Sarasa looked disgusted. She asked, "Do you worship Viator?"

Kimly shrugged. She looked uncomfortable and after a moment she said, "Using the necromancer magic requires a sincere prayer to the god of death. It don't require devout worship. I had to say the prayers to keep from angering my captors. That don't mean I worship Viator."

Cynia nodded, "It would've been really tough to beat that Motlite without her. There are probably more of them out there."

"That's a good point." Rissyl said, "You're right that we probably will need her."

Dalen nodded once and said, "That settles it then. So, back to Rissyl's previous question. What do we do next?"

Randol said, "You have to stay alive, and you have to keep your Magi alive. You don't need to go underground exactly, but you have to be smart. Recruit in all of the cities throughout the empire and the Free Cities to increase your numbers. I suggest getting your trusted Magi spread out as much as possible, and gradually start to bring new people into the order."

Nodding his head the whole time, Dalen said, "I agree completely!"

Randol stood up, "And until you secure the Stronghold, you may use this place as your headquarters and rally point. There is an external exit for this basement, so you don't all have to traipse through my house at all hours."

Several of the Magi thanked him for his generosity.

He smiled and nodded, "It is how I can give. That, and good food. Follow me and we'll have dinner."

Rissyl stood up but he didn't follow the others. He let the others follow

Randol out of the room, but Dalen stayed behind. Rissyl thought perhaps Dalen wanted to continue the debate about Kimly, or ask more information about Jessa.

Dalen said, "Hey Riz, have you heard anything from Firana?"

He was surprised. With everything else that had been going on, it had been several days since he had even thought about the Magi who had been sent to protect Grum'Glin. Rissyl shook his head, "No, I haven't heard anything at all about Firana and the others headed to Grum'Glin. I'm not even sure if the emperor has launched another attack on that city. You should send her a message through the nexus gem."

He thought for a moment and then nodded, "I will, yes." Dalen hurried to catch up with Randol and the others.

Rissyl made his way outside and walked a short distance alone in the dark. A light rain fell and he didn't mind it. He continued to walk away from Randol's house until he found a quiet spot. He lay on his back with both of his arms crossed behind his head as a pillow, and he enjoyed the feeling of the soft rain on his face. His eyes were closed and the light breeze against his wet face felt wonderful. After a dreadfully stressful day, having a moment to relax and rejuvenate was a welcomed relief.

Several minutes later he heard footsteps approaching. He kept his eyes closed. He was sure that he knew who had followed him.

She sat down next to him and took hold of his hand. He lay there quietly until she finally said, "I'm glad that you're safe, I was worried about-"

He spoke before she could finish her statement, "I was hoping you would join me out here. I've made up my mind, I choose you."

She leaned forward and kissed him passionately in the rain.

www.ingramcontent.com/pod-product-compliance
Lightning Source LLC
Chambersburg PA
CBHW060512180626
46817CB00002B/350